GIVE MY LOVE
TO BERLIN

GIVE MY LOVE
TO BERLIN

A Novel

KATHERINE BRYANT

Walrus Publishing | Harrisonville, MO 64701

Walrus Publishing
Harrisonville, MO 64701

For information, contact:
Walrus Publishing
www.amphoraepublishing.com
*Walrus Publishing is an imprint of
Amphorae Publishing Group, LLC*
www.amphoraepublishing.com

Manufactured in the United States of America
Cover Design by Kristina Blank Makansi
Illustration: Shutterstock
Set in Adobe Caslon Pro, Ametis, Gravesend Pro

Library of Congress Control Number: 2024948559
ISBN: 9781940442532

To those whose stories were lost to history. Even though I don't know your names, I promise to remember you.

And to Dave. I will be forever grateful for you.

Soon the day will come when science will win victory over error, justice a victory over injustice, and human love a victory over human hatred and ignorance.
— Magnus Hirschfeld

AUTHOR'S NOTE

In the 1920s, Berlin was considered the gay capital of the world. There were clubs, bars, and restaurants dedicated to the lesbian, gay, and transgender people who lived in the area. Much of the gay community was built thanks to a German physician, Dr. Magnus Hirschfeld, who set up his practice in Berlin during the Weimer Republic. The Institute of Sexual Science was open from 1919 to 1933 and included a massive library with over twenty thousand books and medical journals, a lecture hall, and a surgery.

This era of tolerance came to an end with the Nazi regime. In 1935, the Nazis used "Paragraph 175" of the 1871 German criminal code to target the gay community directly.

Paragraph 175 was a national prohibition added to the Reich Penal Code in 1871. It read:

"An unnatural sex act committed between persons of male sex or by humans with animals is punishable by imprisonment; the loss of civil rights might also be imposed."

However, the law was vague enough that it was rarely enforced. By the mid-1920s, there were many people, including Dr. Magnus Hirschfeld, who were attempting to reform/repeal the law completely.

When the Nazis came to power in 1933, they put a halt to efforts seeking reform of this law. In 1935, after the murder of Ernst Röhm, the NSDAP amended Paragraph 175 to close what were seen as loopholes in the current law. The new law had three parts:

Paragraph 175:

A male who commits a sex offense with another male or allows himself to be used by another male for a sex offense shall be punished with imprisonment. Where a party was not yet twenty-one years of age at the time of the act, the court may, in especially minor cases, refrain from punishment.

Paragraph 175a:

Penal servitude up to 10 years or, where there are mitigating circumstances, imprisonment of not less than three months shall apply to: (1) a male who, with violence or the threat of violence to body and soul or life, compels another male to commit a sex offense with him or to allow himself to be abused for a sex offense; (2) a male who, by abusing a relationship of dependence based upon service, employment or subordination, induces another male to commit a sex offense with him or to allow himself to be abused for a sex offense; (3) a male over 21 years of age who seduces a male person under twenty-one years to commit a sex offense with him or to allow himself to be abused for a sex offense; (4) a male who publicly commits a sex offense with males or allows himself to be abused by males for a sex offense or offers himself for the same.

Paragraph 175b:

An unnatural sex act committed by humans with animals is punishable by imprisonment; the loss of civil rights might also be imposed.

Paragraph 175 Arrest Numbers

Scholars estimate that there were approximately 100,000 arrests for violations of Paragraph 175 during the Nazi Regime. Not everyone arrested under Paragraph 175 identified as a man. During the German Empire and the Weimar Republic, Germany was home to a developing community of people who identified as "transvestites." Dr. Magnus Hirschfeld coined the term "transvestite" in 1910. Initially, this term encompassed people who performed in drag, people who cross-dressed for pleasure, as well as those who today would be considered trans or transgender. Today, in English, the term "transvestite" is outdated and offensive, however, it was widely used at the time.

Some self-identified transgender individuals were arrested under Paragraph 175. These people were assigned male at birth but lived as women. When they engaged in sexual relations with men, the Nazi regime saw this as male-male sex. But transgender women did not see themselves as "homosexual" because they did not consider their sexual relations as male-male sex. Nonetheless, they were punished according to the regime's definition.

PROLOGUE

June 1995

It was early. Only about six a.m. but that was on purpose. Thea wanted the square to be empty. There was a little bit of morning mist still hanging in the Berlin air and the only noise she could hear were the birds chirping off to her left. Her shoes clicked on the cobblestones as she walked into the square, her eyes on the small plexiglass window about twenty feet in front of her.   Yesterday when she was here, there was a crowd of people surrounding the small window, set in the ground, at the center of the square. She didn't have it in her to get emotional in front of a group of strangers, so she left.

She breathed through the lump in her throat. Now she could stand where her grandmother stood and not have to worry about any other people. She felt slightly trapped by the large buildings surrounding her, all columns and marble, and she wondered which of these buildings had survived the war and which had been rebuilt in the '40s and '50s.

The window was closer now, so she slowed her pace and took a deep breath, letting her eyes wander, wondering where exactly her grandmother stood with her friends, watching their lives burn. She closed her eyes and imagined the acrid smell of hundreds of thousands of pages burning and if she focused, the birds chirping faded away and she could almost hear chanting and screams of rage.

Reaching the five-by-five window in the cobblestones, she looked down and felt the air leave her lungs.

Rows and rows of empty white bookshelves were buried under the ground. She had to crane her neck to see them through the small plexiglass window and they seemed to go on forever. She couldn't help it; the tears came. She covered her mouth with her hand so she wouldn't sob out loud. Everything was blurry and for the briefest moment, she could see flames licking the sky when a voice behind her made her jump.

"It's something, isn't it?" An old man stood behind her leaning on a cane, a bag of bird seed in his hand. His English had the thickness of a German accent behind it.

She wiped her face. "My grandmother and her friends were here when they burned all the books. I wanted to see the Memorial for myself."

He nodded. "A lot of us were here. I like to come in the mornings, too, before the tourists." He winked at her. "At least before most of them."

She smiled. "I just wanted to come when there was no one here. It was hard, yesterday, for me to imagine with all the people crowding around the window." She couldn't take her eyes off the ground where the bookshelves were entombed.

He nodded again, his eyes cloudy with age and memory. "There were forty-thousand people here that night in May. Forty-thousand people came to watch the books burn. I come here almost every day, and I still get lost when I look at those empty shelves." His gaze was fixed someplace on the horizon, staring at something she couldn't see.

He blinked and then focused his eyes back on her face. "Did you see the plaque?"

She shook her head and he gestured for her to follow. He

walked about five feet, then stopped and looked down. A small bronze plate was set into the cobblestones.

"Do you know German?"

"No," she breathed.

Standing close, she could see an aged black tattoo peeking out from under his rolled sleeve on the inside of his arm. Numbers. She resisted the urge to reach out and take his hand.

His mouth was set in a grim line. "It says, 'That was but a prelude; where they burn books, they will ultimately burn people as well.'"

Thea stood alone over the empty bookshelves until the first round of tourists and school field trips arrived. The old man's voice kept ringing in her ears.

Where they burn books, they burn people as well.

CHAPTER 1

October 1927

They entered the darkened ballroom after presenting their invitations to the men at the door. The smell of sweat, perfume, and gin hit Tillie in the face, and she swayed briefly in her high heels. Ruth took her elbow to steady her. She could almost see the steam rising from the people crammed into the room, the heat from the bodies dancing together, a stark contrast to the cool evening air outside.

Holding Ruth's arm, she followed Ernesto and James down the stairs and someone in a peacock mask thrust a drink into her hand. She watched the person walk away and it was unclear whether it was a man or a woman, their black skirt flowing out behind them, their heels pushing their height to almost six feet tall. She took a sip and handed her glass to Ruth, who downed the champagne and grinned. She held her black mask up to her face and smirked. "How do I look?" she said loudly, over the noise of the ballroom.

"Magnificent," Tillie shouted back. Ruth leaned forward and ran her nose down Tillie's jawline, making her shiver. Pulling back, she looked around, trying to glimpse the back of Ernesto and James, who were still making their way through the crowd.

"Let's find the others," she said, pulling Ruth along to tail the boys. She recognized the back of Ernesto's blonde head by a corner table in the back of the large room and hurried to catch up. Ruth clung to her hand as they half-jogged through the groups of people dancing and singing and sweating in the center of the dance floor.

As they approached the group in the corner, she could see Dr. Hirschfeld sitting with his boyfriend Karl, his gray eyes twinkling, a smile on his face as he watched the people in the ballroom. When his eyes fell on Ruth, his smile widened. "Ruthie!" He clapped his hands together.

"Hi, Dr. H." Ruth smiled back. She pulled a chair out from the table for Tillie and then one for herself. Ernesto and James were already seated, drinking from sweaty glasses, and leaning into one another talking. "You remember Tillie, right?"

He smiled in Tillie's direction, his eyes warm behind his round glasses. "Of course, how are you, Tillie?"

"I'm great, thanks." She smiled at Karl, who was sitting to Dr. Hirschfeld's left, their hands intertwined. "Are the rest of the girls here?"

Before he could answer, a voice rang out. "Ernesto! Did you bring your beau?" Tillie looked over to see a tall, dark-haired woman hurrying over to the table, flanked by several other women, all in assorted styles of costume. Ernesto jumped up and wrapped his arms around the woman who had called his name.

"Dora!" Ernesto held her tight. "I'm so glad you decided to come tonight." He held a chair out so Dora could sit down at the table with them. The other women followed and sat around the table wherever they could find an empty spot.

"Well, I wasn't going to, I had my knitting and my tea all ready, but Adelaide and Helene convinced me." She nodded to two of the women across from her. "I'm so glad I did, because I get to meet your new friend." Her voice was soft and gentle, and she looked at James with genuine interest. "I'm Dora," she extended her hand.

"She's the house mother at the institute," Ernesto explained, and Dora waved him away.

"Oh, I am not. You make me sound like I'm ninety years old." Ruth leaned in. "She is too, James. She's like the mother we all never had." Dora shook her head, but Tillie could see she was pleased.

Dora took a sip of water and reached to take Ruth's hand. "I'm so glad you could come tonight. Since you moved out of the institute, I feel like I hardly see you. I must get all my Ruthie news from Tillie when she's volunteering at the library."

"Well, you should come to the club to see me, Dorchën," Ruthie said affectionately, squeezing Dora's hand.

Tillie watched Dora's eyes cloud over with anxious worry. "Oh. I don't know. I'm a homebody." She shrugged and drank more of her water.

"Dora, you have the certificate now, you can go wherever you like. The police won't bother you." Dr. Hirschfeld's voice was kind but pointed.

"I've tried telling her." Tillie looked up at the woman sitting across from her. She was wearing a white dress with a matching hat and white gloves.

"Helene," Dora addressed the woman in white. "Just because you feel comfortable galivanting all over Berlin doesn't mean we all do."

Tillie's brow furrowed. "What certificate? What's it for?"

Dr. Hirschfeld cleared his throat. "I've worked with the police and issued Transvestite Certificates to anyone who identifies as such." Tillie glanced at Dora, but her eyes were on the ice in her glass.

"Dora, Helene, Adelaide, and Nissa all have one. And many of my patients have been issued the certificates. They're giving them to both men and women who prefer to live or dress as the opposite sex. If they're carrying the certificates with my signature, they will not be arrested or harassed."

"Hypothetically," Dora added, matching Dr. Hirschfeld's pointed tone.

Ernesto turned to Dora. "That's wonderful, why didn't you tell me? You can come with me to the market on the weekends now."

Dora shrugged again and Tillie could see something else in her eyes. Fear. She nudged Ruth and said, very quietly in her ear, "Change the subject."

Ruth cleared her throat. "Dora, why don't we all do a Sunday dinner this week at the institute?" Dora looked up. "Just like we used to. Tillie and I can come and help set up the lounge, make it an event."

Dora smiled gratefully at Ruth and patted the top of Ruth's hand. "That sounds wonderful."

✝

Tillie breathed in the cool night air as they walked home from the party. She couldn't help stealing glances at Ruth while they walked. She looked like a ghost, despite the flush on her cheeks from the steamy ballroom. Tendrils of black hair were falling forward into her eyes, and she kept pushing them behind her ears. Her hair had a light curl to it and a few pieces were stuck to her forehead after sweating inside all night.

Ruth was all lines and angles covered in muscle and she walked like she was floating. The tuxedo pants Ruth was wearing only went to just below her knee and Tillie could see the outline of her calf muscles with every step they took. Her skin looked like velvet in the moonlight.

"You're staring at me." Ruth looked at Tillie from the corner of her eye, a smirk on her lips. "Can I help you with something?"

"Just wondering if I should be feeding you more red meat." At this, Ruth snorted a laugh and stopped to stare at Tillie.

"What?"

"You're just so pale. You're practically translucent." Tillie nudged her with her elbow. "C'mon, we need to catch up with the boys if Ernesto is going to crash at our place tonight."

Ruth hurried to catch up, muttering under her breath, "I am not translucent" and Tillie giggled.

Ruth reached over and took her hand, kissing Tillie's fingertips. "Do you have to go to work tomorrow?"

Tillie sighed. The downside of having a costume party on a Thursday night was having to work the next morning. "Well, being that I'm the only one with a regular job, yes, unfortunately I do."

Ruth gave her a playful smack on her bottom, which she could barely feel through the skirt of her dress. "We all have regular jobs. They just don't have regular hours. We know the institute will be quiet tomorrow because everyone who spends time there was at the party, which means Ernesto probably doesn't have to go to work, and I don't perform until Saturday night." She pursed her lips thoughtfully. "I think James is on tomorrow night though." Checking her watch, she sighed. "Make that tonight. It's almost two in the morning."

Tillie groaned. "Well, maybe I'll be able to duck out early tomorrow. Fridays are usually slow. My father typically only works a half day and Ernesto's father has his own assistant, so it shouldn't matter if I leave early."

Ruth squeezed her hand sympathetically. "You can fake a headache and come home at lunch. We could spend the rest of the day in bed." She gave Tillie a mischievous grin.

Tillie smiled up at her girlfriend. "Maybe."

They walked the rest of the way to their apartment in comfortable quiet, their footsteps echoing off the pavement in the quiet streets of Berlin.

CHAPTER 2

October 1927

Tillie awoke with a pounding head. She pushed Ruth's arm off her torso as she struggled to sit up, blinking to clear her vision. Ruth mumbled in her sleep and Tillie leaned down to give her a quick kiss on the forehead. She slid out of bed quietly, so as not to wake her, desperate for a cup of coffee. Before she could even pull on her robe, Ruth opened one eye, her other eye still smashed into the corner of the pillow.

"Try to get out at lunch today, okay doll? We can head to the institute and hang with the boys. Maybe convince Dora to take a break from bossing everyone around to sit with us and relax."

Tillie laughed. "Okay, I'll do my best. Fridays at the end of the month are pretty slow. Maybe I'll get lucky, and my father won't even come in. Herr Grandelis will be there, though." She rolled her eyes.

"I don't know how you work with that man. He's awful." Ruth sat up and rubbed her face with both hands.

Tillie shrugged. Ernesto's father had known her since she was in diapers and she and Ernesto took naps together in the same playpen. "I don't have to do much with him, since he has his own secretary. If I don't talk about politics or about Ernesto, then everything is fine."

Ruth made a face. "Do you think if you told him you were a Communist, his head would explode?"

Tillie grinned while she pulled on her stockings. "Probably."

Ruth yawned. "Too bad when he got arrested back in '23 with his buddies at the Putsch, he didn't go to jail."

Tillie raised her eyebrows. "Well, we don't talk about that."

Ruth snorted and reached for her glass of water next to the bed. "I'll bet."

Tillie pushed her feet into her cold heels and looked at Ruth, a sarcastic grin on her face. "Didn't you know, Ruthie? The Nazis are a real political party now. No more throwing beer mugs at waitresses."

Ruth rolled her eyes. "Oh yeah, a real political party. That's just what we need. Those idiots having an actual say." Laying back down in bed and pulling the blankets up to her chin, she added, "And we get those SA weirdos in the club all the time. They still throw beer mugs at the waitresses."

Tillie chuckled and grabbed her coat. "I'll see if I can be back in time for lunch. Love you."

Ruth's voice was muffled from the pillows. "Love you too, doll."

†

Tillie's footsteps were quieted by the carpet as she entered her father's office. There were small movements coming from the records room and Marcia, Herr Grandelis' secretary, poked her head through the doorway.

"Morning Tillie," she called, her arms full of paperwork.

"Morning. Are they in yet?" Tillie pulled off her coat and put her handbag in the bottom drawer of her desk.

"Not yet. But Herr Grandelis has a meeting today at ten, so I assume they'll both be in at some point."

Tillie nodded and groaned internally. Making a mental note to call Ruth to let her know she wouldn't be home for lunch, she sat down at her desk and picked up a thick folder that had been left by her father with a note that read "to be filed." Pushing up her sleeves, she joined Marcia in the filing room while she waited for her father to arrive for the day.

At nine-thirty, Tillie heard her father's voice calling for her from the lobby. She scooped up the papers she had left to file and hurried toward her father's voice, calling "Morning, Papa," as she went.

Her father stood in his doorway, looking over a small notebook. "Tillie, we have a meeting this morning with an old friend of Anthony's." Tillie nodded, setting down the papers on her desk.

"Do you need me to take notes?"

Her father shook his head. "I don't think so. It's just a preliminary meeting. He's thinking of running for office in Bavaria. He's only just returned to the country from Venice." Her father paused. "Or Sweden, maybe?" He shrugged. "I'm not sure. He and Anthony were pilots together in the Great War and then," he paused again, lowering his voice, "he was with us in '23."

Tillie stifled a sigh. "Oh. Okay, then."

"Matilda," a cool voice came from behind her. She turned and Ernesto's father stood on the other side of her desk. "Will you be joining us for our meeting today?"

She gave a small smile. "Yes, Herr Grandelis, if that's alright with you." He nodded but didn't answer.

Turning to her father, he took a deep breath. "Hermann will be here in a few minutes. It's essential that he becomes a client, Vincent. This could mean big things for us as a law firm, should he pass our names along to the Führer."

Tillie turned and caught Marcia's eyes. They both suppressed giggles and Marcia made a face. They both went ahead to the conference room and Marcia whispered, "These men and their obsession with 'the Führer'" she said, her voice mocking.

They gathered water and coffee and set up the conference room while she could hear the men talking behind her. She and Marcia stood on either side of the conference room door while they waited for the men to join them.

She could hear her father's voice booming through the lobby of the law office. Then a separate, equally booming voice echoed off the walls.

A very large man with light eyes smiled at her from the hallway. "Well, hello there ladies." Tillie tried not to wince. He was practically shouting at them. Wearing rings on every finger, a bright armed forces jacket with medals hanging off the chest, he was clinking slightly as he walked, a bright smile on his wide face.

Smiling back, Tillie followed the men into the conference room and Marcia pulled the door closed. They all sat, and Tillie watched the large, handsome man. He appeared to be a bit sweaty, despite the chill in the October air outside. His eyes darted from the door to her father and Herr Grandelis, to his hands, then back again. It reminded her a little of a trapped animal.

"Sir, can I interest you in some coffee?" Tillie stood and picked up the tray, walking it over to him, though it seemed like coffee was the last thing he needed.

"Very good, very good." Inside the conference room, his voice bounced off the walls. Tillie handed him the saucer and noticed his hands tremble, rattling the China ever so slightly. Their eyes met and he set the coffee on the table.

"Hermann, this is Tillie, my secretary." Her father gestured for her to take her seat again. "She's also my daughter," he added, as if he'd somehow just remembered they were related. Tillie gave another smile and nodded at the man. "That's Marcia, Anthony's secretary."

Herr Grandelis cleared his throat and leaned forward on the glass tabletop. "No one is taking notes today, because this is an informal visit." Turning his body slightly, he addressed Tillie and

Marcia. "This is my good friend Hermann Göring. He and I were pilots together when we fought for Germany."

She and Marcia both nodded but didn't speak. Tillie's father leaned back in his chair. "So, Herr Göring. Why don't we dive right in?"

Göring nodded and crossed his long legs under the table. "I had some," he paused, pursing his lips, "trouble two years ago that caused me to have to leave the country for a bit. Just a little illness. Nothing to be concerned about." Tillie watched her father and Herr Grandelis exchange a glance, so fast if she had blinked, she would have missed it. "It appears that I am no longer in the Führer's good graces." He shrugged. "At least, I'm not where I'd like to be."

Tillie and Marcia's eyes met, and Tillie had to drop her gaze to her lap quickly to hide her smile.

Göring didn't notice. "I would like to run for the party in the spring of '28, however the Führer has not yet agreed to back me." He sipped his coffee and leaned into the table, uncrossing his legs. "This is where you come in." He took a deep breath, almost trying to steady himself. "I know some information about the early days of the party. Information that would best remain undisclosed to the public."

Tillie watched her father. He raised one eyebrow, ever so slightly, but the rest of his face remained expressionless. Herr Grandelis kept his face even, nothing betraying his thoughts. Göring waited expectantly, slowly stirring his coffee, his eyes on Herr Grandelis' face.

Finally, Herr Grandelis said quietly, "Go on."

Göring nodded. "I would like to threaten the Führer with a lawsuit to convince him and the party to support my run for representative of Bavaria."

Tillie heard Marcia let out an uneven breath. No one spoke for a moment. Her father broke the silence first. "You want to sue Adolf Hitler."

"No. I do not. I want to threaten to sue him. For him to realize I am indispensable to the cause. I want him to realize that I would be an excellent addition to the Reichstag and give me his endorsement." He took another sip of coffee while his words hung in the air.

Her father and Herr Grandelis exchanged another, much longer, glance. For a moment, the mood in the room was tense and thick. "Well," Herr Grandelis finally said, placing his hands on the glass tabletop and pushing himself up to stand. "I think we can probably draft a letter. Something stern, so he knows we mean business, but not so formal that he wants to drop you from the party."

Göring smiled and stood. "Splendid. I'll be in touch with all the details. I'd like to get a letter to him before the end of the year, ensuring my successful run for the Reichstag in the spring." He strode out of the office, flanked by Tillie's father and Herr Grandelis.

"Well," breathed Marcia, as they both cleaned up the coffee. "That was something." Tillie shook her head as she placed the coffee cups back on the tray. Marcia stopped wiping the table and looked up at her. "What do you think he knows?"

Tillie thought for a moment. "Well, he seems to think it's enough to blackmail the leader of the party into backing him for a position in the government." Tillie bit her lip. "But you'd have to wonder if they'd done something bad enough that threatening to make it public would get you a leading position in the Reichstag, why would you stay with the party?" She and Marcia looked at one another and Marcia shook her head, her face skeptical.

"I don't know, but I don't trust any of these men further than I could throw them." She dropped her eyes to her hands, but then cleared her throat and looked up to meet Tillie's gaze. "Your father included. Sorry, Tillie, but this all seems like it's bad news."

Tillie tilted her head and gave Marcia a sympathetic smile. "It's okay Marcia." Her eyes drifted to the doorway and out into the lobby where her father was standing talking with Göring and Herr Grandelis. "It doesn't seem good, does it."

†

Tillie made the short walk to the institute to meet Ernesto and James for dinner. Her head was still slightly spinning from the meeting with her father, Ernesto's father and Göring and she didn't hear her name being called until she felt a hand on her elbow.

"Doll, didn't you hear me? I was calling your name for almost an entire block." Ruth's face was bare except for her red lips, and she was wearing high-waisted slacks and a white shirt.

"Oh, I'm sorry." Tillie leaned in and kissed Ruth on the cheek. "I had the weirdest day, and I was kind of lost in thought."

"The weirdest day in a law office, huh? Intrigue." Ruth winked at her and linked her arm through Tillie's. "Tell me all about it."

As they walked, the sun quickly setting behind them, Tillie filled Ruth in about their meeting with Göring and Ruth's eyes grew wide.

"What do you think he knows?" Before Tillie could answer, Ruth was squeezing her arm. "I mean, that's a pretty bold move to threaten to sue the leader of a political party just to get his endorsement. Why wouldn't he just run for a different party? Or start his own?"

Tillie shook her head. "I don't know. The entire thing seems so strange, doesn't it." She chewed the inside of her cheek as they approached the institute's steps. "I might have to have a discussion with my father though, don't you think?"

Ruth nodded. "You'd think he'd want to separate himself from people who are engaging in this kind of thing. Blackmail and whatever else."

They stopped at the foot of the concrete steps and looked up at the marble bust of Dr. Hirschfeld staring down at them. The large sign reading *Institute of Sexual Science* was framed between two large trees in front of the building. They could see through the glass doors at the top of the steps that the lounge and front room were crowded with people, all laughing and drinking, with Dr. Hirschfeld in the center, smiling, his arm around Karl.

"You'd think," Tillie answered. "C'mon. Let's go have dinner."

They were just finishing their food, sitting in the lounge, when James walked in, still dressed from his performance at the club. Ernesto jumped up from the couch and threw his arms around James' neck.

Ruth elbowed Tillie and murmured, "You're staring."

Tillie smiled softly. "I know. I'm just happy for them." She turned, pulling her legs up and draping them over Ruth's lap. "Do you remember when we were like that? Do you remember what it was like in the beginning?"

Ruth ran her lips down Tillie's jawbone. "Oh, I remember."

Tillie giggled and shivered involuntarily. "That's not exactly what I meant." Ruth bit lightly on her earlobe.

"You two better behave yourselves." The stern voice made them jump.

Dora stood smiling at them from the doorway. "Dora!" Tillie moved to make space. "Come sit with us!"

"Taking a break from the library to come slum with the lazy folks who like to sit around on a Friday night?" Ruth winked at Dora as she eased into Tillie's vacated chair.

"Oh hush." Dora made to smack Ruth's arm playfully. "So." She nodded across the room towards Ernesto and James. "How's that going?"

Tillie grinned. "Well, I think. What's it been, Ruthie? A month? And they're still obsessed with each other?"

Dora gave a contented sigh. "I've always had such a fondness for Ernesto." Ruth made a disgruntled noise and Dora smiled at her. "Dear, you had James' mother, Bernadette. You didn't need a mother figure. But Ernesto, after his father kicked him out of his house." She cleared her throat. "When he first got here, he was convinced his mother was going to come for him. He talked about it for weeks."

Tillie turned her head to look at Dora so fast, she felt her neck crack. "He did? I didn't know that."

Dora waved her hand. "Oh yes. You remember what happened. His father walked in on him dressed in his mother's clothes."

Tillie nodded and cringed recalling the phone call. Ernesto sobbing, barely using full sentences. *Beaten. Degenerate. Not in my home. Leave before I kill you myself!*

Dora continued, "He kept telling me, 'Don't worry, Dora. She's going to come and get me. She wouldn't choose my father over me.' He was convinced that because his mother knew he wore her clothes, she would come for him. Or at least make sure he was alright." She wiped a small tear from her eye and her voice cracked.

"Poor dear. Eventually he just stopped talking about his mother altogether. I think her not coming for him hurt him more than his father punching him in the jaw the night he was kicked out." She took a sip from Tillie's vodka on the table and gave a small cough.

"Anyway. He needed someone and so did I. So, we had each other. I needed someone to take care of and he was brand new to this part of the city and to the institute." She patted the top of Tillie's hand. "I was so glad when you turned up. He was so lonely here."

"Um. Again. Am I chopped liver? I was living here when Ernesto moved in." Dora leaned over and kissed Ruth on the cheek.

"I know you were, dear, but you and Ernesto were always just surface friends." Ruth snorted into her own drink. "You know

I'm right. Once you're done talking about the weather and who's dating who at the clubs, you run out of things to talk about. Tillie is the glue that keeps you and Ernesto together. Without her, the two of you would have nothing to say to one another."

Tillie laughed. "Dora's not wrong, Ruthie."

Ruth shrugged. "That might be true, but I'm the reason he found James, so there."

Tillie nudged Ruth gently. "Aw, don't get your feelings hurt."

Ruth pretended to blow her nose loudly and fake sobbed, "It's fine" before winking at Tillie.

They were all quiet for a moment while they watched James and Ernesto talking to one another on the couch. "Well," Dora announced after a moment, "that's quite enough snooping."

"Snooping?" Tillie watched as Dora stood up from the table.

"Of course. I came down here to see what my Ernesto was up to. And he's up to that." She pointed over at the boys, whose legs were now intertwined. "I approve, James is lovely, now it's time to get back to work."

"Work," Ruth practically shouted at her. "Dora, it is Friday night, all your friends are here, and the institute closed to the public two hours ago. Sit down and have a drink with us."

Dora put her hands on her hips, looking like a mother surveying her teenage children. "I have things to do, Ruthie." She looked from Ruth to Tillie and then over to Ernesto and James. "You all behave yourselves and don't stay up too late." She patted Ruth on the hand and walked back out the door, waving at them as she went.

CHAPTER 3

October 1927

Saturday morning dawned cold and bright, the sun shining through the bedroom window much earlier than Tillie would have wanted. She squinted into the beams and rolled over, pushing her face down into the crook of Ruth's neck.

Ruth yelped and pushed her away. "Why is your nose so cold?" She rolled as far from Tillie as she could get.

Tillie laughed and sat up, immediately regretting it. Slouching back down under the heavy blankets, she shivered. "I think the radiator needs clunking again."

Ruth groaned and turned to Tillie. "I will wash your work stockings for a month if you get out of bed and fix it."

Tillie leaned forward and kissed Ruth's nose. "Deal."

She took a deep breath and jumped out of bed, gasping when her feet hit the cold floor. Scurrying across the room, she picked up the metal bar they kept propped up against the wall specifically for fixing the radiator. She hit it several times at the bottom to disperse the air pockets that kept it from working. It gave a loud clang and started up again; Tillie could already feel small waves of heat hitting her and she ran back to bed and jumped in.

She touched her freezing toes to Ruth's thigh and Ruth shrieked. "Tillie! Why!" They both fell into giggles and Ruth burrowed herself farther under the covers. "December is going to be dreadful."

"I have to get up, I have a shift at the institute today helping out in the archives." Tillie rolled over and picked up her watch from her bedside table. "Want to walk me?"

Ruth nodded and sat up, shivering again. "Are you coming to the club tonight?"

Tillie could feel the last two late nights starting to catch up with her. "I don't think so, I'll probably stay home and go to bed early."

Ruth made a face. "You're such an old lady."

Tillie tilted her head to one side. "Well, my job doesn't allow me to sleep in every day of the week, so going to bed at two a.m. and then getting to work by eight a.m. makes me tired and cranky." She leaned over, kissing Ruth's bare shoulder. "Do you want me to come tonight? I can for a bit if you'd like."

Ruth gazed over at her, a small smile on her face. "That's okay, doll. You stay home and get some rest. I think both James and I are working on Monday, but the early shift, we'll be done by eleven, so maybe you can come then."

Tillie smiled. "That sounds great." She felt Ruth's cold fingers moving up the inside of her thigh. She raised her eyebrows and looked over at Ruth. Ruth's face had a mischievous grin.

"What time do you have to leave?" Ruth leaned in, still dragging her fingers up Tillie's leg, and kissed her neck.

A sigh escaped from Tillie's throat. "I have a few minutes," she managed to squeak out.

"Oh good," Ruth murmured, her lips on Tillie's collarbone, her cold fingers making Tillie gasp.

✝

An hour later, Tillie was hurrying up the cold street, leaving Ruth behind at a cafe for a much-needed cup of coffee. The institute came into view, and she checked her watch. She was only five minutes late, but she still didn't want to keep Dora waiting.

She rushed through the doors calling out a hello to Helene at the front desk. Her heels clicked loudly through the empty hallways as she tried to get to the library as quickly as possible without running. Pushing open the large wooden double doors, she felt an immediate sense of calm washing over her. Being in the presence of thousands of books was like an instant stress reliever, like all the pages in the room served as a balm for her nerves.

"You're late," a teasing voice rang out from her left.

"Ernesto." She smiled. "I thought I was working with Dora and Nissa today." She slowed to a stroll as she unbuttoned her coat and headed to the main desk in the library.

"Nissa ran down to the kitchen to get coffee and Dora has a meeting with Dr. H." Ernesto picked up a stack of books to start returning them to the shelves.

Tillie nodded and grabbed some books off the towering stack in Ernesto's arms. As they started walking to replace the books, Tillie cleared her throat.

"Hey, do you know a man called Hermann Göring?"

Ernesto tilted his head to the side, thinking. "I'm not sure. Should I?"

Tillie shook her head. "No, I was just wondering. He came into the office yesterday looking for representation. I guess he and your dad were pilots together. And then he was involved in 1923."

Ernesto stiffened for a moment at the mention of his father, but then took a deep breath. "Remind me what he looks like? I feel like the name does sound familiar."

Tillie thought for a second. "He's loud. Loud enough that he makes my dad seem quiet. And he's tall, he sort of fills a room when he walks into it. Blonde, lighter eyes. He seems nervous, maybe? He was really jittery when I met him yesterday."

Ernesto narrowed his eyes, nodding slowly. "Yeah actually, I do remember him. He and his wife came round for dinner a few times, but then they ended up leaving the country. I don't know why, but my dad made it sound like he didn't really have a choice."

Tillie bit her lip. "Yes, he mentioned that he left the country, said he was sick, but wasn't specific."

Ernesto stood on his tiptoes to slide a book back onto the shelf. "So, what did he want?"

"Hm?" Tillie's thoughts were on Göring and the meeting in her father's office. "Oh, here's what's crazy. He came to us because he wants to sue Hitler."

Ernesto scoffed. "The Putsch guy?"

"That's the one. He wants to run for a Parliament seat in the spring but so far, Hitler is refusing to back him. He claims he knows things that, if he threatened to go public, Hitler would change his mind." She shrugged and her hand rested on the spine of the book she was setting on the shelf. "It's all very cloak and dagger."

"That sounds insane," Ernesto laughed. "He's going after the leader of the party with threats? Isn't he worried that he'll just be written off completely?"

Tillie let out a long breath. "You'd think."

"And our fathers were willing to help him do this?" His voice was filled with doubt.

"Yes. That's what's even more strange. They're so obsessed with the party and with Hitler, that I thought for sure they would have immediately said no to Göring. But they agreed. I'm not sure what they think the end game is going to be here, but I can't imagine that threatening the guy who's supposedly in charge is going to get them where they want to go."

Ernesto slid his last book, a pale lavender book, its gold title *The Well of Loneliness*, glinting under the fluorescent lights, onto the shelf.

Tillie reached out. "Wait," she said, grabbing the book out of its spot on the shelf. "That's my 'working in the library' book. I read it when there's no one here and I'm bored." She grinned at Ernesto as he tried to suppress a laugh.

They heard the doors of the library bang open and Nissa called out into the room, "I have coffee."

They started back to the front desk and Ernesto said, "Well it's not like they even matter anyway."

Nissa was setting a tray down on the desk and looked up. "Who doesn't matter?

"The Nazis. Hitler. That whole thing." Tillie picked up her coffee cup and breathed in the aroma, closing her eyes.

To her surprise, Nissa laughed. "Oh yeah, back when I worked," she paused and cleared her throat. "Before I lived here, I worked outside the clubs. You know," she shrugged, "for the men." Ernesto and Tillie's eyes met. It was no secret Nissa had been a prostitute before coming to live at the institute.

"Anyway, there was a man who always would come find me, I don't remember his name, this was a few years ago. And he was there, at the Putsch, with the rest of them. He got arrested, but never went to jail." She sipped her coffee. "Always going on and on about that, like it made him better than the others." She shook her head, chuckling. "He was really high up in the army, I think, but he always talked about what good friends he was with Hitler. I would just smile and nod, say 'sure you are honey.' The more he talked, the less I'd have to see him with his pants down." She winked at Tillie.

She smiled slightly, her coffee cup halfway to her lips. "I wonder what he's doing now. The last time I saw him, he was talking about quitting everything and going to live in the country.

I remember I asked how he would get to the clubs after dark if he lived out in the middle of nowhere."

Nissa laughed to herself and both Tillie and Ernesto couldn't help it, they chuckled along too. "Anyway, you're right. That entire party is a joke." She turned and picked up the third cup off the tray. "Here, Ernesto, drink your coffee before it gets cold."

†

"You're the one who suggested this, don't forget." Tillie was sipping tea at the kitchen table while Ruth leaned back over the counter, cold slices of cucumbers over her eyes. "Also, your shift ended at eleven, so why you thought staying and drinking with James until closing was a good idea is beyond me."

"Tills," Ruth's voice was hoarse. "I love you so much but if you don't shut up, I'm going to throw this cucumber at you." She gripped the unsliced vegetable in her hand and shook it in the air, threateningly.

Tillie laughed into her tea. "We promised Dora dinner like old times, so we have to get going." She stood. "At least we don't have to cook. We just need move the tables around and make it look nice."

When they arrived to pick up James and his mother, Bernadette, James looked just as pale as Ruth and Bernadette wore the same smug expression as Tillie. "Ahhh," she said, her eyes moving from her son to Ruth's face. "I see you're in a right state as well." She clicked her tongue. "Should have stuck to water last night, my dear. It keeps you from getting puffy."

Ruth just groaned but Tillie had to hide her smile behind her hand. "Ready for dinner?" Tillie directed the question to James, but he just shook his head, his face looking paler once he pulled on his dark brown coat.

"Oh I am." Bernadette buttoned her own coat. "I've never been to the institute or met this famous Dora or Dr. Magnus Hirschfeld.

I can't wait." She said Dr. Hirschfeld's name with reverence and beamed, then glanced at James, who closed his eyes and leaned against the wall outside their flat. "You know, if you just threw up, you'd probably feel better."

Stifling a laugh, Tillie turned and linked her arm with Ruth's. "You'll feel better once we get some of Heinz's pot roast in you. Maybe some mashed potatoes to soak up all that leftover gin."

Tillie could tell the cold air perked both James and Ruth up. Once they arrived at the institute, they both had a little color in their cheeks and James had managed a few one-word answers to questions Tillie directed at him.

They walked into the lobby and Adelaide was behind the welcome desk. "Hey, you guys," she grinned up at them. "You here for Dora's Sunday dinner?" She dropped her voice. "Seriously, we should start doing this again, Dora has been on cloud nine all day. She's in such a good mood. Like a mother hen waiting for all her chicks to come back to the barn."

Tillie nudged Ruth and smiled. "See," she whispered into Ruth's ear. "You did good, suggesting this."

They all went down the stairs into the cafeteria, the smells of the pot roast and potatoes wafting towards them. "Hey you guys!" Ernesto called from the counter in the back where he stood talking to the cook, Heinz, and Dr. Hirschfeld.

"C'mon Bernadette, I'll introduce you." Ruth took Bernadette's hand, and they crossed the kitchen dining area leaving James and Tillie behind.

"You feeling okay?" Tillie whispered to James.

He sighed. "Yes, I think so. I'll be able to power through, at least." He turned to look at her. "Your girlfriend and I have too much fun together. It's not good for my health." He smiled, his eyes crinkling, his face warm.

Tillie smiled as she looked over at Ruth, holding hands with Bernadette, talking with Dr. Hirschfeld. "Yes, she's quite fun, isn't she."

All their friends started gathering as Ernesto and James pushed the tables together. Nissa, Helene, and Adelaide came down the stairs first, followed by Karl and Dora. Heinz started bringing out plates of pot roast and potatoes while Dr. Hirschfeld pulled out a bottle of champagne from behind the kitchen counter. Tillie saw Ruth eye it with distaste.

Once they were all seated, Dora at the center, Dr. Hirschfeld stood and raised his glass. "I'm so glad all our friends could gather here tonight for dinner. I think only Heinz might argue against reinstating our weekly Sunday evening dinners." They all laughed and Heinz grinned, sheepishly.

Dr. Hirschfeld's eyes fell on Dora. "Dörchen," he smiled a warm, kind smile at her. "Cheers."

CHAPTER 4

March 1990

Thea stood in the bedroom, her hands on her hips, staring down at the tiny woman in front of her. Her grandmother frowned and tried to wave her away. "I don't know what this fuss is all about."

"Gram." Thea pursed her lips, trying to keep her voice even. Her grandmother sat in an armchair by the window looking through her nail polish, trying to choose a color.

"I'm just a little forgetful, my brain is old." She looked up at her pale, blonde granddaughter and winked. She tapped her temple with a chipped red fingernail. "It's like Swiss cheese up here."

Thea folded her arms across her chest and didn't laugh. "Okay, first, your brain is not Swiss cheese. Gross." Her grandmother chuckled. "And second of all, you were three blocks away with no shoes on." Her grandmother didn't meet Thea's eyes and just shrugged.

Thea dropped to her knees so her grandmother would be forced to look at her. Her eyes, a pale blue, were looking anywhere but Thea's face, determined not to acknowledge what they both knew. Thea took her grandmother's hands into her own. They were soft and wrinkled, blue veins visible through the papery skin.

"Gram," she said softly. "I don't think you can be alone during the day anymore." Her grandmother didn't respond and continued focusing on the nail polish. "When the neighbor found you, do you know what you said?"

Her grandmother finally met Thea's eyes and Thea was startled to see she was near tears. She shook her head and Thea could feel the old woman's hands trembling. "You said you were trying to find Grandpa and Uncle Jimmy." Her grandmother took a deep breath and closed her eyes, tears tumbling down the folds of her face and pooling in the corners of her lips.

"Well, that doesn't mean anything." She hastily wiped the tears away "They aren't here, are they?" Her voice rang with annoyance. "Where are they, anyway?"

Thea's heart felt like it was in a free fall and her stomach turned. "Gram, sweetie. They died." If she had a dollar for every time she had to tell her grandmother they were dead this week alone, she'd have this house paid off.

"Oh." She nodded but Thea could see there was no spark of recognition with the words. Her grandmother didn't remember when her husband had his heart attack at the kitchen table during a Wednesday night dinner when Thea was five years old. Or that he was dead before his fork hit the ground. She didn't remember when Uncle Jimmy went from a spry, fit eighty-five-year-old to a skeleton almost overnight or how he died in the hospital bed in their living room, his partner Michael by his side.

She watched as her grandmother's eyes grew vacant and unfocused. A sure sign she was no longer part of the conversation. Thea lightly patted the top of her grandmother's hand and stood, turning to leave her in the safety of her soft blue bedroom.

"He blamed me. He always loved her more. So, he blamed me."

Her empty eyes drooped, and her breathing slowed. Thea stood watching for a little longer, waiting to see if she was going to open her eyes and continue talking, but then her head slumped forward, and a little snore escaped her throat. Thea shook her head and rubbed her eyes. Half the time, she didn't even know what her grandmother was talking about. Turning and closing the door behind her, she went downstairs to the brightly lit kitchen. Picking up the phone, she dialed.

"Hello?"

"Hi Michael."

"Thea, is everything okay?" She could hear papers rustling in the background and she fought the wave of guilt for interrupting his workday.

"I got called home from work because Gram wandered again."

A heavy sigh. "So, is it time, do you think?"

"I don't really know what else to do. She can't be here alone anymore, and I don't think we can afford to hire someone to be here with her during the day. At least, not someone full time." Thea rubbed her eyes with her free hand. "I wish Uncle Jimmy was still alive to tell me what to do."

Another sigh. "I wish he was still alive too." Michael sniffed, and she heard voices in the background.

"You have to go; we can talk about this when you get home."

Hot shame burned Thea's throat at disturbing him.

"No, sweetie, it's okay." He paused and she heard him whispering to someone, she assumed he'd covered the mouthpiece of the phone because it was muffled, and she couldn't understand his words. "Okay, listen," he said to Thea. "My sister's number is on the bulletin board next to the phone. Do you see it?"

Thea nodded before remembering Michael couldn't see her. She cleared her throat. "Yes." Her voice sounded like a stranger.

"Call Vanessa and let her know what's going on. She might be able to get Gram up the waiting list. Or even get her into the facility now. You never know. Vanessa loves you and your grandmother. You and Matilda are basically family."

Tears started to stream down Thea's face. Michael and Gram were the only people she had left. She didn't want to admit it to herself, but she could feel the seeds of worry blooming in her gut. That once Gram was gone, Michael would see no reason to stay.

"Thea?" She realized she'd been quiet too long.

"Yes, sorry, I'm still here." She wiped the tears from her cheeks.

"I promised Jimmy I would take care of you both and I meant it. We'll get this figured out."

More voices in the background.

A sob bubbled out of Thea's mouth before she could stop it. "Okay," she said, her voice thick.

"Thea, I'm going to come home early from work, okay? We'll have Vanessa over for dinner." She nodded again because she didn't trust herself not to burst into hysterical crying over the phone. Michael's voice dropped to a tender, gentle whisper. "Thea. I know it feels like everyone has left you." She couldn't contain the emotion now. She clutched the phone, her knuckles turning white, the tears burning her face as they fell. "I will not leave you, Thea. We're family."

"Okay," she whispered.

"I'll be home in an hour. Just make yourself some tea and try to stay calm."

Thea gently replaced the phone on the hook when she heard the floorboards creak in the cheery white hallway. She hastily mopped her face with her sleeve and turned, pasting a smile on her lips. Turning to her grandmother, she was all smiles and sunshine.

"Hiya, Gram. You hungry? I was just going to make some tea."

Her grandmother eyed her suspiciously. "Who was on the phone?"

"Oh, I was talking to Michael. He's going to come home from work early today and I think Vanessa is going to come to dinner." She watched her grandmother's face for any sign of confusion. "Vanessa is his sister, remember?"

"*Ich erinnere mich,*" her grandmother snapped, her tone icy and unfamiliar.

Thea clenched her jaw. "Gram, I don't know what you just said." It was happening more and more; when she was tired or having a bad day, she would slip into speaking angry German.

Her grandmother's brain was like an old ship being pulled under the ocean by a tentacled monster. Terrifying arms reaching up from the depths of the sea just to entangle her grandmother and slowly crack the solid wood that used to be her sharp wit and kind smile.

Her grandmother shook her head, like she was trying to push a reset button she couldn't quite reach. "I'm sorry, Thea." Her voice was quiet.

Thea stifled a sigh and gave her a small smile. "It's okay, sweetie. How about some tea?"

Her grandmother nodded and shuffled to the table while Thea watched her. She sat and stared out the large picture window into the backyard, her eyes wide and vacant. "I know they're dead," she said, as Thea put on the kettle.

"What?"

"I know they're dead. Jimmy and Ernie. But sometimes it feels like all the things in my head are made of water. And they're dripping through my fingers." Her voice caught in her throat. "I can't hold on. I can feel myself slipping away and then I'm just gone." For the first time, Thea could hear fear in her grandmother's voice.

"Oh Gram." Thea didn't know what else to say. It was the first time her grandmother acknowledged losing herself.

"I feel so betrayed." Her grandmother's voice shook. "I kept waiting for cancer like Jimmy. Or a heart attack like your grandfather. I kept waiting for my body to fall apart. I never expected my brain to turn on me." She touched her forehead with a wrinkled, trembling hand. "You can never understand what it feels like to know you can't trust your own thoughts," she murmured.

Thea brought two mugs of tea to the table, along with some cookies from Michael's stash in the cupboard. "You're right, I don't know." She sat down and rubbed her grandmother's back.

Her grandmother turned her pale eyes, rimmed with red, toward Thea's face. "I'm so worried that you're going to be all alone."

Thea gave what she hoped was a reassuring smile. "I'm not alone, I have Michael." Her grandmother shook her head.

"I know he loved your uncle, but he's not," she paused. "He's not really family." Her eyes looked past Thea, to somewhere over her shoulder. "He didn't see it all. He didn't know."

"Gram?" Thea tried to move so she was back in the center of her grandmother's gaze.

Her eyes blinked back into focus, and she smiled, picking up her tea. "I mean, he's not your father. Or your grandfather." She sipped her tea. "You know, when your parents died, I promised I would never leave you. You were only two, so I know you don't remember how awful it was. But after the car accident, I sat on that couch in there." She pointed to their ancient brown couch sagging in the living room. "I sat with your grandfather and Uncle Jimmy, and we cried, and I rocked you back and forth while you asked for your mama."

Her eyes filled with tears at the memory. "And I whispered to you that I would never leave you. That it would be okay." Her voice was thick, and she sniffed. "But here you are." She reached out and put a soft hand to Thea's cheek. "You've been left by all of us."

An hour later, Michael walked into the house in the hurried way a lawyer moves. He bustled into the house with his briefcase and, upon seeing Thea standing in the kitchen drinking a fourth cup of tea, he pulled her into a tight embrace.

"My sister will be here at six for dinner." He kissed the top of her head. "How's Gram?"

Thea shrugged. "Freaked out. Sick. Sad." She sipped her tea. "She's sleeping now." Turning her wrist, she looked at her watch and sighed. "Sleeping now means staying up all night, though." Rubbing her face, Thea wondered if this was how parents of newborns felt.

Michael loosened his tie. "It's too bad she couldn't hold on another year. I'm so close to retirement."

Thea tilted her head to the side and stared at him. "You really want to spend your retirement babysitting my grandmother? I know you told Uncle Jimmy you'd be here for us, but you still have a life to live. My grandmother is almost eighty-five. You're barely sixty-five. You have enough time to meet someone new and travel and do all kinds of stuff."

He shrugged. "Jimmy and I were together for almost fifteen years, and they were the best fifteen years of my life. He asked me to take care of you and your grandmother and I intend to." He said it with such finality that Thea felt relief bloom somewhere in her chest. She wouldn't be alone.

They quietly made dinner while waiting for Vanessa to arrive. She hadn't checked on her grandmother for a while, but the lights were still off in the upstairs hallway, and she couldn't hear any movement from her grandmother's room.

Vanessa walked into the house without ringing the bell. Her dark brown skin looked soft and dewy, even though she was thirty-five years older than Thea. Thea shook her head and smiled as Vanessa pulled her into a warm hug. "How do you look younger every time I see you? It's like witchcraft."

Vanessa laughed. "Cold cream and sunscreen. That's the secret."

Michael laughed and pulled her into a hug. "Mama would make fun of you for using sunscreen." Vanessa shrugged and pinched Michael's cheek.

"But I'm sixty and I don't look a day over thirty-five. And you, sir, look like Sammy Davis Jr." She laughed some more when Michael looked horror stricken.

"Sammy Davis Jr. just died!"

They all laughed loudly as they moved to the kitchen, Vanessa still teasing her older brother. As they all settled around their plates, Vanessa's eyes grew soft and her expression more somber.

"So," she began. "Is Matilda going to be joining us for this conversation?"

Thea shook her head. "She's still sleeping. Besides, she'd just argue with us that she's fine and doesn't need to move out of our home."

Vanessa gave a solemn nod. "And do we think it's time for your grandmother to be moved to memory care?"

Thea took a deep breath and then nodded. "Yes. She left the house with no shoes today. Thank goodness the neighbor was outside mowing his lawn. He recognized her from our walks and stopped her." She felt panic rise like a wave before she could stamp it down. "Who knows what would have happened if he hadn't thought to ask where I was."

Michael rubbed her forearm. "She can't be here alone, and I don't think she has the finances to pay for a day nurse while we're both at work."

Vanessa nodded. "Very few people have the finances for that." She took a bite of the salmon Michael had expertly prepared. "Oh, brother, this is good." She chewed thoughtfully and then set down her fork. "We have a waitlist for the assisted living facility now, but there are several rooms open in the memory care wing. She could move as early as next week, provided we can get her finances all set up."

"Next week?" Thea felt her pulse quicken. This was only supposed to be a discussion. It wasn't supposed to go this fast.

"But that's so soon." She looked wildly from Michael to Vanessa and saw their matching expressions of pity.

"Sweetie, she can't stay here," Michael said gently. "We don't really have a plan. We should have been planning better, but here we are. It's time."

Thea dropped her head into her hands, feeling a headache forming behind her eyes. "I know," she said under her breath. "I know it is."

CHAPTER 5

January 1928

Tillie pulled her coat tighter around her shoulders as the tiny white snowflakes swirled around her head and stuck to her hair. She shuddered. "The worst part of New Year's Eve is that it's in January." Her teeth chattered in between each word.

Ruth laughed and pulled her hat down farther over her ears. "It's only another block. Maybe we can crash in an empty room at the institute to save us the freezing walk home."

Tillie pushed her hands deeper into her pockets. "When we walk home, we'll be drunk enough that we won't feel the cold."

They quickened their steps against the bitter wind and Ruth muttered, "Maybe we should have had a few drinks before we left the flat."

The institute came into view and Tillie breathed a sigh of relief. Her toes were starting to go numb. The lights were blazing in the lobby, and she could see there were already groups gathered in the foyer, no doubt the lounge was already full. Opening the door, the warmth hit her in the face and Ruth immediately shed her hat and coat. Shouts of welcome echoed from every corner of the room and someone pushed a glass of champagne into Tillie's hand.

"Tills!" Ernesto was pushing his way through the crowd of people in various stages of undress.

"Ernesto!" Tillie grinned at him and grabbed Ruth's hand to pull her along across the lobby. "There are so many people here, it's madness!" They were sandwiched in between two men dancing together and Dora with her friends all chatting animatedly while drinking from teacups. Dora heard her and leaned forward to kiss her cheeks. Then she gestured to the crowds of people throughout the lounge and the lobby.

"I think the rest of Berlin realized the institute throws the best parties," she yelled into Tillie's ear. "I don't know half of these people and it's pretty clear a few of them aren't our people." She raised a dramatic eyebrow and Tillie laughed.

James took a sip of champagne. "Ew, you mean there are husbands with wives here?" He feigned disgust and they all laughed.

†

Tillie took one last gulp of champagne and leaned over to Ruth. "Ruthie," she could hear her voice slurring, "we should probably head home." They had rung in the new year almost two hours ago and the party had all but cleared out. Ernesto and James sat cuddled on the couch, whispering into one another's ears, Heinz was at a table by the window with a man Tillie didn't recognize, and Nissa was asleep in one of the armchairs. "Everyone's left or gone to bed. We should go."

Ruth nodded and stumbled out of her chair. Catching herself, she grinned at Tillie. "I forgot to ask Dr. H. if we could stay here." She hiccupped. "I guess we won't be cold on the walk home though, huh?" She laughed at herself as she pulled on her hat.

"Ernesto," Tillie called across the room, "we're leaving." He and James pulled themselves apart long enough to wave and Tillie shook her head. "Love you too," she mumbled as she tried to get her arms through the sleeves of her coat.

"Ruthie," she said, on her fourth try. "I think I might have had too much champagne tonight."

Ruth shrugged. "There's no such thing, doll." She looped her arm through Tillie's, and they stumbled beside one another as they walked to the front door.

The air felt like a cold shower on Tillie's drunken face, and she immediately felt quite sober. Ruth made a small noise next to her, like she'd been doused with ice water. "Well," Ruth gasped, "that's one way to sober up." She pushed her hands down into her pockets and they bowed their heads in the frigid wind blowing directly into their faces.

It had stopped snowing and was quiet as they walked. Tillie had expected to see a few party goers, dragging themselves home, but it seemed they were the last ones out. Tillie sighed as she let her body lean into Ruth's while they walked. She could see their flat in the distance when she heard someone call out to them.

"Oy, where you pretty ladies off to?" She felt Ruth's steps falter. Looking left she saw several young men, all carrying bottles of varying fullness, wearing the telltale brown shirts she instantly recognized as the Nazi uniform. Their ties were loose and belts askew, but the red arm band was bright even in the yellow glow of the streetlamps.

"We're on our way home." Ruth's voice was polite but sharp and did not betray the stumbling she had done less than ten minutes prior.

"By yourselves? That's a shame," another of the men shouted. Ruth had slowed, but in another ten feet, they would be forced to walk directly past the men. She felt Ruth's grip on her arm tighten.

"Where are your men?" A third man spoke. His voice seemed darker than the others and there was an underlying hint of malice. The other two men melted back, letting him take the lead position in their group and Tillie could tell he was in charge. Whatever he told the others to do, they would follow. She stared at him, and his eyes looked black in the shadow of the cloudy night sky. Her gaze shifted to the man standing the farthest away. He was blonde and round and didn't look to be a day over sixteen. His eyes darted nervously from the man in the front to Tillie's face.

Tillie watched as the muscles in Ruth's jaw clenched. She could see in Ruth's pale face that she was weighing her options. After what felt like five minutes, she cleared her throat and gave a quick smile . "Oh, you know those Italian men; they can't handle a German New Year's Eve." She felt Ruth's elbow dig into her ribs and took that as a cue to join in with a forced laugh.

The man at the front of the group smiled. "Isn't that the truth? So, your husbands are Italian then?"

Ruth waived a hand. "Oh no, they're just our boyfriends." She gave a bigger smile this time and picked up her pace as they walked. Less than three feet and they would be passing the group. Tillie could see their apartment a block away.

The men moved to block their path. Tillie could feel Ruth's heart quicken and her fingers dig into the flesh just above Tillie's elbow. They stopped walking. "I appreciate you being so worried about us, walking alone, but I assure you, gentlemen, we're just fine. Our flat is right over there." She pointed and smiled again, but Tillie could see the smile didn't reach Ruth's eyes.

The man with the black eyes settled his gaze on Tillie. "You're awfully quiet." He took a step forward and reached out, touching her cheek with his fingertips. "I'd pay a pretty penny to spend some quality time with you, darling."

Tillie felt Ruth's entire body tense up and she wrapped her hand around Tillie's bicep, as if she was going to yank her backwards. Tillie lifted her chin and met the man's terrifying gaze. "I don't think you could afford me even if you wanted to."

The man stared at her for a moment, then Tillie smiled, and he started laughing. He took another step towards her. "What you need is a real German man." He breathed on her neck, and she could smell stale vodka and body odor coming off him in waves. Now Ruth really did yank Tillie back and smiled sweetly at the man.

"This has been so fun, but we really should be going."

She side-stepped the men, pulling Tillie along and Tillie felt a strong hand around her other arm, pulling her back.

"You can go if you want," he nodded to Ruth. "But I think I want to chat more with your friend here." His eyes narrowed on Tillie, and she felt her heart in her throat. Sweat was starting to bead on the back of her neck despite the freezing temperature. His fingers wrapped around her arm, and he pulled her hard into his chest. She stumbled slightly. She threw her hands up and braced herself against him, which he seemed to take as an invitation, and he pulled her in closer. She felt cold fingers on her leg, moving quickly up her thigh. She pushed against him, but his free arm was locked around her waist.

"Please stop," she whispered. She couldn't seem to find her voice.

"Don't worry, you're going to enjoy this," he growled back. She could feel his hand digging into her stockings, trying to rip them under her dress and she closed her eyes, letting her body go limp. Maybe if she stopped struggling, it would be over faster.

Standing stock still, she dropped her hands to her sides. "There we go," his voice was in her ear, and it made the hair on her neck stand. She could feel her stockings slowly ripping under his calloused fingers.

"I said, we should go." Ruth's voice rang out clear and sharp behind her and the man stopped what he was doing to look up over Tillie's shoulder. Suddenly there was a loud crack and the man fell against Tillie, then slumped to the ground. Tillie stood stunned, staring at the man on the ground, his head oozing blood onto the sidewalk. Looking up, she saw the scared blonde boy, his bottle of vodka broken in his hand. He looked shocked at what he had done.

"Thank you," Tillie managed to choke.

"Y-y-you," he stuttered, "you look like my sister." Tillie gave a slow nod.

"What did you do?" The third man shouted, looking horror stricken and then he turned, disappearing into the night.

The young blonde rubbed his face with his empty hand. "I'll tell him we were jumped by commies. He's so drunk, he won't even know." He was quickly regaining his senses and his eyes went to Ruth. "Get her home and get something hot in her. Some food too. She might go into shock." He bent over and hauled Tillie's attacker onto his shoulder. "I'm really sorry about this, miss." He looked genuinely embarrassed at his friend's behavior.

Tillie hadn't moved and realized some of the blood from the man's head had gotten on her shoes. She felt Ruth's hand against her back and her voice saying, "Come on, Tills, let's go home." Ruth's voice sounded very far away. Somehow, she moved her feet to follow Ruth the last few steps to their flat. Ruth led her inside and she fell into a chair at the kitchen table.

Glancing at the clock on the wall, she saw it was after three. Their walk home that should have taken ten minutes had taken over an hour. Ruth put a cup of tea in front of her and helped her take off her jacket.

"Tills," she said softly. "Are you alright?"

"Uh huh." Tillie swallowed the tea, and it stung the back of her throat. Ruth had put bourbon in it. Looking up to meet Ruth's eyes, she suddenly felt exhausted. Setting her cup down, she tried to make a joke. "Well, that definitely put a damper on our evening, didn't it."

Ruth chuckled softly. "Those Brownshirts are such garbage. I'm sorry I couldn't do anything." Her eyes suddenly filled with tears. "Maybe I should start carrying a knife." She bit her lower lip, staring off into space.

"Ruthie, it's okay. I'm fine, nothing really happened. We should have stayed at the institute, that's all." She shrugged and tried to keep her hands from shaking as she picked up her tea again. "Now we know for next time. We're just going to have to be a little more careful." Ruth nodded, but still looked concerned.

Tillie took a deep breath and stood, holding out her hand to Ruth. "Let's just go to bed and pretend this part of the night never happened." Ruth took her hand and smiled, but Tillie thought her smile looked forced. They walked hand in hand to the bedroom, but not before Ruth double checked both the deadbolt and the chain lock on the front door.

CHAPTER 6

March 1928

Tillie placed the medical journal back on the shelf and checked her watch. "You got someplace to be, love?" Dora was standing at the small desk staring at her, her eyes twinkling. Tillie shook her head and smiled. "No, no. I'm just, you know, keeping track of time."

"You're going to see Ruthie perform tonight. I know that look." Dora followed Tillie to the next set of tables, picking up random books as she walked.

Tillie smiled. "No, I'm skipping going to the club tonight, but I'm hoping to get home in enough time to see her before she heads into work."

Dora grinned back. "Well, you can leave a little early then." She looked around the empty library. "The last tour was about an hour ago, so I can't imagine we'll get many more people in here before we close up shop."

Tillie squeezed Dora's arm in thanks, then kept walking along the tables collecting loose books. She picked up another medical journal, this one with a pale-yellow cover, to put back onto the shelves when Dora clapped her hands and exclaimed, "That's my book!"

"What?" Tillie looked down at the journal in her hands.

"Dr. Abraham wrote about me back in 1922, when I first came here." Tillie must have looked confused because Dora chuckled and then added, "I kept getting into spots of trouble. You know, a man in a dress and all that. Finally, the courts released me to Dr. H., and I came here." She thought for a minute. "That must have been, oh, eight years ago, maybe?" She continued. "Dr. Abraham, one of Dr. Hirschfeld's colleagues, did a case study on me after my first surgery and then wrote all about it." She grinned at Tillie. "I'm basically famous," she joked.

Tillie grinned back. "Do you mind if I read it?"

"Of course not, love. That's why it's a book. I wouldn't have let Dr. Abraham put me in writing if I minded. I'm gonna warn you though, some of it even makes me a little squeamish and I'm the one it happened to." She waved a hand. "But then, I don't even like when I see someone get a paper cut, so maybe you'll be fine." She gave a mischievous smile. "I think I'm going to get a second journal in a few years too."

Tillie raised her eyes from the pages she was flipping through. "Oh really?"

"Dr. H. says they can do a second surgery and make me a biological woman." Tillie blushed and looked back at the pages of the journal. "Nothing to be embarrassed about, love." Dora nudged her with her elbow and Tillie smiled and rolled her eyes.

"I'm not embarrassed," Tillie lied.

"Yes, you are, but that's alright. Dr. H. says if I do it, I'll be the first one." She sighed dramatically. "Don't worry Tillie, I promise to remember you when I'm a famous woman in all the medical journals all over the world." She nudged her again; this time she was laughing.

Tillie laughed too and continued to pick up discarded books off the desks to put back onto the shelves.

"Hello, hello." Helene bustled into the library as they were putting books back into their rightful spots. "You ladies are due for a break, so Karl sent me in." Helene sat herself down at the desk, got situated, and pulled out her knitting.

Tillie set the books she hadn't gotten to down on the rolling cart and walked to the desk where Helene was sitting. "What are you making, Helene?"

She smiled. "Some booties for my sister. She's due to have a baby any day now." Tillie picked up the small purple sock and traced the stitches with her fingers.

"They're so tiny," Tillie whispered, more to herself than to anyone around her.

Dora came over and leaned on the edge of the table. "Are you taking these to her, Helene? Doesn't your sister live outside of Dresden?" Her voice had an edge to it and Tillie looked up to see a crease of worry on Dora's forehead.

Helene looked up and met Dora's eyes. "No, I'm just sending them to her." Her voice dropped to just above a whisper. "My parents wouldn't want me there anyway."

Tillie could feel the mood had changed in the room. Dora patted Helene's hand and said, "Well, your sister will love them. They're beautiful."

Helene's shoulders relaxed a little and she said, "I'm thinking of knitting a blanket to match, but I'm not sure if I'll have time."

"Say no more, you and I will have a knitting party tonight, love." Dora stood up from the table. "I bet we can finish the booties and a baby blanket by the end of the weekend." Dora's hand was still resting on top of Helene's, and she squeezed.

Tillie felt almost inappropriate standing watching them and their sisterly love for one another. Dora gave Helene's hand another pat and then turned to Tillie. "How about a cup of tea?" Tillie nodded and Dora looked at her watch. "We'll be back in about twenty minutes, Helene. Is that alright?"

Helene nodded. "Take your time, Dörchen," she said, affectionately.

Tillie and Dora settled down with their tea in the lounge, which was empty. The institute would be closing soon for the night. Tillie tapped her cup thoughtfully and Dora asked, "You alright, love?"

Tillie nodded; unsure she should say anything. Dora went back to sipping her tea, watching her. Before Tillie could stop herself, she said, "Why didn't you want Helene to visit her family? You all have those certificates from Dr. H. You should be fine to travel."

Dora met Tillie's eyes, her soft gaze unblinking. "Tillie, you can ride on a train and people would look at you and think you are a lovely, German woman. Even if you were riding with Ruth, as long as you weren't holding hands or kissing, everyone around you would assume you were just two friends, out for a day trip."

Tillie opened her mouth to say something, but Dora held up her hand. "My point is you can hide. In plain sight. Me, Adelaide, Helene, Nissa; we can't. People know exactly what we are. To them, we are men in dresses."

She picked up her tea. "We might be safe here, and with the certificates Dr. H. pushed the police to issue, we might be safe walking to the market or to the clubs." She shrugged and then said, "Well, we're hypothetically safe. Reality is a little different. But walking to the Belle Club to see Ruth perform and taking a train to Dresden to visit a family member are two very different things."

Tillie sat for a moment, then said quietly, "I'm sorry, Dora. I didn't mean to seem so naïve."

Dora waved a hand. "Nonsense. How would you know when you've never lived someone else's life? It's not a safe world for people like you, Tillie. But it's less safe for people like me and Helene. That's all."

Tillie nodded. Then Dora added, "Plus, you know exactly how Ernesto's father reacted when he saw him in stockings and heels. Could you imagine how a good German father would react if his son was actually his daughter?" She laughed and shook her head.

"There's a reason we have Christmas here every year with Dr. H. and Karl."

"I didn't know you celebrated Christmas here altogether, that's lovely," Tillie said, smiling.

Dora looked up from her tea and smiled again at her, but this time her smile was sad. "Tillie, do your parents know you're with Ruth?"

Tillie laughed out loud. "Good Lord, no."

Dora nodded. "You can hide. In plain sight." Tillie felt her stomach sink and her eyes filled with tears. "Most of the girls here haven't seen their families in at least ten years. I know I haven't."

"Dora," she whispered. "I'm sorry, I didn't know."

Dora leaned forward and patted the top of her hand, something Tillie was accustomed to. Dora did it often, to everyone. "Now you do." She gave her a small smile and Tillie smiled back over her teacup.

✝

After her shift ended, Tillie walked back to the flat, Dora's medical journal in her arms, ready to spend the evening with a cup of tea in an armchair reading and waiting for Ruth to get home from work.

She was deep in thought, and she didn't hear her name being shouted behind her. She was only steps from their apartment when she heard "Matilda Rose!" She jumped and turned, her heart beating fast. Only one person referred to her as Matilda Rose.

Her parents were walking quickly up to her, her father in a long dinner jacket and her mother wearing elbow length gloves and a fancy hat pinned into her blonde hair.

"Mama, Papa, what are you doing here?" Tillie sputtered and gave a nervous look up at the third window from the left. She hoped either Ruth had already gone or that she didn't hear and open the window, wondering who Tillie was talking to.

Her mother leaned in to kiss her on the cheeks. "We're out for the night, dinner and a show." Her mother was wearing a long black dress and a black fur. "We saw you walking and wondered what you were doing on this side of town."

Her father was staring at her, a small frown on his lips. "I thought your flat was by the office." His tone made it clear it wasn't a question. Before she and Ruth moved in together, her flat had been by the office.

"Oh." Tillie thought quickly. "Yes. Well, Ernesto lives on this side of town." She swallowed and forced a smile.

Both her parents relaxed considerably. "Well, where is he? Is this his building?" Her mother looked up at the building, her eyes curious. Just then, Tillie heard the interior door open, and her stomach sank.

"Tills, who are you talking to?" She heard Ruth behind her and watched as her parents looked from Ruth to her, their faces sinking into confusion and distaste.

Tillie turned to see Ruth leaning out of their building in her silk robe, her face already made up for her shift. Before Tillie knew what was happening, Ruth walked outside in her robe and stood next to her.

"Hi, I'm Ruth." She stuck her hand out to Tillie's mother, as her mother stared back, her mouth slightly ajar.

Her mother recovered quickly and snapped her mouth shut. "Hello Ruth. I'm Alice, Tillie's mother and," she gestured to Tillie's father, "this is Vincent." Her eyes traveled up Ruth's body, and Ruth pulled her silk robe tighter.

"Ruth lives across the hall from Ernesto," Tillie breathed, praying Ruth picked up on the lie.

"I'm sorry that I look so disheveled," she said quickly. "I'm getting ready for work." Tillie watched her mother and father's eyes widen. Ruth added, "I'm a waitress."

Her parents nodded, still looking uncomfortably at Tillie. Ruth turned. "Ernesto wanted me to keep an eye out for you, he had to run out, but he'll be back in a bit."

"Oh," Tillie said. "Right. Okay, thanks Ruth." Ruth nodded and smiled at her parents once more before hurrying back into the building.

Her parents watched her go and then her father cleared his throat. "What exactly is Ernesto doing living in this district, anyway?" His arms were folded, and she could feel his disapproval washing over her.

"He has a job with a museum," Tillie lied. "In the archives." It was sort of true, he did help in the archives at the institute sometimes. "He didn't want to have roommates, so this side of town was the best option." At least that part was the truth. Ruth moved to this building years ago precisely because she didn't want to have a flat mate. She could tell her mother believed her, but her father was still appraising her, his eyes narrowed.

"I don't want you mixing with people who could get you into trouble, Tillie." Her father's eyes flicked back up to the building behind her.

"Of course, Papa."

"You're a respectable girl, and I expect you to act like a lady." Tillie took a deep breath and nodded. Her father stared at her for another moment. "Tell Ernesto we're expecting you both for Sunday dinner tomorrow night."

"I'm not sure we'll be able to make it," she said, trying to keep her voice even.

Her mother sniffed and pulled on the edge of her glove. "We're not asking, dear." She looped her arm through her husband's. "We will be having dinner with you and your beau tomorrow night." Tillie bit her lip and nodded.

Her mother leaned in and kissed her cheek goodbye and Tillie could smell roses and a hint of vanilla wafting off her neck.

"Have a good evening, Mama." Her mother's returning smile was cool, and they turned, heading up the road toward the less dingy parts of Berlin and out of Tillie's district.

Tillie sighed, watching them go, then turned and headed into the apartment where Ruth was still standing at the top of the stairs, outside the open door of their flat.

She hesitated, biting her thumb nail. "Doll, I'm so sorry," she rushed forward, wrapping her arms around Tillie's waist. "When I looked out the window, your mother was dressed like someone from the club. I just thought maybe you knew them from the institute."

Tillie blinked and looked at Ruth. "You thought my mother was a transvestite?" Ruth went pink but Tillie laughed so hard, she had to wipe tears from her eyes. Ruth looked at her warily, her mouth turned up into a smile, but her eyes were still concerned.

"Are you okay?" Ruth asked, when Tillie finally stopped laughing. They walked together into their tiny apartment.

She nodded. "My parents are expecting me and Ernesto for dinner tomorrow night, so that should be fun." Ruth made a face.

"Did you tell them you and Ernesto are a couple? Should I be jealous?" Ruth winked and tickled Tillie's side.

Tillie squirmed and stuck out her tongue at Ruth. "Yes. So very jealous." She shook her head. "No, my father sort of assumed Ernesto and I were a couple because we're always together." Tillie shifted uncomfortably. She hated lying. "And I just didn't correct him." She put her hand on Ruth's cheek and stared into her hazel eyes. "I was hoping to make it back before you had to get dressed and head to the club."

Ruth checked the clock on the wall and said, "We've got a little time. I don't have to be at the club for another forty-five minutes." She untied the belt on her robe and it fell open. Tillie crossed her arms.

"Are you trying to seduce me, Ruthie?"

Ruth pressed her own body against Tillie's and braced her hands on the counter behind her. Tillie dropped her arms to her sides as Ruth's mouth met her own and she whispered, "Maybe."

Tillie leaned into Ruth's kiss and whispered back, "You already finished your makeup." Ruth traced Tillie's lips with her finger and leaned down to kiss her neck.

"That's okay, it's just makeup." Tillie shivered involuntarily as she felt Ruth's lips tracing her collarbone. She slid her hands under Ruth's robe around her pale waist and the robe fell to the floor. Ruth took Tillie's hand and led her to the bedroom, a trail of clothes left behind them on the floor.

†

The next evening, Ernesto was fidgeting next to Tillie at her parents' front door. "I can't believe I agreed to this," he growled at her.

"I promise to buy your drinks for the rest of the month," she murmured back, as her mother opened their front door, arms outstretched.

"Hello dear," her mother said as they walked into Tillie's childhood home. They heard voices coming from the kitchen.

Tillie set her handbag down on the table in the hallway. "Who else is here?" she asked.

Her mother started down the hallway toward the kitchen. "Didn't your father tell you? Anthony, Madge, and Tommy are here for dinner as well."

Ernesto froze next to her, then grabbed her elbow hard enough to leave a bruise. "My father is here?" he hissed.

All Tillie had time to do was shake her head in disbelief and whisper, "I didn't know" before her mother ushered them into the kitchen where an older version of Ernesto stood next to a petite brunette woman in a deep purple dress.

A gasp came from a boy sitting quietly at the table, drinking a glass of milk. "Ernesto!" He jumped up, ran to Ernesto and threw his arms around his waist.

"Hiya Tommy," Ernesto said quietly. "That's an interesting outfit you have on." The boy, who was fourteen, was wearing black shorts, a tan button-down shirt, a dark scarf tied around his neck, and a red armband with a large black swastika featured prominently on his bicep.

The boy beamed. "I've been in Hitlerjugend an entire year. I graduated from the Jungvolk when I had my birthday. We did a big camping trip last weekend and in August, I'm going for a whole week with Herr Gruber and my friends and," his voice dropped to a whisper, "the Führer is going to be there."

Ernesto nodded and met Tillie's gaze. He gave Tommy's hair a ruffle and said, "Well, that sounds like fun." His little brother nodded and went back to his milk at the table.

Anthony Grandelis was coldly staring at Ernesto as Tillie watched her father cuff him on the shoulder. "Thought we might bury the hatchet, at least for one night so Tillie and her beau could have dinner with us," he said, chuckling.

At these words, Ernesto's mother choked on the piece of cheese she was eating and had to take a drink of water. She turned her small gray eyes toward Tillie. "You two are a couple?" Tillie shrugged, forcing a smile. "For how long?" Her voice was sharp.

Mercifully, Tillie's mother shoved champagne flutes into everyone's hands and said, "Madge, stop interrogating them. We've only just gotten them to admit it." Her mother was laughing but Tillie couldn't help noticing both of Ernesto's parents staring at her with suspicion.

They all sat, listening to Tommy talk about his adventures in the Hitler Youth, his friends that were part of the group, and the awe in his voice as he spoke about the leader of the HJ, Herr Grüber.

As Tommy finished telling a story about practicing how to march in parades led by Hitler himself, quiet descended upon the table.

Tillie cleared her throat. "I didn't realize the Nazi party was so popular."

Tommy opened his mouth to respond, but Herr Grandelis held up a hand to stop him. He said, "All Germans should be part of the Nationalsozialisten."

He gave the party's title emphasis. "The Führer is going to save Germany, *Matilda*." Tillie winced at the way he said her name. Herr Grandelis eyed Ernesto. "But then, the Nationalsozialisten party is for true Germans. There are certain people we wouldn't allow. Ones that do not belong." Ernesto dropped his gaze from Tommy back to his plate of food and concentrated on chewing his carrots.

Herr Grandelis continued, watching Tillie's face carefully. "So. How long have you two been a couple?"

Tillie set down her fork and said, "You know, I'm not even sure. A year maybe?"

"Interesting," his father said, then went back to eating. There was an uncomfortable silence until Tillie's mother spoke back up.

"Ernesto, who is that young woman who lives across from you?" Tillie coughed on a carrot.

"What woman?" Ernesto looked confused.

"When we ran into Tillie yesterday, a young woman ran out of your apartment building. Gracious! She was practically naked . Saying that you had asked her to look for Tillie and that you were on your way home."

Her father interrupted. "Speaking of which, I know that district might be closer to your job," Ernesto looked with wide eyes at Tillie who shook her head imperceptibly, "but you really don't belong in that area of town. And Tillie *certainly* doesn't belong there, even if it is just for visits."

He got up and retrieved a small piece of paper from the desk on the opposite wall. He handed it to Ernesto as he sat back down. "That's the number of a chap we do business with. He owns property all over Berlin. Surely, he'll be able to find you something more suitable."

"Tillie, we were walking to the restaurant from Ernesto's apartment when we saw a group of men," her mother's voice dropped to a whisper, "dressed as women." She shook her head. "Have you ever seen such a thing over there? Really, Ernesto, that is no place to be encouraging our daughter to spend her time."

Tillie's eyes flickered to Ernesto's parents. His mother had gone very white and was staring at her wine glass, but his father met her gaze, his eyes cold, his head tilted to the side. Tommy shifted in his chair and looked from his parents to Ernesto without blinking.

She cleared her throat. "No, I've never seen anything like that." Her mother nodded, satisfied with that answer and quiet descended upon the small table once more.

For the rest of the dinner, Tillie barely listened to the men discussing work or the women discussing local gossip. She focused on getting Ernesto through the dinner and getting out. She was so relieved when her mother brought cups and saucers to the table following dessert.

"You know, Mother, we both have early mornings tomorrow, so Ernesto and I should probably get going."

"Oh, of course. Let me wrap some leftovers for you to take, though. Ernesto, you're looking far too thin." Her mother fussed over them as they said their goodbyes to the other guests. Ernesto's parents gave a stiff, forced farewell to Ernesto—it was the only thing they said to him the entire night. Tillie wondered if her own parents noticed.

Tommy hugged his brother again and whispered, so only they could hear, "I miss you, Ernesto."

Ernesto whispered back, "I know, buddy. I miss you too."

They were at the front door when Tillie's mother said, "Oh shoot, I left your food back in the kitchen."

Tillie wanted Ernesto out of the house as soon as possible so she said, "That's alright, Mama, I'll get it." She hurried back to the kitchen, only to see Herr Grandelis alone, getting another cup of coffee. She gave a stiff smile and reached for the wrapped plate on the kitchen counter.

"What I don't understand," he started slowly, quietly, "is what you're getting out of this."

"I'm sorry?" Tillie's heart skipped.

"You and I both know you and Ernesto are not a couple," he snapped, his voice low and menacing. "So, tell me, Matilda, what exactly are you getting out of this?"

"I- I- I really don't know what you're talking about," Tillie said, a cold sweat breaking out on the back of her neck.

His eyes narrowed and his face took on a vulture-like stare. Tillie started to back out of the kitchen. "I know exactly what he is," he said, coldly. "And I know you do too." Tillie didn't say anything. "Are you like him?" he snarled. "Are you just as deranged as he is?"

Tillie felt a wave of sickness flow over her and then she said slowly, "I honestly don't know what you're talking about, but I have to go." His eyes narrowed and she could tell he didn't believe her, but she kept her face calm and willed herself to walk at a normal pace out of the house. She kept it together until she saw Ernesto waiting for her at the end of the walkway. As soon as he turned to look at her, her face crumpled and the tears came.

She and Ernesto walked in silence, Tillie wiping tears from her face, while passing multiple groups of the Jungvolk on their way. Ernesto shook his head, watching the small blonde boys wearing red armbands pass them. "Thank God that didn't exist when I was a little kid. My father would have signed me right up."

He shuddered. "Poor Tommy, he has no idea what he's even part of."

"He doesn't believe us," Tillie said, quietly.

"Who? My father? Of course, he doesn't," Ernesto laughed. "Why would he? He knows I like men and now, I suspect, he thinks you like women. At least that would be the assumption I would make if I were him."

Tillie closed her eyes and felt the dinner churning in her stomach, threatening to come back up. She swallowed hard. "What do we do?" She turned to look at Ernesto.

"Do? What do you mean?" He raised his eyebrows at her.

"I mean, what if he tells my father? What if I get fired?"

Ernesto waved a hand. "He's not going to tell your father and you're not going to get fired."

"How could you possibly know that?" Tillie could feel a pounding behind her eyes.

"Because he's embarrassed. He's embarrassed to have a son like me and telling your dad would mean he would have to tell the truth about me." Ernesto shook his head. "He'd rather die than admit he raised a son like me."

She rubbed her forehead. The evening had zapped all her energy. She was going to be so relieved once she got home and she could sit and have a cup of tea. She sighed, suddenly so completely exhausted, she wasn't sure she could make it the rest of the way.

Ernesto walked her to her building then kissed her on the cheek. "So. That was fun." He winked at her, and she laughed. "Let's never do that again, yeah?"

She shook her head, still laughing, and watched as Ernesto turned to walk the block up to James' apartment.

Pushing the door open, still chuckling to herself, she was surprised to see Ruth sitting at the kitchen table, with no makeup, in her robe.

"Hey, I thought you were working tonight?"

Ruth looked up at her, her eyes tired. "I was too anxious about how your dinner went. I wanted to wait for you to make sure you were okay."

Tillie smiled and crossed the small kitchen to take Ruth's hand in her own. Their eyes met and she cupped Ruth's face in her free hand. She leaned down and kissed her lightly. "It was fine. I'll tell you all about it, but right now I just need to take off this dress and these shoes and have a cup of tea."

Ruth smiled back. "Why don't you go change and I'll make you something and then you can fill me in."

"That sounds perfect," Tillie already had one shoe in her hand, and she went to the bedroom to take off her dinner dress.

As she settled down at the kitchen table, cozy in her robe, sipping her tea, Ruth crossed her arms and peered at her over her own mug. "Okay, so. What happened?"

As Tillie started telling Ruth about her evening with her parents, her eyes grew wider and wider, and she only interrupted with scoffs and eyerolls.

"So, Ernesto's father is a Nazi, he doesn't believe you and Ernesto are a couple, and Ernesto's little brother is a Hitler-in-training?"

Tillie nodded, sipping her tea. "That's the sum of it, I suppose."

Ruth blew out a long, low whistle. "Shit."

"I know it." Tillie shook her head. "You should have seen Tommy. I know you don't know them, but I remember when Tommy was a tiny little boy. Just this round little blonde thing that would cry if he dropped his toast." She set her mug down. "Ernesto told me Tommy doesn't even like to kill spiders." It came out just above a whisper, a sadness settling into her chest.

Ruth reached out and rubbed Tillie's arm. "That sounds really hard, to see a kid you know being forced into this."

Tillie nodded, her eyes stinging. "I remember when the Putsch happened. When they followed Hitler and tried to overthrow the government in Munich."

Ruth's mouth set into a grim line. "I remember too. It was right before we got together, '23, right?"

Tillie nodded again. "My mother was devastated. The shame she said it brought onto our family horrified her. But my father wasn't arrested and neither was Herr Grandelis, so they all sort of forgot about it. Or at least, pretended it never happened. I just don't understand why they would …" She trailed off and rubbed her face, the headache coming back just behind her eyes.

A crease formed between Ruth's eyes. Tillie reached out and tried to smooth it with her fingertip and Ruth laughed. She swatted Tillie's hand. "I hate it when you do that."

"I hate when you look so worried. It's fine." She shook her head. "I mean, it's not fine. I wonder if this time, they'll all end up getting arrested." She sighed.

"I don't think there's anything you can do, doll," Ruth said, reading Tillie's mind. "People are going to make their own choices." She shrugged.

"Do you think working for my father could put me in association with them, if something like 1923 happens again?"

Ruth bit her lip, thinking. "Honestly, I don't know. Probably not, since you're just the secretary, but who knows." She let out a long sigh. "Those kids, though; Tommy and the rest of them. That's what I can't stop thinking about."

"Meaning?" Tillie leaned forward, concerned at the worry coming across Ruth's face.

"Well, they're kids. And they're being, I don't know, trained or conditioned to be a certain way. To believe certain things." She rubbed her arms like she was cold. "The kids are what make me nervous. Watching them marching around, throwing up their little hands in salute. It's unsettling."

Tillie wrapped her fingers around her mug. That's exactly how she felt. Unsettled.

CHAPTER 7

April 1928

Tillie arrived at her parents' house wearing a dark green dress she had dug out of the depths of her closet. Her instruction from her mother was to look as nice as possible, so she even rummaged around in Ruth's makeup for lipstick and rouge. Taking a deep breath, she rang the bell, checking her watch to make sure she was on time.

Her mother opened the door looking harried. "Come in, come in." She waved Tillie inside. The small front room had a bar set up with champagne and bourbon glasses lining the table. The kitchen was full of platters of finger food and the main living room was missing the couch and comfortable chairs, replaced with three round tables all set with her mother's finest cutlery.

"Mama, this looks great." Tillie looked around in amazement. "I thought you needed my help to set up. It looks like you're done already."

"Oh, I spent all yesterday getting things together. I wanted you to be early so that I knew you'd be on time." Her mother wiped her hands on her apron and went back to stirring the gravy on the stove. "You know what your father says, early is on time, on time is late."

Tillie kept her face even. "Okay, well I'm here now. What can I help with?"

"You can double check all the alcohol and that the tables are set up correctly." Tillie nodded and escaped to the bar while her mother flitted around the kitchen like a hummingbird, checking plates, stirring pots, and washing dishes somehow all at once.

She was just filling the ice buckets when her father came down the stairs. "Hello, Matilda, don't you look lovely." He walked over and kissed her on the cheek.

"Hello, Papa. How are you?" She smiled at him, while pushing the bottle of champagne farther down into the ice bucket.

Her father fidgeted a little and looked around the room. "You know, Tillie, I wanted to ask you about something. I'm sure it's nothing but, well, you know." Her heart started to beat faster, and she looked up at him.

"What is it, Papa?"

"Well, you know Anthony and Ernesto don't get along."

Tillie nodded, not meeting her father's eyes.

"It's just, Anthony doesn't believe you're a real couple," he hurried through the words like ripping off a band-aid and he still refused to make eye contact with her.

She forced a laugh. "What?"

"He claims he knows for a 'fact'"—he used air quotes to stress the word, while making a face— "that you're lying about being a couple." His voice dropped to a murmur, "Though how he could know anything when he doesn't speak to his own son is a mystery to me." He raised his voice again to address Tillie. "Any idea what would make him think that?"

When she didn't respond right away her father added, "You know, I wanted to invite him tonight, but Anthony lost his temper with me over it. Said Ernesto isn't a 'true German' which is absurd. But, well, he refused to allow Ernesto to come. Said it wouldn't be good for business." He shook his head. "Of course, when I ask him why or how he could know such a thing, he changes the subject and tells me it doesn't matter."

He started to fix himself a drink, and Tillie watched through a haze. She blinked several times trying to clear her vision and calm her racing heart. Her father sipped his drink, not noticing his daughter's distress.

"I told him, differing politics is no reason to cut ties, but he seemed to think having Ernesto here, with his political leanings, wasn't a good idea." He chucked Tillie under the chin, and she looked up at him, still trying to calm the panic rising in her throat. "I know you'll be on your best behavior, even if you don't agree with the political stance of our guests." He smiled, his eyes crinkling in the corners.

It took a moment for Tillie to register her father's words through the blanket of worry and fear that had settled over her. Tillie came out from behind the bar. "Who did you invite to dinner, Papa?"

As if on cue, the bell rang and Anthony Grandelis walked through the door without waiting for someone to answer, his wife and Tommy, dressed head to toe in his Hitler Youth attire, following behind. Herr Grandelis was wearing a red band around his upper arm, a black swastika inside a white circle plainly visible across the room.

Tillie's stomach churned when she saw him, the anxiety rising like a lion in her gut. He'd all but ignored her since the disastrous dinner with Ernesto, though she kept waiting for a confrontation. She constantly felt on edge around him, like she was slowly turning the handle of a jack-in-the-box, waiting for him to pop.

"We'll discuss this later," her father whispered, and he strode off to shake Herr Grandelis' hand and welcome him to dinner. After shaking hands, Anthony reached into his coat pocket and pulled out a second armband and handed it to her father.

They strode together into the kitchen, without another glance in Tillie's direction. She watched them go and stood very still, willing herself to take a few deep breaths. She wiped her palms on one of the linen napkins behind the bar, then dabbed the nervous beads of sweat that had formed on her forehead.

"Matilda!" her mother hissed from the kitchen doorway. Tillie jumped and looked over at her mother.

"Go stand by the door to take people's coats as they arrive." Tillie nodded and moved to the entrance to wait for the bell to ring.

The first of the dinner guests to arrive was a very small man, only a few inches taller than Tillie. He had a pointed face, almost like a rat, dark cold eyes, and thin lips that did not smile when she opened the door. She offered to take his coat and he nodded and handed it to her without speaking. She watched as he walked toward the kitchen, noticing he had a slight limp and then she watched as Herr Grandelis welcomed him.

"Joseph! How lucky we are to see you. I trust your trip up from Weimar was a good one?"

The man called Joseph answered with a curt "Yes" and Tillie heard a cork pop and a clink of glasses. Tillie listened long enough to hear her father begin to make conversation when the bell rang again. Hurrying back to the door, she opened it to a familiar face taking up the doorway.

"Matilda," Hermann Göring boomed. "How lovely to see you again." He gave her a jovial smile and shrugged off his coat to place it into her outstretched arms.

"Hello, Herr Göring." Tillie smiled. "How are you doing, sir?"

"Oh, I'm splendid. This is my wife, Carin." The woman peeking out from behind Göring's massive frame was small and pale with a pretty heart-shaped face.

Tillie gave a small smile. "Hello, it's lovely to meet you." The woman reached out a birdlike hand to Tillie and nodded her head.

Göring gently removed his wife's coat to hand it to Tillie. "Has Herr Goebbels arrived yet?"

Tillie paused. "I think so. One other guest has arrived. Everyone is in the kitchen. I can walk you."

He waved a hand, "Not necessary, I'm sure we'll find it. Thank you, Matilda." Tillie nodded and took their coats up the stairs, making a mental note to look in the files at work for a man called Goebbels.

Still waiting for the third guest, Tillie was straining her ears to try and hear the conversations going on in the kitchen. She could just make out the booming baritone of Hermann Göring's voice talking to her father about money and investing in the party using their business resources when the bell rang for a final time. The man at the door was slightly balding, with glasses and a wispy mustache. He looked like a professor and Tillie wondered if he was another lawyer.

Offering to take his coat, he smiled and handed both his coat and his wife's to Tillie before walking into the kitchen to join the others. He, too, was wearing the red armband and Tillie noticed a very small swastika lapel pin on his wife's collar. Tillie didn't bother to introduce herself this time and went immediately upstairs without showing them to the kitchen.

She stood in her parents' bedroom, placing the last of the coats on the pile that had formed on the bed. She listened at the door for a moment to ensure no one was going to come up the stairs, before slumping into the chair by the window to clear her head.

She didn't recognize any of the men besides Herr Göring, but it was obvious they were all part of the Nazi party. She was still sitting in her mother's armchair holding her head in her hands when the door creaked open. She jumped up.

"Tillie, are you alright?" It was her mother.

"Oh yes, Mama. I'm sorry. I just have a little headache. I'll be right down." Her mother nodded but closed the door behind her.

"I know you aren't a big fan of the National Socialists, dear, but truly they all have the best interests of Germans in mind." Tillie nodded, waiting for her mother to finish. "This group of men, Herr Himmler, Herr Goebbels, Herr Göring, and the Führer of course, will rescue Germany," she said, her voice sounding grateful. "They're going to rescue the real Germans, and they will restore our country, our purity, our morality..."

Tillie took a deep breath. "Of course, Mama."

Her mother smiled and opened the door. "Just give them a chance. They're so intelligent and have wonderful plans for the country. Just listen to their ideas. I promise you'll be impressed." She paused. "It's too bad Anthony was so dead set against having Ernesto come, I think he could have learned a lot tonight. Especially from Herr Goebbels. He's a very inspirational speaker." She turned and held the door open. "Come down and help me serve dinner."

Tillie said, "Yes, Mama," and followed her mother down to the kitchen and to the group of waiting dinner guests, her eyes on the red armband wrapped around her father's bicep.

She stood against the wall with a water pitcher in her hand. The women were all murmuring to one another, but Tillie was focused on listening to the men.

Herr Göring was reminiscing with Ernesto's father about being pilots in The Great War and she wondered if Hitler had received the letter that her father sent on behalf of Göring. The small man with the pointed face cleared his throat and the rest of the table fell silent. Tillie recognized that he was clearly in charge. She saw her mother turn to him, her eyes wide and sparkling.

He folded his hands, almost in prayer, his fingers in front of his lips. "So," he began slowly. "We are all preparing for the upcoming election next month. Hermann, how do you feel about your chances in Bavaria now that the Führer has given you his endorsement?"

Tillie's eyes went to her father to confirm that they had indeed sent the threatening letter to Adolf Hitler, but he was staring at Goebbels with rapt attention.

Göring grinned and he slapped the table. "Well, I feel excellent about them, Joseph. I feel very strongly that I'm going to win this election and we'll start to turn the tides. How do you feel about your race in Berlin?"

For the briefest moment, a look of annoyance crossed Goebbels' face. Tillie wondered if he felt he was above these other men somehow. But he recovered and gave an oily smile. "I feel very good, thank you for asking."

He turned to the man with the wispy mustache. "Heinrich, we are not having a Nuremberg rally this year, in order to make our rally next year much grander. You are planning to do the films for this event?"

The man called Heinrich nodded. "It will be much longer than the film shown at the rally last September, but I think it will be worth the extra time."

Goebbels nodded. "I think I would like to view it, whenever it is completed, if that's alright with you." His tone suggested there would be no disagreement. "And your position at the Schutzstaffel. How has that been going?"

Himmler shifted in his seat, looking uncomfortable. "Fine. Since becoming deputy, I've been able to reorganize things and I think you'd agree the creation of the Gaus has been helpful to our cause."

Goebbels nodded again but did not respond immediately. Himmler readjusted his glasses and continued. "We should have a good number of participants for Nuremberg next year."

Tommy spoke for the first time. "Excuse me sir, what are the 'Gaus' you're talking about?"

Herr Grandelis' eyes shifted to his son's face, and he snapped, "Tommy," but Goebbels held up a hand.

"Anthony, the boy has a right to ask questions." He shifted in his chair, so his eyes fell on Tommy. "You see son, we've divided our great country of Germany up into smaller sections. Sort of like pieces of pie." His voice was so soft, everyone laid down their utensils to listen.

"Each section or Gau has a leader. I'm the Gauleiter in Berlin." Tommy's mouth was slightly open, and he was nodding along with Goebbels' words, his brow furrowed. "We work towards the Führer and make sure our presence is known within our piece of the pie. There is one person above me, in charge of a larger piece of the pie, and there are those below me.

"My piece is then divided into even smaller sections and your father," he gestured toward Herr Grandelis, "is the Krieslieter of this section of the city. He reports directly to me." Tommy nodded and smiled.

"Then there are more men below him called Ortsgruppenleiters, and they are in charge of the smaller neighborhoods."

"That makes sense, sir. Break things apart into manageable chunks to ensure the party's message is being heard everywhere." He picked up his fork, apparently done with asking questions.

Göring patted Tommy on the back and beamed. "What a smart kid you have here, Anthony. He's exactly right." Tillie swallowed, wondering just how many pieces Germany was divided up into.

Goebbels gave an icy smile and changed course. "The Führer and I have been discussing increasing our presence within the …" he paused, a look of distaste on his face, "less desirable neighborhoods of Greater Berlin. I will include announcements in the paper to gather support. But we will be relying on the Kreisleiters and the Ortsgruppenleiters to take the helm on this."

Tillie's father interrupted. "The paper?" he asked.

Goebbels' small, hard eyes turned to her father, and they were full of malice. Her father flinched under the angry glare, but he waited for Goebbels to finish.

"My paper, *Der Angriff*," Goebbels said finally. "I write and edit a newspaper." His cold eyes swept over the table back to Herr Grandelis. "I'm surprised," he said in a slow, pointed voice, "you've not read it. Surely my Kreisleiter would have copies of my paper at your office." Herr Grandelis dropped his eyes and didn't respond. "We'll have to remedy that…" His tone was soft and dangerous.

"Of course, sir," Herr Grandelis replied before Goebbels could finish his question.

"As I was saying," Goebbels continued, "the Führer and I were discussing increasing the presence of our men in the less desirable neighborhoods." He folded his hands in his lap and leaned back in his chair.

This time it was Frau Grandelis who interrupted. "Excuse me, Herr Goebbels. Forgive me, of course, I'm just curious though," she stammered, sounding nervous. "Won't marching through neighborhoods without support cause people to get angry with the party?" This time, to Tillie's surprise, Goebbels' face softened.

"On the contrary." He lowered his voice, like a grammar schoolteacher speaking to a confused child. "When those who do not support us get angry and cause a scene, we can point it out to all of Germany." He leaned forward, his eyes dancing. "We can point at them and say 'See? Look at how these people behave. They are not civilized Germans.' No matter what happens, chaos will work in our favor, dear woman."

Tillie stared at him, her mouth falling open. "Tillie!" She jumped at her mother's shout and realized her arms had grown slack and water was pouring onto the floor out of the pitcher.

"Oh dear. I'm so sorry." She looked up and saw that all the eyes at the table were on her. Herr Grandelis was staring at her with something close to contempt on his face. She felt herself flush and quickly said, "You're just such an articulate speaker, sir. I was taken with what you were saying." She forced a smile. "Excuse me, I'm going to go get a towel."

In the kitchen she set down the pitcher and closed her eyes. She took a deep breath and rubbed a tense spot in the back of her neck. She heard a throat clear behind her and she spun around, afraid of another confrontation with Ernesto's father, but it was not Herr Grandelis standing in front of her. It was Joseph Goebbels.

He surveyed her with his small eyes, his hands clasped behind his back. When he didn't speak, Tillie raised her eyebrows and said, "Can I get you something, Herr Goebbels?"

He took a step forward and Tillie noticed his limp looked more pronounced than it had earlier in the evening. "You are Vincent's daughter, yes?" She nodded. He pursed his lips. "Tell me, how old are you?"

Tillie bristled. "I'm twenty-four, sir."

"And you work? I mean to say, you support yourself?"

She met his stare. "Yes. I'm a secretary at my father's law office."

The corners of his mouth twitched, and he lifted his chin while he surveyed her. "Is that so?" he said. Something about his tone made Tillie feel nervous.

"Matilda, is it?" She nodded. "You know, the Führer is always looking for pretty German girls to help the cause." She remained silent while his eyes roamed her body.

"I'll be working more closely with your father and Herr Grandelis in the coming months on different projects." He tore his eyes away from the lower half of her body and met her eyes again. "Loyal workers are important." She nodded again, still unable to speak.

Frau Grandelis walked into the kitchen behind him, admiration on her face. "Herr Goebbels," she said, "I believe dessert is going to be served soon."

"Wonderful, thank you my dear," he said in a calm voice, still staring at Tillie. "Matilda, I look forward to talking with you again." He walked out of the kitchen and Frau Grandelis glowered at Tillie, then turned to follow him.

Tillie sagged against the counter, feeling the sweat run down between her shoulder blades, just as her mother bustled into the kitchen. "Did you have a nice chat with Herr Goebbels, dear?" she asked as she started spooning fruit and cream onto small dessert plates.

She dropped her voice to a whisper. "I prefer Herr Göring. He's much more personable than the other two but according to your father, the other two men are just as powerful." She stopped and looked contemplative. "Maybe even more so. So only good things can come, I suppose." She smiled conspiratorially at Tillie before she blinked, seeing her daughter for the first time. "Are you alright? You're as white as a sheet."

Tillie found her voice. "Yes. I still have a headache."

Her mother frowned. "Alright, well help me serve the dessert." She stared at Tillie for another beat and shook her head. "You should go to bed as soon as you get home tonight. I'm sure it's just exhaustion."

Tillie didn't respond as she took the plates from her mother to take to the dining room.

The dinner guests didn't discuss business again until coats were being handed out. "I'll be stopping by your office before the election next month," Goebbels began, to her father and Herr Grandelis. "Just to check in and make sure we're all set. And I'll make sure to get the law office on the list of drop off locations for my paper."

He turned to walk out the door, putting his hands into his pockets. "Oh, I almost forgot." He pulled something out of his pocket and handed it to Herr Grandelis. It was another armband, only this one had gold embroidered leaves in the center and gold piping along the edges of the band and around the black swastika.

"This is the official armband for the Kreisleiter. Please attach it to your coat." He nodded at them all, then turned to leave without waiting for a response. They all stood for a moment, quiet in the doorway.

"Well," said Göring, "that was a lovely meal, Alice. Thank you so much for having us." He shook everyone's hands as he swayed a little on the spot. "Matilda, you are lovely. It was so nice to see you again." She gave him half a smile . He put his hat on, and he and his wife were out the door, followed by Himmler and his wife.

As the door closed, Tillie's mother let out a long breath of air. "Well," she looked around at the group left standing in the doorway. "How about coffee?"

Tillie didn't really feel her shoulders relax until she heard her front door click behind her. Ruth was at work and wouldn't be home for several more minutes, so Tillie decided to change into her night clothes and try to make sense of the evening while she waited.

She was just sitting down with a vodka and ice when the phone rang. "Hello?" she said, wondering who could be calling this late in the evening.

"Tills. How was the dinner? Anything happen with my dad?"

"Ernesto," Tillie sighed into the receiver. "Oh, not with your dad, no."

There was a pause. "What does that mean?" She didn't say anything right away and he said, "Tills? Are you still there?"

"Yes. It was just a long night is all. Nothing happened really, I can fill you in later. Your father and my father are just keeping some pretty interesting company these days."

"Oh really?"

Just then Ruth walked in from her night at the club, still dressed in her tuxedo. "Ruth just got home, want to come over and I can fill you both in?"

"James and I will be there in ten minutes."

Ruth raised her eyebrows at Tillie as she hung up the phone. "How was your dinner?" She gestured to the phone. "I take it that it was eventful, given that Ernesto is on his way here at midnight."

Tillie grinned and kissed her girlfriend. "You have no idea. Is it okay if he comes over? You're not too tired, are you?"

She smiled back. "No, just let me wash my face and change."

They were all sitting around the small table ten minutes later, Ruth changed into her robe sipping tea, James still with makeup on from his own shift at another club up the street, and Ernesto, his foot shaking under the table with impatience. They all looked at Tillie. She took a deep breath and began talking.

She spoke for close to twenty minutes recounting the party. The men who attended, the things they discussed, the new armband presented to Ernesto's father, and most importantly, what Joseph Goebbels said about marching in the neighborhoods and the pie analogy Goebbels used to describe their presence all over Germany.

When she finished, she folded her hands in her lap and met their eyes. They all stared back at her, a mixture of horror and bewilderment on their faces.

Ruth tilted her head to the side, her teacup in her hand. "It almost sounds like they're building an army." They all turned to look at her.

James blinked a few times and said, "What?"

"Well, they've got Hitler at the top, right? Then there are a few people below him, then this Goebbels guy and probably a few more just like him, then people like your dad below him. And God knows how many people below your dad. Like little foot soldiers, it's all trickling down from Hitler."

James made a noise and they looked at him. "It seems like they're everywhere, doesn't it?" he said. "The kids like Tommy," he gestured to Ernesto, "and the Brownshirts. And now they're trying to, what, take over Germany one neighborhood at a time?" They all nodded, and he went on. "I agree with Ruth. It seems like they're building an army. Or at least trying to. It sounds insane."

"It also sounds like your father is in deep. I mean, I can't imagine these men having dinner with random business owners in Berlin," Ruth said to Ernesto.

Ernesto rubbed his face and then shook his head. "My father believes in their message, and I know from that awful dinner we had," he nodded at Tillie, "that Tommy is obsessed with Hitler. I imagine my father must be, too, Tommy has to be getting it from somewhere. Plus, my father has known Herr Göring since 1916. They've all been there since the beginning. They were all at the Putsch. Göring was shot during the coup. I wonder if Himmler and Goebbels were arrested in '23 with Hitler."

James yawned and it was contagious. Ruth was next, then Tillie. "Well, we're not going to solve this tonight," she said, stretching her arms. "I suppose I'll just keep an eye on what they're doing at the office?"

They all murmured an agreement while standing up from the table. The boys turned to leave, and Ruth walked them out while Tillie washed all the mugs. She felt Ruth wrap her arms around her waist and lean into her against the sink. "I missed you tonight at the club."

Tillie leaned back against Ruth and sighed. "Trust me, I would have much rather been there tonight." She shook her head and then turned around to face Ruth. "You know what's weird?"

"What?"

"When my mother found me sitting upstairs, she said to me that 'the National Socialists were going to save Germany.'" Tillie folded her arms across her chest. "But the Nazi Party is barely a party. How many seats in Parliament do they even have right now? Ten? If that?"

Ruth shrugged. "That sounds about right."

"So how are they going to save Germany when they barely exist here?"

Ruth shook her head. "I don't know." She reached forward and took Tillie's hand. "But I do know we can't do anything about it right now." She felt Ruth squeeze her fingers. "It's late, let's go to bed."

Tillie nodded and followed Ruth to the bedroom, turning lights off as she went. They got into bed and Ruth wrapped her arms around her, kissed her neck, and breathed "Goodnight, doll," into her ear. Tillie melted into Ruth's arms and tried to forget about the evening at her parents' house as she drifted to sleep, Ruth lightly snoring next to her.

CHAPTER 8

May 1928

Ruth sat down onto the sofa next to Tillie and draped her legs over Tillie's lap. She had the day's paper in her hands. "Did you see this?"

"All that talk of 'pie' and taking over the neighborhoods and they just fell apart." Tillie shook her head and chuckled as she read the paper in Ruth's hand.

Ruth laughed too. "Not even three percent of the vote. How embarrassing for them."

Ernesto flopped down next to them on the red couch and sighed. "Dr. Hirschfeld has a lecture tonight, so I've been helping Heinz in the kitchen all morning to make sure there's enough appetizers for all the guests coming. I have twenty minutes to sit here." He moaned as he propped his feet up on the chair across from him. "Remind me of this moment when I volunteer to work in the kitchen again. Because I do not enjoy it." He rubbed a spot on the back of his neck, his hands covered in what looked like flour.

Tillie chuckled. "You don't enjoy doing anything unless it involves James," she teased.

He smiled. "Well, that's true enough. How long are you going to hang out today?"

Tillie checked her watch. "I have an interview with Dora to start picking up volunteer shifts giving tours in the museum. I think she's trying to help get everything ready for tonight, so she asked if I could wait." She shrugged. "And I can. Ruth came because she's not working this weekend and when she doesn't work, she can't figure out what to do with herself." She grinned as Ruth playfully hit her with the newspaper.

Ernesto sighed and said, "I miss the museum." He leaned over and picked up the paper that Ruth had thrown down onto Tillie's lap. He chuckled. "I bet my dad is so angry. Only gaining twelve seats."

Tillie made a noise in her throat. "I'm genuinely afraid to go to work on Monday after this."

Ernesto laughed, his eyes still skimming the paper. "Huh."

They looked over at him. "What is it?" Tillie asked.

Ernesto shook his head. "It looks like our dads got Göring what he wanted. He won the election in Bavaria." He tossed the paper back onto Tillie's lap and then heaved himself off the couch. "I'm back to the kitchen, ladies. Think of me often." They laughed at him as he dragged himself out of the lounge to help Heinz finish cooking.

Tillie picked the newspaper back up again and saw Hermann Göring's face staring back at her. He was just a shade too puffy and round to be handsome. Next to him stood Goebbels, looking miniscule and foxlike in the shadow of Göring's massive frame.

She read the caption aloud. "'Hermann Göring takes one of twelve seats for the National Socialist German Workers Party along with Joseph Goebbels.' Well, at least they both won. So, my dad and Herr Grandelis won't be totally insufferable."

Ruth moved her legs so she could curl up against Tillie's side, reading over her shoulder. Tillie leaned into her and bit her lip. "Although, Goebbels winning is a little concerning. After hearing what he said at that dinner last month. He's frightening, but you should have seen everyone at that dinner table listening to him speak. He takes all this," she waved down at the paper, "very seriously." She let the paper drop back into her lap and looked up at the ceiling. "You know, I didn't vote in this election." She turned to Ruth. "What about you?"

Ruth shook her head. "No, I worked a double at the club. I was tending bar, then had to perform. I didn't have time."

Tillie stared down at the faces of the two men who had suddenly become such a presence in her life. "I wonder if we should be paying more attention."

Ruth opened her mouth to respond when Dora materialized at the door of the lounge, her face just as kind and serene as it always was, despite the chaotic day at the institute. "Hi, love. You ready?"

Tillie smiled and handed the newspaper to Ruth. "You bet."

Ruth leaned over and gave her a quick kiss on the cheek. "Good luck, doll."

†

Tillie awoke, a bundle of nerves churning in her stomach. The interview with Dora was only two weeks ago, but it felt like a lifetime since she'd been trained on how to give tours at the museum. She fiddled nervously with the zipper on her sweater while she took deep breaths, trying to ease her wobbly legs and the tightness in her chest. "Don't be nervous," she whispered to herself as she walked, "you're going to do fine."

She went up the staircase to the building, Dr. Hirschfeld's kind face stared down at her from the top of the stone pedestal. She smiled and breathed in, pulling the fresh June air down deep into her lungs, all nervousness gone.

She had just reached the top step when she heard shouting coming from somewhere below her. She turned and there were several young men standing in a group together, leaning against the stone wall at the base of the steps to the institute.

"Did you say something?" She peered down at them. They were all dressed in a similar fashion, dark pants and a lighter, tan-colored shirt. Brownshirts. Her heart skipped a beat. They couldn't have been more than twenty and their boyish faces were staring up at her on the steps above them. She scanned their faces, looking for the boy that had saved her on New Year's Eve.

The boy who stood in front twisted his mouth into a sneer and cold fear erupted in Tillie's gut. He pushed off the half-wall and came up two steps, his eyes narrow and accusing.

"I said, what's a nice German girl like you doing going into that cesspool?" He nodded toward the Institute of Sexual Science behind her.

She swallowed and stepped back, her hand on the railing. If she ran, she could probably make it to the doors before they caught up with her. But she saw in his eyes that he was calculating too, and the other men standing at the bottom of the stairs started to make their way up the steps toward her.

Another man, this one with hair so light it sparkled in the June sun like snow, spit at her and then said, "You know, you really shouldn't be involved with the disgusting people that come and go from this building." His voice was icy and threatening. She took another step back.

The first boy leaned over, bending at his waist, his eyes still on hers. "Hey little girl. Are you a Jew?" he hissed, and she saw movement out of the corner of her eye. It was then she realized that two of the men had come up the outside edges of the stairway while the two others had distracted her. She was surrounded. None of the boys' faces looked familiar.

The blonde's eyes flitted to just above Tillie's shoulder, and she felt a large hand on the small of her back. She jumped and stifled a scream.

"Don't you boys have anything better to do?" The voice was menacing and angry. "Get out of here before I call the police."

The leader of the group laughed. "The police are on our side, you queer," he snarled. They retreated, still watching Tillie and her savior on the steps but then turned and walked away, talking loudly to one another as they went.

Tillie let the air out of her lungs and felt lightheaded. She stumbled a bit and the man behind her reached out a steadying hand. "Are you alright?" he asked.

She nodded but found she couldn't speak. Her hands were trembling, and she was fighting back tears. She turned and looked up at him, relief washing over her. "Karl," she breathed and then she felt her knees falter. He put his hand under her elbow to help her up the last two steps and guided her to the front doors.

She finally found her voice. "What on earth was that about?" She gestured back down the steps to where the men had stood.

He shook his head. "The election. Those Brownshirt kids are getting more brazen every day." His hand was still firmly under her elbow as they walked through the doors.

"Adelaide," Karl said to the woman sitting behind the front desk, "could you go and get Tillie a cup of tea? I'm going to walk her to the library to meet up with Dora." Adelaide stood as they passed her.

"Tills, are you alright?" Adelaide's dark eyes were full of concern.

Tillie gave a weak smile, "Yes, I'm fine. Really, I don't need any tea." She could feel the shame like a hot potato sitting in the pit of her stomach.

Karl patted her back and said to Adelaide, "Those boys were back, and they were harassing her while she was on her way in."

Adelaide's eyes narrowed, full of venom. She muttered something under her breath that sounded suspiciously like "piles of shit." She turned to Tillie, her face softer, and said, "If they're ever out there again, you can go around and come in through the back door by the lodging rooms, where you go when you come visit Ernesto."

Adelaide gave a nod of sympathy and put a little sign on the front desk that said *Back in five minutes* and turned to head down one of the hallways. "I'll bring your tea to the library," she called over her shoulder.

By this time, Karl had let go of Tillie's elbow but still had a hand on the small of her back. His eyes were light and his face long, with a receding hairline and a widow's peak. He had the serious face of someone in charge and was wearing a suit with a polka-dot tie. "Here we are," he said, pulling open the wooden doors of the library.

Dora was sitting at a desk in the front, copying something from a book into a large ledger. She looked up and saw Karl practically carrying Tillie and jumped from the desk, hurrying to meet them.

"Oh, my word, is everything alright?" She peered into Tillie's pale face. "Did you faint, love?"

Tillie smiled. "No, really, I'm fine. All this fuss is really unnecessary." Dora took a step back and crossed her arms in front of her, eyes narrowing. Tillie got the impression of a mother, standing before a child caught with their hand in the cookie jar. Instead of asking Tillie more questions, she turned to Karl.

"Those kids were back on the steps." Karl pulled a chair out for Tillie to sit down.

"Oh." That was all Dora said, but her face flushed, and her jaw clenched.

Tillie tried again. "Really, I'm fine. It was a little scary, but I'm ready to get to work." Karl's mouth was set in a grim line as Adelaide walked in carrying a steaming cup of tea. She brought it over to where Tillie was sitting and when Tillie took it, the cup shook in the saucer, rattling the China together.

"Fine, huh?" Dora said, her arms still crossed. She looked up at Karl and nodded. "I've got it from here, Karl. You can get back to whatever you need to do. I'll make sure she drinks all of it."

Karl watched Tillie take a small sip of tea and then nodded back. "I'm going to call Ernesto at the end of your shift to walk you home." Tillie didn't bother to argue, she knew it would get her nowhere.

Karl followed Adelaide out of the library and Dora pulled up a chair. She reached over and patted the top of Tillie's hand. "What a way to start your day." She sniffed. "They yell at me too. I want to say you get used to it, but you don't. Not really. Every time, your palms sweat and your heart races, and you're just waiting for them to do something. To come after you."

Tillie looked at Dora. She was staring at the teacup on the table, her brown eyes misty and her voice hoarse.

Tillie reached over and put her hand on top of Dora's. "Thank you. I think I'm alright now."

Dora nodded and said, "Finish your tea, love. Then we'll head upstairs and you can get started on your first tour. I think there's a group coming in at one o'clock."

Tillie picked up the saucer and took another sip, this one longer, and closed her eyes. She let the chamomile wash over her and she tasted honey and felt a bite at the back of her throat. Adelaide must have added whiskey to her tea. The warmth started to spread down her throat and the ball of shame in her stomach started to untangle. Her shoulders relaxed and her hands were no longer shaking. She opened her eyes to see Dora smiling at her.

"Leave it to Adelaide to get you drunk before a tour," she winked. "Come on over here and I'll show you how to enter people's names into the tour ledger while you finish your whiskey. I mean, your tea."

Tillie laughed and moved over beside Dora at the desk, content to spend the rest of her shift sipping tea in the quiet of the library.

CHAPTER 9

April 1990

Thea rubbed a hand over her face and rolled her shoulders to try and loosen the knot that was starting to form in her neck.

"You okay?" Michael watched her, his eyes sad and worried.

"Yeah, I just hate that it's come to this, you know?" He nodded and they continued to pick through the closet full of clothes, the smell of lavender and powder filling their noses.

"How much do you think she needs?" He pulled another sweater off a hanger and tossed it to the growing pile just outside the closet door.

Thea shrugged. "I'm not even sure. It's not like she's going to be going out to dinner or drinks." Her voice shook and she could feel a hot prickling sensation behind her eyes.

"But she'll be going to the cafeteria for her meals, so you know she'll want to look her best." He reached over and rubbed her arm. "I mean, you always gotta wear your red lipstick, right?" He grinned at her, and Thea laughed, wiping the tears from her eyes.

"I definitely packed her lipstick. She still wears it. When she has good days." Thea exhaled. "Okay." She crossed her arms in front of her chest and resolved to stay focused. "I'm going to say, probably one outfit per day, plus pajamas. And enough outfits to go, I don't know, two weeks before needing to send the laundry out?" She looked over at Michael for confirmation.

He nodded. "I think that sounds reasonable." He pulled out a dusty hat box from behind a stack of shoeboxes. "What about this?"

Thea nodded. "She specifically told me to make sure all her hats come." He shrugged and put the box on the bed with the other clothes needing to be folded and packed into the suitcases sitting open and empty.

She looked at her grandmother's clothes hanging down like the branches of a willow tree, some dresses collecting dust on the shoulders. "Nothing lace, silk, or cashmere. Nothing dry clean only. That stuff we can keep here."

She pulled a black dress off the hanger and the smell of dust and dried flowers hit her. She went to throw it into the pile when she heard the crinkle of paper in one of the pockets. She pulled the folded paper out of the pocket of the dress and saw that it was the program from her grandfather's funeral.

A small sob escaped her throat. "Michael." He looked up, alarmed at the sound of her voice. "Look." She handed him the program.

He took it and his eyes softened. "Oh, Gram," he said. He flipped the yellowed brittle program over and said, "Didn't your grandfather die twenty years ago?"

Thea nodded, covering her mouth with her hand. The dress suddenly felt heavy. "I'll bet she never wore this dress again." She shook her head, trying to swallow the lump that had formed in the base of her throat. She looked down at the black dress in her hands, her vision blurring at the edges with tears. She put the dress in the donate pile.

✝

Michael brought the last of the suitcases down and put them into Thea's car. "Are you staying to have dinner with Gram after you drop off her things?"

Thea shrugged. "It'll depend on what kind of day she's having. The intake nurse said that the memory care patients eat in their own cafeteria with locked doors, but that if they're having a bad day, they just bring their food to their rooms." Her voice caught on the words 'memory care.' She took a deep breath as Michael folded her into his long arms and kissed the top of her head.

"I know this is hard, but this is the best thing for her." He was quiet for a moment and then said in an even quieter voice, "And for you." Thea nodded into his chest, the tears finally spilling over and staining his light blue pullover.

"I should go." She got into her car and pulled out of the driveway, giving a halfhearted wave to Michael standing on the porch, his arms hanging at his sides.

She parked at the assisted living facility and was pulling suitcases out of her trunk when a voice startled her into almost dropping her grandmother's makeup bag.

"Hello, Thea." The voice was warm and smooth like tea with honey and Thea relaxed.

"Hi Vanessa." She stood next to Thea and helped with the last of the bags and then laid a hand on Thea's arm.

"Tell the truth. Are you alright?" Her deep brown eyes were so much like Michael's and were full of care and concern. Her hair was braided down to her waist, and she kept her soft, cool hand on Thea's arm, giving her a light squeeze.

"Um. I mean, I'm not great." Thea laughed a little, then wiped another tear. It seemed she could do nothing about the tears at this point, they just came.

"I know." Vanessa's lips were set in a grim line, and she bent to pick up one of the suitcases. "This isn't easy for anyone."

Thea couldn't speak around the knot in her throat, so she just nodded and followed Vanessa obediently through the main doors of the facility.

It smelled like cleaning supplies with an undercurrent of old and sick. Thea felt a wave of nausea as she continued to follow Vanessa through the winding corridors until they reached the memory care wing.

Vanessa turned. "Okay, so when you come to visit, you'll just let someone at the front desk know that you're here and they'll unlock the doors for you. Or just call me before you leave your house, and I can make sure someone is waiting for you."

She pulled a large ring of keys from her belt and unlocked the door, holding it open. Thea walked through and the hospital smell grew even heavier. She swallowed and tried to focus on what Vanessa was saying.

"After you get checked in and the doors are unlocked for you, you'll be able to visit Gram as long as you like. If she's having a good day, you're more than welcome to take her to the courtyard to get some sunshine or eat with her in the cafeteria." Vanessa smiled and rubbed Thea's back with her free hand. "I know we already went over all this, but sometimes it takes a few times to really process all the information we throw at you."

Thea remained quiet and looked around at the sterile, wide hallways, the older people shuffling back and forth with flat eyes and tried to suppress a shudder.

"The memory care courtyard is fenced in, but you can hardly see the fence, it's disguised pretty well with bushes, trees, and flowers. There are benches and tables out there; it's nice. And, the cafeteria is just down the hall that way." She pointed down another hallway, Thea noticing her bright red fingernails for the first time.

"Your nails look like my grandmother's lips," the words were out before she knew what she was saying.

Vanessa stopped and turned, her eyes sympathetic. She didn't say anything, just leaned in and hugged Thea, squeezing hard. Thea could smell cocoa butter on Vanessa's skin and a floral scent wafting from her braids. She closed her eyes and breathed deeply. "You smell good," she murmured, and Vanessa laughed.

"This is a lot for a twenty-five-year-old," Vanessa whispered into her ear. "You're doing great."

They finally reached her grandmother's room and Vanessa gave a light knock, then pushed the door open without waiting for an answer. "Hey there, Gram." Vanessa set down the suitcase and straightened, moving out of Thea's way. "You have a visitor. And she brought you all kinds of goodies." She patted Thea's arm one more time and said, "Dinner is in about an hour, if you want to stay. I'll leave you to it. If you need me, have one of the nurses page me." To her grandmother she called, "I'll see you soon, Matilda. You have a nice visit with Thea."

Her grandmother was sitting by the window in a large armchair. She looked small and frail, and her pale blue eyes stared into the courtyard, looking at something Thea couldn't see.

"Hey Gram," she called softly. "I brought you some things, your clothes and makeup." On good days, her grandmother remembered her name and her face, she smiled and put on her red lipstick and laughed and made jokes. On her not so good days, she asked over and over about her grandfather and confused Thea with Jenny, Thea's mother. On her really bad days, she didn't speak at all.

Her grandmother turned and smiled. "Thea." Her voice was warm and strong. Thea breathed a sigh of relief.

"Hi." She crossed the small room and sat on the bed near her grandmother, reaching out to grasp her small, wrinkled hand. Her bones felt so delicate it was like holding a baby bird. "How are you doing? Do you like it here so far?"

Her grandmother blinked a few times. "Here?" Her voice sounded confused, and her eyes darted around the generic room.

They hadn't had time to put up any pictures yet. The nurses recommended putting up as many pictures of family as possible because it helps the patients acclimate, even if they don't recognize the faces staring back at them.

Thea's brow furrowed but her grandmother looked around and gave a vacant smile. "Oh yes, this hotel is lovely, dear. Are you in a room down the hall?" Before Thea could answer, she turned back to the window and her gaze fell on the trees and the grass in the courtyard. Her grandmother gave a contented sigh and said, "Tell Ernie I want him to wear the green tie for dinner."

Thea exhaled and said, "Okay Gram. I'll tell him. I'm going to start unpacking some of your stuff." Her grandmother didn't respond.

She set to work unpacking suitcases, putting the hat boxes in the closet, and hanging photographs, not stopping until the nurse came to the room to ask if they wanted to eat in the cafeteria. She looked back at her grandmother, still sitting gazing out the window. She hadn't moved in an hour. "I think we'll just eat in here, if that's okay." The nurse nodded and disappeared to bring back their food trays.

"Gram," Thea said, keeping her tone light, "it's time for dinner. Are you hungry?" Her grandmother didn't move and for a terrifying moment Thea wondered if she'd died, sitting in the armchair. "Gram?" She moved closer to the chair and then brushed her grandmother's arm with her fingertips.

Her stomach flipped when she saw that her grandmother's face was wet with tears. "Gram?" She knelt down in front of the tiny old woman and rubbed the tops of her legs. "Are you alright? What is it?"

"They're all dead," she said in a hoarse, strained whisper, the tears streaming silently down her face. She turned her vacant eyes to Thea, not seeing her. "We left them behind and they all died." Her voice started to rise until she was almost screaming. "We left her, she's there and she's dying. I can smell the gasoline. Help her."

Thea grabbed her grandmother's shoulders and gave her a small shake. "Who? Who died?" She rubbed her grandmother's small hands and tried to get her grandmother to focus on her face. "Gram?"

Her grandmother turned her head to look directly at Thea. Her watery eyes were wide with a terror that Thea couldn't see. "I left her. *Ich habe sie zuruckgelassen. Ich sah sie brennen.*"

Thea tried not to feel exasperated. "I don't speak German, remember Gram? I don't know what you're saying."

Her grandmother blinked and turned back to look out the window at the small courtyard. She didn't answer.

Thea heard the door click open and a nurse bustle in with dinner trays. "Hey there, Miss Matilda, I have your dinner for you." The nurse must have seen Thea's face, because she stopped. "Are you alright?" Thea nodded, then looked at the nurse. "Actually, is there a physician on staff that I could speak to?"

Thea sat in the warm office, a round graying man with glasses sitting across from her. He gave her a welcoming smile. "So, you wanted to ask me some questions?"

Thea nodded. "I was just curious if it's possible my grandmother could be experiencing hallucinations or delusions of some kind with her dementia."

The doctor agreed. "It's possible. There are types of dementia that involve hallucinations. Visual and auditory. Did she say she saw something that wasn't there?"

Thea shook her head. "Today she talked about leaving people behind and how they died. She keeps speaking in German, so who knows what else she's talking about. But talking about these supposed dead people seems to be very unsettling for her. And today, she talked about smelling gasoline."

The doctor made a note and said, "Well I'll tell you, everything you've mentioned is common for people experiencing dementia.

Unfortunately, it's hard to know if it's a hallucination or if it's just a memory she's reliving at this stage. She's a bit unreliable as far as asking her questions about how she's feeling, so we'll just have to rely on the nurses to keep track."

Thea bit her lip. "Okay, well thank you for your time."

He leaned forward and shook her hand. "Of course. Please call if you have any other concerns."

Driving home, she couldn't stop thinking about the wide-eyed fear on her grandmother's face. By the time she pulled into her driveway, she was crying.

When she walked into the house, she was trembling and Michael rushed her inside, onto the couch and under a quilt, shoving a mug of tea into her hands. Despite curling her fingers around her warm beverage, her teeth still chattered.

"She said she smelled gasoline?" he stared at her, a mixture of horror and concern.

"Yes." Her shoulders shook and Michael rubbed her arm with his large hand. "And she talked about leaving dead people behind."

"Behind where? What on earth could she be talking about." It wasn't a question.

CHAPTER 10

April 1990

Thea sat in the office chair staring at the antique rolltop desk in front of her. The stack of papers tilted precariously to one side and Thea took a large swig of wine from her even larger goblet before scooting her chair in and getting to work.

It didn't help that her grandmother seemed to save everything. There were bills for yard work and refrigerator repair that were from when her grandfather was still alive. As she leafed through each stack, her trash pile grew and grew.

Michael poked his head into the study. "Hey, how's it going?"

"Oh, fine." Thea tipped the last of her wine into her mouth. "I'm pretty sure I've kept three things out of the one million documents I've found so far."

Michael laughed. "Your grandmother wasn't known for being tidy." He came in and sat on the loveseat across from her with his own glass of wine. "I was going to order a pizza for dinner. How does that sound?"

Thea absently said "sure" as she pulled drawers open and threw away old receipts for dry cleaning and jolly rancher wrappers. After the third handful of wrappers, she looked up at Michael, exasperated. "What is going on with these wrappers?

Did my grandmother not own a trash can?"

Michael smiled and shook his head. "Jim and I had been together about a year, so it was probably 1976. You were ten or eleven, do you remember?"

Thea nodded. "Yes. Gram hated you." She winked at him, still throwing handfuls of wrappers into the trash bag at her feet.

"Yes, well, I think she thought I was too young for your uncle." He paused, staring at his wine glass, his eyes far away. He inhaled and his eyes cleared. "Anyway, your grandmother was having a hard time being alone after your grandfather died and then when Jim and I started getting serious, I think she felt like she was going to be alone forever."

"She went on this huge health kick. She went vegetarian like she was some kind of hippie." A deep laugh formed in his belly, and he rubbed his face, shaking his head. "Anyway, she also decided that was the year she was going to quit smoking."

Thea's eyes lit up. "Oh my gosh, that's right. I totally forgot." She looked down at the yellow and clear wrinkled wrappers in her hands. "She used these to quit." The sadness washed over her. "She never seemed lonely to me." She tipped her hands into the trash bag and watched the Jolly Rancher wrappers flutter like confetti down into it. Her eyes lifted to meet Michael's. "But she was, wasn't she."

He nodded, his smile melting into a grim line. "Yes. She was lonely." They were quiet for a moment. Thea stared at the remnants of her grandmother's life, wanting to put her hands over her eyes and pretend she was ten years old again.

"Well, this is depressing," Michael joked, trying to alleviate the sad fog that had settled over the room. Thea chuckled. He stood. "I'll go order the pizza while you finish up. How about *Unsolved Mysteries* and wine tonight?" He laid his hand on her shoulder and squeezed as she leaned forward and opened one of the smaller drawers near the top of the desk.

"Huh."

Michael stopped at the door and turned. "What is it?"

Thea squinted, trying to read the blurry newspaper print. "It's a newspaper clipping." She flipped it over and caught a date on the back. "It's from 1942." She held it up so he could look at it. Under the newspaper clipping was an envelope and she recognized her grandmother's neat script, though most of the words were smudged to the point of being unreadable.

The postmark was from 1941 and there was a bright red stamp directly over the addressee in the center of the envelope with the words *Return to Sender*. Then underneath that stamp were smaller words. *Returned by Censor. Undeliverable.* Michael had his bifocals on and was reading the article while Thea inspected the envelope. She looked up at him and said, "Well? What does it say?"

He shrugged. "It's just an article about Hitler and what was going on in Germany at the time." He smoothed the newspaper with his finger. "I don't know why she'd keep this though." He peered over the top of his glasses at the envelope in Thea's hand. "What's that?"

She shook her head. "I don't know. A letter my grandmother tried to send." She handed it to him, and he held it at arm's length to read the slanted penmanship.

He squinted at the words. "I can't make out any of the words."

Thea stood to make sure the little drawer was empty and saw a small corner of something stuck in the crack between the drawer and the desk. Pulling, she realized it was a photograph.

"Oh man," she smiled, seeing her grandmother looking so happy and young. Michael took the photo from her.

"I think that's Jimmy too. I wonder where this photo was taken." He flipped the photo over and read the cramped writing on the back. "The Belle Club, 1928." He held the photo between his thumb and his forefinger. "I wonder where the Belle Club was, I've never heard of it."

Thea laughed and plucked the photo from his fingertips. "How old were you in 1928?"

He made a face. "Good point. I was four. Maybe five."

Thea touched her grandmother's smiling face in the photo. "I forgot how tiny she was next to my grandfather." For a moment, she just gazed at them. Her grandparents standing in front of a booth, drinks littering the table. Her uncle was seated behind them. "I wonder who this woman is sitting next to Jimmy." She was beautiful. "Maybe a cousin or something?" She looked up at Michael.

He shook his head. "I don't recognize her." He handed the envelope back to Thea while continuing to study the photo. "Can you make out the addressee on this envelope? I can't figure out what it says under the stamp."

She took the envelope and squinted at it, really looking at it for the first time. "Oh man. I think it says *Germany*. I wonder if she was writing to family. Should I open it?"

Michael tore his eyes from the photo. "Didn't she come here with Ernie and Jimmy when she was really young?"

Thea was still staring at the envelope. "Yeah, I think right after World War I, but maybe they still had family back in Germany." She looked up at Michael, but his brow was furrowed, and the photo was an inch from his nose.

"What is it?" Thea stood to look at the photo too. He didn't say a word, just pointed to a spot in the picture. There, barely noticeable in the shadows of the grainy black and white, where her uncle's legs were bent under the table, was her grandfather's hand intertwined with her uncle's and resting on his thigh.

Her eyes met Michael's, and they both looked at the envelope lying on the desk.

"We should open it," Michael said, his voice hoarse. "I'll get the wine."

✝

They sat next to one another, the bottle of wine completely empty, the letter from her grandmother fanned out over the coffee table between them.

"Well." Michael began. "That was …" he paused, raising his eyebrows at the neat cursive, "certainly a letter, wasn't it?"

Thea couldn't speak. She kept replaying parts of the letter in her head. *I miss you. I love you. My body aches for yours.* She exhaled and downed the last dregs of wine in her glass.

"This is a love letter." She picked up the first page and stared at the greeting. *My Darling.* "In 1941, she was already married to my grandfather. My mother was born barely two years after she tried to send this letter." Thea shook her head. "Who could she have been writing to?"

Michael shrugged, still staring at the photo of her grandparents from 1928. He flipped the photo over again, biting his lip. "The Belle Club," he said slowly, his eyes narrowing on Jimmy and her grandfather and their intertwined hands under the table in the photo.

His eyes lifted to meet Thea's. "What if," he stopped and picked up the last page of the letter and his eyes scanned the words at the bottom. *You have my heart. Until we're together again. Give my love to Berlin.*

"What if what?" Thea asked. The wine sloshed in her stomach, making her feel uncomfortably full and empty at the same time.

Michael's eyes were glassy and far away as he ran his fingers over the photo. His voice lowered to just above a whisper. "Nothing. What if nothing." He rubbed his hands over his eyes under his glasses. "I'm going to be so hung over tomorrow." He patted her shoulder and set the last page of the letter and the photo gently back on the table. "Don't stay up too late, kiddo."

"Wait, you're going to bed?"

He stopped in the doorway and looked back at her. "I am. You should too. This," he gestured to the table, "is not a mystery that is meant to be solved. If your grandmother or Jimmy or your grandfather wanted us to know about whatever this is, they would have told us about it." Thea squared her shoulders and clenched her jaw. "I know you think I'm wrong, Thea," he said. "But who are we going to ask about this? Let's just let this go, okay?" He turned without waiting for an answer and Thea could hear the stairs creaking as Michael retired to his room.

She picked up the envelope and squinted at it, trying to decipher the name underneath the bold red letters with the words *Return to Sender*.

The next morning, Thea walked through the stark hallways of the memory care facility, reaching into her bag and clutching the photo and the letter in between sweaty fingers just to double check they were still there and hadn't vanished between the time she left her house and now. Michael had still been sleeping when she awoke and for that, Thea was grateful. Something about the look in his eyes when he said the words 'what if.' He had an idea of what this was all about.

She pushed her grandmother's door open while knocking. "Morning, Gram," she called brightly. She peeked around the edge of the door and saw her grandmother, looking small and frail, in the hospital bed. She was gazing out the window, her shriveled hands in her lap.

Thea walked into the room and the smell of disinfectant overwhelmed her senses. "Gram, it's me. How're you doing?" She sat at the foot of the bed and rubbed the top of her grandmother's tiny foot.

Her grandmother blinked her drooping eyes and turned. Thea could see recognition in her eyes, a smile forming on her grandmother's lips. Thea breathed a silent sigh of relief. "Hello, Thea." Her grandmother reached forward to place a cold hand on top of Thea's on the bed. "What are you doing here today?"

Thea lifted the photo from her bag. "I found this. I thought you might want to hang it up here." She eyed her grandmother's face carefully as she passed her the black and white photo. Her grandmother took the photo from her, still smiling, and looked down. Then she dropped the photo like it burned her fingertips.

"Where did you find this?" Her voice was strained and hoarse. The photo lay harmless on her grandmother's lap but she was recoiling from it like she was afraid it was going to bite her.

"Oh, I'm sorry Gram. I found it in your desk while I was cleaning up. That's you, isn't it? With Grandpa and Uncle Jimmy?" Thea reached forward and picked the photo back up. "I found a letter with it." She paused, unsure if she should keep going. Her grandmother's face had lost all color and her hands were trembling. She added, "There was a newspaper article too."

Her grandmother's eyes closed, and she rested her head against the headboard of her bed. "Oh," she breathed. "Yes. I read that article so many times, I used to have it memorized." Her voice was still quiet, and her face was the color of chalk. She took a deep breath. "You found a letter?"

Thea pulled the paper, soft with age, out of her purse and set it on her grandmother's lap. "I'm sorry, Michael and I opened it. After finding the photo, we were curious." A small smile twitched on her grandmother's lips, and she picked up the letter. The paper rustled as her hands shook. She ran a hand over the first page, smoothing out the wrinkles of the paper.

"I wrote as often as I could. In the beginning, I always got a letter back from her. A week, maybe two and I'd have news from her." A tear rolled down her grandmother's cheek. "When I sent this letter, the weeks stretched with no reply. I was so worried and then I got it back in the mail. Return to sender." Her voice caught in her throat. She watched her grandmother's hands petting the paper like it was a beloved pet. "Then your grandfather found that article in some newspaper and ..." her voice trailed off.

"And?" Thea prompted.

"And that was it." Her grandmother stopped touching the letter and pushed it back toward Thea's hands laying on the bed.

"Who was the letter to?" Thea's brow furrowed with frustration trying to get her grandmother to say more.

Her grandmother turned her head away and looked out the window again. She paused before she spoke. "A friend," she finally said. She made a noise in her throat and Thea realized it was a laugh.

"Gram," Thea started. She wanted to ask why Uncle Jimmy and her grandfather were holding hands under the table.

"I'm so tired, dear. Do you think we could talk about this later?" Her grandmother's eyes were still turned out the window, not looking at her.

"Oh. Yes. I just wanted to know about Grandpa and Uncle Jimmy. But we can talk later." She knew it wasn't fair to upset her grandmother further, but she wanted to see her reaction. Her grandmother's eyes snapped to Thea's face.

"What?" she asked, her voice sharp as a knife.

Thea was startled. Her grandmother never used such an angry tone, even having an episode. "Oh. Um, well," she stammered. "In this photo," she pointed. "They're holding hands." She watched as her grandmother's jaw clenched and her throat moved, swallowing hard. She reached out, picked up the photo and huffed.

"It must have been a trick of the light, dear. I don't see anything." She leaned over and put the photo in a drawer in the bedside table, careful not to let Thea see it again. "Now, I'm going to take a nap. I'll see you later." Without looking in Thea's direction again, she slouched down under the covers and left Thea to sit and stare at the small lump in the center of the bed, the room filled with a stifling quiet.

CHAPTER 11

March 1929

Ruth poked Tillie in the back. "Doll, you're late. It's seven-fifteen."

Tillie rolled over to stare at the clock on the bedside table. "Ugh." She sat up, careful not to move her head too fast, tasting the gin still lingering in the back of her throat. "I blame you wholeheartedly."

Ruth laughed. "Hey, it's not every day you turn twenty-five. We had to celebrate."

Tillie pulled the pillow over her head. "My birthday isn't until tomorrow. We could have celebrated then." Her head was pounding.

"No, we couldn't because both James and I are working tomorrow. Just call in sick. Honestly, Tills, you never do. And because it's *before* your birthday, no one would even know." Ruth winked at her and then rolled back over in bed.

Tillie sat up for a moment and then grabbed her robe. Hurrying across the cold kitchen floor, she made it to the phone and dialed her father's number. "Hello, Papa?" She made her voice sound scratchy and held her nose so she would sound congested. "I'm feeling a little under the weather today, I don't think I should come in."

She expected her father to tell her to go back to bed but he didn't respond right away. Her heart beat a little faster, wondering if he could hear that she was faking. "Tillie, I'm sorry to have to do this to you when you sound so miserable, but could you try to come in today?"

"Oh." She was surprised. "Um, yes, I think I have some cold medicine around here someplace." She forgot to keep holding her nose. "Is everything alright?"

"Well, we're supposed to be having a meeting with Herr Göring, Herr Goebbels, and Herr Himmler about the rally in Nuremberg in August, but Marcia is already going to be out today. Something about a family holiday." He paused and she could hear that he was nervous. "I could really use your help today in this meeting. Herr Goebbels likes you and we really need someone here to take notes."

Tillie held in a sigh. "Of course, Papa. I might be a little late, but I'll be in." She quietly hung up the phone and padded back to her room to get out a dress and stockings. "Sorry Ruthie," she whispered. "I'm going to go in."

Ruth's muffled voice came out from under the pillow. "I knew you would."

†

They were all gathered in the larger conference room, Goebbels at the head of the table. Tillie sat up straight, her pen in her hand, ready to take notes.

Goebbels cleared his throat. "Well, because we had to postpone last year's rally, we are prepared to make this rally the best yet." He nodded to Himmler, sitting a few seats down from him. "Your film is almost complete, yes?"

Himmler nodded. "It's substantially longer than our film from 1927, but I believe it will far exceed your expectations." When Goebbels didn't respond, Himmler added, "I also think adding in fireworks would be a nice addition to the rally. Perhaps music as well?"

Herr Grandelis leaned forward in his chair. "My son Tommy is part of the Hitler Jugend. They have been practicing multiple formations while marching, including a brilliant swastika with torches. It really is a marvel to behold."

Goebbels gave a thin smile. "Well, I think that sounds splendid." He turned to Tillie. "Matilda, please take care of that for me. Contact Kurt Grüber and set up the HJ to be a part of the rally in August. Fireworks, music, and the marching of the Brownshirts and the HJ will all be part of our celebration. This rally is going to be the best we've had."

Tillie hurried back to her desk with her assignments in her hand. She wanted to get away from Goebbels as quickly as possible. She was just turning the corner when she heard the icy voice behind her. "Matilda, won't you wait a moment?"

She took a deep breath and then turned. Plastering a smile across her face she said, "Herr Goebbels, what can I do for you?"

He walked toward her and again she noticed his limp. Her eyes lifted from his foot as soon as she realized she was staring at it. Hoping he didn't notice, she said, "That meeting was very productive. I think the rally is going to be wonderful."

He smiled, though it didn't reach his eyes. "I agree. I think it will be very successful. The Führer will be pleased."

Tillie had no response to this, so she just nodded and smiled. "So, did you need me for anything else, Herr Goebbels?"

"Ahh, yes. Your father mentioned you often visit a part of Berlin that is ..." he paused and pursed his lips, "a stronghold for those that oppose the party."

Tillie's felt her heart in her throat. "Oh?" Her voice sounded high and thin.

"Yes, something about a good friend that lives in that area?" His eyes narrowed. "Possibly a boyfriend?" Tillie didn't respond so he kept going. "While your personal life isn't my business as you are not my daughter, I'm hopeful that this issue will resolve itself as you become more involved with the party. However, that's not why I'm approaching you. In that area of Berlin, we are lacking representation."

Tillie nodded but was unsure where he was going with his little speech.

"We would like to go about securing the neighborhood much in the same way we've done others in Berlin, with an influx of information. However, my Kreisleiter in that area is not having much luck in terms of campaigning. Plan B is," he smirked, "well, I'm sure you've heard about Plan B in other neighborhoods that don't want to listen to reason."

He reached out and touched her forearm, and she had to will herself not to pull away. "Matilda, you are a good German girl. I would advise that you stay away from that neighborhood in the future. Encourage your," he cleared his throat, "friend to move to a more desirable location. Nothing good is going to come in that part of town."

Without waiting for a response, he turned and limped down the hall, leaving Tillie stunned and shaking in his wake.

✝

"Wait, he said what?" Dora reached over to pour gravy onto her potatoes. Karl, Dr. Hirschfeld, and Heinz were all staring at her, their eyes wide.

"I know. It's crazy. All but guaranteeing the Brownshirts will be descending on our neighborhood. Evidently the people who live here don't want to listen to 'reason.'"

Ruth snorted. "Reason. You mean all those ridiculous posters that are everywhere? The flyers littering our sidewalks? The stupid propaganda newspapers that are stacked in our clubs and cafes?" She took a bite of roast chicken. "If that's reason, I'm the Queen of England."

James looked from Ruth to Tillie. "But what do we do? If the Brownshirts show up?" Ernesto rubbed his arm and gave him a reassuring smile.

Karl answered. "Nothing. Don't engage with them unless you're sure you can get someplace safe immediately after. We've had a problem with those men outside on the steps for over a year now and it's just getting worse. There are more of them and different ones on different days. Most of our patients have to come through the back at this point because of the harassment."

Dr. Hirschfeld shook his head. "It's really a shame to have so much anger at someone who is doing nothing to affect your life whatsoever. Those men must have very sad souls." The table was quiet for a moment.

"They attacked me once." Tillie's voice was quiet, but everyone looked at her. Ruth immediately put down her spoon and put her arm around Tillie's shoulder. "On New Year's Eve, walking home. It was awful." She took a deep breath. "We need to start being more careful. If these men are going to start showing up here, trying to start fights with our people, we need to make sure we don't do anything to provoke them."

Heinz made a noise in his throat. "So, we just lay down and take it then?"

Tillie shook her head. "I don't know the right answer. All I know is they're inciting violence on purpose. They *want* us to look scary and unhinged. Goebbels admitted that's what they were planning to do two years ago. To make the German people believe they're in danger from people like us, they have to be afraid of us. They've done it with the Communists and now they're coming here. We just have to be ready."

They all exchanged glances. Finally, Dora spoke. "I just don't really understand how this can be allowed. All this fighting. Where are the police? Where is the government to keep us safe?"

Karl sipped his wine. "I'm afraid the police are part of the groups marching. I'm not sure the police are going to do us any bit of good at this point." His gaze settled on Dora. "Not that they ever really have."

The sun was just beginning to set as Tillie and Ruth set out for their apartment after dinner. Ruth laced her fingers through Tillie's hand and leaned into her. "Are you alright, doll?"

Tillie looked up, a little startled. "Yes, why?"

Ruth shrugged. "Well, it just seems like this must be really difficult. Having to listen to those men, know what they're trying to do, and then have to come back here and tell us about it. Tell us to be careful." She touched Tillie's skin just under her eyes. "You look tired and like you've lost weight. This can't be easy."

Realizing she was close to tears, Tillie shook her head. "I keep telling myself that they're insignificant, you know? The party is tiny. Outside of my father, Herr Grandelis, and these three men who have somehow become fixtures at our offices. I don't know anyone else that's a Nazi. Not one person."

Ruth chuckled. "Well, most of our friends are Communists or Socialists. We don't exactly surround ourselves with the conservative types." She winked.

Tillie laughed. "No, I know. It just seems like they're so small. They have twelve seats in Parliament. That's nothing. So, I shouldn't feel so nervous about all the things they're doing. But I do." She shook her head, biting her lower lip. "They're so organized, Ruthie. More organized than any other party. Everyone has a job, a purpose, and the end goal is to take over. Organized enough that unless something happens, eventually, they'll be able to be the biggest party in Germany."

Ruth scoffed. "I'll believe it when I see it. Besides, there's no sense in worrying about something that hasn't happened yet."

Tillie nodded and put her head on Ruth's shoulder while they walked. "I suppose you're right. I just wish I could feel this at ease when I'm at the office surrounded by red armbands and propaganda papers stacked on my desk. It just feels like no one is really taking them seriously. Outside of you, James, and Ernesto, I mean. And the people at the institute. Regular, normal German people don't seem to care about the things that they say."

Ruth unlocked their door. "Tills, we don't know any regular, normal German people, so I'm not sure how you could really know that."

Tillie rolled her eyes and laughed. "Fair enough." She took a steadying breath. "I know you're right. Right now, everything is going well. We're finally recovering from The Great War, and they hardly got any votes last year. We just need to hope the fighting dies down." She shrugged. "And hope they don't decide to go after anyone besides the Communists, I suppose."

Ruth looked at her, her face suddenly serious. "Well, besides the Communists and the Jews, you mean."

"Oh, Ruthie, I'm sorry. Yes, of course. I just meant that they're attacking the Communists in the streets."

Ruth's eyes narrowed and her voice grew soft. "They are, aren't they."

"You can't think they'd do that to the Jewish people living here?"

Ruth shrugged. "Some of them already have. You've seen the stories of Jews being beaten by a Brownshirt on their way home. You just never know." She paused. "Hitler hasn't made it a secret that he hates us." She bit her lip.

Tillie didn't say anything for a moment. She could see all the pictures printed in *Der Angriff*, blaming the Jewish people for The Great War, for the loss of jobs that followed the loss of the war. According to the Nazis, it seemed all the bad things that had happened were everyone else's fault.

She laid a hand on Ruth's arm. "The Nazis are using people's fear of Communists to breed more fear and hate." She gave Ruth a reassuring smile. "But how would they make people afraid of the Jews? I just don't think the German people would fall for that."

Ruth gave a small nod, but Tillie could see the worry in her eyes.

CHAPTER 12

May 1990

Thea sat at her desk, staring at the letter in front of her. The letter, the photo, and her grandmother's reaction had been rolling around her brain like loose marbles for two weeks. She stood and decided to go have lunch with her grandmother in the hopes that maybe she felt like talking.

She arrived to have lunch when a nurse met her in the hallway. "Your grandmother is having a bit of a rough day, I'm afraid." The nurse's face was tight and sad. "I'm not sure how much you'll be able to visit with her today."

Thea nodded and slowly pushed her grandmother's door open. She took a deep breath before looking around the corner. "Hey Gram." She kept her voice soft and even, not wanting to startle her.

Her grandmother was sitting on her bed. She was dressed, but it was clear she hadn't been out of her room in some time. Her hair stuck up in the back and the room smelled musty with an undercurrent of sickness and dirty skin. Her grandmother's face was wet, and her nose was red.

"Gram?" She took a few steps toward the bed and realized she had several photos on her lap. The photo from her desk was in the center. The pink hatbox from her grandmother's closet sat open on the nightstand and Thea could see it was full of yellowing photos and handwritten letters.

Easing herself on the bed, she laid a hand on her grandmother's tiny foot. It felt cold even under the heavy cotton socks. Tillie could see the slip resistant rubber visible on the soles.

Her grandmother sniffed. "Did I ever tell you about them?" She didn't look up from the photos.

"No, you didn't." Thea's heart was pounding, and she forced her breathing to slow.

"Well, your father didn't want us to tell you the truth. I always felt bad about that." A skeletal finger traced the faces on the photo closest to her. Thea bit her lip, realizing her grandmother had her confused with Jenny, Tillie's mother. She didn't say anything, wanting her grandmother to continue. "Did you know you were adopted?"

Thea blinked and then blurted out, "Are you talking about Jenny? Jenny was adopted?" For the first time, her grandmother raised her tired eyes to Thea's face.

"Yes, you," she snapped. "Who else would I be talking about?" Thea nodded, not daring to interrupt again but her heart was racing, and her mind went blank from shock.

"Your father and I, we loved one another, and we thought we could," her grandmother paused, "well. You know." She blew a long breath out. "Jimmy wouldn't hear of it. He was furious when we told him. But we didn't think people would keep believing us if we didn't have a child."

Thea's brow furrowed in confusion. She just sat and waited, hoping somehow her grandmother would weave all the pieces together. That everything would make sense. After a few beats of silence, Thea couldn't stand it. "Why couldn't you and Gr—I mean, Dad, have a child?"

Her grandmother suddenly swept all the photos onto the floor and put a hand to her face. "Because Jimmy didn't want us to.

He was jealous." Her grandmother's voice was bitter. "He always blamed me for her death. And when Ernie said we needed a child, Jimmy was livid. He only agreed when we promised to adopt."

She shook her head. "And even then, he was awful about it. It was only after you came that he calmed down." Her hands were balled into tight fists, her knuckles white. "I think he just liked playing house with Ernie. Pretending you were theirs." Angry tears trickled down her face.

Thea bent over and picked up a photo she had never seen before. Her grandmother looked about twenty and she was standing next to the woman from the photo she had found in her grandmother's desk. The woman was very tall and wearing a tuxedo. They had their arms around one another.

"Is this her? The woman who died?" She gently placed the photo back onto her grandmother's lap.

Her grandmother stared at the photo without touching it and a strangled sob escaped her lips. "Oh Jenny," she moaned. "*Sie war mein ein und alles.*"

At that point, her grandmother collapsed into hysterics, so much so that Thea had to call a nurse to come and sedate her. She watched her grandmother sink into sleep and felt the guilt and shame seeping from her every pore. She worried the nurse could see it, rising off her like steam.

✝

She sat at her grandmother's desk, staring at the letter and the photo, trying to decipher what her grandmother had said. She had taken the photo of her grandmother and the woman. On the back of the photo there was a name and a date. *Ruth and me. 1929.*

Staring at it, she pulled out a legal pad and began writing things down. She made a list of all the places her grandmother might have hidden more photos or letters. She was trying to figure out where else to look for clues when Michael walked into the office without knocking and started to ask what she wanted for dinner.

"What the hell are you doing?" His face grew splotchy, and she could see the annoyance and impatience in his dark brown eyes.

"Okay, listen. I went to have lunch with her and I ..." She could feel the wave of disbelief wash over her and she wasn't sure how to even start.

Michael stood in the doorway; his arms crossed. "Well?" he asked, his voice tight.

"Did you know my mother was adopted?"

He dropped his arms to his sides and his face went from annoyed to confused. "What? That can't be right."

Thea recounted everything her grandmother said about her mother and the adoption. "I couldn't get her to talk more about it after she started crying, but I just don't understand what's going on." Her eyes grew hot and while she didn't remember her mother, she could feel the regret that her mother didn't know anything about this before she died.

Michael looked down at her and his face was full of pity. "Thea." His voice was gentle and sympathetic. "Do you really not understand what happened? What was really going on?"

She stared at him and shook her head. He sighed and pinched the bridge of his nose. "They were gay. All of them."

"What? What are you talking about?"

"This woman, Ruth. Was that her name?" Thea nodded. "I'm positive she was your grandmother's partner. Your grandfather and your uncle were a couple. I mean, obviously he wasn't really your grandmother's brother." He made an exasperated noise in his throat. "Or maybe he was, I don't know. Your grandparents got married to hide." Thea realized her mouth was hanging slightly ajar and snapped it closed. "They adopted your mother to make it look real."

"But." She looked down at the photo in her hands. "That makes no sense. Uncle Jimmy was with you. And you two never hid."

Michael took a deep breath and crossed the room, settling into the couch and putting his elbows on his knees. He rubbed his face and he looked older than she'd ever seen him look.

His voice dropped to a whisper. "Jim and I got together five years after your grandfather died. And it was the seventies. That's completely different from 1930." He gestured to the photo.

"But," Thea said again, but this time didn't have anything to add. All the pieces clicked into place. She raised her gaze to meet Michael's. "Why would they lie?"

Michael barked out a laugh. "Why would they tell the truth?" He shook his head and leaned back on the couch.

She watched him and then said, "You knew." His eyes snapped to meet hers. She stood, her body suddenly filled with adrenaline and anger. Her eyes flashed as she walked toward him across the office. "You knew."

He held his hands up. "No." He stood and placed his hands on her arms. She glared at him. "I mean, I didn't know. But after we found the first photo and the letter, I suspected maybe that was what was really going on. I just didn't want to push your grandmother if that was the case. She had her reasons for not telling anyone and now we're going to respect that." He pulled her in for a hug, but her arms hung at her sides.

She wormed her way free of his arms and she saw concern in his eyes. "I just," she began, but he shook his head a second time.

"Let your grandmother have her memories. She doesn't need to know we know. Or that we suspect. We need to just let it go."

Thea felt the photo still between her fingers and looked down at the two smiling women. Her voice caught in her throat. "But what happened to Ruth?"

Michael dropped his arms from her shoulders. He sighed. "My best guess? Based on the letter we found, plus that article snippet in the desk, she was probably killed in the Holocaust."

Thea crossed to the desk and pulled the article back out from the drawer. Scanning it, she saw it announced Hitler's plans for the Jewish people of Germany. The newspaper was smudged in places, with fingerprints around the edges. It was soft, almost like fabric. She could tell it had been read many times over. Looking up at Michael, she saw he had tears in his eyes.

"I don't know why Jimmy never told me," he said. "If he and your grandfather were really a couple, that would have meant they had been together," he stopped to do the math in his head.

"Well, my grandparents were married for something like thirty-five years when Grandpa died. Maybe a little less," Thea interrupted. Michael slowly closed his eyes and shook his head.

"Ernie would have been the love of his life." Taking a deep breath, he took off his glasses. "And here I thought I had been his longest relationship." He smiled sadly. "Except fourteen years isn't exactly a lifetime, is it." He wiped the tears from his eyes.

Thea walked over and hugged him. "Michael, I saw the way my uncle loved you. Even if he and my grandfather were a couple, that doesn't diminish his love for you." He sniffed and rested his head on her shoulder. "In fact," she pulled back to look him in the eye, "I would argue it makes it that much more special. For him to be able to love someone again after losing the person he spent most of his life with. He chose you for that. That's really amazing." She gave him a reassuring smile, and he smiled back.

He nodded and mopped his face with a handkerchief from his back pocket. He took a second deep breath and let it out like a tire leaking air. "So," he said, looking down at the list on the desk, "what's the plan now?"

Thea shrugged. "I just want to know what happened. I want to know about my mother. I figure I'll start going through every place in the house I can think of to try and find something. More photos, newspaper clippings. She had to have kept more than just this one thing, right? If she had an entire life before this," Thea gestured to the room around her, "she has to have some sort of record of it all. If she lied about all of it, there has to be something here."

Michael nodded. "You'd think."

"Have you ever found anything in Uncle Jimmy's room?"

He shook his head. "But honestly, I haven't really looked." Thea nodded. It wasn't like Michael to snoop.

"Well, that's my plan for now, I think. I'm just going to tear the house apart."

✝

The next day when Thea walked into the house after work, Michael was sitting at the kitchen table surrounded by old photos.

"What's all this?" Thea set her keys and purse down on the kitchen counter and slid into one of the high-backed chairs.

"I found these in a chest in the back of my closet." He looked at her over his glasses. "The chest had a false bottom."

Thea raised her eyebrows. "Really?" Picking up a photo, she saw her grandfather with several men she didn't know, her Uncle Jimmy sitting on his lap. "Oh my."

"Oh my, indeed," Michael joked. He took off his glasses and rubbed his forehead. "I still can't figure out if your grandmother and Jimmy were actually brother and sister, but your grandfather and your uncle were absolutely a couple."

Thea picked up another photo, one of her mother as a baby sitting on her grandmother's lap. Her grandmother is looking at the camera, but her grandfather is gazing at Jimmy's handsome young face. "Huh."

"What?" Michael looked up at her.

"Who do you think took some of these?" She picked up another with just her grandfather and Jimmy embracing in front of a Christmas tree.

Michael shrugged. "It looks like they had a pretty tight-knit group of friends." He pushed a few photos over to her. "There's a core group in a lot of these photos. Two women and three other men, plus your grandparents and Jimmy."

Thea picked up another picture where they were all holding champagne glasses. The two women were kissing. It looked like maybe it was New Year's Eve. Her grandmother must have been the one taking this photo because she wasn't in it.

"I know in the '40s there were groups of gay men and women that hung out with one another. I mean, I was so young, I don't know a ton. But I've heard things from the elders."

Thea cocked her head to the side and giggled. "I'm sorry, 'the elders'?"

He waved his hand at her. "The elder gays. You hush. Anyway, it's not surprising that they found a community of people."

"There's nothing from before they moved to this house, though?" Thea dug through the stacks of photos on the kitchen table, her grandparents smiling up at her from every corner.

Michael shook his head. "Nothing. It's like they didn't exist before they got here."

Thea chewed her lip. "What did Jimmy tell you about his childhood?"

Michael leaned back in his chair and crossed his arms. "Not a lot. He was close with his mother. He was out to her, even in the '20s when he was really young. She lived in the UK and died in the '50s after World War II. His father was killed in World War I and he had been an only child. Before working for the public library, James worked as a waiter in a club."

"What about where he grew up?" Thea tried to remember seeing baby pictures of her grandparents and the only one she knew of was a split frame with her grandmother on one side and her grandfather on the other. She couldn't think of any photos she knew of with her grandparents as kids or teenagers.

Her brow furrowed. She recalled the one time she had asked her grandmother about her own parents.

"My parents died a long time ago," her grandmother had said. "But we weren't very close." She had shrugged and kissed the top of Thea's head and that had ended the conversation.

Michael shook his head. "Jimmy didn't like talking about his childhood. It upset him and so I never pushed. I assumed that because he had lost both his parents, it was just too painful to talk about. I always thought he grew up with your grandparents in Germany, but I thought they came over after World War I since that's when his mother moved to France."

Thea's eyes roamed over the photos strewn across the dark mahogany tabletop. "It's all so strange. I feel like I didn't even know them." She lifted her eyes to meet Michael's gaze. He gave her a thin smile.

"I know, kiddo." He sipped from his mug of tea and repeated again, softer this time, "I know."

CHAPTER 13

January 1930

Tillie shivered under the blankets and Ruth moved closer to her, wrapping her arms around her shoulders. "Why don't you put on another layer of clothes?"

Tillie shook her head. "Then I would have to get up." Ruth giggled into Tillie's shoulder.

"Should we turn on the radiator?"

Tillie bit her lip, thinking about her frozen feet. "No," she said finally. "We should save our money. It's just going to get colder next month."

Ruth nodded. "Well, the institute will be warm. Why don't we get up and get dressed? We can spend the day in the library. I don't go into the club until six."

Tillie let out a long breath. "Okay." She wiggled her toes inside the two pairs of woolen socks and could feel that they were stiff with cold. "Let's just lay in bed for a few more minutes." She felt Ruth's smile on the back of her neck, and they snuggled together, trying to warm up their shivering arms and legs.

Tillie woke again with a start at a loud knock on their front door. Ruth lay snoring next to her, and she realized they must have drifted back to sleep. She sighed and peeled the heavy blankets off, feeling the frigid air of the bedroom penetrating her layers of clothing. She wrapped her bathrobe around her and hurried to the front door to keep the knocking from waking Ruth.

She winced touching the cold doorknob as she slowly opened the door. James stood in the doorway, his cheeks red and his eyes watering from the winter wind outside. "James," Tillie stepped aside to let him in, "is everything all right?"

He walked in and sat at their kitchen table without removing his coat. He sniffed and wiped his nose. "Is Ruthie here too?"

"Do you need me to go wake her up?"

James sighed and nodded. Tillie could see tears in his eyes. She squeezed his shoulder and went back to the bedroom. "Ruthie," Tillie whispered loudly. The body shaped mass under the pile of blankets stirred. "Ruth, James is here. Something's wrong."

Ruth sat bolt upright and swung her legs out of the bed. "What do you mean 'something's wrong'?" She ran her hand through her hair to flatten it and threw on her bathrobe. "James?" She called into the dark hallway. "James, what's going on? Is it your mother? Is Bernadette alright?"

Tillie followed Ruth into the kitchen, where James stood and embraced Ruth. There were tears on his face. Tillie bit her lip and watched them in the center of the kitchen, hugging. He drew a shaky breath. "My mother's shop has to close. There are no customers." His voice cracked. "She started with just closing twice a week, thinking that she'd save on the electricity. But," he sighed, "no one is having dresses made. She can't keep the shop open by selling needles, thread, and buttons." He sniffed, his eyes still down. "She made the most money on designing and sewing costumes for the performers at the clubs. But all the performers are getting fired or their shifts cut. The clubs are closing so no one is having new costumes made."

He dropped his head into his hands. "We tried. We really did. But ..." His voice dropped to a whisper. "It's over now." He cleared his throat and lifted his head. "Which means we can't keep our apartment. I'm here to ask if my mother can move into your extra room." He didn't meet Ruth's eyes.

Tillie watched him. "Where are you going to go?"

He swallowed, still looking down at his hands. "I'm moving into Ernesto's room at the institute. Dr. H. already promised all the empty rooms to his patients that have been the hardest hit, so there's no space for my mother." He finally lifted his eyes to look at Ruth. "She doesn't have anywhere else to go," he whispered. "Her sister lives in France, so she mentioned going there, but I can't imagine her going so far away."

"James," Ruth's voice was soft and calm. "Of course, Bernadette can stay with us." She held his hands. "It's not even a question. She can move in today if she needs to." He let out a long breath and wiped the tears from his face.

"Oh Ruthie, thank you." Tillie crossed the kitchen to hand him a handkerchief and he gave a watery smile as he took it from her. "I feel like I'm failing her," he said, his voice cracking. "I don't make enough at the club to support both of us, especially not now. And now there's no room for her where I'm going."

"You're not failing her." Ruth sat down and pulled James into the chair next to her. "Everything is hard right now and you're doing the best you can. She made it an entire month after the crash. That's longer than a lot of other businesses. And just because she's closing her shop now, doesn't mean it's going to stay closed."

James nodded, but his face looked skeptical. "Can you afford to take in another person?" His eyes darted to Tillie, knowing she was the one to answer.

She smiled. "We'll figure it out. Don't worry."

Tillie slowly closed the door when James left and turned, her eyes meeting Ruth's. Ruth had a crease of worry between her eyebrows. "Can we really afford another person right now?"

Tillie took a deep breath and then shrugged. "We'll have to. We can't just turn her out into the street." She lowered herself into a chair and pulled her bathrobe tighter around her and rubbed her face. "It'll be fine. I'm sure this will pass soon."

Ruth let out a long sigh. "I hope you're right. We're hardly getting anyone into the clubs right now. My shifts have been cut in half and four of the other performers have been fired." She fought a shiver. "I'll honestly be surprised if any of us have jobs by March."

Tillie bit her lip. "Well, I can't imagine my father's law firm closing. So, I'll at least still have a job." She looked up at Ruth. "We'll be okay." She tried to sound confident, but her voice sounded small and thin. Ruth gave her a small smile. "I know, doll." She left the kitchen and went back to the bedroom, closing the door softly behind her.

⸸

The day Bernadette moved into their flat, dark gray clouds hung low in the sky, casting everything in a greenish light. Bernadette and James were quiet, and their eyes were rimmed in red. They moved slowly, bringing in her suitcases and a small amount of furniture.

Tillie tried to smile while they moved things around to make room for Bernadette, but she could feel it didn't reach her eyes. The worry on Ruth's face, combined with the sadness on Bernadette's, over losing her shop, her home, and most of her belongings weighed Tillie down.

James pulled Ruth aside as Tillie was moving things around in the hallway closet. "I tried to get her to leave all my father's old clothes, but she was hysterical about it. I finally convinced her to only pack a suitcase full of his things." He rubbed his face and Tillie could tell he was trying not to cry. "I'm sorry she's bringing so much to move into your apartment; I just couldn't bear to keep fighting with her about it."

Ruth smiled at James and gave his arm a squeeze. "It's really fine. We'll figure it out." She met Tillie's eyes and Tillie could see the depths of Ruth's sadness.

When she was finally moved in and James had left to take his small box of things to Ernesto's dorm at the institute, the women all sat around the kitchen table, sipping vodka.

Bernadette took a long drink and then said, "Girls, I really appreciate you letting me stay with you." Her voice broke and she cleared her throat, wiping a tear away from her cheek. Ruth opened her mouth to say something, but Bernadette held up her hand. "I know having another person here is going to put a strain on your finances and I just really can't thank you enough." She trailed off and sniffed. "I'll do my best to help out."

Ruth rubbed Bernadette's arm. "Bernadette, you're family. We'll figure out the rest of it as we go, but you absolutely do not need to feel like you owe us anything. This is what family does for one another."

Bernadette nodded and stood from the table. "I'm so tired. I'm going to go to bed." She glanced at the door. "You know, Jimmy and I have never lived apart." She sniffed again and shook her head, wiping her eyes as she walked slowly to the guest bedroom at the end of the hall.

†

Tillie made her way to the train station, hurrying through the cold streets. It was a normal occurrence to pass by groups of people burning money to keep warm, families huddled together in doorways of boarded up stores and shops, and small children crying from hunger.

The first few weeks, Tillie would cry on the train ride after passing the toddlers with no shoes and the men gathered on street corners shouting out at her, but she'd grown accustomed to it. If the people on the street saw you crying for them, it just made them angry.

Walking the short block from the train station to her parents' home, Tillie marveled at the quiet in her parents' neighborhood. Here, there were no crying children outside without shoes. Almost as if the crash hadn't touched these homes.

"Hello Mama," Tillie pushed open the front door. Her parents' home felt warm and inviting; they could still afford heat.

"Tillie, dear, what are you doing here?" Her mother emerged from the kitchen, wiping her hands on her apron.

"Oh, Papa wanted me to come by on my way to the office and then we'd go to work together. He didn't say why though." She looked around. "Is he here?"

"Yes, he's upstairs getting dressed. Why don't you come into the kitchen for some breakfast while you wait for him?"

On the kitchen counter her mother had spread out bread and jam, coffee, tea, a hardboiled egg, and some homemade applesauce. Tillie clenched her jaw. Her refrigerator at home contained hard bread, some government butter, and vodka. Bernadette was doing the best she could in the breadlines, but they usually could only rely on soup and stale bread. Maybe some potatoes on a good day. Certainly not coffee or jam.

"Mama, this looks great." Her voice sounded flat, but her mother didn't notice.

Her mother shrugged. "It's not our normal breakfast, but it will have to do." She sighed. "I just wish we weren't having to pay for food for the entire country." She turned to Tillie. "You know your father has started sleeping with a bat next to his side of the bed?"

"Good Lord, why?"

Her mother's voice was incredulous. "In case those disgusting Communists try to break into our home." Her eyes widened and her voice grew fearful. "They're going to come after us, Tillie.

After all of us, you mark my words. Unless the government does something about it."

Tillie's mouth hung open and she just stared at her mother, unsure of what to say. A copy of Goebbels' paper *Der Angriff* caught her eye on the kitchen table. "Mama," Tillie fought to keep her voice from sounding accusatory. "Why are you reading this garbage?" She walked over and picked up the paper, waving it slightly. "You know nothing in this paper is true, right? It's all lies to make people like you afraid."

"Matilda Rose," her mother hissed, "do not talk about Herr Goebbels and his paper that way. First of all, Herr Goebbels is your father's boss, which means he is *your* boss as well. Second of all, it is *not* all lies. Don't you see the violence the Communists are causing? Riots and looting everywhere you look. I barely feel safe enough to leave the house."

Tillie blinked. "What do you mean Goebbels is Papa's boss?"

"*Herr* Goebbels, Matilda," her mother corrected her. "Your father has been given the position of Ortsgruppenleiter. Which means he reports to Anthony as the Kreisleiter and to Herr Goebbels as the Gauleiter. He's in charge of our entire neighborhood."

Tillie rubbed her forehead and abruptly left the kitchen. "Papa," she yelled up the stairs. "I'm here. What is it you need from me?" She felt sick to her stomach.

She could hear his footsteps across the bedroom, then saw him appear at the top of the stairs. "Tillie, I'm so glad you could make it."

She gave a stiff nod. "Yes. Well, what exactly did you need from me? I do have some filing to finish, and I usually get to the office about an hour before you do. I should really get going." The house had gone from warm and inviting to sticky and uncomfortable. She could feel sweat building up on her neck under her hair.

Her father's eyes narrowed. "Are you alright Tillie?" As he got to the bottom step, he reached out and touched her cheek. "You look pale."

"You're working for Goebbels now?" She couldn't mask the annoyance in her voice.

Her father, on the other hand, looked delighted. "Your mother told you the good news! Yes, isn't it exciting? He appointed me the Orstgruppenleiter last week. I'm overseeing our entire neighborhood. Passing out flyers to each house and talking with the neighbors about the Führer and the party. The reason I wanted you to come over this morning is because I would like to plan a parade in the neighborhood, and I need your help with it."

"You want me to help you plan a Nazi parade?" She couldn't keep her voice calm.

Her father's eyes turned sharp. "'Nazi' is a disgusting, derogatory word. You will not use that language inside my household, Matilda."

"Fine. You want me to organize a parade for the National Socialists then." Her father appraised her and then shook his head.

"It's alright, I can see by your face you'd rather the Communists take over and murder us all in our sleep." Tillie opened her mouth to respond, but her father held up a hand. "It's fine, I'll ask Marcia to do it. Clearly, you're not *comfortable*," his voice mocked her, "although I can't imagine why on earth you wouldn't be lining up to join the party as well." Her father's face had grown red, and a vein was popping out of his forehead. Tillie had hardly ever seen him this angry.

He went to walk into the kitchen, leaving Tillie in the hall when he stopped and turned back to face her. "You know, Anthony wants to fire you. He says that you're going to be bad for our law office once the Führer is president. That having someone like you that so obviously opposes our agenda is bad for business."

Tillie's eyebrows shot up. "And what exactly is that agenda?"

He paused, his finger on his lips. "Our agenda is to *save* Germany. To rid the country of those that caused us to fall so far in the first place and put them in their natural place. Our agenda,

Matilda, is to restore Germany to greatness. What Germany was before the disgrace of The Great War. Why anyone would not want this is beyond my comprehension. But mark my words, Tillie, if you do not get on board, being my daughter will not protect you from losing your job."

Tillie managed to make it to the office, but she couldn't even remember the ride on the train. She felt like she was suspended in water. Her arms and legs felt sluggish, and her thoughts were clouded. Her father had ignored her when he arrived and called Marcia in almost immediately. Tillie went to hide in the filing room and counted the minutes until she could escape to the café across the street at lunchtime.

"Hey!" Marcia whispered hoarsely from the other side of the filing cabinets. "Tillie, are you still in here?"

Tillie sighed and stood. "Yes, I'm here." She held up a hand and waved in the direction of Marcia's voice.

Marcia's footsteps sounded hurried as she walked to the back of the filing room. "What in the world is going on?"

Tillie's eyes felt tired and itchy. "What do you mean?"

"Well, for starters your dad just complained to me about you 'not being a team player' for about ten minutes. So that was awkward. And then he made me promise to help him with some ridiculous parade through his neighborhood. I have to call Herr Goebbels to get approval *and* I have to go to some Hitler Youth meeting to ask for participants." She rubbed her temples. "That's about the last thing I feel like doing."

Tillie slid down to the floor and leaned against the backside of the filing cabinet. The metal felt cool on her back through her silk blouse. "I know Marcia. I'm sorry. It's my fault you got roped into planning this." She swallowed her shame. "I didn't really refuse to do it, but I wasn't …" she paused, "*enthusiastic* about it. At least not enthusiastic enough for my father." Her voice was quiet.

Marcia watched her for a moment, then smiled. "Good for you."

Tillie blinked and looked up at her. "What?"

"Good for you," she said again, louder and slower. "No one is going to be able to talk sense into these men. But tiny actions can add up." She lowered herself onto the floor next to Tillie. "I really don't want to go to the Hitler Youth meeting." She groaned. "Those kids are so creepy."

Tillie looked over at Marcia, her dark curls framing her young face. Tillie never really noticed but Marcia was very pretty. "Marcia, are you married?"

Marcia looked startled momentarily but then laughed. "Yes, actually, I just got married last year. Why?"

Tillie shrugged. "It just occurred to me that I don't know anything about you. I consider you my friend, but I don't know anything really, except that you prefer blue ink over black." She nudged Marcia's shoulder with her own.

Marcia giggled. "Well, I'm married to a lovely man. He had been working as a laborer but with everything," she gestured to the front of the office, "he lost his job. We had to move back in with his parents, but his father is a doctor so we're doing okay now." She shrugged. "Plus, we have my job here. I see all those people outside, people who have lost everything, and I should consider us lucky that we had someplace to go."

Tillie nodded. "I'm sorry you're being roped into this Hitler Youth thing. I can go with you if you'd like. You know, Herr Grandelis' son is in the Hitler Youth. I'll bet that's the meeting you're going to."

Marcia raised her eyebrows. "Oh, you're probably right. Man, they're really in this aren't they?"

Tillie dropped her voice. "Did you know they were both involved in the coup in 1923?"

Marcia turned, her hand flying to her mouth. "You're kidding! I had no idea. What happened?"

Tillie pulled her legs in to get more comfortable on the floor. "Well, my father wasn't super involved with the Nazis yet, but Anthony was, even then. They were both so terrified of Communists. I was only working here part time after school. There was a third lawyer here; he and Anthony were part of the march into Munich behind Hitler and Göring. The other lawyer was shot and killed. Anthony ran after Göring was shot. I think my father left before the march began, but he refuses to talk about it."

"Oh, my goodness. Did anyone ever know they were involved?" Marcia's eyes were wide and transfixed on Tillie's face.

"I don't think so. The other lawyer's family acted like he was just in the wrong place at the wrong time and my father and Anthony never discuss it. I caught Anthony reading Hitler's book once, but when I went back into his office, it was gone. I think until about 1925, he didn't want anyone to know he was still following the party." Marcia shook her head but didn't respond. "What about your family?" Tillie could feel the heat creeping up her face—shame in her own family's beliefs.

"Oh, no. My husband's family is Jewish. We all vote for the Social Democratic Party." Marcia was looking down at her fingernails at the chipping paint.

"How can you work here?" Tillie's voice was a whisper. "Knowing how much they hate your husband and your family?" Marcia had to have seen the disgusting cartoons Goebbels put in his newspaper every week, the way they blamed Jewish people for the loss of The Great War, the way they talk about Jewish people like another species.

Marcia shrugged. "It's a job, Tillie. So many people are out of work. Besides," she stood and reached down to help Tillie up from the floor, "they're loud, but they're outnumbered. They aren't even the fifth biggest party in Parliament. There's nothing to worry about."

Back at her desk, she could hear her father banging around inside his office. Taking a deep breath, she tapped at his door with her fingernail, then pushed it open.

"Papa?" Her voice shook. She cleared her throat. "Marcia was just telling me that she's planning the parade for you." Her father's face was cold as he stood in front of her, his arms crossed over his chest. "It sounds like a lot for just one person to do. I …" She swallowed then hurried on. "I would be happy to help her. I'm sorry about how I acted this morning."

His face did not soften. "I don't want you to do anything you don't want to do, Matilda."

"It's not that, it's just …" Tillie grasped for an excuse. "Well, I've been having to wait in the breadlines and I'm just very tired and it doesn't seem like these," she started to say 'Nazis' but corrected herself. "That the party is doing anything to make things better. They're just marching and throwing around posters and newspapers and starting fights. It's exhausting to watch when you're cold and don't have enough to eat."

Looking up at her father, she saw she had struck a nerve. His horror-stricken face at the news his only daughter was cold and hungry made her insides unclench slightly. "You're having to wait in the breadlines?" His voice was strangled now, like something was stuck in his throat.

"Well, yes. Everyone who isn't wealthy is having to wait in breadlines right now, Papa." It wasn't exactly a lie. They were having to wait in breadlines, but only because her salary couldn't support herself, Ruth, and Bernadette. On the rare weekend when Ruth did well at the club, they didn't have to wait in the breadline at all. They were still treading water, most of the time anyway.

Her father stared at her. "I'm so sorry, Tillie, I didn't realize. I'll see to it that we raise your salary." He lowered himself into his chair. "As for what the party will do to help, once we're able to make Germany great again, you'll see. You'll see how it's better. For all of us."

At this, Tillie tilted her head to the side. "Well, I don't want a raise, especially if Marcia doesn't get one. I'm fine, really. But, Papa," she sat down in the chair across from him. "How? How is the party going to 'make Germany great again'?" She folded her hands across her lap. "How specifically?"

Her father smiled. "The Führer is going to end unemployment, create a strong government, squash the Communists, and he will give us back our strong army. All things that will help our country."

Tillie sat quite still, trying to decide if she should continue pushing her father after he'd accepted her apology. He took her silence as acquiescence.

"Well," he drummed his hands on his desk. "I have a few things to do, but I'm glad you'll be helping Marcia and I hope that you're ready to be a team player from this point forward." He started to usher her out of his office. "You should make more of an effort to read Herr Goebbels' paper, you'll see. The Führer and the party are going to do great things, Tillie." He shut the door behind her.

She set her notepad back on her desk and looked at her father's closed door. "But how?" she whispered to herself.

CHAPTER 14

August 1930

Tillie sat at her desk, straining to hear what was going on inside her father's office. Herr Goebbels had been in every day this week and one day both he and Göring were here, talking in hushed, serious voices and going straight into Herr Grandelis' office without waiting to be invited.

Tillie knew why they were so tense. The elections were two weeks away and The Nazi Party was trying to get more Parliament seats. Tillie could tell that even Göring was feeling the stress; his normal jovial presence was replaced with a sullen, nervous man who seemed on edge every time she saw him.

She tapped her foot, the nervous energy needing to go somewhere, moving papers back and forth trying to look busy. She, Ruth, and the boys were all planning to vote this Sunday. On the surface they all joked and laughed about the Nazis. How ridiculous Hitler was wandering all over the country screaming at audiences of crazed men and women waving swastika flags and Goebbels with his newspaper and his threatening posters hung up and down the streets of Berlin. But inwardly, Tillie felt like a string pulled taut ready to snap.

As she watched the important men parade through her

father's office wearing the red armbands, none of it felt funny. It was hard to remember the jokes she and Ruth had told about the party when she walked past the children marching through the streets with torches singing Hitler's praises. When she had to attend speeches with her father to listen to Goebbels talk to the German people, his audiences watching him just like her mother did at that first dinner party. Their eyes were full of anticipation and something that looked like rapture. There was a small voice in the back of her head, getting louder every day, and it was saying to her, *"It could happen. They could win. People are listening to them. People like them."*

When Tillie heard her father's door open, she put her head down and picked up a pencil, pretending to be jotting down some notes. She looked up when she heard her name being spoken.

"Matilda," the soft voice said, and she met the cold, small eyes of Herr Goebbels. "It's lovely to see you today." She forced a smile. Göring, her father, and Herr Grandelis were still inside her father's office, chatting. He leaned in and she could smell the mixture of sweat and his sour breath.

"I'm looking for a secretary. Someone to help keep my files in order, someone to answer my phones, and I've heard from your father that you are an asset to his business." Tillie swallowed, trying to remain composed under his stare. "Would you be interested in a job at my office?" His smile showed yellowed, slightly crooked teeth and there was an absence of any emotion from his beady black eyes.

"Sir, that's such a generous offer, but I really couldn't leave my father." She smiled and hoped her tone came across as grateful and sincere, but her heart was hammering inside her chest.

He nodded and said, "I completely understand," then rapped his knuckles on her desk and added, "if you ever change your mind, you'll let me know." It sounded like an order.

The other three men came out of her father's office, and they all bustled to the front door, her father dropping a folder on her desk as they went, saying, "Tillie, file those for me please. We're taking Joseph and Hermann to lunch." She didn't even have time to nod before they were all out the door.

As soon as they were gone, Tillie picked up the phone and dialed Ruth, praying she would answer.

"Hello?"

"Oh good, you're home." Tillie breathed a sigh of relief, just hearing her voice.

"Hey, doll. Is everything okay? You sound weird."

"Do you want to meet for lunch? Or bring lunch to the office? My father is gone for the afternoon." She could hear a teacup being set down into a saucer in the background.

"Sure, I'll bring over some sandwiches." Ruth paused. "Doll, are you sure you're alright?"

Tillie made a noise in her throat. "Herr Goebbels and Herr Göring are always here, and they make me so jumpy. They're all on edge about the elections this weekend and Herr Goebbels just asked me if I would be his secretary. He made it sound like he was asking, anyway, but I wouldn't put it past him to order my father to hand me over." Her voice shook.

"Oh dear," Ruth replied, her voice sympathetic. "I'll be there in about thirty minutes, does that work?"

"That would be lovely. When you walk through the main lobby, there will be another secretary walking around; Marcia has dark hair and she's Herr Grandelis' personal secretary. She's here somewhere, if she stops you," Tillie paused, not sure what to say.

"I'll say I'm your neighbor and bringing you lunch," Ruth finished, a softness to her voice. "It's okay, Tills, I know how this works when your father is involved."

Tillie rubbed her eyes, feeling them start to sting. She cleared the lump in her throat. "Okay, I'll see you in a bit."

"Okay, doll, I love you."

Tillie smiled and said, "I love you too."

They were just settling down on the couch in the lounge when Marcia walked in to get her own lunch and her eyes fell on Tillie and Ruth, sitting just a hair too close on the couch, their knees touching.

"Oh," she said softly. "I didn't know anyone was in here." Her eyes moved to Tillie, "I assumed you went to lunch with *them.*" She sounded exasperated.

Tillie swallowed a bite of her sandwich and subtlety moved her body away from Ruth. "Oh, no, I wasn't invited to lunch," she said, before adding, "this is my friend, Ruth. She was just passing by and stopped in for a girl's lunch." Ruth gave a little wave.

Marcia looked from Tillie to Ruth and tilted her head to one side while she watched them. Tillie fidgeted in the silence and Ruth cleared her throat, but then Marcia nodded and sighed.

"Are you ready for this ridiculous parade?" She sat down at the table, taking out her own lunch and lifting her sandwich as a kind of cheers in Ruth's direction.

Tillie nodded and wiped her hands on the napkin in her lap. "I suppose. We've got all the youth volunteers signed up, all the flyers have gone out in the neighborhood, and we have the speakers lined up. I'm not sure what else there is to do."

Marcia nodded and chewed thoughtfully. "My father-in-law keeps trying to get me to quit and come work at his doctor's office." Her voice was quiet. "When my husband found out about me helping to plan the parade, he was furious."

Tillie could feel Ruth shift next to her. "It's hard, you know?" Tillie looked over and Ruth had set down her own lunch and was leaning forward, her elbows on her knees. "Watching the person you love most having to sacrifice their beliefs just to stay employed. Jobs are so scarce right now. So, what do you do? I know how hard this is for Tillie so I'm not going to make it harder for her. Do I wish she could find another job? Yeah, absolutely. But I also know the reality right now and that's not likely. So, we all do the best we can."

Marcia met Ruth's gaze and smiled slightly. Tillie pretended to itch the side of her nose and wiped away a small tear. Ruth leaned forward to pick up her sandwich and let her knee touch Tillie's for just a moment. Tillie glanced at Marcia and wondered if she saw.

Marcia's eyes rested on the space between Ruth and Tillie's knees for a moment, then she looked up and took another bite of her sandwich. "That Goebbels is a creep, isn't he?"

Tillie laughed and Ruth sat back to continue eating her lunch. "He's something alright." They all giggled, and the room became quiet again while they ate their lunches.

Marcia sighed as she cleaned up her mess. "Back to work, I guess." She stood and smiled at Ruth. "It was lovely to meet you, Ruth. Tillie, you're so lucky to have such a nice friend to bring you lunch. Wish my husband would bring me lunch." She winked.

Marcia moved to throw away her trash. "You know, I bet we could get paid overtime for this ridiculous parade. We're there representing the law firm." Marcia nodded to herself, as if deciding. "I'll make sure to get overtime notes signed by Herr Grandelis before then." She grinned at the girls still sitting on the couch. "At least we can make a little money watching all those fools march around with their flags and their torches."

"Brilliant idea. Thanks, Marcia."

She smiled again and turned to walk back into the office. "See you in a bit," she called over her shoulder.

Ruth bit into a bite of leftover potato and leaned into Tillie. "Well, she's very nice."

Tillie nodded, peering into the bag to see if there was another fork to share the potatoes. "I know, she's great. I really like working with her."

"Pretty too." Tillie looked up and Ruth's eyebrow was arched.

"Pretty and married. To a man. Don't be jealous, Ruthie." Ruth grinned into her potatoes and Tillie kissed the side of Ruth's neck.

Just then, Marcia stuck her head back into the lounge and whispered, "They're back. Apparently, they forgot about a phone call they were supposed to have." She blinked and Tillie knew Marcia had seen her kiss Ruth's neck. Marcia gave a small encouraging nod. "Ruth might want to stay here and wait until they leave again. Or sneak out once they're in the conference room."

Tillie groaned. "So much for our relaxed lunch." They rose to clean up their trash, putting the sandwiches back in the bag Ruth had brought and then Ruth stood by the trash can with a look of mild worry on her face.

"What do you want me to do? Stay here and wait for them to leave again?"

Tillie rubbed her face and then said, "Wait here." She hurried out of the lounge through the main lobby and into her father's side of the office, where the men were hurrying out of their coats and speaking to one another in terse, clipped voices.

Goebbels was shooting daggers at both her father and Herr Grandelis and when he spoke, his voice was low and dangerous. "This does not reflect well on any of you." She stood for a moment, then cleared her throat.

"Gentlemen, you can absolutely blame me for missing your phone meeting." They all stopped and turned to stare at her. "If you would like me to initiate the call and apologize for my error, I can do that. Let's just step into my father's office." She hoped her smile was convincing.

Goebbels stared at her for a moment longer and then turned to Herr Grandelis. "Where is that useless secretary of yours? Why isn't *she* offering to fix this for us?" His face was contorted with rage, but his voice didn't rise above a strangled whisper. He turned back to Tillie and motioned for her to follow him into her father's office without so much as a thank you. She hurried after him and took the phone from his outstretched hand.

The voice on the other end said, "Hello, Julius Streicher's office."

Tillie cleared her throat. "Yes, hello. I have Herr Goebbels for Herr Streicher. I apologize for the late call. I took a long lunch, forgetting I needed to be here to connect the associates."

There was a pause on the other line and then, "Hold, please." Tillie handed the phone back to Goebbels and he covered the mouthpiece.

"Go get the others," he hissed.

She nodded once and went back out to her desk where the other men were standing around looking sheepish. She motioned for them to go in and they all shuffled through her father's door. She stood for a moment, waiting to make sure she heard voices, then hurried out of her office, across the lobby, and into the lounge where Ruth was standing with Marcia, whispering.

"They're in the meeting. Let's go," Tillie motioned for Ruth to follow, and Ruth grabbed the bag from the table, said a quick goodbye to Marcia, and went to follow Tillie out of the office.

"Matilda!" She froze and realized she and Ruth were still holding hands. She let go and took a small step away from where Ruth was standing. Her eyes met Ruth's and they were full of apprehension.

She turned and saw Herr Grandelis walking toward them. Ruth scooted towards the wall and tried to make her body as small as possible.

He was staring at her, his narrow gaze in the spot where they had both just been standing, fingers intertwined. Realization dawned on his face, his eyes widened, and a dangerous smile formed on his lips.

She decided to pretend everything was fine and she put on a cheerful smile. "Did everything get worked out?"

Goebbels trailed behind Herr Grandelis and he smiled at her, showing his yellow teeth. "Thanks to you, yes." Tillie fought

a shudder under his gaze. "Your father is lucky to have you."
He turned to Herr Grandelis. "Maybe I should have given the
position of Kreisleiter to Vincent." Herr Grandelis dropped his
eyes, his face changing back to a stone mask in an instant.

"Thank you for smoothing over the situation, Matilda," Herr
Grandelis said, his voice low and angry. Tillie nodded. It was the
first time he spoke directly to her in over a year.

At that moment, Goebbels' eyes fell onto Ruth, standing
against the wall. He tilted his head and crossed his arms, then
said, "Who is your friend, Matilda?" His voice was even and
calm, but Tillie thought she could detect an underlying menace.

"Oh, this is Ruth, a friend of mine. She stopped by for a girl's
lunch." Tillie stood stock still as Ruth smiled and gave a small wave.

She cleared her throat and said, "It's so nice to meet you both.
I've heard so much about you from Tillie. I apologize for being
here, we thought you all were gone for the day." Tillie watched as
Ruth forced a tense smile. "I was just leaving, though, so you all
can get back to work."

Goebbels stared at Ruth; his eyes locked on her face. "Ruth,"
he said, his tone delicate. "That's a Jew name."

She raised her chin a fraction of an inch. "Yes, it is." Her eyes
were hard and she was no longer smiling.

Goebbels narrowed his eyes at her, turning them into small
slits in his pointed face. He said to Tillie, still staring at Ruth,
"You should keep better company, Matilda."

Tillie didn't say anything, but she felt Ruth bristle.

"I think the company she keeps is just fine," Ruth spat back.

"I would hate for you to lose your position based on the
people you have in your confidence," he said, still staring at Ruth.
Then he added, in a much lower voice, "You just wait, my dear,"
his lips curling into an icy smile. He turned to walk back into the
main office and said over his shoulder, "Matilda, I expect you still
have work to do."

Herr Grandelis remained standing in the entrance, watching them. "So," he said, his eyes moving from Ruth to Tillie, "you protect Ernesto and he protects you." He gestured to Ruth, then he turned and walked back into the office without another word.

CHAPTER 15

September 1930

The morning of the parade dawned clear and blue. There wasn't one cloud in the sky and Tillie grew more annoyed about it as she walked the final few blocks to her parents' house. She'd at least wanted rain or clouds to match her sour mood.

She heard them before she saw them. The roar of voices grew louder and louder. Young shrieks and shouts mixed with older voices washed over her as she rounded the corner to the spot where the parade was supposed to begin. She stopped dead, a small gasp escaping her throat.

The street was bathed in red, white, and black. Nazi flags hung from every window. A row of Hitler Youth in the back had giant flags attached to their belts and another group of youth were carrying instruments. Nazi flags embroidered in gold and red fluttered in the wind attached to drums, trumpets, flutes. Men, women, and children lined the street ahead, cheering and giving the Hitler Salute to one another in greeting and waving at friends or neighbors.

Tillie realized she hadn't moved, and her breathing had turned rapid. She felt a hand on her shoulder and jumped. Turning, she met Marcia's eyes. They were wide and full of fear.

"Oh, my goodness," she breathed. Her hand gripped Tillie's bicep. "Who are all these people?" she whispered. "I thought there would only be fifty people here to watch this nonsense. Maybe seventy-five people at the most." Tillie could feel Marcia's hand shaking. Tillie's heart was pounding in her throat as she took in just how many people were in attendance for a parade that she and Marcia had thought to be a waste of time.

"Tillie, Marcia!" Her father's voice rang out from behind them. Tillie turned slowly and saw her father, beaming at them. "This is wonderful!" He clapped his hands together and grinned even more. He didn't seem to notice the complete panic on Tillie's face or the fear on Marcia's. "What a wonderful turnout." He looked around and raised his eyebrows. "I do hope someone is here from *Der Angriff*. It would be such a shame for Herr Goebbels not to know how splendid this came together."

Marcia cleared her throat. "Sir, there's a reporter from *Der Angriff* at the end of the parade route. I already arranged it, on Herr Grandelis' orders." Her voice was so quiet, Tillie had to lean in to hear her.

Her father looked delighted. "Well, now, you girls have thought of everything, haven't you?" He patted them both on the back and then started forward, pushing them along.

"Come on now, let's get a good seat. You don't want to miss the final product of all your hard work." Tillie was next to her father, stumbling along, still trying to fight the shock of the sheer number of people shouting, cheering, and waving flags. She saw her mother, standing on the sidewalk surrounded by neighbors all wearing red armbands.

"Marcia, are you alright?" They had stopped walking. Tillie snapped out of the fog that engulfed her and saw Marcia looking pale and sweaty.

"I'm sorry, sir, suddenly I'm not feeling so well. All the people maybe? I'm a tad claustrophobic." Marcia pulled away from

Tillie's father, backing away from the crowds of people back to the entrance of the neighborhood. Tillie met Marcia's eyes and Marcia gave her an apologetic look.

"I think I should just wait at the beginning of the route. You can come get me if you need me. I would hate to swoon and ruin your morning." She gave a shaky laugh, but Tillie could see Marcia was on the verge of complete panic.

Tillie gripped Marcia's arm. "You go ahead, Marcia. I've got it all under control." Marcia nodded and turned to hurry away.

"She's going to miss all the fun. What a pity." Her father put his hand on Tillie's back again and steered her toward where her mother stood waiting. "We'll check on her once the parade ends. Now, let's see if we can pick out all the youngsters we know when they walk by." He took his place on the sidewalk next to Tillie's mother and turned to her. "Tommy is leading the band today, isn't that exciting? Anthony must be so proud."

Tillie nodded without answering and watched as the boys started marching. The drums echoed in her ears, and she felt like she was under water. Her mother squealed. "Look! There's Tommy!" Raising her eyes, Tillie watched the small blonde boy leading the group of Hitler Youth. Some of them couldn't have been older than six years old.

Tommy carried a massive red flag, the black swastika blowing back and forth in the light fall breeze. His eyes fell on Tillie, and he grinned. He bore a striking resemblance to a younger Ernesto. The boys following him all had small drums around their necks, playing some sort of march. A group of girls followed dressed in crisp white shirts and long skirts. Two teen girls led with a banner held between them that read *The League of German Girls*.

Tillie looked around her at her parents' neighbors, smiling, shouting, and waving. The crowds were three or four people deep in some places, small children sitting on shoulders waving tiny flags. As they passed, she watched everyone around her raise their right arm in salute. A tiny flaxen-haired girl across the street pushed her way to the front of the crowd and Tillie could see she was shouting "Heil Hitler."

Her throat felt tight, and she felt a pointy elbow in her ribs. She looked over at her mother. Alice's arm was in the air, and she widened her eyes at Tillie, looking annoyed. She gave Tillie a stern nod and Tillie slowly raised her arm, feeling the rest of her body go numb.

†

They all sat sipping coffee around the tiny cafe table early Monday morning. Tillie could see Ernesto's eyes were puffy and Ruth had deep purple circles from lack of sleep.

Ruth rubbed her face for the third time and started again. "Well," but then she paused. It was the second time she'd tried to start the conversation and the second time she faltered, unsure of what to say.

James swallowed his coffee. "Well, indeed." He sniffed and his eyes swam with tears.

"I'm not even sure what to do now," Ernesto said, his voice hoarse. His eyes met Tillie's. "What do we do now?"

James wiped the tears and looked up, setting his face in what Tillie assumed was supposed to be hopeful. "Maybe it won't be a disaster."

Tillie shook her head. "You should have seen that parade, James." Her voice was quiet. "This is bad."

Ruth waved her hand at the newspaper splayed out on the table between them, announcing the election results from the previous day. "Yeah, I'd say this is bad."

Ernesto pulled the paper closer to him. "Six million votes." His voice sounded empty and hollow. "They have one hundred and seven seats now." His voice lowered to a whisper. "How could this have happened?"

They all dropped their eyes. Tillie cleared her throat and finally spoke. "People are listening to them. You should see the way my mother looks at Goebbels. Or the way my father talks about Hitler 'saving Germany.' At this point, it's happened and now we need to make sure we're paying attention." She rubbed her face and felt guilt bubble up, hot in her stomach. "And maybe not plan parades in their honor in the future," she added.

Ruth reached over and rubbed her arm. "Tills, you would have been fired if you hadn't helped plan it. You didn't have a choice."

Tillie shook her head. "There's always a choice. I should have let them fire me."

Ruth clicked her tongue. "Tillie at this point, you're the one person left with a steady income. You know as well as I do that you can't lose your job. You did what you had to do."

James sighed and pulled the paper closer to him. "Well, we're not the only ones upset about the results." James pointed to a smaller column on the next page of the paper describing the fighting that went on between the Nazis and the Communists the previous evening. "Bet there are a few dead men today," James mused, and Ernesto laughed without humor.

Tillie finished her coffee and set her cup down on the table. "All we can do now is wait. There's another election in two years. We just need to get to 1932." James and Ruth sighed and nodded, but Ernesto didn't respond.

No one else said anything until it was time for Tillie to get up and walk to work. "Well," she said, checking her watch. "I should go. We can talk more tonight, I suppose."

All the heads at the table nodded, still not speaking. Tillie turned to walk the last three blocks to work, lost in her own thoughts.

Tillie walked through the lobby of her father's office into the lounge to get a cup of tea. Marcia had her back to the doorway and was standing at the sink.

"Good morning, Marcia," Tillie mumbled.

Marcia turned, her eyes just as red and puffy as Ernesto's were and her cheeks were still wet with tears. Tillie walked over to her and wrapped her arms around the woman's small shoulders.

"We helped, Tillie." Marcia's voice was a whisper. "We did this. We helped them win all those seats. They're the second largest party in Germany now. Because of us."

Tillie sighed. "We would have lost our jobs if we hadn't helped plan that stupid parade."

Marcia pulled away to turn and look Tillie in the eye. "I'm not just talking about the parade. The meetings, the notes, the phone calls. We're helping them run their law office." Marcia put her hands on each of Tillie's shoulders and gave her a small shake. "Tillie. We work for the Nazi party."

Tillie backed away. "No, we don't. We work for my father and his partner. They just happened to be involved in the party. There are other clients besides the Nazis."

Marcia tilted her head to the side, pity on her face. "Tillie. There are no other clients. Not anymore. Your father, Herr Grandelis, they're on the Nazi payroll now. We may as well be working in Goebbels' office. That's how far in they are."

Marcia turned to leave, wiping the tears from her cheeks. "I'm leaving. I can't stay here, not anymore. I should have quit a year ago. I should have quit the day we had that meeting with Göring." She paused in the doorway. "That parade was a mistake. I'll have to live with that shame inside me for the rest of my life."

Tillie blinked, then busied herself with making her tea, trying to keep the tears from spilling out onto her cheeks. As she walked across the quiet lobby to her desk, she could hear her father on the phone in his office, his voice loud and excited. She paused, her hand resting on the stack of folders left for her to file. She waited until she couldn't hear her father's voice, then knocked on his door.

"Papa?"

Her father looked up, a wide smile across his face. "Yes, Tillie?" His smile faltered when he saw her standing, pale and red-eyed in his doorway. "Are you alright?"

She nodded and walked into his office, lowering herself into the chair in front of his desk. "Papa, I haven't seen some of our regular clients in quite some time."

Her father looked confused. "What do you mean?"

"Our regulars. The Shermans, where have they been? Or what about" she stopped to think. "What about Gladys from across the street? The cafe owner. You've represented her since you started the practice. I haven't seen her in over a year."

Her father leaned back in his chair; his eyes narrowed. "What are you getting at, Matilda?"

She took a deep breath. "It just seems like all we do is follow Göring and Goebbels around. That those two men are our only clients. Where is everyone else?"

Her father looked down at his hands, folded across his lap. He spoke slowly. "We have been asked by Herr Goebbels to represent the interest of the National Socialist German Workers Party exclusively. Is that what you're asking?"

Tillie felt bile rise into her throat and her breathing quickened. She clenched her jaw and swallowed hard.

"Is that a problem for you, Matilda?" Her father's voice was low and icy.

She shook her head because she didn't trust her own voice. Rising and leaving his office, she walked straight to Marcia's desk.

"You were right. There are no other clients." She put her hand on Marcia's. "Go work for your father-in-law."

Marcia looked up into Tillie's face, her eyes full of concern. "What about you?"

Tillie bit her lip and looked back at her father's closed door. She thought about Ruth and Bernadette and the food she was singlehandedly putting on their table. "I guess I'm here until I figure something else out."

CHAPTER 16

December 1930

When Tillie arrived at work, her father accosted her before she even sat down at her desk.

"Matilda!" Tillie gave a little jump at her father's voice coming from inside his office. Typically, she was the first person at the office and hadn't expected her father for another forty-five minutes.

"Good morning, Papa. You're in early today." She went back to unpacking her work bag and putting her scarf and hat into her bottom desk drawer.

"Yes, I wanted to catch you first thing." He handed her a large, thick folder filled with loose papers. "I need you to file these today."

She stared at the file in his hands without moving. "Today? All of them?" The file looked massive.

He raised his eyebrows. "Is there a problem?"

"No, no of course not." Tillie paused. She had made plans to have lunch with Ruth at eleven-thirty at the cafe down the street. Fridays were normally quite slow; she hadn't planned to have to file random papers all day. "I just have plans for lunch."

Her father's lips twitched upward. "Meeting Ernesto?"

If she lied and said yes, he might let her leave. She cleared her throat. "Yes, as a matter of fact." She watched her father's smile widen.

"Well, who am I to stand in the way of special Friday lunch plans?" He held the file out to her. "Just get as much done as you can until five, then finish the rest Monday."

She took the file from her father with a grateful smile. She turned to head to the main filing room and opened the file as she walked. She saw the handwriting and stopped. "Papa, are these your notes?"

Her father looked up from his writings. "Oh, no. They're Anthony's notes from some important phone calls he's had over the past few weeks. He fired his third secretary last week and instead of hiring someone new, Herr Goebbels instructed him to have you handle his files. He seems quite impressed by you after planning such a successful event with the parade. Joseph can be difficult to please and he's been watching you over the past few weeks. Most of the notes from our meetings are confidential, so Joseph clearly thinks you're an asset to the party." Tillie swallowed hard and then changed the subject. "He fired Anita? Why would he do that? She was excellent. And his third secretary since Marcia left."

Her father shrugged as he went back to his paperwork. "She couldn't prove her heritage." He said it in the same way he'd say someone had misplaced their keys. Tillie stared at him. He felt her eyes and looked up at her. "Is there something else?"

"No," she managed to whisper. She cleared her throat. "I'll go get started."

Tillie made it to her desk and slid into her chair, her hand resting on the top of the thick file. She looked at her clock; she had close to three hours until she had to leave to meet Ruth.

She opened the file to the first page and saw a date scrolled across the top. October tenth. The notes on top were from two months ago, a few weeks after the election. She flipped the file all the way to the last page. December fifth. Today was December sixteenth. Tillie couldn't make sense of most of the words and notations and flipped back to the top page. At the bottom of the page dated from October, she saw the words *"German Bloodline Laws."* They were underlined.

†

An hour and a half later, she hadn't filed a single paper but had read through almost half the stack. She felt nauseated. There were multiple pages of notes from phone calls with Hermann Göring and several with Himmler that seemed to be all about recruiting young men and college students to be some sort of citizen watch, but Tillie had trouble making sense of Herr Grandelis' shorthand. It was in line with what they discussed at her parents' dinner party but, it also seemed like Göring used Herr Grandelis as a jumping off point for ideas.

Other papers didn't reveal who the conversations were with, but they were lists upon lists of men's names, written in a pyramid style, with Adolf Hitler at the top.

There were dates of elections, and it was clear from the notes that the Nazi party was planning on Hitler running for president in the next election. There were charts with Nazi party's membership numbers in the years preceding 1930 and Tillie was horrified to see that the numbers were steadily growing.

She had to make a decision. She sat for a moment, then went to her father's office. "Hey, Papa?"

He was standing putting on his hat and buttoning up his coat. "What is it, Tillie?"

"Are you leaving for the day or just for lunch?"

"I'm heading to meet Anthony and a few colleagues for lunch, but I don't think I'm coming back. Why?"

Tillie tried not to look too pleased. Both her father and Herr Grandelis were going to be out of the office for the rest of the day.

"Oh, no reason. My lunch ended up becoming dinner, so I'm going to finish filing as quickly as I can to get out early, is that okay?"

Her father smiled. "Of course, dear. Tell Ernesto I said hello."

Tillie nodded and walked quickly back to her desk. She picked up her phone and quickly dialed her home phone.

"Pick up, pick up, pick up," she whispered.

"Hello?"

"Oh Ruthie, good, you haven't left yet."

"No, I was just about to head to the cafe. Is everything okay?"

Tillie paused. "Oh yeah, my dad just gave me a ton of work to finish today. I don't want to have to stay late tonight, so I was hoping you wouldn't mind if I just worked through lunch instead." Tillie looked at the pile of papers on her desk and closed her eyes, trying to shut out all the awful things she'd just read.

"That's fine. Why don't you meet me at the institute after work and we can have dinner with the boys?"

Tillie's eyes lingered on the notes on her desk. "That sounds great. I'll meet you there."

"Okay doll. Love you."

"Love you too." Tillie gently placed the phone back in its cradle before flipping the notes back to the beginning and scooted her chair in, resting her fingers on her typewriter. "Okay." She said to herself. "Let's get started."

It took her until nearly six o'clock to finish copying all the notes from Anthony's phone calls and she sped through getting as much filed as possible. She didn't want to leave all the notes unfiled for Monday. Surely her father would find that suspicious.

When she arrived to meet Ruth, the institute door was locked. She knocked, the large folder containing all the typed notes banging against her leg. She could see Helene hurrying toward the door with a smile on her face.

"Hey there, Tills. Everyone is down in the cafeteria." Tillie gave Helene a quick hug.

"What are you doing up here all by yourself?" She hoisted her bag up onto her shoulder, the file poking her in the back.

"Just getting some last-minute things done." Helene smiled and went back to the front desk. "I'll see you for your tour shift tomorrow, right?"

Tillie smiled back. "Absolutely." She walked down the deserted stairway to the warm sounds of laughter and friends sharing a meal. She spotted Bernadette, James, Dora, Ernesto, and Ruth sitting at a round table near the back of the cafeteria, their plates cleared away and their drinks in hand.

Tillie watched them for a moment. They were laughing at some joke she was too far away to hear. The stack of notes seemed to get heavier on her arm as she watched the people she loved most enjoying their time together and the warmth she felt watching them faded to worry and fear.

Ruth noticed her and waved, but upon seeing the look on Tillie's face, her smile contorted into confusion and concern. Tillie took a breath and walked to the table, towards the family she made for herself.

"What's wrong?" Ruth pulled out a seat for her.

Dora stood. "Tillie, dear, I'm going to get Erwin to fix you a plate. You look pale as a ghost."

Tillie sat very still for a moment, taking in each of their faces before sighing. "I know you all remember the parade I helped plan for my father and the law firm."

Ernesto raised his eyebrows as they all nodded. Dora set a plate down in front of Tillie and she felt her stomach turn. Taking a small sip of water, she pulled the bag up on the table. "Well, my father admitted that they no longer have any other clients. They're working for the Nazi party. And only the Nazi party."

Bernadette shook her head and clicked her tongue and Ruth reached over to take Tillie's hand. Staring at Ruth's fingers intertwined with her own, she tried not to let the shame of being a part of the entire charade overcome her. She chewed the side of her cheek. "Today my father also informed me that I'm to start working as Anthony's assistant."

"Who's Anthony?" Dora was leaning forward on her elbows, a line of worry etched across her forehead.

"My father," Ernesto said quietly. "He and Tillie's father run the law firm together." Dora nodded and gestured for Tillie to continue.

"I was given a stack of notes to file today. Just notes from phone calls and meetings, all from your father." She glanced at Ernesto. Pulling her hand out of Ruth's grasp, she opened her bag and pulled the large folder out. "I made copies."

No one said anything for a moment. Then Bernadette broke the tense silence. "Why?"

Tillie opened the folder and picked up the first page. She cleared her throat and glanced at Ruth before reading "Bloodline Laws. Point Four. Only one with German blood can be a citizen. Therefore, no Jew can be a German citizen." She set the paper down and looked up at the faces surrounding the table. "That's just the first page."

"I don't understand," James leaned forward against the table. "What do they mean, 'no Jew can be a German citizen'? We were all born here. What could they possibly be talking about?"

Dora was pushing some of the papers around on the table and everyone was picking up a sheet, reading all the notes Tillie had typed up. A small gasp escaped Dora's throat and she turned the paper towards them. "Did you do this Tillie?" It was a map of Germany, with the word *LEWD* written in large letters across Berlin.

Tillie shook her head. "That one I just took. I couldn't bear to copy it." She shrugged. "Plus, I'm not exactly an artist. Drawing a map of Germany escaped me." She watched as the paper trembled in Dora's hand. Ernesto rubbed her back.

"What do we do?" James' voice was small and quiet.

Tillie shook her head. "I honestly don't know. Hope Hitler doesn't win in 1932?" When Bernadette put a hand to her mouth and closed her eyes, Tillie gestured to the stack of notes. "They want him to run. And being the second largest party in Germany now, I have no reason to believe he won't win. Or that he'll come awfully close to winning."

Ernesto held up a sheet of paper. "What does this mean?"

Tillie turned to look. "Back at that dinner we had when I first met Goebbels, he explained that they've divided the country into sections."

"Like a pyramid," Dora interjected, looking over Ernesto's shoulder at the crude drawing Tillie copied earlier that day.

Tillie nodded. "Exactly. So, see this?" She pointed to near the bottom of the list next to the drawing. "That's my parents' neighborhood. My father's name is next to it, which means he's in charge of the neighborhood. He's in charge of ensuring the party is reaching that particular part of the city."

Ernesto nodded and then pointed. "My father is here. Does this mean he's in charge of more than just a neighborhood?"

"Yes. Remember I told you about the armband Goebbels gave your dad at that dinner? Your dad is above mine in the pecking order and works directly under Goebbels. He's in charge of all these neighborhoods."

Tillie ran her finger down the list. "So, if we're thinking of it as a pyramid, he's in charge of all these pieces that hold up his piece. And all these pieces make up Berlin, which is run by Goebbels. Each city has its own person in charge."

"And they all work under Hitler." Ruth rubbed her face and leaned back in her chair.

Tillie nodded again. "Hitler is at the very top of the pyramid. They're very organized." She looked around at all her friends sitting at the table, their smiles gone, the laughter from the evening a forgotten memory. "I'm sorry everyone. You were all having such a nice time and I ruined it."

Dora shook her head. "No dear. It's good. We need to know what's happening."

"So," James blew out a long breath, "what do we do now?"

Tillie bit her lip. "I'm not sure. I can keep watching what they do. I can keep making copies of notes when I'm able, listening at meetings. But, I'm not sure where they're going with all this."

She waved a hand over the stacks of papers strewn across the table. "I'm not even sure they can do half the things they're talking about. They might be the second largest party in Germany, but they still don't have the majority. How do they think they're going to accomplish everything they want to do?"

CHAPTER 17

July 1990

Thea walked quickly through the brightly lit hallways of the memory care building. She arrived right at mealtime with the hopes her grandmother was having a good day.

"Hi Gram," she announced cheerfully as she entered her grandmother's room. For the first time in several months, her grandmother was sitting at the small vanity applying bright red lipstick and she was dressed in a sweater and slacks.

"Well, look at you." Thea walked over to her and placed her hands on her grandmother's pointy shoulders and kissed her powdery cheek. Her grandmother smiled at their reflection.

There was a knock at the door and a voice saying, "Hey there, Miss Matilda, are you ready for some dinner?" and a tiny red-haired nurse's assistant entered the room. "Oh," she said in surprise. "You must be Theadora." She reached out a hand. "I'm Claire. It's lovely to meet you." She looked like a sprite dressed in dark blue scrubs. Thea smiled and took her hand.

"Nice to meet you. Thea is fine." Claire leaned around Thea and winked at her grandmother.

"You weren't kidding," she and her grandmother shared a conspiratorial chuckle.

Thea raised her eyebrows at the tiny woman, and she waved a hand. "Your grandmother told me you'd correct me if I tried to call you by your full name. Even though it's beautiful."

Thea shook her head and rolled her eyes. Her grandmother gave a dramatic sigh. "She was named for my husband's mother. That woman was a saint." Her voice grew small. "She didn't deserve what happened to her. In the end." Thea could tell her grandmother was starting to slip away but before she could catch her, tiny Claire reached out her hand and patted the top of her grandmother's.

"Hey, there, Miss Matilda. Why don't we go down to the cafeteria and get some dinner? I'm even on my break so I can sit with you, and we can eat together. Won't that be nice?"

Thea watched as her grandmother's eyes cleared and she nodded. Claire leaned over her grandmother and gave her white curls a little bounce in the mirror. "I mean, you're all done up, we can't waste all that effort, can we?" She gave another wink and squeezed her shoulders. Thea smiled at them, making a mental note to mention Claire to Vanessa.

They all left her grandmother's room and Thea's mind started to race as they walked down the hallway to the dining area, Claire chatting animatedly with her grandmother about lipstick or nail polish or something. They all got seated when Thea pretended to get annoyed with herself.

"Oh, my goodness. I left my purse in your room, Gram." Two sets of eyes turned to her, and her grandmother waved a hand.

"That's alright, doll, your handbag is fine in the room," her grandmother set her napkin on her lap before they even had water in their glasses.

Thea could feel Claire's eyes on her. She tried again. "No, I know it is, I just was planning on leaving from here because I have a few errands to run." Her grandmother raised an eyebrow. Thea hoped her smile didn't look as forced as it felt. "It's okay,

I'll be right back." She stood. "You have Claire here to keep you company."

Claire shrugged and turned back to her grandmother and started talking about an art class they offered to the residents and Thea hurried back down the hall to her grandmother's room.

Once inside, she closed the door behind her and crossed to the tiny closet. Pushing the soft clothes aside, she scanned the shelves for the pink hat box. She only had a few minutes to find what she was looking for and her heart continued to drum inside her chest. Finding nothing in her grandmother's closet, she turned, her hands on her hips, looking around the small bedroom.

Her eyes settled on the side table next to the bed. The top part had a skinny drawer, for papers and pens, but the bottom drawer was large. Large enough for a hat box. Pulling open the drawer, she inhaled. The pink box was wedged inside the drawer, barely fitting. Thea reached into the drawer and slowly worked the hat box out of its tight squeeze.

She could hardly breathe as she lifted the lid off the box, the edges squeaking slightly. There were stacks of photos and yellowing papers in the box and Thea had to remind herself to stay focused. She couldn't be distracted by the smiling face of her grandmother from sixty years prior.

She spied what she was looking for buried under a loose photo of a group of people standing in front of a large brick building with the bust statue of a mustached man in the background. The sign of the building was in German. When Thea picked it up, she saw her grandparents standing off to the side with her uncle and the woman named Ruth. Behind her grandfather was a tall woman with a kind, soft face. Thea flipped the photograph over. In her grandmother's neat writing she read: *Row one– Me, Ernesto, James, Ruth, Heinz. Row two– Dora, Nissa, Adelaide, Karl, Helene, with Dr. H. 1929*

Her eyes fell on the name Dora and flipped the photo over again. Could her great-grandmother be in this photo? None of the people in the photo looked old enough. Shaking her head, she set the photo on the bed and grabbed the paper that had been hidden beneath it. A letter with her grandmother's name in the greeting, the return address in the upper right-hand corner with a name clearly visible. Ruth Birnbaum. She took a breath and gave a small smile. She had a name and an address in Germany.

Her heels echoed in the hallways as she hurried back to the dining room. She had been gone less than five minutes, but she still felt like it took too long. The envelope was safely placed in her purse, along with the photo of the group in front of the German building. She wanted to see if she could find her great-grandmother in any of the photos her grandmother kept in the albums at home. To compare all the faces.

Claire and her grandmother looked up, forks in hand, when Thea returned to the table. "What kept you, dear?" her grandmother asked.

"Oh, sorry, I stopped in the restroom and then got a little turned around. All the hallways look the same here."

Claire stared at her for a moment and then said, "Why wouldn't you just use your grandmother's bathroom?"

Thea felt her heart stop and her face flush. She froze and then a little bubble of laughter erupted from her throat. "I completely forgot she even had a bathroom in her room." Which was true. Otherwise, she would have come up with a better lie.

Thankfully her grandmother laughed and said, "You know, doll, I forget there's a bathroom in there almost every day." She and Claire turned to her grandmother with wide eyes. "What, I can't make jokes about my," she took a drink of water, "predicament?"

Claire chuckled and took a bite of her mashed potatoes. "Miss Matilda, you're the best." Thea let out a slow breath and picked up her own fork, willing her pulse to slow, her mind on the photo and envelope in her purse.

†

When she arrived home, Michael had left a note that he was out to dinner with friends, so she went to her grandmother's old office and dug out the dusty photo albums from the bottom of the bookshelf in the far corner of the room. She chose what looked like the oldest album and started at the beginning.

The photos were all in black and white and they were of her grandparents and her uncle from when they all lived in this house together. After quickly flipping through four of the eight books in front of her, she discovered that, so far, there were no photos of her grandparents as children, none of her great-grandparents, and none of Ruth in any of the books.

She leaned against the couch, the photo of the group of smiling people on the floor in front of her. She turned the photo to read the sign across the brick building. *Institut für Sexualwissenschaft.* She chewed her lip. She needed someone who could read German.

Shaking her head, she picked up the envelope and ran her finger across the return address. Ruth Birnbaum, Berlin. Picking up one of the thickest photo albums, she noticed a tiny piece of paper stuck in the space between the shelf and the base of the shelving unit. She set down the photo album and got down onto her hands and knees, gently pulling on the corner of the paper.

As she pulled, a paper with slanted handwriting came out from under the shelf and Thea sat back on her heels staring at it. It looked like it was all in German. She looked back at the shelf, the paper resting in her hands. She squinted at the photo, then she stood and went to go get a screwdriver.

After prying the shelf open, she stared at a giant stack of papers hidden away in the hollow base of the shelving unit. Scanning them, her mouth fell open and she gathered everything up into her hands.

When Michael's key turned and he walked into the dark kitchen, Thea was waiting with the envelope and the photo she'd taken from her grandmother. He jumped when he flipped the light on and saw her sitting there. "Good Lord, what are you doing?" His hand was on his chest. "Are you trying to kill me?" He came and sat down with her at the table. "Why are you sitting in the dark?" His brows knitted together, and he looked at her with concern.

"I got her name." She pushed the envelope toward him. "And I found this photo." She set her hand on the stack of papers. "Then, there's these." He raised his eyes from the envelope and picture of her grandmother's friends to the two stacks of papers on the table.

"What are those?"

She slid the first stack of papers toward him. "This is what was in the safe. I never really looked at any of these before, but it's my grandparents' marriage certificate. Plus, my mother's birth certificate, as well as mine. My mother's birth certificate has to be from after they had it changed, after they adopted her. Plus, their passports."

She dropped her eyes to the second stack of papers. "This stack was hidden in the bookshelf. My mother's adoption papers were in there. Her birth parents aren't listed. She was adopted from some home for unwed mothers. I don't know if there's any way to find out any more information about it, to be honest." She swallowed the lump in her throat.

"And here's my grandparents' birth certificates, marriage certificates, and Jimmy's birth certificates." She held up two pieces of paper. "He has two. One has his last name as Weber, which is my grandmother's maiden name. And one has his last name as Levin."

She met Michael's gaze. "Not only that, but Uncle Jimmy was married to this Ruth person."

At that, Michael's eyes narrowed, and he reached out to take the papers. "What?" He started leafing through them while Thea sat, her hands in her lap.

"I'm not sure what I'm looking at here," Michael murmured. "Are these the marriage certificates?"

Thea nodded. "One is for my grandparents, and one is for Jimmy and Ruth. His last name on the marriage certificate is Levin, same as on this birth certificate." She held up one of the certificates she found. Michael took it from her outstretched hand.

"His parents and your grandmother's parents' names don't match." He looked up at her over his glasses.

"No," she said. "And that's not all. I'm named for my great-grandmother, right?" He nodded, eyes back on the birth certificate in front of him. "Well, here's my grandfather's birth certificate and his mother's name was Ursula."

Michael looked up at her again. "What? No, I heard countless stories about Dora and how amazing she was, and I didn't even know your grandfather. Both your grandmother and Jimmy loved her like a mother."

He scratched his chin. "Maybe Dora was a nickname?" Thea made a face at him, and he shrugged. "I don't know, none of this makes any sense. I mean," he gestured to the papers on the table, "I understand why they would lie about being a couple because it was 1930. But why would they all marry each other before coming to the states? Or have fake birth certificates. Why they would talk about how amazing Ernie's mother was without telling us her real name."

Thea picked up the last of the papers from in front of her. "I found three passports in the safe with the other paperwork. Two of them belonged to my grandparents, then there was Uncle Jimmy's with the last name Weber. Then I found four other passports hidden in the bookshelf."

She gestured to the four passports on her left. "My grandparents' passports are in German but look pretty standard. But then there are two more. A second one belonging to Uncle Jimmy and one belonging to Ruth."

Michael picked up her grandmother's German passport. "Why is her last name listed as Wagner in this one?"

Thea shrugged and rubbed her eyes. She could feel a headache forming. "My grandfather's passport has his picture with the name 'Aaron Wagner.' I have no idea why since all the other paperwork they have has their correct names."

Michael picked up James' hidden passport and flipped it open. "This listed his last name as Levin." There was a large J stamped on the inside over the picture. He ran his finger along the J and his eyes grew wide with horror. "Is this what I think it is?"

She nodded. "We thought they left Germany right after the first world war. But they didn't." She gestured to all the papers strewn across the table. "Based on this, it looks like they were somewhere in Germany in the '30s. Uncle Jimmy and Ruth were Jewish. These other papers must be forgeries. I don't know why my grandfather and grandmother had completely different identities, but they did. Jimmy and my grandmother weren't brother and sister. They all got married, forged papers, and they ran." Goosebumps rose on her arms, despite the warm temperatures outside. "They were running from the Nazis."

Michael's hand was over his mouth, his eyes still wide. He picked up Ruth's passport and touched the black and white photo. Her pale skin and black hair made her look like Snow White.

Michael's voice dropped to a whisper. "But then why didn't she make it out?"

CHAPTER 18

February 1931

Tillie awoke to banging on their door. Ruth groaned next to her and they both could hear Bernadette in the kitchen, her voice startled. "For goodness sake, Ernesto, you're going to bang this door down. Is everything alright?"

Tillie sat up as Ernesto came barging into their bedroom. "Ernesto, what is it?" His face was pale and his eyes wide.

"Today is Dora's surgery." He began pacing their bedroom and Tillie waved Bernadette away from their doorway.

"It's okay Bernadette, everything's fine."

Bernadette nodded and turned to go back to the kitchen. "Why don't I just make some tea."

Ruth rolled over and pushed herself into a sitting position. "Ernesto, Dora's surgery has been planned for over a year now. What's wrong?"

Ernesto wrung his hands and continued to pace. "She told me this morning that one of the doctors called her by her old name." His eyes filled with tears. "Dr. H. corrected him, and the doctor made a note of it and Dora said it hasn't happened again, but …" His voice caught in his throat. "The doctor called her by her old name. Her birth name. What if he doesn't care enough to pay attention during the surgery? What if …" he trailed off.

Tillie's brow furrowed. "Wait. Was it Dr. Levy-Lenz? Or Dr. Gorhbandt? Those are the doctors working on her case now. I can't imagine either of them making such an error."

Ernesto shook his head. "No. It was one of the doctors helping with anesthesia." He rubbed his face. "But don't you think that's even more important?"

Ruth met Tillie's eyes. "Of course, Ernesto. Of course, it's important. But the doctor was corrected, and Dr. H., Dr. Abraham, and Dr. Levy-Lenz will all be there during her surgery. She has three very important people in her corner. Nothing is going to happen to her."

Ernesto paused at the door and turned to look at Ruth. "We don't know what it's been like for her. Not really." His voice dropped to a whisper. "We don't know. And she could die. She could die in front of the doctor who didn't even have the decency to ask her real name."

"Ernesto," Tillie began but he held up a hand.

"I'm going back to the institute to sit with her until she gets called back. I just wanted someone else to know, to want to be there for her. To make sure she knows that we know who she is."

Bernadette appeared in the doorway, blocking Ernesto's path back out of the apartment. She reached out and took his hand. "Ernesto, dear, come have some tea with me while the girls get dressed. I'm sure they'll want to go back with you. Where's James?"

Ernesto sniffed and wiped his eyes. "Back sitting with Dora, waiting for me."

Bernadette smiled and led him into the kitchen, giving Tillie and Ruth a meaningful glance. Ruth sighed. "I guess we're getting up now."

When they emerged dressed into the kitchen, Bernadette was still holding Ernesto's hand and they were talking quietly. His eyes were still wet, but he seemed calmer.

"We're ready to go, if you are." Tillie took a swig of tea from Bernadette's mug on the table. Ernesto nodded and stood.

"Ernesto," Bernadette said in a soft voice. "Remember how loved she is. Take your love for her and push it outward so others can feel it. And she'll be just fine."

Ernesto leaned in and hugged Bernadette, whispering his thanks to her. "And tell my son I expect to see him tomorrow for dinner."

He chuckled and nodded. "Of course."

Tillie and Ruth followed Ernesto to the front door. "We'll call you later Bernadette, to let you know how it's going."

Bernadette smiled and began taking the teacups to the sink. "I'll just be here. You keep Ernesto from going crazy, okay?"

They both grinned and Ernesto rolled his eyes, closing the door behind them.

✝

They all sat in the lounge, trying to avoid one another's gaze.

"When will they come get us?" Ernesto was biting his thumb nail.

James looked up from his newspaper. "Ernesto, Dr. H. told us he would come let us know once Dora was out of surgery. Karl told us it would be at least six hours, and it's only been," he stopped to check his watch, "four hours since Dora went back. Try to stay calm."

Helene stood up and smoothed out her dress. "I'm going to get a cup of tea. Ernesto, I'll bring you back some. Anyone else?"

Ruth stood. "I'll come help you." She squeezed Tillie's hand and added, "Try to get him to calm down, would you?" Tillie nodded, then stood and walked over to Ernesto. He was standing staring out the window chewing his lip.

"You alright?" She rubbed his back.

He nodded. "It's just." He cleared his throat. "She's like my mom, you know?" His voice became thick. "I need her to be okay."

"She will be. Dr. Levy-Lenz knows what he's doing, and a lot of the work was already done during her first surgery with Dr. Abraham." Ernesto nodded. "Dora will be fine." He nodded again, blinking back tears.

"I just keep thinking about how excited she was this morning before they took her back." He laughed through his tears. "She told me she was about to go make history." Ernesto tried to hold in a sob and made a small squeaking noise. He turned to Tillie. "Tills," he whispered. "What do I do if she dies?"

"She's not going to die," Tillie responded firmly.

Ernesto nodded again, still staring out the window when they heard a voice from the door. "Well, Dora will be pleased to know she essentially caused the institute to cease functioning while she was under anesthesia," Dr. Hirschfeld was leaning against the doorway, chuckling.

Ernesto turned, his face full of emotion. "How is she? Is she alright?"

Dr. Hirschfeld held up his hands and smiled. "She's doing beautifully. Dr. Levy-Lenz wanted me to come give everyone an update, and I wanted to check on Karl, as he's running things single-handedly right now." He gave a pointed look to all the other employees sitting playing chess and knitting in the far corner of the lounge. A few of them had the decency to look sheepish.

Dr. H. continued to smile, his eyes twinkling. "Dora is lucky to have such a wonderful group concerned about her well-being. Dr. Levy-Lenz thinks maybe another hour or two. I'll let you know when she's being moved to the recovery room." Ernesto gave a huge sigh of relief and squeezed Tillie's hand when Dr Hirschfeld turned back around.

"You know, Erwin was making pot roast with veggies this afternoon. And I believe he's making cobbler for dessert." He winked at the group. "Perhaps the time would go faster in the cafeteria over dinner." He left the room to go find Karl. "Just a thought, of course," he called back to them. They all looked at one another, shrugged, and filed out to head down to the cafeteria.

Ernesto sat down at the table across from Tillie and nervously tapped the saucer under his teacup. "You're driving me crazy, Ernesto," Tillie said, sipping her own tea.

"You know, I was just on my way back up," Ruth said, the irritation plain in her tone, sitting down with two cups of tea, one in each hand.

"I think we were starting to annoy Dr. H. with our hovering," Tillie told her while Adelaide sat down on the other side of her, and James slid in next to Ernesto.

Adelaide chuckled. "I imagine so. Poor Karl is probably so annoyed at all of us. Being so worried for Dora that we can't even do our jobs. I attempted to file the same bit of paperwork three times before Karl sent me to the lounge; he was so exasperated."

Ruth elbowed Tillie. "And where does your father think you are this fine afternoon, Matilda Rose?"

Tillie rolled her eyes. "Well, it just so happens that I got the day off today. I told them I had plans with Ernesto." She gestured to Ernesto sitting across from her. "Which is not a lie, because look. There he is."

James shook his head and laughed. "The fact that he's *met* Ernesto and still thinks the two of you are a couple might be the funniest part of that whole charade."

Ernesto pretended to be offended. "What exactly are you getting at, James?" They all were laughing so hard now, that the other employees in the cafeteria were staring.

"I think," said a voice behind them, "he's saying that it's quite obvious that women are not your, shall we say, main interest." Erwin was carrying plates of pot roast and sprouts and setting them down in front of the friends, now howling with laughter.

Ernesto shook his head. "You all are terrible. Why am I the issue here?" He took a bite of pot roast and groaned. "Oh Erwin, that's incredible." Erwin smiled as he continued handing out plates to Ruth and Adelaide. "I'm just saying," Ernesto continued, gesturing to Tillie with his fork, "have you seen this girl and the way she stares at Ruth?" Tillie raised her eyebrows. "It's like they want to devour each other."

Ruth and Tillie exchanged glances. "I'm sorry," Ruth said. "'Devour' each other? Seriously?"

Adelaide collapsed into giggles. "Well, he's not wrong. The two of you are …" she paused trying to catch her breath, "you're a bit much." Ruth shook her head and Tillie rolled her eyes, continuing to eat.

"I don't even know why we're talking about this. My parents think we're a couple and that's all that matters," Tillie said, in mock annoyance.

Everyone at the table continued to chuckle while finishing their dinner and Tillie was thankful for the brief distraction from worrying about Dora. Ernesto seemed to be calmer now that they were all laughing together.

They were all sitting around the cafeteria enjoying coffee after getting their fill of the cherry cobbler Erwin had made when Karl walked in. "Magnus sent me down to get you. Dora's out of surgery." That was all he said before turning around and heading back up the stairs. They all looked at one another for a moment, then jumped up, yelling their thanks to Erwin and Heinz before racing up the steps, Ernesto in the lead, taking the stairs three at a time.

Dr. Hirschfeld was standing with Karl by the administration desk. "That was quick," he said, eyes twinkling. Karl shook his head, muttering under his breath about excuses and lack of hard work.

"Well?" Ernesto asked, leaning forward.

"She did beautifully," Dr. Hirschfeld clapped his hands, clearly delighted. "She's in recovery now and Dr. Levy-Lenz said she did exceptionally well. She's resting and you'll be able to see her in a few days."

"We can't go see her now?" Ernesto tried to keep his voice even.

"We want to keep her safe from any infection," Dr. Hirschfeld said, "but in a few days, she'll be up for visitors."

"I trust you'll all be able to work now," Karl added, under his breath. Dr. Hirschfeld gave an amused look in Karl's direction.

"Alright then. Well, I'm off to get some work done before retiring. Since we're closed now, Karl, why don't you join me?" Karl looked up at him, his expression resigned and still annoyed. "The rest of you are welcome to stay the night. I'm sure the lounge could be made up to be comfortable , that way no one has to walk home in the dark." He smiled at the group standing in front of the desk and then he and Karl turned to walk back to his office, holding hands.

He went a few feet, then turned back. "You know, when Dörchen came to me, she was all alone." He looked up at the group of them standing huddled together at the desk, all wiping tears of relief from their eyes. He smiled again, more to himself. "How lucky we all are, don't you think?" Then he turned and he and Karl disappeared down the hallway, fingers intertwined.

James reached out and squeezed Ernesto's arm as he wiped tears from his eyes and Ruth wrapped her arms around Tillie's shoulders. Tillie met Ernesto's gaze and she smiled. How lucky, indeed, she thought.

✝

After work several days later, Tillie brought a vase of flowers to the institute to leave in Dora's room. Ernesto had seen her two days after her surgery and she was still in a great deal of pain and sleeping on and off, so Tillie wanted to sneak in without disturbing her. She waved to Adelaide sitting at the front desk, and to the group of young men in the lounge sitting with Erwin and Heinz.

She had never been to the hospital wing of the institute and was starting to wander through the hallways trying to figure out where Dora's room was when she heard voices. She stopped outside one of the rooms. The door was ajar. She heard Ernesto's voice coming from inside.

"It was the longest day," he was saying, his voice shaking.

"Oh, love. I told you everything would be fine. Shh. It's alright," she heard Dora's voice, weak but clear drifting through the door.

"You're the best mother I've ever had," now she could tell he was crying, his voice disjointed through stifled sobs. She heard bed linens rustling and his crying was muffled.

She heard Dora's voice again, this time quieter. "Ernesto, you heard Dr. H. Everything went great. I'm fine now, just a few more days in bed and then I'll be better than new." She heard Ernesto let out a shaky breath.

"I know, I was just so worried. I'm so relieved that it's over."

"Me too, love, me too. And now I get another journal to my name," Dora's laugh was soft. "Dr. Levy-Lenz says there are other people out there like me. I'm the first one to become a woman with surgery and now other people who want this surgery can come here too, once everyone knows about it."

Her voice grew stronger. "It's very exciting, Ernesto." She sighed. "There are people like us out there who are all alone, love. They need to know we exist. They don't have best friends or institutes or libraries filled with books or people like Dr. Hirschfeld looking out for them." Tillie heard Ernesto sniffle. "They don't have family like we do. Someone had to be the first, the one to open the door. And now other people can follow."

"I'm just so glad you're okay," Ernesto sighed and then they were quiet. Tillie took that opportunity to walk into the hospital room with her flowers.

When she pushed the door open, she saw Ernesto lying on Dora's bed on his stomach next to her and she was patting the top of his hand. She had her head back on the pillow, her eyes closed.

"Tillie!" Ernesto exclaimed as she walked in.

"Hello you two. I didn't want to bother you, but I thought you would like some color to brighten up your room." Tillie turned to set the flowers down but saw that the entire room was full of flowers and notes, there was hardly an open spot for her small vase. Tillie laughed and turned to Dora, "Aren't you Miss Popularity."

Dora shrugged. "What can I say? I think everyone is just glad I'm not bossing them around in the library right now."

Ernesto snorted. "Well, that's probably true."

Dora made a noise of mock indignation. "Apparently, we're done with the 'thank goodness you're okay, Dora' attitude, hmm?"

Ernesto rolled his eyes. "My feelings of being relieved you lived through the surgery and being annoyed at how bossy you are in the library can coexist just fine, thank you."

Tillie set the flowers down in a small space on the windowsill. "So how long until you're back to work, Dora?"

"Another two weeks or so before I can work again, but just a couple more days in bed. I get to stay here and be waited on hand and foot for a little longer," she teased, patting Ernesto's hand again.

Ernesto checked his watch. "Speaking of which, we should let you rest, Dörchen." Dora smiled. "I'll be back to check on you during dinner. We can eat together."

"That sounds wonderful, love. I'll see you then," she patted his face and they smiled at one another. Her eyes drifted up to Tillie and she added, "It's dark. You should walk Tillie home."

Ernesto stood and looked at Tillie, "Shall we, darling?"

Tillie smiled and said, "Absolutely. Dora, I'll see you soon, okay?" Dora nodded and smiled warmly at Tillie, then Tillie took Ernesto's arm, and they walked out, leaving Dora to rest.

As soon as they were out of earshot of Dora's room, Ernesto gave a huge sigh. "God, I'm glad that's over."

"Are you alright?" Tillie could see the bags under Ernesto's eyes. He looked exhausted.

"Yes, I'm fine. I was worried about her, that's all. It was a lot bigger of a deal than she let on to all of us. The surgery, I mean."

Tillie nodded. "She probably didn't want to worry anyone."

Ernesto nodded back. "I'm sure that was part of it." They grew quiet, walking in companionable silence.

"How are things going at the office?" Ernesto glanced at her, his eyebrows raised. "We haven't talked much about my father the last few weeks."

Tillie shrugged. "It's much of the same. I've been sitting in on meetings, taking notes for your father and mine. Answering phone calls. Goebbels and Göring are in and out every other day it seems."

They linked arms as they walked out into the frigid winter air and turned in the direction of Tillie's apartment. "Do you think they're still planning on pushing Hitler to run for president?"

Tillie nodded. "Oh yes. That's a done deal. It will be interesting to see if people really turn out for him though." She turned to look at him. "I'm beginning to wonder if the Nationalists are just the loudest of the bunch and that's why we see them everywhere we turn. Perhaps most of Germany is like us, quietly waiting for the swastikas to fade away."

Ernesto nodded. "That would make much more sense than an entire country thinking someone like Goebbels has any sense, wouldn't it?"

Tillie chuckled thinking of Goebbels and his rat-like face. "He really is just unbelievably unsettling, isn't he? My mother is so fond of him and for the life of me, I can't figure out why."

Arriving at her apartment, she took Ernesto's face in her hands. "Everything will be fine. After seeing Dora and what the institute has been able to accomplish for her, I truly believe that everything is going to work out."

CHAPTER 19

April 1931

Tillie rubbed her temples and tried to blink away the headache forming behind her eyes. It had been a little less than four months since Goebbels assigned her services to a somewhat reluctant Herr Grandelis. Not only did she have double the work, but it had also become quite clear that whatever was being planned and discussed, both her father and Ernesto's father were smack in the middle of it.

She had taken to going through his files, through his desk, and through his office after hours. Tillie knew that if she was ever caught, she would be fired but that wasn't enough to keep her from continuing to copy anything that looked suspicious. She had seen her friends panic the first time she shared her notes, so at this point she decided to keep everything to herself until there was something real to report on.

Tillie took a sip of tea and continued to look through the latest files she discovered in her boss's office. There was the map with *A.H.* at the top of the lists, a pyramid similar to the one in the first round of notes from back in January, but then there were other lists and crude drawings. There was another small map of Germany with a star near Munich and the name *Himmler* written in tiny letters next to the star. Under Himmler's name was a list including the words *"dissidents, communists, asocials, socialists, non-Germans."*

Looking at the clock and realizing it was almost eight p.m., she gathered up the copies of the notes she'd made and went to return Herr Grandelis' paperwork to his desk when she heard the doorknob rattle and then there was a soft knock at the front door. Tillie froze. She had a handful of confidential Nazi documents gathered into her arms, most of which had been locked in her boss's desk. There was another knock and she heard Ruth's voice behind the door.

"Tillie?" She whispered through the door. "Are you in there? Are you alright?"

Tillie breathed a huge sigh of relief and hurried to the locked door to let her girlfriend in. She opened the door and Ruth's face was pale and terrified staring at her.

"Where have you been?" Ruth demanded. "I've been worried sick. You were supposed to be home two hours ago. When I called, it just rang and rang." Tillie glanced at her desk and realized she'd taken the phone off the hook to focus and forgot to replace it.

Ruth strode into the office, wringing her hands. She whirled on Tillie. "I can't even count how many late nights you've had this month. Tell me what's going on. Now."

She stood with her hands on her hips, tears in her hazel eyes, making them look more green than normal. She had no makeup on, so Tillie knew she had been worried. She never left the house without at least her red lipstick. Ruth met Tillie's gaze and dropped her arms to her sides. "Please," she whispered.

Tillie nodded. "I know. I'm so sorry. I'll tell you everything but," she looked around the office, suddenly feeling nervous that all the lights were on. "Not here. We should go." The thought struck her for the first time that if Herr Grandelis was a Nazi lawyer, people might be watching the office. Her heart began to race. She hurried the papers back to Anthony's office and locked them back into his bottom drawer.

Tillie gathered up her notes from her desk and started turning off lights while Ruth watched her. "Tills, what are you doing?" She sounded as confused as she looked while Tillie hurried around the office, making sure everything was in its place.

Once all the desk drawers were locked and all the lights were out, Tillie beckoned Ruth. "C'mon," she whispered again. "Let's go home." Ruth reached out and took her hand, still looking worried and nervous. Tillie squeezed Ruth's hand and then immediately let go before they walked out into the lobby.

She leaned away from Ruth and tried to look out into the cold night, squinting to be able to see past the shadows. "We can't hold hands here; someone might be watching. You walk out first and meet me at the cafe down the street. That way if anyone asks tomorrow, I can say you were bringing me my house key." Ruth stared at her.

"What? What are you talking about? Who would be watching us?"

Tillie just shook her head.

"Just please go. I'll meet you at the cafe." Tillie stood in the lobby trying to keep her breath steady, waiting for Ruth to leave.

"Doll," Ruth breathed. "You're scaring me."

Tillie met her gaze. "I know."

They met outside the cafe and neither felt like stopping so they walked the rest of the way home in silence. Ruth kept looking over at Tillie, but kept her arms folded, her fists clenched, knuckles white. Tillie kept her eyes up, looking around to make sure no one was following them.   When they reached their apartment and were safely locked inside, Tillie gave a huge sigh of relief. Ruth spun to grab Tillie's arm and said sharply, "Tell me what's going on."

Tillie nodded and put her work bag onto the small kitchen table while Ruth sat down across from her. Tillie could feel Ruth's eyes on her as she pulled open a hidden seam in the lining of the bag, pulling out a blue folder that was otherwise hidden. When she turned and went to the pantry, she heard Ruth pull the folder across the table. "You have to read them in order," Tillie told her over her shoulder. "Just a minute."

Pushing several cans of food to the side, she exposed a small hole in the wall. Tillie pulled on it and a square of the wall came out, revealing a hiding spot, about a foot across and a foot deep. Ruth gasped while Tillie pulled two more massive files out of the hole and returned to the kitchen table.

She sat back down and gestured to the brown folder. "These are the papers I showed you at the institute." Then she pushed the green folder forward toward Ruth. "This one is new," she said. Ruth reached out with a shaking hand to open the folder.

Two hours later, there were papers everywhere. Tillie was less worried about the mess and more worried about Ruth's colorless face sitting across from her.

"So, when you kept saying 'it's just more of the same' that wasn't exactly the truth," Ruth began.

Tillie nodded, looking around at all the paperwork. "I've been secretly copying anything and everything that looked relevant." She drummed her fingers on the brown folder. "I didn't want to worry you, so I've been hiding everything. Since December."

Ruth dropped her head into her hands. She looked back up at Tillie through her fingers. "Shit, Tills. This is," she waved her hand over the papers. "What *IS* this?"

"I think they plan to take over the country, Hitler as president and all of these other men in places of power."

"I don't understand this though." Ruth picked up the map of Germany with the star by Munich. "Are they going to try to make Munich the capital?"

Tillie shook her head. "I don't know. I'm wondering if they're going to build a jail there. See where it lists *political dissidents, communists, and socialists* under the map?" She pointed. "I wonder if they're going to start arresting people who speak out against them." Ruth dropped the paper back on the pile with disgust.

Ruth bit her lip. "I wonder how many Nazis there are now." Tillie could tell she was thinking of her parents in Munich and her sister in Dachau. "Maybe I should call Cecelia and see if she knows anything."

"Ruth, you haven't spoken to your sister in ten years. I can't imagine you would be able to just call her up and ask her about the Nazis."

Ruth tapped her fingers on the table. "Well, can you ask your dad about it?"

Tillie raised her eyebrows. "You mean just casually bring up that I've been stealing their information for four months and then ask him if the Nazis are building a jail in southern Germany?"

Ruth laughed. "No, I mean when you get something like this," she tapped the map of Germany in the center of the table, "you play dumb. 'Papa, what does this mean?'" She batted her eyelashes and gave a vacant smile.

"Cute."

"If you act like you're stupid, they won't be careful around you. That's all I'm saying. They already think you're one of them, given you've been able to do all this without anyone knowing what you're up to."

"That's true." Tillie crossed her arms. "I don't even know why I'm doing it—other than hoping somehow it protects us and our friends."

Ruth was quiet for a minute. "Well, I think it's good to know what they're up to. And we'll be able to support the other political parties. Maybe even form some kind of resistance."

Tillie took a deep breath. "I suppose."

Ruth stood and stretched. "We should at least let everyone at the institute know what's going on. Try to drum up support for the other candidates running. Get people involved in voting."

Tillie nodded and started scooping up the papers to return them to their hiding place.

"Tills," Ruth stood in the doorway to their bedroom. "Why did you think someone was watching the law office? Why are you hiding these folders in a hole in the wall?"

Tillie stopped and turned toward her. "It hadn't occurred to me before tonight but if Anthony is working directly under Goebbels as the Gauleiter, then it's possible the law firm is being watched." She rubbed her arms, feeling a shiver travel up her spine. "It's possible they're watching me, I suppose." She looked back down at all the papers still littered across the table. "I don't know, it just feels safer keeping them where I can't see them." She bit her lip and met Ruth's gaze.

Ruth shook her head. "If they were watching you, they'd know you're not with Ernesto and they'd know you work at the institute. They would know everything, and you wouldn't have a job anymore. If they were watching you, that means they consider you a threat. They absolutely don't." She grinned. "You're just a nice German girl, remember?"

Tillie laughed and rolled her eyes. "I'm going to clean this up, I'll be in in a minute." Ruth disappeared through the bedroom door and Tillie turned to stack up the papers.

A small noise behind her made her turn and Bernadette was standing in the kitchen, her eyes tired.

"Oh, Bernadette. I'm sorry, did we wake you?"

She shook her head. "Tillie." She came into the kitchen and lowered herself into a chair, a wool shawl wrapped around her shoulders to keep out the chill. "I've been around a long time. Longer than you, obviously." She gave a small smile.

Tillie sat down across from her. "Is everything okay, Bernadette?"

"I overheard what you and Ruth were discussing." Tillie watched Bernadette's face, her eyes remaining fixed on an invisible spot on the surface of the table. "I think it would be best for you all to start talking about leaving."

Tillie blinked. "Leaving what?"

Bernadette finally lifted her gaze to meet Tillie's. "Leaving Germany. I'm going to talk to my sister in France. Things are going to get worse before they get better." She sniffed and then stood. "I'm going to encourage James to come with me to France. You, Ruth, Ernesto are all welcome, of course. It's time."

She didn't wait for a response, she just turned and walked out of the kitchen, leaving Tillie at the table staring after her.

CHAPTER 20

October 1931

Ruth rubbed her face with tired hands. "Do you think we should meet with Dr. H. and the rest of the employees at the institute?"

James met Ernesto's eyes and bit his lip. "I'm not sure. Would any of them even believe us?"

Ruth shook her head and put her hand on Tillie's arm. "What do you think, Tillie?"

Tillie took a deep breath. "I think we should at least make sure Dr. H. and Karl are prepared; we should at least warn people about what might be happening." She shrugged. "Another election is coming up in July. We should make sure people know that it's coming up, so they know to vote." Ernesto nodded in agreement.

"I'll make a list of things that are most important. I can go over all the notes I've taken over the last year or so and we'll go from there."

Ruth smoothed back her curls; Tillie noticed that she had once again skipped her makeup and hadn't done her hair. The stress of always talking about the Nazis was taking its toll on all of them. There were small creases forming on Ernesto's forehead. James had puffy, purple circles under his eyes, and she rarely heard any of them laugh with any real feeling anymore. All they did was talk about Goebbels, Ernesto's father, her father, and what they could be planning.

Tillie felt the rage bubbling inside her making her chest tight. She slammed her fist down onto the table and the other three jumped. "What?" Ruth demanded.

"I am tired of this. I'm tired of us always being nervous, of always talking about these wretched men. I'm tired of not sleeping. I'm tired of all of it." By the end of her rant, she was standing and shouting, though she hadn't meant to raise her voice.

They all stared at her, eyes wide and shocked. Slowly, quietly, Ernesto began to laugh. Then James joined in and then Ruth, and Tillie stared at them before dissolving into her own giggles. The well inside her body broke and she felt the waves of hysteria inside her, rising to the point that she didn't think she'd ever stop laughing.

After close to five minutes, clutching a stitch under her ribs and wiping her eyes, Ruth rose and got a bottle of vodka out of the freezer. "How about I make martinis?" They all nodded, and Tillie caught her breath.

"I'm sorry," she said, still chuckling. "I've just had enough." She shook her head and the chuckling turned to a quivering chin and a prickling behind her eyes. "I'm tired of these men and their ideas and I'm tired of listening to them talk circles to one another." James and Ernesto sat across from her blurred as she fought to keep the tears from spilling over.

Ernesto moved over beside her and rubbed her back. "I know." Tillie was relieved he didn't try to make her feel better. Ruth handed her a glass filled with ice and vodka, and Tillie took a long sip of the cold liquid, feeling it burn her throat then expand into warmth inside her belly. Her arms and legs began to feel lighter as she kept drinking, ignoring the looks between the other three.

She set down her half empty martini glass and looked up at her three best friends. "Bernadette is right. I think we should start thinking about getting out." Without waiting for a response, she stood and walked into the bedroom, closing the door behind her.

†

Tillie watched Heinz and Erwin serving their friends and the other employees dinner in the cafeteria. Dr. H. had agreed to let them speak to all the employees after the evening meal and she could already feel the butterflies in her stomach. Bernadette squeezed her hand and smiled at her. "It'll be fine, dear. Don't worry. They'll listen to you."

Tillie nodded but couldn't muster a smile back. She watched as Karl cleared his throat and stood, tapping a knife to his glass.

"Friends, Ruth and Tillie would like to have a word with you. They are trusted members of this community, and we owe it to them to listen to all they have to say."

Tillie stood with Ruth rising next to her. She cleared her throat. "As you all know, my day job is working for my father's law office. It has come to my attention in the past few months that," she paused unsure of how to continue.

Ruth laid her hand on Tillie's arm. "The Nazi Party is continuing to rise." Ruth's voice was strong and didn't waver. Her eyes flicked to Tillie for the briefest moment. "I cannot tell you how I know, but I believe they are trying to form their own army."

Uncomfortable laughter began to bubble up from a few of the employees in the back of the cafeteria, but she saw Karl and Dr. H. exchange a panicked glance. Her eyes fell on Dora, sitting with Helene and Adelaide. Dora was biting her lip and Adelaide's hand was tightly wrapped around Nissa's wrist.

A voice rose from the back of the cafeteria. "Ruthie, darling, we adore you, but this is nonsense." Looking up, Tillie could see Friedrich and Arthur, two of the boys who worked on the grounds as gardeners.

Friedrich stood. "First of all, have you even listened to the Nationalists message? Hitler wants to restore Germany to what it was before the war." He sat back down, and Arthur patted him on his back, a few of the other employees nodding in agreement.

Arthur spoke next. "You don't have to agree with his message and if you don't, just don't vote for anyone in the party."

Tillie took a breath. "I believe they are going to start targeting specific groups of people. They are making Germans afraid of the Communists. They continuously write in their papers about how the Jews are the reason Germany is falling apart." Her eyes settled on Dr H. and Karl. "I believe we will be next. Our community."

She watched as Dr. H. nodded and she felt the fear clench her stomach. Ruth folded her arms and narrowed her eyes at the table where Friedrich and Arthur were sitting. "I didn't believe anyone would vote for them, that anyone would take Hitler seriously. But they're the second strongest party in Germany now. We have to do something."

"Ruth," Heinz rose and patted her on the shoulder. "We appreciate that you're concerned about a group you don't agree with and I'm on your side. Those young men in the Nazi Party have a tendency to create havoc wherever they go. But they hardly even have power. They're not even the biggest party in Parliament."

While a few of the tables in the cafeteria were starting to talk amongst themselves, Tillie's eyes were on Karl and Dr. H. Their heads were together, and she could see the concern on both their faces.

Friedrich cleared his throat. "We can disagree with someone's politics and continue to get along."

He, Arthur, and the rest of the young men sitting at their table got up to leave the cafeteria. Ruth watched them go, her eyes bright and narrowed. She took a breath as if to argue, but the other employees were rising from their chairs, already done hearing whatever she had to say.

Tillie saw Ruth's shoulders slump and one single tear drop from her left eye, tumbling down her face like a stone. She quickly wiped it away with pale fingers and pulled herself out from underneath Heinz's hand, still resting on her shoulder.

He shrugged and turned to leave with Erwin. Tillie lowered herself back into her chair and a tense quiet settled over the room. She heard Dora's chair scrape the floor. "Dr. H." Dora's voice was tight and low. "Magnus, is she right?"

Dr. H. took Karl's hand. He squeezed it and raised his eyes to look at Dora. "I'm planning on leaving soon on a speaking tour. It is my belief that being Jewish and doing the work that I do, I am a target of these Nazi men. I'm not sure if Tillie is right, that they'll come after ordinary citizens. I believe you are safe within the walls of the institute. I, however, am not."

No one spoke. Bernadette leaned forward on the table. "You mean to tell me, you are leaving all these people here, all the people you've helped, that you claim are your family, because you don't think you are safe here any longer? But you're not advising them to leave too?" Her voice was sharp, and Tillie could tell she was angry.

Karl held up a hand. "That's unfair. Magnus could be arrested at any moment by these goons. He's the face of this institute and therefore, he is in the line of fire."

Dr. H. rubbed the top of Karl's hand. "I will be back in a year or so, after the election, once this all settles down. Karl will remain here with all of you. If I thought it was that unsafe, I would never leave any of you here, I promise you that. It is unsafe for *me*. Germany is still perfectly safe for the rest of you, provided you stay within our community."

Dora was standing unnaturally still. "And what of us, Magnus?" Tillie could see tears sliding down her face. "Adelaide, Nissa, Helene, and myself? Are we supposed to stay locked inside the institute until this all blows over? I'm in as much danger as you are here, and you know it." Her jaw clenched. "And you're leaving us here to fend for ourselves."

She turned to walk up the stairs, gesturing for the other women to follow. Bernadette shook her head and trailed them up the stairs. She turned back at the last moment and pointed at Dr. H. "You should be ashamed of yourself. At least try to get the girls out."

Tillie couldn't pull her eyes from Dr. Hirschfeld's face. He looked older than he had in years and there were tears in his eyes behind his round glasses. He shook his head and grasped Karl's hand tighter. Looking up at Ernesto's angry face, he blinked, and the tears fell down his face.

"You have to understand, Ernesto." He swallowed hard to keep his voice from quivering. "Here, inside these walls, it's still the safest place for Dora and the other girls. America isn't safe for them. Italy, France." Dr. Hirshfeld waved a desperate hand. "I can't keep them safe in those countries while I travel. They are still safest here, with the people who love them and can protect them. Here they have everything they need." He rubbed his hands under his glasses and Karl wrapped an arm around his shoulder. "I just don't know how to keep them any safer."

✝

Tillie tapped the glass of gin in front of her, not drinking, as they all sat quietly at Ruth's club. After the meeting at the institute, they all needed a drink. The crowd was noisy around them but none of them had anything to say.

James drained his glass. "Well. Dr. H. is leaving. My mom is leaving at the end of the year. She wants us to go with her." He glanced over at the rest of them. "Should we? I'm sure France is lovely."

Ernesto was staring at his own glass. "I can't leave Dora here alone."

James nodded. "I assumed as much. And I'm not leaving you. So, I guess my mother will enjoy her French holiday alone." He chuckled. "She'll be thrilled, she can hardly stand her sister. I think she was hoping she could bring a group of queers with her to be a buffer."

Ruth gave a little laugh and shook her head. "I don't want to leave. This is our country. How dare they think they can just run us out." She took a long swig of vodka.

"Well," Tillie began, "maybe Heinz is right. How much power could they possibly have? They aren't even the largest party, like he said. And Dr. H. is right. Dora is safest within the walls of the institute. We just need to get to the next election, and this will all blow over."

Tillie hadn't noticed the extreme noise of the bar until it was absent. The crowd had fallen totally silent.

She raised her eyes from her glass and Ruth's face was white, her eyes set on the front door. Tillie shifted in her seat to follow Ruth's gaze. Standing at the entrance of the club were two tall blonde men, their faces stern, and their eyes hard. Their armbands stuck out like a slash of red paint on a black and white canvas. Ruth's hand tightened on Tillie's arm. They watched as the owner of the club hurried to the doorway, shouting and gesturing for the men to leave. One of the men raised his right arm stiffly and shouted "Sieg Heil!" before they left the club.

Ruth sucked her teeth and took a long drink. "They will not scare me out of my country." She slammed her glass down onto the table, spilling vodka onto the black tablecloth, making a large, dark stain. She stood and announced to the three of them still sitting, "I'm not going to run. And neither are any of you."

The next morning, Tillie had the tired, jittery feeling of too much coffee and not enough sleep while she walked to her train. Everything felt too bright and shiny. Rubbing her temples, her eyes fell on the newspaper left strewn on the seat across from her.

Adolf Hitler stared back at her, walking in the middle of a street surrounded by soldiers in black pants and tan shirts. She leaned forward and picked up the paper, reading the caption.

"Adolf Hitler walks with Rudolf Hess, Julius Schaub, Wilhelm Bruckner in Bad Harzburg for meeting with Alfred Hugenberg to discuss overthrowing of Brüning Government."

Turning to the inside of the paper, she saw a photo of Hitler posing with Hermann Göring and she could see the pointed face of Goebbels in the background. There was little in the way of information about what went on in Bad Harzburg, just that the right-wing groups met together in opposition to the Brüning Government. The way the reporter had written about the Nazi Party, Hitler, and Göring, it was clear they thought the men to be a joke and the story to be a waste of time. Taking one last look at Goebbels and his cold stare behind Hitler, she closed the paper and laid it back down on the seat of the train where she found it.

At her desk, there were stacks of *Der Angriff* waiting to be placed around the office and lobby. Peering into her father's office and seeing he hadn't arrived for the day, she opened Goebbels' newspaper, wondering if there was more information here from the meeting in Harzburg.

While there was no story about Harzburg, Tillie read about a large parade that was held over the past Sunday in Braunschweig. Her eyes scanned the page, and she focused on the number of people listed in attendance at the parade.

"Our men came out in force to show loyalty to the Führer. One hundred thousand men participated in the six-hour march and received badges in honor of their sacrifice and as a gesture of appreciation for their allegiance."

One hundred thousand. The weight in her chest felt heavy and the air in the office was suddenly stifling. There were photos of the SA and SS officers marching through the streets, followed by Hitler, closely flanked by guards. Nazi flags in black and white dotted the photo, clenched in the hands of men, women, and children smiling for the cameras and holding their arms up in salute. She could only see one mention of Harzburg on the page. "*This event was a show of strength that blots out the memory of Harzburg and serves as an answer to Brüning. While Harzburg may be a tactical half-way stage to our goals as a party, our showing at Braunschweig clearly demonstrates the political leadership of the anti-Brüning front is in our hands.*"

Tillie was shaken from her thoughts by her father's booming voice. "Getting some reading in before starting your day, Matilda?"

She shook her shoulders and looked up at him. "Just trying to keep up to date with the goings on."

He picked up a copy of *Der Angriff* and nodded. "We're so close, Tillie. The elections next year are our chance to take Germany back. Our country, our soil, our voice, they have all been stolen by people who have no right to be here or to speak for us. With these elections, we'll be able to make Germany for the Germans, like it was before the Great War. We'll finally be free again. "

He set the paper back down and dropped his voice. "You know, there's talk of Herr Goebbels being promoted. If the Gauleiter position opens, I'm going to encourage Anthony to take it, so that I can take the Kreisleiter position."

His eyes glazed and a look of reverence crossed his face. "Imagine, Tillie. If Anthony is Gauleiter, the Führer might even come to the office." He blinked twice and chuckled. "Yes, well, anyway. Distribute these throughout the lobby, please." He didn't bother to wait for a response before striding into his office and shutting the door with a click that sounded like thunder.

CHAPTER 21

September 1990

Thea sat on the floor of the den while Michael rested on the couch, a glass of wine in his hand. All the different papers and photographs they had found throughout the house were strewn around Thea's feet. She was surrounded by the smiling faces of her grandparents, their friends, and her uncle from over the years.

"Well," Michael took a sip from his wine, "according to one of my partners, if Ruth was put into a camp, there would be a record of her with the Red Cross once the camp was liberated."

Thea nodded, drinking her own wine. "Okay, so what if she's dead?" Picking up a photo of her grandparents, her mother as a toddler, and her uncle in front of a bunch of palm trees, she couldn't help staring at her grandmother, trying to pick out any hint of sadness behind her eyes.

"Well, then we won't find her?" Michael shrugged. "I honestly don't know. There are a few places where Jewish people can try to track down family members, but I don't know if they'll work with us since we aren't technically her family."

He pulled a notepad out of the briefcase on the couch next to him. "We have an in-house investigator that is tracking down some of the Red Cross information, plus they suggested trying to go through The Church of Latter-Day Saints in Utah."

Thea looked up. "The Church of Latter-Day Saints? Like, Mormons?"

Michael nodded. "Apparently they have a pretty extensive genealogy collection." He picked up the letter Thea had taken from her grandmother's hatbox. "We have this address. Let's just write to it and see if they know what happened to her?"

Thea nodded and bit her lip.

Michael was staring at her. "What's wrong?"

"I just keep thinking about the tragedy of it all. Grandpa and Uncle Jimmy getting to spend their lives together. Then Uncle Jimmy getting to be with you. They got to live their lives, even if it was behind closed doors. They still had one another."

She touched one of the photos directly in front of her, her grandmother standing alone, unsmiling, at the edge of the frame with four or five couples, her grandfather and her uncle holding hands in the center. "I just can't imagine a life lived like this." She wiped a tear before it trickled down her face. Looking up at Michael, she saw he was crying too. "It must have been so hard for her."

Michael wiped his face then gulped the last of his wine. "Okay so, here's my next question. Do we tell your grandmother we're looking for Ruth?"

Thea shook her head. "No. Odds are she's dead. She likely died back in '42 after her letter was returned. Or, you know, she just got old." Thea shrugged. "I don't think telling Gram would do any good. She'd just forget we told her after a day or two anyway."

"You're probably right. And if we don't find out anything, it remains a mystery. I can't imagine that would be very comforting to her."

The next morning, Thea had three separate letters in front of her. One to the Church of Latter-Day Saints Genealogy Program, one to the address on the returned envelope, and one to the American Red Cross. They all said the same thing; she was searching for a good friend of her grandmother's, that the woman possibly was placed in a concentration camp in 1942, that she was likely around thirty years old at the time, and her last known address was likely in Berlin. It was hardly any information, but it was their only shot. Taking a deep breath, she addressed each envelope and put them in her purse to drop off at the post office on her way to work.

✝

Several weeks went by and Thea found herself checking the mailbox multiple times per day. She would run home at lunch to check the mail, just in case it came early, then again when she got home for the day. Often Michael would get home later than her, so he would check for good measure on his way inside the house as well.

After five weeks of nothing, she couldn't take it anymore. She was in the kitchen slamming cabinets and stomping around making dinner when Michael walked through the front door. "Ugh!" She shouted as soon as she heard the door click shut. "I cannot keep doing this. There must be something else we can do besides just waiting." She turned around to see Michael standing in front of her and grinning, holding a much-abused-looking letter in his hand.

"It's from Berlin."

Her eyes widened and she snatched it from his fingers. Her breath caught. Looking up at him, she whispered, "They wrote us back, but what if they don't know anything?"

He shrugged. "Then we're in the same spot we're in now." Thea nodded and ripped open the top of the letter. She started scanning, but Michael made a noise in his throat. "Read it out loud," he snapped.

Thea smirked at him and started reading.

"*Dear Thea,*

I hope my letter finds you in good health. I apologize if my response took some time to get to you. I had to double check a few things prior to writing back to you. Interestingly, my grandparents were part of the resistance during World War II. There were many stories about my grandparents and their bravery during that time. I did know that they hid several of their friends over the course of the Nazi Occupation, though there is no real record of who those friends were. They were arrested and held briefly as political dissidents but then were able to return to their home after the camp, and they were released to my great-grandparents. I'm assuming a bribe was likely involved.

Anyway, I inquired with my father to see if he recognized your grandmother's friend, Ruth, or if he had heard her name. While the name did not sound familiar to my father, he was also born in 1948, so that would have been after Ruth, if she had been here in hiding. My grandparents had a false bookcase and behind it, there was a small room where their friends remained hidden. I believe it was also the headquarters for their resistance meetings at one point. The room is my daughter's playroom now; she loves showing it off to her friends. Unfortunately, there wouldn't be anything left in the room itself.

I did speak to a good friend of my grandmother's, Elizabeth Schafer, and she DID recall Ruth and recognized both her and your grandmother from the photo you sent. Elizabeth was married to a friend of theirs, a man by the name of Henry. She didn't know what happened to Ruth or your grandmother, so she was quite thrilled to hear that your grandmother had escaped to America. She believes Ruth lived with my grandparents in hiding until around 1941 or 1942 but cannot remember after that point as many of them were arrested for aiding the resistance.

I'm sorry I cannot be of more assistance. Unfortunately, both my grandparents have since passed away, so I am unable to inquire about this further. I wish you the best of luck in finding Ruth. I would love it if you would keep me abreast of your progress in finding her.

    Sincerely,

    Christoph Hayes

Thea finished reading and looked up at Michael, who was still standing in his coat with his briefcase in his hand. "Well, that's more than we knew before."

Thea nodded. "So, we know that Ruth was in hiding with the resistors until at least 1941." Her eyes widened as she stared at the letter. "Do you think she was a spy or something?"

Michael started shaking his arms out of his coat. "Who knows? This is great though because we've found people who knew her. We're on the right track." Taking a deep breath, he strode into the kitchen. "Let's eat, I'm starving."

Suddenly Thea felt famished too. She smiled at the letter from Christoph in her hand. It was a start. They were going to find her.

A week later, the phone rang at Thea's desk at work. She'd barely said "Hello" when Michael's voice was practically shouting in her ear.

"Get this!" He sounded like he was pacing back and forth. "The PI from my office just informed me that the Red Cross started a new program specifically for families of Jewish people who were living in Europe during the war. It could be why they haven't gotten back to us yet, because they had to forward our letter to this new division."

"Okay," Thea said, slowly.

"It's called The Red Cross Holocaust Victims and Tracing Program." He let out a long breath, like he'd been holding it in. "Can you even believe it? I have a phone number; we just need to call them."

"Wait, are you serious?" Thea put down her pencil and the bank numbers she'd been working on.

"Yes. It's for finding people that were detained in a labor camp or killed during the Holocaust. You call, give them the information, and they do the rest."

Thea picked up her pencil. "Give me the number."

✝

Hands shaking, Thea opened the door to her local Red Cross building. The building was bright and smelled faintly of cleaning solution. An older woman sat behind a counter and when the bell rang above the door, the woman looked up and smiled.

"May I help you?"

Thea swallowed and nodded. "Yes, I was directed here to complete an Inquiry Form."

The woman's face softened. "Oh, of course, dear. Let me get it for you." Disappearing into a back room, Thea was left in the lobby standing at the desk. She had the letter with the Berlin address, Ruth's name, and an approximate date. She hoped that would be enough.

The woman reappeared with a paper in her hand. "Okay. Now, here's how this goes. We'll fill this out together, then I'll send it to the tracing program in Baltimore where it will be assigned a case number. From there, they send out inquiries to museums, other Red Cross offices, different archive organizations, and to a few satellite offices in Israel." Thea nodded. "Once they find anything out, they'll contact you and let you know what they've found."

"What if they don't find anything?" Thea's voice quivered.

"Well," the woman paused, "this program is brand new, but so far, they've always found something." Her voice was kind and soft. She picked up a ballpoint pen and sat down. "Now, let's get started. What's the name of the person you're trying to find?"

"Ruth." Thea took a deep breath. "Ruth Birnbaum."

CHAPTER 22

July 1932

Tillie fanned herself sitting at the little round table in their kitchen. The sweat ran between her shoulder blades and her breasts in steady streams, pooling in her belly button and the base of her spine.

"I do not think I've ever been this hot," she moaned, while Ruth got them a second batch of ice from the freezer.

"My eyelashes won't stick. I had to stop wearing them to the club because the glue won't set. It's too hot." Ruth collapsed into a chair, sucking on a piece of ice and pushing Tillie's glass back toward her across the table.

Their front door sprang open, and James and Ernesto walked in, their hands full of fliers, looking as melted as Tillie felt. James' normally bright eyes looked tired and dull, and he went straight to the sink for a glass of water.

Ernesto sank down into the chair next to Tillie. "We papered the neighborhood." Sweat seeped through his shirt on his chest and back and his normally bouncy blonde curls hung limp and damp on his forehead.

He set the fliers down and Tillie studied the graphics. A man being impaled by a crown emblazoned with a bright red swastika with the words "The People Die from this System" across the top in bold yellow lettering. Across the bottom the words "Elect Social Democrats" in red letters leapt out from the inky black background.

"These are great," Tillie breathed. "And after Hitler lost the presidency, I'm feeling so much more optimistic about how this election is going to go." She smiled up at Ruth, who smiled back.

She looked around the table remembering how they had felt three months ago. With Adolf Hitler running for the presidency, she'd awaken with fear and dread like anchors in her gut. The same feelings hung over them all like a fog, permeating every aspect of their lives. She watched Ruth and James laughing with one another now and placed a hand on her belly, breathing deeply.

She could still feel terror in the very pit of her stomach, solid like a lump of coal. The smell of the multiple packs of cigarettes Ruth and Ernesto had gone through the day of the last election still clung to the floral curtains in the kitchen and they had gone through almost three bottles of vodka between the four of them.

If she closed her eyes, she could almost taste the hangover that followed, the air tense and electrified. The apprehension of waiting to know the future of their country was so heavy, Tillie almost broke under it. When they woke up the next morning, teeth fuzzy and heads pounding, Hitler had lost, and Tillie felt a breath release that she didn't even know she'd been holding. Now, taking the flier in her hand, her shoulders felt loose and free, despite the sweltering heat. Ruth reached over and took her hand. "Are you okay?"

Tillie nodded. "I really am. I think things are going to be fine now." She smiled. "We still have work to do, of course," she said, thinking of all the Nazi flags that lined her route to work now. "But I think we're on our way."

†

Tillie took Ruth's arm in her own as they walked home from voting on Sunday. The sun beat down on them and the crook of Tillie's elbow immediately became sweaty but when she pulled away, Ruth tugged back, smiling at her and leaning to kiss her neck. James and Ernesto walked in front of them, hand in hand, and despite the heat, her steps felt light.

Feeling Ruth's hand squeeze her arm, Tillie looked up and felt the muscles in her neck tighten. About twenty-five yards ahead of them, a large group of young men with swastikas attached to their biceps like armor were screaming at the people walking by.

Their Nazi flags whipped high above their heads and posters of Hitler were held tight in their hands. She watched Ernesto and James drop their hands and move inches apart while the Hitler Youth screamed at them and spit in their direction. As they got closer, she could hear them chanting "Jews Out, Hail Victory" over and over. Tillie's chest began to burn, and she realized she wasn't breathing. Inhaling through her nose, she kept her eyes forward as they drew nearer to the men. They looked deranged as their faces contorted with rage.

Tillie's breath caught as she heard a voice shouting at Ernesto. "Hey. You. Jew lover. You a queer, too?" She felt a wave of cold over her entire body. It was Ernesto's brother, Tommy.

"Don't stop, don't stop," she whispered, watching Ernesto slow his steps as he also registered the voice he heard over the yelling crowd.

She heard Ruth breathe into her ear. "What is he doing?" They were almost in front of the group of men now and Ernesto had completely stopped walking, his gaze settling on his younger brother in the front of the crowd.

"That's his younger brother." She heard Ruth inhale sharply.

"We cannot stop in front of these men," she hissed to Tillie, digging her nails into the flesh of her forearm.

"I know that, but it's his brother," Tillie whispered back. They slowed their pace while the men continued to shout at them, directing most of their hatred to Ruth. Tillie knew with her blonde hair and light blue eyes that she was relatively safe from their vitriol.

They were close enough to Ernesto that she could hear what he was saying. "Tommy, what are you doing?" His voice was thick and desperately sad.

Tommy didn't answer right away. His eyes darted to the older boys surrounding him and he fidgeted where he stood. Behind him, a larger dark-haired man crossed his arms, his eyes narrowing at Ernesto and James. James stood next to Ernesto, his eyes darting back to Tillie and Ruth, and Tillie could see the nervousness and fear on James' face. "Blood and honor," the man started yelling. The other men surged forward around Tommy joining in. "Blood and honor," they were all shouting, and soon, the group swallowed Tommy like a large shark devouring a small fish. As Tommy vanished from view, Ernesto took a step forward.

"Tommy?" He shouted out; his voice drowned out by the screams of the men. James reached out and grabbed Ernesto by the elbow and pulled, trying to lead him away from the group.

"C'mon." Ruth yanked Tillie forward and they both tried to help James steer Ernesto away from the terrifying men. "Ernesto, it's not safe here. We have to go!" She had to shout to be heard over the cries of 'Blood and Honor' all around them. Ruth pulled on his free arm while James continued to tug forward as the group shouted and jumped up and down, working themselves into a frenzy. Tillie could see the tears running down Ernesto's face, but he wasn't calling for Tommy anymore.

One glance over her shoulder and she saw Tommy's small round face, stuck within the crowd of men, his eyes wide, his mouth a thin, grim line. Their eyes met for the briefest moment, and she thought he gave a little shake of his head, before he was knocked sideways by a larger boy holding a poster of Hitler slamming a caricature of a Jewish man to the ground.

Tillie turned, following Ruth and James as they guided Ernesto to safety, feeling her hands trembling and her heart pounding in her ears. By the time they made it back to the apartment, the optimism they felt after voting had faded with the setting of the July sun.

They sat around the table. The stillness of the evening accentuated by Ernesto sniffling into his drink. Every so often, he would shake his head and mutter "Tommy" under his breath.

Tillie felt her insides writhing like snakes every time she looked in his direction. She had seen the fear in Tommy's eyes when she looked at him, standing so small in that cloud of hate. He looked like a person stuck inside a nightmare.

After several drinks, James and Ernesto decided to go back to the institute. Bernadette sat, rubbing Ernesto's back until they stood to leave. She leaned in and gave him a quick kiss on the forehead before giving a grim nod to her son. Any words of understanding or encouragement would have rung false and empty.

James turned to his mother. "Can I use Papa's old hat? Something to cover my hair while we walk home." Bernadette hurried to her room to gather the last of her husband's things to give to James. Tillie could see James' face was paler than usual. His lips lacked any color, and it was then that Tillie realized James was afraid to walk home.

The boys left and Tillie, Ruth, and Bernadette stood awkwardly in the kitchen. Bernadette cleared her throat. "Depending on what happens tomorrow with this election, I will likely be moving to my sister's at the end of the summer. If not the end of the summer, then surely by the end of the year."

Ruth slowly sat back down. "Bernadette," she began, but Bernadette put up a hand.

"I know you all aren't coming with me. I've already spoken with James about it. He won't leave Ernesto and Ernesto won't leave Dora and France isn't safe for Dora." She sighed. "I wish you all would reconsider." She leaned against the doorway and put her hand to her forehead. "It's going to get worse. Exponentially worse before it gets better."

"Not if they lose tonight." Tillie tried to clamp down on the panic bubbling up inside. "If they lose tonight," her voice trailed off.

"If they lose tonight, there's another election in November. Then another at the beginning of next year. Meanwhile the streets are being lined with Nazi flags, the parades are everywhere, and hundreds of thousands of people are lining their children up to be a part of the Hitler Youth. They are teaching their children to spit on us, to hate us. Jews are the villains in the stories they tell. They are not going away, even if they lose every election from now until the end of time."

Ruth and Tillie were quiet as Bernadette watched them. "Please," she said, her voice a whisper. "Please consider coming to France. You will always be welcome."

She turned and left the kitchen. Tillie's eyes fell on Ruth. She was feeling the same panic she had three months earlier during the presidential election. "Ruth," she hardly recognized her own voice. It was strained and hoarse. "Should we leave? Convince the boys to leave?"

Ruth rubbed her face with the back of her hand. "I don't want to leave. This is our home, Tillie."

"But what if we're not safe here anymore? Bernadette clearly thinks it's not safe here. Marcia left the country six months after she quit the law firm. Obviously, some people believe that it's going to get worse. Should we go too?"

Ruth pushed herself up from the table. "No." Her voice was firm. "We are not leaving." She met Tillie's gaze, her eyes hard.

"Dora can't leave. Adelaide, Helene, Nissa. They can't leave. So what? We just leave our friends here to fend for themselves? No. We're not doing that."

"Ruth, that's not what I'm suggesting we do, but …"

Ruth interrupted her mid-sentence. "That's exactly what you're suggesting we do." Her voice dropped to a whisper. "That's exactly what Bernadette is doing. Leaving her child behind because right now things are hard."

"Ruth," Tillie couldn't keep the shock out of her voice, "that's not fair."

Ruth shook her head. "Fine. Believe what you want. If you want to go, then go. But I'm not leaving." Without waiting for a response, she turned and walked to the bedroom, closing the door behind her.

†

The next morning, the pounding on their door awoke them. The haze coming through the window signaled it was just after dawn. Ruth rubbed her eyes and quickly got up while Tillie took time to put on her robe. They staggered to the front door while the banging continued.

"What?" Ruth swung the door open, her voice sharp and furious. Ernesto stood in the doorway, James just behind him looking exhausted. Ernesto's eyes were wide with dread. In his hands he held up that morning's paper.

"The results," he said, his voice sounding hoarse and strained. On the front page was a huge picture of Adolf Hitler.

Ruth moaned. "No."

His hand crumpled the paper so that all Tillie could see was Hitler's shoes. The tears were flowing freely down his face. "They won almost one hundred and thirty more seats. Fourteen million votes. I can't …" his voice caught, and a sob escaped his lips.

Ruth put a hand on her chest and fell into a chair. "Oh no." Tillie looked from Ernesto's white knuckles around the paper to Ruth sitting at the table, her head in her hands. Bernadette appeared in the doorway between the kitchen and the hall, her bathrobe pulled around her.

Tillie reached out and took the paper from Ernesto to read what it said. "The National Socialist German Workers Party has successfully become the largest party in Parliament after yesterday's election," she read aloud. "The party of Adolf Hitler won a total of two hundred and thirty seats, adding one hundred and twenty-three seats won with fourteen million votes by the citizens of Germany. While they did not gain a majority in Parliament, they currently hold thirty-seven percent of the seats." She swallowed, feeling a wave of nausea creeping up into her throat. Looking up at Ruth and Ernesto, their faces tight with panic, she set the paper down on the table.

Bernadette's face was despondent. "I suppose that means I'll be moving to France at the end of the summer." James rubbed the tears from his face while Bernadette looked at each of them. Her voice turned desperate. "Please come with me. Please."

They all sat in silence—the loss of hope palpable. Bernadette finally turned and left the tiny kitchen.

CHAPTER 23

March 1991

Thea took a deep breath outside her grandmother's room. As she pushed the door open, she heard her grandmother talking in a low voice.

"Gram, who are you talking to?" She walked through the door and looked around. There was no one else in the room.

Her grandmother looked at her and blinked. "Jenny. What are you doing here?"

"I came to check on you; just to see how you're doing." Thea sat down in the armchair by the window. Her grandmother's room smelled like talc and unwashed skin. "How's it going?"

Her grandmother gave a noncommittal shrug.

"Who were you talking to just now?"

"What?" She turned and looked at Thea, her eyes narrowed.

Thea tried to breathe in extra patience. "When I walked in, I heard you talking to someone. Were you on the phone?"

"I was talking to Dora."

Thea raised her eyebrows. "Dora? As in, Grandpa's mom?"

Her grandmother waved her hand. "No." Her voice had a sharpness to it that Thea didn't recognize. "Your father lived with Dora before he moved in with me. She was like a mother to him." She dropped her eyes and they filled with tears. Her voice was quiet, barely above a whisper. "We left her behind. Sometimes I tell her how sorry I am that we left her. I hope she can hear me."

Thea sat motionless, her stomach in a freefall. Should she be looking for Dora as well? Maybe she was still alive. "Gram, when did you leave Germany with Grandpa and Uncle Jimmy?"

For a moment her grandmother stared at her. Then she shook her head. "It doesn't matter." Her tears fell silently down her face. "I can't go back. Not now."

Thea leaned forward and took the old woman's hand in her own. She judged the situation, debating whether or not to tell her grandmother what she was doing.

She decided to go for it. "Gram, there's this new program that's been started." Her grandmother kept her eyes down, looking at their intertwined hands. "I've been able to ask them to find out what happened to Ruth. I'm waiting to hear back." She rushed on before her grandmother could interrupt her. "I could try to find Dora too. I just need her last name."

Her grandmother lifted her eyes to gaze at Thea. "I know what happened to Dora. I know what happened to Ruth. They're dead. Just like everyone else." She yanked her hand away. "I don't need some program to tell me what I already know."

She stood and went into the bathroom, slamming the door behind her, leaving Thea sitting alone in the armchair, wondering if she had made a huge mistake telling her grandmother about her plans.

✝

Thea walked into her dark house feeling defeated. The kitchen light was on and she could smell something delicious cooking.

"Hey Michael, I'm back."

"Hey Thea." He appeared in the doorway from the hallway to the kitchen. He was wearing one of her grandmother's old aprons. Thea smiled.

"What are you making? It smells great."

He grinned at her. "Chicken Parm. Come sit down and have a glass of wine. It's almost finished."

She sat down and watched him moving through the kitchen, checking in the oven, tasting things from the stovetop, cutting some crusty bread on the cutting board. She sipped her wine and felt the knot between her shoulders loosen.

"I went and saw my grandmother today."

He turned and gave her a sad smile. "I take it from your face, it didn't go well."

Thea shook her head. "She's worse every time I go in to see her. I don't think she's recognized me once in the last month. She always calls me Jenny." She took a long sip of the red wine, closing her eyes to swallow. "I walked in on her talking to herself today and when I asked her who she was talking to, she said she was talking to Dora."

Michael raised an eyebrow. "Your grandfather's mother?"

"According to my grandmother, they weren't related. She was some woman that he lived with for a while. She said he was like a mother to her. But then she got all cryptic about how they left her behind." She rubbed the back of her neck. "So, I told her that we were looking for Ruth."

Michael couldn't hide the surprise on his face. "And how'd she take that?"

Thea shook her head. "She said it didn't matter. That they were all dead. That she didn't need 'some program' to tell her things she already knew." She laid her head down on her forearms.

Michael brought a plate of steaming chicken and pasta over to the table and set it down next to her. " Do you think she's right? That Ruth is dead?"

Thea sat up and picked up her fork. "I don't know. It's been months and we haven't heard anything. It's like a needle in a haystack."

She took a bite and chewed thoughtfully. "Not to mention, we can't even try to look for Dora because I don't know what Dora's last name was. And if she was just friends with my grandfather, it's possible she could still be alive, especially if she was the same age as they were." She swallowed and felt the knot in her shoulders fade away. "This chicken is so good," she breathed, shoveling another huge bite into her mouth.

Michael smiled. "Well, let's hope that they end up having good news about Ruth and then we'll go from there. Maybe she knows what happened to Dora."

The next morning, before Thea was out of bed, Michael burst into her room, his eyes wild and his face flushed.

"What?"

"The Red Cross is on the phone."

Thea threw back the covers and sprinted down the hallway after him. She picked up the second telephone in her grandmother's office and forced out a shaky "Hello?"

"Hello, is this Theadora Brandon?"

Thea cleared her throat. "Yes."

"We have some good news for you. We were able to trace Ruth May Birnbaum from Berlin to the camp Dachau. After Dachau was liberated, she and her niece were placed in France at a Red Cross station. From there, they departed to Canada, then they relocated to the United States." Thea held her breath. The person on the phone continued. "Would you like her current address?"

She heard Michael gasp into the phone in the kitchen. "She's still alive?" Thea couldn't believe it.

There was a sound of papers shuffling and then the woman on the other end of the line said, "As of last year's census, she was still alive and living in northern Vermont."

Thea realized she was crying. "I would like her address very much," she said in a trembling voice. She heard Michael through the receiver give a small whimper. Grabbing a pen, she wrote down the address the woman gave her and stared at it.

"I'm sorry, what?" Thea mumbled into the phone.

"I said, good luck, dear. I'm glad I was able to deliver some good news to you."

Thea wiped her eyes. "Thank you. Thank you so much." She set down the phone and walked into the kitchen, the address clutched between shaking fingers.

Michael was leaning against the counter, the phone still in his hand. "Thea," he whispered. "She's alive." Thea nodded and he wrapped his arms around her. "This is amazing," he said into her hair.

She pulled away, still holding the address in her hand. "What do we do now?"

He looked down at the paper and gave a contented sigh. "We should probably deliver your grandmother's letter."

CHAPTER 24

January 1933

Ruth dry heaved into the sink while James rubbed her back and whispered words of comfort into her ear. Ernesto and Tillie sat at the kitchen table in a tense silence, another newspaper between them. This time, the front page was announcing Adolf Hitler's appointment to Chancellor.

Tillie watched as her beautiful girlfriend threw up in the sink and Ernesto sat with silent tears running down his face, his eyes staring into nothing. The air felt heavy. The weight upon Tillie's shoulder, the one that had been there since the previous July when the Nazi Party became the largest party in Germany, felt like it would crush her. She took a deep breath but releasing it did nothing to ease the sinking feeling in the bottom of her stomach.

Ruth rinsed her mouth and sunk into a chair, her face clammy and white. James sat down next to her, continuing to rub her back. Ernesto stood and readied a mug of tea, placing it in front of Ruth, the tears still dripping down his cheeks into the collar of his shirt. She picked up the tea, hands trembling, and closed her eyes.

James stared at the paper for a moment. "At least my mother left already." Tillie watched his eyes meet Ernesto's and could tell they were thinking the same thing. *"It's time for us to go, too."*

Tillie kept opening her mouth to say something, but no words came. She didn't even know where to start. Staring around at her friends at the small kitchen table, it felt like there were no words left.

Ernesto and James stayed at the apartment until the sun began to set. They left to go back to the institute with the promise to call when they arrived.

"Ruth," Tillie began as she closed the door behind James.

"Don't say it." Ruth was still pale, but she was less sweaty as she took small sips from her tea.

"We have to go. Bernadette was right." Tillie jabbed a finger onto the newspaper. "This is going to go from bad to worse. If we go to France, we have a chance to try and find a place for Dora and the other girls. We could help other people from our community get out, too." Tillie felt the frustration burning her stomach. "Ruth!" she shouted. "The least you could do is look at me."

Ruth slowly lifted her eyes from her tea. "I'm not leaving, Tillie. This is my home. I'm not leaving."

"So what? You'll let me leave without you? You'd do that?"

Ruth took a sip of her tea, her eyes bright with tears. She swallowed hard. "No. No, of course not." She closed her eyes and shook her head, as if trying to shake the idea away. "No."

Tillie nodded but felt a cold brick of fear in her gut. "I'm going to bed." She glanced at Ruth, still unmoving at the table, her tea cold in front of her. "Don't stay up too late."

Ruth gave a small nod and Tillie went into the bedroom to stare at the ceiling until she felt Ruth come in and sink down beside her.

Walking into her office the next morning, she felt the exhaustion deep in her bones. Once she had finally fallen asleep, she slept like the dead. The mixture of emotional upheaval and too many vodka-and-sodas made her body heavy, and it was like walking through quicksand to get to her desk.

She heard male voices coming from her father's office and she attempted to get to the ladies' room without being seen. The idea of having to interact with her father and his associates today made her head pound. She had taken three steps when she heard the familiar low voice behind her. "Matilda." Breathing slowly, she turned. Joseph Goebbels stood before her, carrying a champagne glass, his beady black eyes glinting with satisfaction.

She couldn't force her mouth into a smile. Her face felt like clay. "Good morning, sir. I was just on my way to the ladies' room. Can I help you with something?" Her voice was flat, and she thought she saw annoyance flash across the small man's face before he broke into a pointy smile.

"Come celebrate with us." He gestured his champagne glass back toward her father's office. "The Führer has successfully gotten one step closer to the presidency. I have been promoted, which means the Gauleiter position has fallen on your boss, Herr Grandelis."

Lips curled showing his yellowed teeth, he took several steps in Tillie's direction, and she had to fight the urge to turn and run. "You know what that means, don't you?"

Tillie shook her head, not trusting her voice to be calm and even. "Why, it means your father has been made Kreisleiter." His smile was so distorted that he took on the look of a wolf mid-snarl.

The corners of Tillie's vision started to blur and get darker, and her legs went limp. They felt like noodles beneath her. She listed to one side and Goebbels' voice sounded very far away when he asked. "Matilda, are you alright?" It was as if she stepped into a hole in the middle of the room. The feeling of cold and darkness surrounded her, and Goebbels disappeared from in front of her as she plunged into nothingness.

When Tillie opened her eyes, she saw her father staring down at her, his forehead creased with worry. She recognized the jovial booming voice from behind her father asking, "Is she alright, Vincent?" Göring was here as well, she thought to herself.

She forced herself into a sitting position, even though stars burst in her vision and her head swam in darkness a second time. "Tillie, darling, should I call a doctor?" Her father's voice was quiet and concerned. She shook her head but didn't dare try to stand.

Another voice she didn't recognize asked the room, "What happened?"

The icy voice of Goebbels pierced the tense quiet of the room. "I told her that her father had been promoted to Kriestleiter and over she went." His voice almost sounded amused, there was a current of laughter just below the surface and she could tell her father heard it too. His jaw tightened and his eyes narrowed.

Tillie cleared her throat. Her eyes fell on the new armband wrapped around her father's bicep. Gold and red popped out at her, bright against his black suit. She took a deep breath and met his eyes, now filled with something else besides worry. She thought she saw fear behind his gaze.

"Oh goodness," she began, her voice weak. "You know, my flat mates and I must have celebrated a little too much last night. I overslept this morning, then skipped breakfast in my rush to arrive."

She forced a girlish giggle, and it made her cringe. "Really, I'm fine, I just need a little something to eat and maybe a cup of coffee." A look of relief washed over her father's face, and she felt a desperate sadness. He nodded and left, she assumed to get her breakfast that she wasn't the least bit hungry for.

As she adjusted her dress and moved to a more comfortable position on the floor, her eyes locked with Herr Grandelis. He stood behind Goebbels, arms folded, a look of smug satisfaction on his face. The edges of his lips twitched, and he raised his eyebrows at her, before saying, "Good German girls don't spend the night drinking with their flat mates, regardless of the reasons."

Göring laughed and clapped Herr Grandelis on the back. "Oh, come now, Anthony. Certainly, you can give the girl some leeway. It's a time of celebration." He winked at Tillie and steered Herr Grandelis out of the room, leaving her with Goebbels to wait for her father to return.

She could feel his eyes upon her, but she kept her face down brushing off invisible lint from her skirt to avoid his gaze. She heard him inhale but before he could speak, her father rushed back in with bread, cheese, chocolate, and coffee from the cafe across the street. He helped her up into a chair.

"Here you are, darling. Why don't you phone Ernesto to come walk you home later today." Tillie gave her father a weak smile.

"Thanks, Papa." She nibbled on the chocolate and sipped the coffee.

"You just sit here and relax, don't worry about working too much today. I dare say we likely won't be doing a lot of business anyway, eh Joseph?"

Tillie finally chanced looking at Goebbels and saw he was staring back at her with a curious mixture of pity and what looked like annoyance.

"Ernesto," he began, his voice low and careful. "Isn't that Anthony's son?"

The air in the room shifted. She saw her father's face tighten, and he turned to Goebbels. "Yes, it is."

"From what Anthony has told me, Ernesto is not appropriate company for a good German girl to be keeping. Wouldn't you agree, Vincent?"

Tillie could see her father trying to figure out the best way to answer the question. After a long stretch of silence, her father looked at his hands and said, "Well, I think it depends on what you think is appropriate. Ernesto has always been a good boy and he and his father have always had a strained relationship." Tillie could see a vein just above her father's temple pulsing and beads of sweat were starting to form above his lip.

"I think an alleged Communist is not an appropriate person." Goebbels' voice was hard and deadly quiet. "I'm sure you understand that it would not be …" he paused, *"prudent* for Tillie's safety to continue seeing such a man that is so obviously beneath her."

Her father bristled. "Herr Goebbels, with all due respect, we have no reason to believe that Ernesto is anything of the sort." Tillie could see her father's face turning a deeper shade of red. "And frankly, I find it a little offensive that you would suggest that my daughter, someone who has become indispensable to our law firm, would be spending her time with anyone unworthy."

Goebbels stood for a moment, his hands behind his back. Tillie didn't move as she watched the two men stare each other down. After a beat, Goebbels bowed his head and said, "Of course, Vincent. I'm just relaying what rumors I've heard regarding Anthony's oldest child. Perhaps if we all had dinner together and I was able to meet this Ernesto, my views would change." His eyes flickered to Tillie. "I didn't mean to offend you, Matilda."

Her father wasn't expecting Goebbels to back down. "Yes, well, I appreciate that," he stammered. "I think if you'd met him, you'd see that Ernesto is a lovely young man. I'm not sure what happened between him and Anthony, but I've never had anything but good experiences with Ernesto."

Goebbels nodded, but he was still watching Tillie. "I do hope you're right." Then he turned and left the break room, leaving Tillie with her father.

"Matilda," her father's voice was pleading. "Please tell me Ernesto isn't a Communist. Please tell me I didn't just defend you to one of the most powerful men in Germany with a lie."

Tillie took a breath and forced a smile. "No, of course not Papa. Ernesto isn't a Communist."

Her father let out a sigh of relief. "Thank goodness. Well, I'm off to get some work done. Rest in here as long as you need to, dear."

Without waiting for a reply, he followed Goebbels' footsteps through the lobby back to the office, leaving Tillie still sitting, cheese in hand, feeling thoroughly spent.

Ernesto arrived at the law office an hour later and Tillie sat waiting for him out in the cold to keep him from having to face his father. "What happened?" His face was pale and sweaty. "I got here as soon as I could."

She shrugged. "My dad is Kreisleiter. Your dad is Gauleiter. Everyone has been promoted. Also, apparently your father is openly telling people you're a Communist to explain your estrangement."

Ernesto rolled his eyes. "Super." He helped her stand up from the cold bench where she'd been waiting.

"Let's just go," she said, her voice flat and full of exhaustion. "I can't be here anymore." Ernesto nodded.

"What," an angry voice behind them rang out, "are you doing here?" Tillie's heart fell. She should have known Ernesto's father would be waiting for him.

Ernesto didn't even turn around. "Picking up a friend," he said in a low voice.

"A friend, hmm?" He dropped his voice to a low hiss. "I know what both of you are. Mark my words, you and your disgusting friends, your days are numbered here." He slammed the office door behind him.

Ernesto stood very still for a few moments before taking a deep breath and offering his arm to Tillie. "You ready?" He kept his voice even and didn't look at her face.

She nodded, taking his arm. "Let's go home, Ernesto."

CHAPTER 25

February 1933

They all sat together drinking tea in the lounge at the institute. Ruth was curled up reading in a corner of the bright red couch, Ernesto and James were playing chess, Dora and Adelaide were knitting, and Tillie was just returning from her shift in the library. They were all getting used to being in the institute without Dr. H. He'd been gone almost an entire year on his speaking tour, with no return date set. Ernesto glanced in her direction and gave her a small smile. She was just sitting down with her own tea when the door to the lounge burst open and Erwin stood, red-faced and sweating.

"Turn on the radio," he said breathlessly. "The Reichstag is on fire."

There was a brief silence, followed by gasps and someone yelling to go get Karl from his office. Erwin disappeared at a jog to go round up any of the other employees left in the building. The seconds it took Tillie to stand and rush to the radio felt like hours. They all crowded around the desk in the back of the lounge and the room became deathly quiet.

A static voice came over the radio, sounding tinny and thin. "The Reichstag fire appears to have started sometime just before ten p.m. A concerned citizen phoned Berlin Police stating that the dome of the Reichstag was burning in brilliant flames. Valiant effort on the part of the Berlin Fire Department was unsuccessful in containing the blaze. Chancellor Hitler, Joseph Goebbels, and Hermann Göring were on the scene relatively quickly and watched from across the street. Göring was overheard blaming the Communist Party for the fire and the Reichstag officials are currently gathering this very evening to determine next steps."

Karl leaned forward and switched the radio off. The silence that bloomed over the group made Tillie's ears ring. Karl sucked his front teeth and then stood. "For those of you still here, just sit tight. I'm not sure it's wise to go out and venture home just yet. There are a few bottles of vodka down in the freezers in the cafeteria, or I'm sure Heinz and Erwin can make some tea. I'm going to have to phone Magnus." His face was solemn as he left the lounge; everyone still standing around the radio.

Tillie walked back to the couch to sit, her legs felt heavy and unstable. She traced a small stain on the arm when a hand took hers and she felt Ruth's lips on her fingertips.

"This is bad, Ruth," she whispered. She didn't want anyone else to hear. "This is what they've been waiting for."

"I know." Ruth sat down without letting go of Tillie's hand. They sat together without speaking, Ruth's thumb making small circles on the inside of Tillie's wrist. James and Ernesto made their way over and sat down with them.

"Well, what do you think they'll do now?" Ernesto's tone was light, but his face was serious. He took a long drink of whatever it was Erwin was handing out.

"If they blame the Communists, I'm sure they'll start arresting people as early as tomorrow," Ruth answered, her voice just as light as his. To Tillie it sounded like they were talking about what to have for dinner. She watched James down his entire glass in one gulp, wipe his mouth, and then pick up the glass that she thought was supposed to be hers. He met her eyes, and she gave a nod, then he swallowed that one as well.

Dora and Adelaide stood off to the side, whispering to one another. Dora met Tillie's eyes and Tillie saw they were full of tears. "Dora," Tillie said. "Come sit down."

Dora took Adelaide's hand, and they joined the group in two of the overstuffed armchairs.

"I was just telling Adelaide we should try to get in touch with Dr. H. Try to join him in France once he arrives there." Ernesto reached out and took Dora's hand.

"James' mother is in France. We could all go. I'm sure we'd be safe there." Tillie looked at Ruth. Her eyes were fixed on a spot on the carpet, and she didn't nod along with James.

"Adelaide thinks it's safer to ride things out here, but I'm not so sure." Dora chewed a fingernail. "I keep saying to myself that it will all work out and be fine, but things just keep getting worse."

Erwin came over and leaned against the couch. "Who do you think set the fire?"

James shrugged. "Does it matter?"

Erwin frowned. "I guess not."

Adelaide cleared her throat. "Maybe it was an accidental fire? Buildings catch fire all the time." No one responded, and Tillie could tell none of them, not even Adelaide, believed it was an accident.

Karl appeared back in the doorway. "Magnus sends his best and wants you all to know you're welcome to stay as long as you need. He also wanted me to let you know we'll be closing to the public starting tomorrow. Only employees and those known in our community are welcome. No strangers will be permitted to enter the building unless they're here on the recommendation of someone we know." Karl nodded once, then left the lounge.

Dora sighed. "I'm going to bed." She patted Ernesto on the cheek. "Goodnight, loves." She looked at Ruth. "You should stay here tonight. I can go get some extra blankets from the dorm closet to set you up in here."

"Thanks Dora, but I think Tillie and I should go. I think it'll be worse tomorrow morning walking home. Once the fire is out, the SS will have nothing to do but arrest people."

Dora nodded. "If you change your mind, you know where all the extra blankets and pillows are."

Ruth stood, pulling on Tillie's arm. "C'mon." She looked down at James and Ernesto, a look of concern on her face. "Do you think you're okay here? They won't come here, right?" James shook his head and Ernesto sighed into his drink.

"I think we're okay. Why don't you two stay here tonight?"

Tillie shook her head. "No, we should go home." She looked over at Ruth. She had come to the institute right after her shift at the club. "Ruth, you're still wearing your tux."

Ruth just shrugged. "Does that matter?"

"What if they stop us? What will they do to a woman dressed like a man? I don't think it's safe for you to be dressed that way." Tillie felt the panic rising in her throat and it made it hard for her to swallow.

Ernesto tilted his head to one side, looking from Tillie to Ruth and then to James.

"James, you go with Tillie. Walk her home then turn and come back. I'll stay here with Ruth while she changes and then walk her home. I'm sure one of the girls has something that will fit her. It'll be like we're two couples out for the night."

He picked Ruth's hat off the small table where she left it after her shift and handed it to James. "Here. Borrow her hat so your hair is covered."

Tillie hurried to say, "That sounds like a good plan. "Thanks, Ernesto," before Ruth could dismiss the idea as ridiculous.

James nodded and held out his arm to Tillie. As they walked out into the frigid February air, they could hear shouts and screams around them. Tillie tightened her grip on James' arm, and she noticed his breathing speed up.

"It's okay," she whispered in his ear. "We're just two people out for an evening stroll. No one is paying attention to us."

There was a smokey haze floating over the streets, like they were walking through a dream, and the acrid smell of burning wood stung Tillie's eyes and throat. They could see a red glow just on the horizon and Tillie looked down at her feet. Seeing the Reichstag burning gave her such intense feelings of panic and fear, she didn't think she'd be able to keep walking if she stared at it any longer.

"I'm going to be afraid to read the paper in the morning," James said, before taking out his handkerchief and covering his mouth. The smoke grew thicker with every step they took.

Tillie chuckled. "I'm always afraid to read the paper."

James nodded, laughing along. "Aren't we all." They arrived at Tillie and Ruth's building, and he squeezed her hand. "Here we are. I'm sure I'll see you tomorrow, Tillie."

"Be careful walking home, James," she said over her shoulder. He waved and turned to hurry back down the way they came. The red glow in the distance had grown larger in the time it took for them to walk home and Tillie stood watching it, wondering how long the building would burn.

The next morning, Tillie called her father to let him know she had a terrible cold and wouldn't be at work. The kitchen floor was so cold on her bare feet, it almost burned. She carried two cups of coffee back to the bedroom and curled next to Ruth's warm body under piles of covers. Slipping her arm around Ruth's waist, she leaned in and kissed Ruth's neck. Slowly at first, but then with more urgency, until Ruth awoke and arched her body toward Tillie's mouth.

"What's the special occasion," Ruth joked between kisses.

"I just don't want the world to be real for a while," Tillie answered, and Ruth took her face into her hands.

Their eyes met and Ruth pulled Tillie into a deep kiss, tracing her lips with her tongue. Ruth pushed Tillie back onto the bed and she felt Ruth's hands touching every inch of her. Closing her eyes, she lost herself in Ruth's hands, her fingers, and her lips and forgot about the rest of the world.

Wrapped in tangled sweaty sheets, they sipped their coffee and laughed with one another, then made love several more times, before a hesitant knock echoed through the apartment.

Ruth rested her head against the inside of Tillie's thigh. "I guess our little honeymoon is over."

Tillie pushed her body up and Ruth laughed, then ran her tongue along the bone of Tillie's hip. Before they could go any further, though, the knock sounded again, this time louder.

Tillie groaned and fell back to the bed and Ruth gave her stomach a quick kiss before jumping up and putting on her robe.

Turning to look at the clock, Ruth gasped. "Tills, it's after one o'clock," she laughed. Giving Tillie a light smack on her bottom, she said, "We should do this more often. I feel five years younger."

They were still giggling when they opened the door to Dora, Adelaide, Karl, Ernesto, and James. Tillie's blood turned icy as she took in their horrified expressions and saw a newspaper clutched in Karl's hand. She moved to the side gesturing them inside and Ruth said, "I'll put on some tea" in a solemn voice.

Once they were all comfortably strewn around the kitchen, Karl began to read. His voice was loud and clear despite the small sniffs and strangled sobs coming from Dora and Adelaide.

"The burning of the Reichstag was intended to be the signal for a bloody uprising and civil war. Large-scale pillaging in Berlin was planned for as early as four o'clock in the morning on Tuesday. It has been determined that starting today throughout Germany acts of terrorism were to begin against prominent individuals, against private property, against the lives and safety of the peaceful population, and general civil war was to be unleashed."

He turned the page and then continued, only the slight quiver of his lip betraying his calm demeanor.

"By Order of the Reich President for the Protection of People and State."

He took a deep breath and Dora rose, stifling cries into her hand. She left the room, too overcome to listen to him continue to read.

"Articles 114, 115, 117, 118, 123, 124 and 153 of the Constitution of the German Reich are suspended until further notice. It is therefore permissible to restrict the rights of personal freedoms: freedom of expression, including the freedom of the press, the freedom to organize and assemble, the privacy of postal, telegraphic and telephonic communications. Warrants for house searches, orders for confiscations as well as restrictions on property, are also permissible beyond the legal limits otherwise prescribed."

Ruth drew a sharp breath in through her nose. "The President has taken away all our freedoms?" She looked widely around the room. "What does that mean?"

Karl carefully folded the paper and set it down on the table. "It means we're not safe. It means the Nazis have won."

CHAPTER 26

May 1933

The pounding on the door startled Ruth and Tillie out of their quiet dinner. They both stared at the door, tense, wondering who could be banging on their door after dark.

Ruth nodded to Tillie and got up from the table as the banging continued. She moved towards the door to look through the peephole when they heard James shout, "Open the door!"

Ruth rushed to the door and unlocked it; James came flying into the room past her into the kitchen. He was pale and sweating, trying to catch his breath.

"The books. All of Dr. Hirschfeld's books. They …" He closed his eyes. "They're stealing all his books," he choked out as tears leaked from his eyes. Ruth looked over at Tillie with alarm.

"What? What are you talking about?"

"Them! The Nazis. The creepy Hitler Youth. They broke into Magnus' library. They're destroying his lab, tearing apart his office, trying to destroy his notes and his writings. And they're stealing his books. We were in the lounge when the Nazis came.

"Ernesto and some of the others ran to the back library to try to save something. Anything they could find." For a moment, time seemed to stand still in the tiny kitchen. They all looked at one another, Tillie's hand covering her mouth, Ruth standing pale next to the refrigerator, and James, still panting from his run over.

Ruth chewed the inside of her cheek, then leaned forward to get her house key from the kitchen counter. She looked at the others. "Let's go."

Her words snapped them into action. They raced out the door, Ruth locking it behind them. Tillie shouted to them as they ran down the steps of the apartment building, "Are we going to get more help or should we get back to the institute?"

James took the steps two at a time. "The institute. We need help Ernesto and the others save what they can."

They ran as fast as they could through the streets of Berlin. The air had a chill in it even though it was the first week of May. They rounded the corner just in time to see a large group of young men carrying armfuls of books and pushing wheelbarrows down the steps of the institute. They were filled with papers, library books, and notebooks Tillie recognized from Dr. H.'s therapy office.

Her stomach dropped when she saw Arthur and Friedrich walking with the Nazi youth, their arms full of books. She grabbed Ruth's arm and pointed, and Ruth nodded. She started scanning the area for Ernesto, hoping she'd find him in the crowd of onlookers.

She caught sight of him, with other employees of Dr. Hirschfeld on the other side of the square, watching the men as well. There were so many of the Nazis; at least 100 and the air seemed to grow around them as they walked. Their bright red armbands looked like blood in the light from the streetlamps. Tillie shivered.

Tillie, Ruth, and James shrank into the shadows while the men passed them through the square, then raced into the building to see how bad it was. The bushes in the courtyard had been ripped out and there was dirt everywhere. Tillie winced as the glass crunched under their feet. Ducking, she stepped through the frame of the door, avoiding the sharp claws of the broken glass, reaching angrily inward, tinged red with the blood of those that weren't as careful. Ernesto and the other employees of the institute entered behind them, and Tillie could hear the gasps of shock and people crying as they walked through the lounge area. She heard someone in the back say, "Thank goodness Magnus is in France right now."

A different voice. "Has anyone phoned him?" A murmur broke out among the employees as they dispersed, some going to check the offices, others going to try to phone Dr. H. in France. Ruth took Tillie's hand, and when Tillie looked over at her, she saw that Ruth was crying. She looked over at James and he was white with terror, staring at the lounge.

The couches where they used to spend afternoons and evenings drinking and chatting had been ripped apart and thrown around the room. There was white stuffing like piles of snow all over the floor. Tillie stifled a shocked laugh at their favorite couch, comically looking like Santa Claus, white fluff spread over the bright red fabric. There was destruction in every direction.

After picking up the welcome desk, Adelaide pointed to the small holes in the walls and the nails on the floor. "They must have taken the artwork," Adelaide whispered. There were broken ink bottles everywhere and dark stains spread out over the carpet in pools that made the furniture look like it was bleeding.

Dora came running toward them. Her eyes were bruised, her nose looked painfully crooked, and there was blood on her dress.

Tillie gasped. "Dora! Are you alright?"

"His office is empty. They took everything." A sob ripped from her chest. "Even all our medical charts are gone." A few audible gasps could be heard from the others in the group. She shook her head. "I tried to stop them but there were too many. I think my nose is broken." As she cried, her tears mixed with the blood on her face and made red-tinged spots on the collar of her dress. "I haven't been back to the library yet."

All the employees exchanged glances and the group headed down the hallway, terrified of what they were going to find.

There was a small group that had already made it back to the library just standing at the doorway. The silence told Tillie exactly what they were going to see. Ernesto was in front of her, and she heard him whisper, "Oh my God."

She and Ruth pushed to get next to him to see into the library but there was nothing left to see. All the shelves were empty. There had been close to thirty thousand books in the massive room and now every single book was gone. Most of the shelves were broken and stray pages littered the ground. The tables, desks and chairs were overturned and lying haphazard along the now empty stacks. . The ladders used to go back and forth among the books on the top shelves looked like broken bones hanging at odd angles, some just dangling at their hinges.

The silence hurt Tillie's ears. Ruth spoke first. "What are they going to do with all the books?" She turned to look at Tillie, then her eyes moved to the rest of the group. "What could they want with all our books? All the work Dr. Hirschfeld has done?" No one answered her. They could hear the sobs coming from Dora. Both her medical journals were gone.

Then they heard the screaming.

"They're coming back!" Adelaide was running toward them from the front of the building. "The Nazis. They're on the road, shouting, marching back here. They have torches." For a split second no one moved. She turned a corner about six feet from them, still running. "There's an exit that way, I'm going to go back around to make sure everyone else is out."

Dora shouted, "Adelaide, wait, I'm coming too!" Then she shouted back over her shoulder, "Leave through the exit by the dorm rooms. Hide yourselves in the alleys behind the building!" She took off running after Adelaide, her feet pounding the green tiled floor like a drum.

At that moment, Tillie felt her arm being grabbed by Ruth on one side, and Ernesto on the other. She heard Ruth's urgent voice in her ear. "Run."

The feet around her sounded like a stampede. She felt hands pushing her forward and as they ran down the hallway, it seemed like the exit door continued to get farther and farther away. More screams came from people still behind her. "They're setting the building on fire."

Another voice, "There's so much smoke."

She heard James' shout, "Is everyone out? Is everyone with us?"

The door flew open, spilling them out behind the building. They all turned as one back to their beloved institute, the place where they all belonged and saw the wisps of smoke curling from a few of the back windows.

Tillie rubbed her arms and looked around. "We should probably keep moving, in case some of them come out here." Murmurs of agreement went up and the group started to move to one of the alleys to the side of the building. There were loud pops and crackles, and Tillie was too afraid to turn back around.

A voice rang out among the footsteps. "Where's Dora?" It was Erwin, from behind them.

"Where is she? Where's Adelaide?"

Adelaide's voice came from their left, she was leaning against one of the buildings. She spoke, her voice a harsh rasp. "She was right behind me, but said she needed to check the bathrooms and make sure everyone was out." Her voice broke into coughs. "She told me to run." Adelaide slumped down the brick wall behind her, dissolving into coughs and gags.

More voices sounded, calling her name. "Dora?" The voices were getting more frantic, running back toward the burning building. "Dora?"

Ernesto grabbed Tillie and started back toward the flames and smoke, shouting Dora's name. Tillie gestured to him, and they jogged around to the other side of the building where the dormitories were located and started shouting her name through the broken windows.

"Dora, can you hear us?" They could hear men's voices inside the building, shouting and more glass breaking. The front of the building was engulfed in flames, and she squinted into the broken windows trying to make out Dora in the haze of swirling smoke.

Deep in her chest, she felt a heavy sense of dread. Ernesto was shouting Dora's name, but Tillie had stopped and was standing, watching the building burn. "Ernesto," she said quietly.

He turned back to her. His blonde hair was wild, mixed with ash and dust, making a bird's nest on the top of his head. His face was caked in soot from leaning through the windows shouting for Dora.

Tillie shook her head "If she's still inside," Tillie trailed off. Ernesto turned and vomited and when he straightened there were streaks running down his face, his tears mixing with the soot and ash stuck to his skin.

They walked back to the others who stood watching the building burn when a sound started to travel to where they were standing. It became louder and louder and rose over the popping and crackling of the fire.

"Seig Heil, Seig Heil, Seig Heil," it was coming closer to where they were congregating.

Still looking for signs of Dora inside the inferno, Ernesto broke away from James, tears still streaming down his face.

"Murderers," he screamed at the large group of young men. They were waving their torches, chanting, and marching back down the main road.

The others in their group started whispering and Adelaide grabbed Ernesto's arm and tried to pull him back. "Ernesto," she hissed. "Stop it!" A few of the men marching in the back of the large group looked over into the shadows where Ernesto was standing. One or two of them stopped marching to stare.

Ruth's eyes narrowed and she started forward. Tillie heard her breathe in, readying to shout along with Ernesto but Tillie, seeing the danger in drawing attention to themselves, grabbed Ruth's wrist and shook her head. Then she said, "Ernesto, sweetie, you can't yell at them right now. If they hear you, they'll come for us."

Ruth stood next to her, arms crossed. Tillie could see Ruth out of the corner of her eye—the anger was coming off her in waves and her jaw was clenched.

She hissed in Tillie's ear, "Let them come over here. Let them see what they've done to us."

Tillie shook her head. "Ruth, those men don't care what they've done to us." Ruth's face fell and she dropped her arms to her sides in defeat.

"I know. They don't care." She stepped forward next to Ernesto. "Come on. You'll come stay with us." She wiped the tears from his face and took his hand in hers. They took one last look at the burning building and then turned to walk home.

Tillie and James had to each take one of Ernesto's arms. His body shuddered while he sobbed, and he struggled to put one foot in front of the other. He kept moaning, "But where is she?" over and over as they helped him move forward.

The sound of running footsteps from behind made them stop and turn. Heinz came toward them, covered in black soot and ash. "I found her. On the other side of the courtyard. She got out." He doubled over in a fit of deep coughs.

Ernesto pulled away from Tillie and Ruth and started running. "Where?" he shouted. Heinz pointed and that was all Ernesto needed. Ruth, Tillie, and James took off after him, running back toward the flames. They could tell the fire was going to take hours to burn out. The flames looked higher than ever. Ernesto rounded the corner and shouted, "Dora! Oh, thank God."

Dora was lying on the ground and from where they were, it looked like she was covered in ash. As Tillie got closer, she heard Ernesto scream as he kneeled down over her. She and Ruth ran to him and realized Dora wasn't covered in ash. Her entire body had been burned from head to toe. Her hair was almost gone, her fingers curled into painful claws. Her clothes were melted to her body in places and her calves and feet were black and charred. Tillie fought the urge to vomit when she saw the blood on the inside of Dora's unburned thighs.

Her eyes were open but as Tillie watched her it became clear she physically couldn't close them. Her skin looked scaly and gray. Adelaide and Erwin came running up behind them and Erwin shouted, "Oh, Dora!!" before Adelaide broke down into sobs.

Adelaide asked in a shaky voice, "Is she dead?" Almost in response, they all heard a broken, painful rasp come from Dora. She was still breathing, but barely. They all froze.

"Dora?" Ernesto whispered. "Oh honey." Tillie could see her eyes moving from looking directly up at the sky to where Ernesto was. Ernesto looked up at the crowd that had begun to surround them. "What do I do?" Everyone looked around, no one knew what to say.

Tillie knelt down next to Ernesto. The smoke coming off Dora's trembling body shimmered, and the gasoline smell filled her nostrils. "They set her on fire," she whispered, more to herself than anyone else.

She looked around, suddenly fearful the men would come back and noticed that the fire had spread across the entire building. The institute was engulfed in flames, but there were no sirens. No one was coming to help them.

"TILLIE!" Her head snapped around when she realized Ernesto was shouting at her. "You have to help me drag her farther away from the building." She shook her head looking down at Dora, whose wide eyes were going in and out of focus.

"It will be too painful; we can't move her." Tillie sat down on the pavement beside him and rubbed his back, while Dora rasped another painful breath and watched them. "Dora, honey. You have some burns, but I think you're going to be alright." Tillie hoped her voice sounded soothing. She watched as Dora's eyes went out of focus again. Tillie blinked back tears and kept her voice even. "Listen to my voice, love." She swallowed hard to break up the rock in her throat. "If you go to sleep, you'll wake up feeling so much better." Another raspy breath. Tillie could hear crying around her, and Ernesto's body shook with silent sobs next to her. "Dora it's okay, sweetie. Just go to sleep. We'll see you in the morning."

Dora's fingers moved, just a little, and she managed to rest her hand on top of Ernesto's. Her eyes met Ernesto's and Tillie thought she was trying to blink. Tillie saw her fingers move, ever so slightly, like she was squeezing Ernesto's hand under her own. She took another raspy breath, then her eyes went out of focus again. The rasping sounds stopped, and her fingers were still.

Ernesto broke into a wail and the others standing around Dora's body began to sob. Tillie stood up and buried her face into Ruth's arms and James took her place next to Ernesto. After several minutes, James looked up at them and said in a whisper, "We should go, before they come back." The others nodded and began to disperse, looking back at where Ernesto sat crying into James' arms.

The group was still standing watching their only home burn when Karl announced that he knew of a friend's flat where they would all be welcomed. His voice sounded far away.

Adelaide rubbed Tillie's back and whispered, "Be careful walking home," then dissolved into the darkness after Karl and the others. Soon it was just the four of them. James, Ernesto, Ruth, and Tillie stood next to the burning building and Dora's lifeless body, the flames casting sinister shadows wherever Tillie looked.

Ruth cleared her throat. "We need to go."

Tillie nodded but Ernesto let out another wail. "We can't just leave her here alone," he sobbed. James looked up at Ruth and Tillie, still rubbing Ernesto's back, his eyes red and puffy.

"We have to, sweetie," he whispered. "We can't do anything else for her." James nodded to Ruth, and she nodded back. Wiping away her own silent tears, she let go of Tillie and leaned down, helping James lift Ernesto to his feet. "C'mon, darling. Time to go home." Tillie stood, watching as they each put an arm around Ernesto's back and helped him walk.

Tillie looked around for something she could leave. A flower from a bush, a pretty rock, something so Dora wouldn't be left all alone in the dark. She couldn't find anything, so she took off her sweater and laid it over Dora like a blanket. She knelt down, the smell of burned flesh and gasoline causing a wave of nausea. She patted the top of what was left of Dora's hand and whispered, "Goodbye Dora."

She turned and followed Ruth and James, dragging Ernesto away from his adopted mother's body, listening to the small pops and crackles of the building on fire, punctuated by Ernesto's sobs.

✝

Several days later, she and Ruth were sitting at the kitchen table for dinner. "Should I get the boys? Maybe we can get Ernesto to eat?"

They were debating on whether to bother the boys when there was a light knock on the door. She and Ruth looked at one another, terror on their faces. The soft knock came a second time and when Tillie swung open the door, Adelaide and Nissa stood in their doorway, their faces stricken in horror.

"Oh, what now?" Ruth groaned. She could tell by Adelaide's face she was bringing more bad news.

"They're marching." She looked like she was going to be sick. "They have torches and they're marching through the streets."

Tillie still stood with her hand on the doorknob. "Marching to where?"

Adelaide spoke this time, her voice shaking. "They're burning the books."

Ruth's eyes widened in shock and terror. "What?"

"They're marching to the main square. Erwin and Heinz are staying over there with someone, they called us. They're burning our books in the square."

They exchanged glances and Ruth sighed. "I'll go get James and Ernesto." There was none of the hurry they had on Saturday. The boys came out from their bedroom, but they moved with resignation.

Tillie rose from the table and went to grab her sweater before she realized she had left it with Dora. She went into the bedroom and grabbed a sweater from Ruth's closet and a coat to give to Ruth. She walked back into the kitchen where James, Ernesto, Adelaide, Nissa, and Ruth stood. Their faces were pale and grim. She handed the coat to Ruth. "Here, in case it's cold. Let's go."

They walked slowly, like they were on the way to a funeral. To Tillie, it felt like they were. There were still a few men marching with their torches in the street, shouting as they walked, but for the most part the streets were empty.

As they drew closer, the men with torches grew in number and Tillie could feel Ernesto's rising tension in being so close to the Hitler Youth. She took his elbow in one hand and Ruth's hand in the other. "We should find a place where we can see but where we won't be in any danger." Ruth nodded and they veered to the left, cutting down an ally where they could continue toward the center of the square without being surrounded by torches and chanting.

There was a group of people standing on the steps of an apartment building across the street from the large pile of books surrounded by youth with torches. They started up the steps and Tillie could see that both women standing there were crying.

Wheelbarrows of books were being dumped onto the fire while the students dressed in the Nazi uniform stood by and cheered. Then Tillie saw it. At the top of one of the wheelbarrows, a bright yellow spiral bound book. It had to be Dora's case study. She felt Ernesto stiffen next to her and she knew he saw it too.

She sensed him looking for a way in, trying to figure out how best to get the journal, when a large, blonde boy heaved the contents of the wheelbarrow into the fire. They watched as the only record that Dora ever existed shriveled and wilted in the flames.

Ernesto let out a loud cry and turned into James' arms. Ruth pulled Tillie in closer, and Tillie stood there with her eyes closed, face buried in Ruth's neck, until she heard James draw a sharp breath.

They all followed his gaze and a line of youth with torches were following a soldier in an SS uniform holding what looked like a long pole. Tillie squinted to try and make out the large blob on the end of the pole, but it was Ruth who recognized what it was.

"Is that" she reached over to grab Ernesto's arm, "is that Dr. Hirschfeld's statue?" Ernesto nodded, too stricken to speak.

Tillie recognized it now. The marble bust of Dr. Hirschfeld from the entrance area of the institute. She had been so overwhelmed with all the destruction she hadn't even noticed it missing on Saturday. Ruth clutched her chest as she watched the men surrounded by women twirling the Nazi flag like batons. They marched down the middle of the road, heading straight for the large bonfire of books with Dr. Hirschfeld's marble bust.

They could hear someone speaking into a microphone in the square. Tillie heard the words "Exaggerated Jewish intellectualism is now at an end" coming from a voice that raised the hair on her neck.

"Goebbels," she whispered. Ernesto looked over at her through the tears, his brow furrowed.

Tillie cleared her throat. "It's Joseph Goebbels. That's who's speaking." The voice sped up, reaching a crescendo to match the flames stretching into the black sky.

"That is the mission of the young," Goebbels cried. "And therefore, you do well at this late hour to entrust to the flames the intellectual garbage of the past."

His voice rang out, reverberating off the buildings near the square so it sounded like he was everywhere, surrounding them. Screams and cheers rose from the crowd and Nazi flags waved in front of the massive pyre.

The groups of students continued to march toward the inferno with Dr. Hirschfeld's statue in front. Tillie watched as the glow of the flames distorted the eyes of the Nazi Youth, making them shine and dance. James whispered, "We should do something" but didn't move from the steps. Tillie knew there was nothing they could do. They watched as Dr. Hirschfeld's marble bust made its way to the bonfire, while the people with torches walking behind the soldier chanted. She held her breath as they got closer and closer to the fire and then, with a flourish, he heaved Dr. Hirschfeld's statue into the fire while all the people around him cheered. A sob escaped from Ruth's chest, and they clung to one another as their life from the institute burned.

All they could do was turn and walk back home, tears streaming down their faces.

CHAPTER 27

June 1991

Thea sat in her car and looked at the two-story house across the street. With its white facade and butter yellow front door and shutters, it looked bright and sunny. Welcoming. Like it was smiling at her. She looked down at the letter in her hands and her fingers shook slightly.

"Don't be nervous," she whispered to herself, turning off the car. Taking a deep breath, she left the cool shadows of the rental and stepped out into the midday heat. Her shoes echoed on the path up to the front door, the house glittering like snow under the watery Vermont sun. She had hardly walked ten feet when the sweat began to drip down her spine. She could hear the bugs buzzing in the trees all around her.

She stood in front of the yellow door and had to squint. The air was so thick and humid, she felt like she could swim through it. Thea took another deep breath and knocked. She waited, rolling from the balls of her feet to her tiptoes and back again. As she waited, she glanced around at the front of the house. The lawn, if you could call it that, was brimming with life. Every inch except for a few stone paths was built into a raised garden bed. Lavender, garlic, and rosemary peeked out from other bushes that Thea couldn't name.

She heard footsteps and stopped rocking, pulling herself up to her full five feet and lifting her chin.

The door swung inward to reveal a pretty, older woman with a heart-shaped face and a smattering of brown freckles across her tan skin. She was barefoot and wearing a sundress with buttons down the front. Her long gray hair was braided to one side and draped over her shoulder.

"Hi, may I help you?"

Thea cleared her throat. "I hope so. I'm looking for Ruth Birnbaum."

The older woman frowned. "Why?"

Thea held up the envelope in her hand. "I have something for her."

The woman narrowed her eyes and opened the door farther, putting her hands on her hips. "I'm sorry, my aunt is resting. I can take whatever that is and give it to her though."

"Oh. Well." Thea looked down at the envelope and shook her head. "I'm sorry, I really would prefer to give this directly to Ruth." The woman tilted her head and stared at Thea, her eyes bright and distrustful.

"No one calls her Ruth anymore. If you really need to give her something, you can leave it with me or in the mailbox. Have a nice day." With that, she swung the door closed in Thea's face, the distinct click of a deadbolt resounding through the quiet afternoon leaving her standing under the burning sky.

Back in the safety of her car she sat for a moment, wondering what to do next. She looked up at the sunny house and saw a swish of curtains in the upstairs window. She was being watched.

"Ugh." She growled to herself. She certainly wasn't leaving before getting this letter to its intended recipient. She bit the inside of her cheek, the annoyance building. "Screw it," she murmured. She got back out of the car, slamming the door behind her, and jogged up the path. Knocking again, she stepped back to look back at the window on the second floor where she saw the curtains flutter.

The older woman answered again, this time with a scowl on her face. "If you don't leave, I'm going to call the police."

Thea held up her hands. "Please, just hear me out. And then I'll go."

The woman crossed her arms in front of her. "You have approximately one minute."

"Uh. Okay. So, I'm here because I have this letter to give to your aunt. It's from my grandmother or at least, it was. I found it with all my grandmother's things, and it was returned as undeliverable back in 1942. I thought I would find your aunt and bring it to her." Thea took a deep breath. "And, well, that's it, I guess."

The woman furrowed her brow. "What do you mean, 'that's it'? Who even are you?"

"My name is Thea Brandon. Your aunt and my grandmother knew each other in the '30s and '40s. And maybe the '20s, too. I'm a little bit unsure of the timeline, exactly."

The woman's face hardened further. "We were a little preoccupied in the '40s." Her eyes narrowed. "I can't imagine she was keeping up with her correspondence while we were in Dachau. Please go."

Shame and anxiety rose like a wave inside her gut. She closed her eyes. "I'm so sorry," she said but it came out in a whisper. She could feel the hot tears pricking the backs of her eyelids and she fought to remain composed. She opened her eyes and realized the woman had dropped her arms to her sides and was staring, still suspicious, but now with some curiosity as well.

"What is it that you want, exactly?" The woman didn't look as angry, but Thea could still feel she was on thin ice.

"They knew each other." Thea took a breath. "That's all I know really." She held up the yellowed envelope. "It was marked 'Return to Sender' but I thought I could deliver it if I could find her. I thought I could deliver it for my grandmother. When I asked her about who Ruth was, she fell apart."

Thea's voice dropped to a whisper. "I've never seen her so upset. Not even when my grandfather died." She didn't really know what else to say.

She could see the woman's curiosity getting the best of her. Her resolved eyes flickered, and she checked her watch. "Look, can you come back tonight around seven? My son will be home then."

Thea nodded. "Of course, tonight at seven. I'll be back."

The woman nodded once and then closed the door and Thea heard the lock click into place a second time. She walked back to her car, her back slick with sweat. The curtains in the upstairs window moved again and she wondered who was up there watching her.

At seven p.m. sharp, Thea clicked back up the path relishing the cooler evening air. It was still hot, but more manageable without the sun frying her like an egg on the sidewalk. She knocked again and heard heavier footsteps than she had earlier that day.

The door swung open to a handsome face, dark brown eyes with high cheekbones, and a polite, wary smile on his lips. "Hi there, I'm Robert." He put out a bronze hand, large enough to make Thea's hand disappear. He looked a few years older than Thea. He stepped back from the door to let Thea pass through. "Come in."

Thea walked into the house, and it appeared just as cheerful inside as it did on the outside. The hallway leading into the kitchen was bright and a mirror hung above a side table making the space feel larger. Robert led her into a white kitchen with yellow cabinets and a large gray kitchen table with benches. It felt like she'd stepped into a farmhouse.

The woman from earlier sat at the kitchen table, a mug in front of her. She was still frowning. "Please," Robert said, gesturing to the bench. He sat down across from her, next to his mother.

"Okay, well first of all, thank you for seeing me. I know you didn't want to." She met the woman's dark eyes, and the same bright distrust from the afternoon stared back at her. "I'm so sorry, but you never told me your name."

The woman blinked. "Oh." She shifted on the bench and inhaled through her nose. "It's Miriam."

Robert squeezed Miriam's hand and then said, "Where are our manners? Let me get you a cup of tea." He got up and went to the cupboard, the clink of mugs and a tea kettle echoing through the room.

An awkward silence hung in the air while Miriam sipped from her mug. "So." She set her mug down and folded her fingers around it. "You said you needed to give something to my aunt."

Thea took the letter out of her purse and set it on the table. "Yes. As I said earlier today, your aunt and my grandmother knew one another. I think they lived in Berlin together, but I'm not sure."

Miriam held up a hand. "And as *I* said we were in a camp in the '40s. Along with almost everyone else either of us knew. Plus, Ruth Birnbaum isn't exactly an uncommon name. She doesn't even go by Ruth. She's gone by her middle name since I was ten years old when we …" she paused and cleared her throat. "When we left Germany," she finished. "Are you sure your grandmother isn't confusing my aunt with someone else?"

Thea swallowed hard. The fact was, she wasn't sure. All she had were the photos and what the Red Cross told her. Looking at the envelope in her hands, she started to feel swirls of panic deep in her stomach. The air between them was thick, and Thea tried to figure out what to say next when the sound of a soft cough made her jump and turn.

A brittle old woman stood in the doorway leading into the kitchen. She had eyes the color of amber with flecks of green and a shock of white hair. Her skin was translucent, and Thea could see the blue veins lining her hands under the age spots.

"Aunt May!" Miriam jumped up from the table. "What's wrong? Do you feel alright?" The old woman smiled as Miriam fussed over her.

"Yes, yes, I'm fine." Her voice quivered with age and was soft and gentle. "I heard more voices than usual and decided to come down and say hello." She winked at Thea.

"I wish you wouldn't come down the stairs by yourself."

"Pish. Miri, I'm fine." She waved off the concern, moved with surprising ease to the table and sat down next to Thea.

"May Birnbaum, pleasure to meet you." She held out her hand and Thea took it. It was smooth and cool, and she smelled like oranges and soap.

She smiled. "I'm Thea Brandon. It's nice to meet you."

May nodded and took the cup of tea from Robert. "So," she began, "to what do we owe the pleasure of you sitting at our kitchen table this evening?" Her face was soft and kind.

Thea swallowed hard. "I believe you knew my grandmother."

May sipped her tea. "Is that so? I've known a lot of people. What's your grandmother's name?"

"Matilda Weber." She paused. "But my grandfather used to call her Tillie. It was a pet name my grandfather used."

The smile vanished from the old woman's face, and she swayed. Robert was setting the tea down in front of Thea and rushed to May's side. "Aunt May, are you alright?"

She gripped his arm, her knuckles white, and stared at Thea. "Did you say Tillie? Tillie Weber?"

Thea turned her eyes to Miriam, who looked as horror stricken as she felt. She nodded, unable to speak. The old woman looked pale and more fragile than she had five minutes before. Tears were swimming in her eyes, and she looked down at Thea's hand, the envelope resting under her bright blue fingernails.

"What's that?" She pointed.

"Oh. This is why I'm here actually. I found this in my grandmother's desk." She picked up the envelope and handed it to May. She could see the paper quivering in May's grasp, from old age or from shock, Thea wasn't sure. She watched May's watery eyes take in the addressee and run her gnarled fingers over the 'Return to Sender' stamp in the center.

"February 1941," she murmured, reading the postmark date. "I was in Dachau by then." She wasn't talking to anyone in the kitchen now. She was lost in her own memories.

They all sat quietly, Robert continuing to crouch next to his aunt, rubbing her arm. Miriam, biting her lower lip, kept glancing from May to Thea, as if unsure what to do next.

May sniffed and then looked up at Thea. "She wrote to me often when they first left Germany. First at our old apartment, then through a mutual friend. I was living in his cellar; he had me hidden while we worked with the resistance." Thea nodded, encouraging her to continue.

May took a deep breath. "We were caught, of course." She smiled and shrugged. "Most of us were. We had a few good years, though. Fighting back." Her gaze turned warm as she settled her eyes back on Thea's face. "Your name is Thea?"

She nodded. "Well, it's Theadora. I was named after my great-grandmother. My grandfather's mother." She amended, "At least, someone that was close to my grandfather. I never met her though."

At this, the tears that were brimming on her sparse lashes fell and her face crumpled. With a quivering lip, she nodded. "Her name was Dora."

Thea nodded again, confused at this reaction. "Did you know her?" May put a hand to her mouth and, closed her eyes as the tears ran freely.

At this, Miriam stood. "I think it's time for you to go." Her voice was sharp and cut through the emotion in the room like a knife.

Robert, who now was sitting on the floor in between May and Thea, looked up at his mother. "Mom, clearly May knows the woman who wrote this letter."

"She is ninety years old," Miriam hissed between clenched teeth. "This cannot be good for her."

May's eyes popped open, and she glared at Miriam. "First of all, I'm not a child. Second, sit down because we're not done here yet." Miriam lowered herself back into her chair, a crease of worry between her eyes.

"Aunt May, are you sure?"

At this, May's eyes narrowed further. "For heaven's sake, Miri. I'm not dead yet. Stop acting like I'm made of glass." Robert hid his snort of laughter under a fake sneeze on the floor next to Thea.

She looked down and their eyes met. He smiled warmly and winked at her, and she felt a smile tug at her own lips. He patted her hand perched on her knee and he pulled himself up to stand.

Leaning forward, he whispered, "They fight like this all the time, don't feel awkward." Then he walked around to sit at the head of the table. He folded his hands in front of him and then said, "Well, I believe you have some mail to open, Auntie May."

With shaking hands, she pulled the soft paper from the already opened envelope and scanned it, smoothing the wrinkles with her hands. A small smile tugged at her lips at the end of the letter.

"Give my love to Berlin," she gave a quiet chuckle. "That's how she signed every letter. I think she missed the city as much as she missed me." She put the papers to her face and took a deep breath. "She would always spray her perfume on the paper." She closed her eyes and held the letter to her chest.

After what felt like an eternity, May set the letter down. Without looking at Thea she said, "You said you found this?"

Thea nodded. "In her desk."

"Do you mean that you had to go through her things," she paused, then swallowed hard. "Did you have to go through her things without her?"

"Yes. When she moved out, I started going through her study and her bedroom and I found this letter. So, I decided to try and track you down. She had never mentioned you and, honestly, I just needed something to do after she left." She shifted, embarrassed at how sad and alone she sounded.

May's head snapped up. "When she *moved* out?"

Thea nodded, confused again. "Yes, she had to move out about a year ago. Into a memory care facility."

May reached out and gripped Thea's arm with a surprisingly strong hand. She squeezed and whispered, "Is Tillie still alive?"

Watching May's face, Thea smiled. "Yes, she's alive."

May deflated like a balloon and buried her face into her hands, sobbing. "She's still alive," she kept repeating, over and over. No one said a word; they all let May cry and Robert stood, his long arm brushing Thea's hand to give May a tissue.

"I have to see her," May hiccupped. "Where do you live? Where is she?"

At this, Thea turned to look at Miriam, terrified of the woman's angry stare. "Uh," Thea began. "We live in Ohio." She heard Robert click his tongue and Miriam scoffed.

"Ohio. That's hundreds of miles. Aunt May, there is no way." Miriam shot daggers across the table at Thea, who suddenly felt very, very small.

"Um, Ms. Birnbaum?" Thea took the old woman's hand in her own. May dabbed her eyes with the crumpled tissue. "The thing is my grandmother," Thea stopped, not wanting to upset the old woman further.

She waved a hand after dabbing her eyes. "Please, sweetie, call me May."

"May." Thea took a deep breath. "My grandmother, she has

dementia." She dropped her eyes to focus on the wrinkled hand clinging to hers. "It's why I didn't really know exactly who you were. I couldn't ask her about what I had found. She hasn't recognized me in months. She used to have good days but," she stammered, "not really anymore." Thea brushed a tear from her eye and tried to keep her voice even. "I don't know if she would know you."

May let go of Thea's hand and put a finger under Thea's chin, tilting her face up to look into her hazel eyes. They were still wet with tears and looked even more green. Her face was kind but determined. "Doll, Tillie would know me, even on her deathbed."

Thea shook her head. "She doesn't even recognize her own reflection sometimes. She doesn't remember when my grandfather died or my uncle." She couldn't keep the tears in any longer. They ran down her face as she looked into May's hazel green eyes. "I just don't want you to be disappointed."

May's head tilted to the side. "Your grandfather died? Ernesto?"

"Um. Ernie. Yes. He had a heart attack back in 1970."

Her eyes looked past Thea, contemplating. "And your uncle. James?"

Thea furrowed her brow. "Yes," she answered slowly. "He had cancer. He died last year."

May shook her head. "They were all here. All this time. I thought they stayed in Portugal; I had no idea they came to the States."

Thea stared. "I never knew they were in Portugal. I thought they came to the States right after World War I."

May, still wearing an expression of profound grief, settled her gaze on Robert. "Darling, can you make us more tea? It seems I have a few stories to relay to Tillie's granddaughter."

CHAPTER 28

July 1934

Everything felt gray. Tillie looked around her small kitchen. Ruth stood at the sink washing dishes and the boys sat at the kitchen table drinking tea, but it seemed the color had been leached out of everything around them.

Tillie pulled on her coat. "I'm heading to work." They all nodded in her direction, but no one smiled or looked up. She leaned in and kissed Ruth on the cheek. "Maybe try to get out of the house today?"

She glanced back at the boys sitting at the table. Ruth nodded and pushed her body into Tillie's. "Have a good day, doll. We'll be here when you get home."

She was surrounded by red flags and Nazi armbands on her train ride. Multiple people on the train put up their arm to those wearing the emblem of the Nazi party on their biceps, praising them for their allegiance to Adolf Hitler. Tillie tried to look small on the train and focused her eyes out of the train window, ignoring the flashes of red, black, and white they passed on her way to her father's office.

Upon arriving at the office, Tillie saw the stack of *Der Angriff* on her desk waiting to be placed around the office, in the kitchen, and in the waiting room. Sighing and removing her coat she picked up the latest copy of Goebbels' paper and began to scan the articles. The words *Röhm Putsch* jumped out at her, and she sat down, focusing more.

There was something about a supposed coup that was being planned by Ernst Röhm. She and Ernesto both knew of Röhm; he sometimes came to the clubs, and it was no secret that he was a friend of Dr. Hirschfeld. Röhm, Tillie recalled, had even been to a few of Dr. Hirschfeld's lectures in the past.

She read on, noticing the continued emphasis on the danger Röhm posed, his plans to overthrow the government, and how the Brownshirts were not true Germans.

"These men have been removed, these stains to our German moral fiber and we will not allow those who wish to do us harm to continue with these acts against our beloved country. The Führer has addressed the Reichstag and we have come away knowing that these executions were, in fact, the only possible step in continuing to keep our country safe from those that wish us to fail, to do us harm, to ruin our purity. Moving forward, we will not allow these unsavory characters to sully our mission. The officers who so honorably serve us will henceforth be keeping lists of those who fall into step with those that engage in degenerate acts. Those acts will be considered a threat to our very way of life and will not be tolerated."

Tillie felt her blood turn cold. Röhm was dead; murdered by his own government. And it was clear they would be coming after the rest of them. She set the paper down and stood, trying not to panic. She felt snakes in her gut, writhing and gnawing at her insides, and she fought the urge to vomit. Pulling her coat back on, she pushed in her chair with trembling fingers.

"Tillie, darling, what are you doing?" Her father arrived at the office and was striding across the carpet to get to his own office, a smile on his face and a small pastry in his left hand.

Tillie swallowed. "Papa, I'm not feeling so well. I think I should go home." She hoped her voice didn't sound as small and quivery as she felt.

Her father frowned, taking in her appearance. "You do look a bit peaked. I don't want to let you leave if you're under the weather. What if you swoon on the train?" He shook his head. "No, darling, better to stay here and rest." His eyes fell to the *Der Angriff* on her desk, and he looked up to meet her pale face.

"Yes, well." He stammered. "The paper has you upset today, hasn't it? You never did have the stomach for violence." He sighed and walked toward her, wrapping his arm around her shoulder. "Darling, listen," he began. "These men were dreadful. Criminals. Degenerates. They engaged in acts against God and country and our Führer was just ensuring they didn't do anything to jeopardize our future."

He patted her on the back while Tillie's vision swam. She tried to tune out his words as she walked to the kitchen, but he just kept talking, following her. "Sometimes, killing is necessary, dear, when we're protecting what's rightfully ours. Herr Goebbels will be in to see me in a few minutes, I'm sure he'd be willing to discuss this with you further, if you'd like."

It was all Tillie could do just to shake her head and collapse onto the sofa in the kitchen. Her father shoved his uneaten pastry into her hand and stroked her hair. "Tillie," he said softly. "The Röhm Purge was a necessary evil. What would happen if good men just stood by doing nothing?"

Tillie continued to sit in stunned silence and watched her father walk out of the room before hurling the Danish at the wall. Crumbs of flaky crust and bits of jelly exploded upon contact, giving Tillie an overwhelming feeling of satisfaction. Taking a deep breath, she reached up to try and rub out the headache she felt beginning behind her eyes, only to feel tears running down her cheeks. Her father's words rang in her ears.

What would happen if good men just stood by, doing nothing?

After a few moments, she willed herself to stand and venture back out into the office. She sat down at her desk, trying to decide what to do next.

"Matilda?" The voice made her jump and look up. Joseph Goebbels stood over her, his face creased with a mixture of concern and annoyance. "Why are you still in your coat?" He folded his arms over his chest. "Are you feeling feverish?"

Tillie shook her head and cleared her throat. "No, sir. I just arrived a few minutes ago and went to the kitchen first, so I just hadn't had a chance to remove my coat."

He nodded, but his expression didn't change. "I'm here to speak to Anthony, is he in yet?"

Tillie shook her head a second time. "Not yet, sir." She met his gaze and started to shrug off her coat.

"Did you read the paper today, Matilda?" His eyes were narrow, and his head slightly tilted.

"Yes, sir." Her voice was barely above a whisper.

"There are two kinds of people in Germany right now, Matilda. Those that are National Socialists and those trying to destroy our country." He paused. "There is no third option."

She dropped her eyes to her desk and her heart pounded so hard she was convinced he could hear it.

"Those that support our cause will be rewarded. And those that do not," he paused again and dropped his voice an octave, "will not."

Before Tillie could respond, footsteps sounded in the lobby and Anthony Grandelis appeared in the doorway of the waiting room flanked by several other men Tillie didn't recognize. "Joseph, am I late or are you early?" He looked at his watch.

Goebbels waved a hand. "Oh, I'm early. I always enjoy arriving in time to have a chat with Matilda." Tillie could see Herr Grandelis behind Goebbels rolling his eyes.

"Yes, well, we've all arrived so let's let Tillie get started on her day. I believe we have a rally to begin planning."

Goebbels nodded without taking his eyes off Tillie. He blinked and then turned, following the group of men into her father's office, closing the door behind them.

✝

Tillie rubbed her eyes and looked over at the small clock on her bedside table. It was six a.m. Groaning, she willed herself up out of bed with as little movement as possible so as not to wake Ruth. The apartment was quiet and dark; Tillie was the only one used to waking up for a regular job so even on the weekends she was up hours before the rest of the group.

She settled down at the kitchen table and spread out the most recent information she'd taken from her father's office. She knew they were helping to plan the latest rally in Nuremberg, but she was more interested in the maps she found in her boss's desk pinpointing different spots throughout Germany. There was a star over Dachau, north of Munich. Another just north of Berlin, a third star near Weimer, and a fourth near Hamburg.

She was squinting at the paper while reading through some of Anthony's shorthand when there was a soft knock at the front door. So soft, Tillie wasn't even sure she heard it. When it came a second time, Tillie rose from the kitchen table, quickly throwing a blanket over the notes she'd been pouring over.

Cracking open the door and peeking through the chain, Tillie saw a small woman standing in front of the door nervously looking over her shoulder. Tilting her head to the side, Tillie could see she shared Ruth's dark hair and chiseled cheekbones.

"May I help you?" Tillie asked through the slit in the door.

The woman cleared her throat. "I'm looking for Ruth."

Tillie didn't move the chain. "And you are?"

The woman folded her hands in front of her and looked right into Tillie's eyes. She had the same small green flecks in her irises. "I'm her sister."

Cecilia Meyer sat with her long, white fingers wrapped around a steaming mug of tea while Tillie tidied the kitchen. Ruth's sister was looking around, her eyes wide. "So," she began. But she didn't say anything else.

"Um, Ruth is sleeping. I can get her," Tillie picked up the last of her notes and shoved them into the pantry without putting them away in the hidden cubby behind the canned peaches. Cecilia nodded without responding.

Tillie pulled the bedroom door closed behind her and hissed, "Ruth!" The figure under the white blanket stirred and a soft moan escaped from the large mound. "Ruth!" Tillie said again with more urgency.

"What?" Ruth sat up, her hair sticking up in odd angles, large purple circles under her eyes.

"Your sister is here." Tillie pulled her bathrobe tighter around her body.

Ruth's eyes grew round, and her face drained of all color. "My sister? Cecilia? That's not possible."

"Well, I'd say it's very possible, as she is sitting at our kitchen table drinking our tea right now."

Ruth jumped out of the bed and then staggered a bit. Trying to smooth down her hair and pull on a pair of pants at the same time, she lost her balance and went crashing to the floor. Tillie closed her eyes, rubbed her forehead, and felt a bubble of laughter rising.

A creak behind them made Tillie jump. There in their bedroom doorway was a shorter, rounder version of Ruth, her hands on her hips. She tilted her head to the side to address her younger sister on the floor. "Hello, Ruthie."

Once Ruth was properly clothed, they all sat around the kitchen table, the silence hanging like a wet blanket between them.

Tillie snuck into the spare bedroom and hissed for the boys to stay where they were no matter what. James asked about having to go to the bathroom and Tillie nodded at the water jug on the bedside table. James followed her gaze, then looked back at her, eyes wide with horror. Ernesto just groaned and flopped back into their bed.

Tillie made her way back to the kitchen in time to see Ruth narrow her eyes in Cecilia's direction. "Should I even bother to ask how Mother and Father are? It's not like they care how I am."

Cecilia bit her lip for a moment, then looked up and met Ruth's eyes. "Mother and Father don't know that I'm here."

"Of course not." She made an impatient face and raised her eyebrows. "Why are you here? Are you alright?"

Cecilia's eyes snapped to Tillie for just the briefest moment. "Of course, I'm alright," she responded curtly. "It's you that," she stopped, taking a deep breath to calm herself. "I'm here because I wanted to warn you."

Ruth's brow furrowed. "Warn me? About what?"

Cecilia tapped her fingers on the side of her mug. "There's a place. A building." She took a deep breath. "A jail. It's near our farm. We see the Nazis bringing in truckloads of people. Prisoners. They don't come out. It started just before the Reichstag fire and hasn't stopped."

She met Tillie's eyes, then Ruth's. "If anything, since the fire last year, the number of people going in has doubled." She took a sip of tea. "We've been warned not to go near the fences or the gates. Two of my husband's friends were sneaking around the perimeter last May. The men were forced inside of the prison and kept overnight." She shook her head. "They were not permitted to discuss what happened, but they made it clear to the rest of us to stay away from the fence."

Tillie stood and went to the closet. Retrieving a stack of papers in a purple folder from the closet, she came back to the table and laid them out. "You live in Dachau?"

Cecilia nodded and Tillie opened the folder. In it were notes about Dachau, the prison camp for Communists, and lists of others they were planning on including to arrest and take there.

Cecilia's eyes grew wide. "Where did you get those?" She recoiled from the papers and looked around the room, as if she expected Hitler himself to jump out from behind a curtain.

"My father works closely with high level members of the Nazi party," Tillie couldn't keep the bitterness out of her voice.

"Wait." Ruth's voice was sharp and both Tillie and Cecilia jumped. Ruth lowered her voice and then asked, "Why would you need to warn me about this?"

Cecilia's eyes narrowed. "Because I know you. You live this life," she gestured to Tillie and then around their tiny kitchen, "and I know you'll be next. You think these men hate Jews?" She laughed without humor. "They hate your kind more."

Ruth reached over and took Tillie's hand. Cecilia's eyes rested on their intertwined fingers, and she shifted in her chair. "We know," Ruth said, her voice like ice.

Tillie felt Ruth's hand squeeze her own and knew she was thinking of Dora lying on the ground after being set on fire by the Nazis. Being attacked and then burned like she was nothing but trash. Tillie closed her eyes trying to force the memory from her mind's eye.

Ruth stood and smirked at her sister. "Thank you for coming, but as you can see, we have some inside information. We already knew about the jail in Dachau. I appreciate that you were concerned enough to come and warn me though."

Cecilia stood and nodded. "We're planning on leaving Germany soon. We'll likely go North to Aunt Muriel's. Mother and Father are refusing, you know how much our mother hates Poland. But I'm hopeful we'll be able to convince them." Her eyes flicked to Tillie. "I would suggest you do the same."

Tillie smiled and opened her mouth to respond that they also had plans to get out, but Ruth interrupted her. "We will not be leaving Germany. But thank you." Cecilia's eyes rested on Tillie's face for a moment before she turned, walking out their front door without a goodbye.

CHAPTER 29

August 1934

"He's dead!" Tillie looked up from her desk where she was organizing a few Nazi client folders for her father.

Herr Grandelis was taking long strides across the office and his voice rang out. "Vincent, did you hear me?"

Tillie's father poked his head from his office door. "Who's dead?" His voice was full of alarm.

"Hindenburg." Herr Grandelis' eyes were bright, and his face was flushed.

"You must be joking." Her father opened his office door and welcomed Herr Grandelis in, leaving the door cracked behind them.

Tillie moved her chair closer and leaned forward, closing her eyes to try and hear what they were saying. "What do you think will happen now?" her father was saying.

"Well, I would think that the Führer would be set to take the presidency," Herr Grandelis responded. "Hindenburg was the only thing standing in the way of a complete party takeover. Without those traitors in the SA, it's only a matter of time."

Her father said something in response that Tillie couldn't make out and Herr Grandelis laughed. She heard footsteps coming toward her, so she pushed herself back to her desk. Her father exited his office first and patted her shoulder. "Tillie, this calls for a celebration. I think we should plan a dinner for tomorrow evening. Phone your mother to let her know to get started on the menu. I'm sure all the phone lines are quite busy but call and leave a message with Herr Goebbels and Herr Himmler inviting them to dinner at my house for tomorrow." He turned to Anthony.

"Do you want to touch base with Herr Göring or would you like Tillie to call him?"

Herr Grandelis' eyes swept over to Tillie and then nodded. "She can send him an invite as well. I have things to deal with."

Her father clapped his hands. "Wonderful. Tillie, why don't you invite Ernesto as well? Let's show Herr Goebbels what a fine citizen your beau is?"

Tillie nodded and kept her eyes on her desk, but she could feel Herr Grandelis' stare on her face. He cleared his throat. "Are you sure that's wise, Vincent? I really don't know my son's political affiliation these days and I'd hate to cause undue stress to our relationship with our clients."

Her father scoffed. "Nonsense. Tillie isn't a Communist and neither is Ernesto. You're judging him for things he believed at sixteen. He's a man now; I'm sure his political leanings have grown."

Tillie risked a glance at Herr Grandelis' face and regretted it immediately. His skin was blotchy and red, and she could see a vein popping out of his forehead. She could tell he was doing his best to keep his voice measured and calm. "Vincent, inviting Ernesto is a mistake." He didn't wait for a response and turned to storm back to his office, slamming the door behind him.

Her father shook his head. "I just can't understand someone who would write their child off so completely over something that happened ten years ago."

"Can I skip the invite for Ernesto?" Tillie's mouth was dry.

Her father paused, then nodded once. "No. Invite him. I think it would be good for Anthony to see Herr Goebbels influence Ernesto a bit. Anthony will see that Ernesto is a good German boy who just didn't understand politics when he was sixteen. Maybe then all of this nonsense can be forgotten."

Her father turned to her with a twinkle in his eye. "You and Ernesto are such a handsome German couple. Despite what Anthony may think." A smile started to bloom on his face. "You know, Herr Goebbels is planning to bring the Führer to our office at some point and I would love the opportunity to show him our commitment to continuing good German bloodlines."

†

"Come in, come in." Her mother bustled Ernesto and Tillie through the doorway and helped them out of their coats. "Don't you two look lovely." Her mother smiled at them for a moment, then reached forward to tuck a strand of Tillie's coppery brown hair back into the bun set at the nape of her neck.

"Herr Goebbels is coming tonight, so we need to look our best." She sighed. "Your fathers are very important men in the Party, which means *you* are going to be watched." Her mother raised her eyebrows at them. "This is important. You need to be the perfect Germans tonight."

Tillie nodded, while Ernesto answered, "Yes, ma'am."

They followed her into the kitchen. Tillie's hand gripped Ernesto's so hard, her knuckles were white. Standing around a large crystal punch bowl were Ernesto's parents, his brother Tommy, and her father. "Ahh, don't you two look lovely." Her father hurried over and gave her a kiss on each cheek. Then, he stood back and scrutinized her.

Furrowing his brow, he addressed Tillie's mother. "Alice? Can you take Tillie and rouge her cheeks a bit? Maybe get her some lipstick. She looks so pale." Her mother nodded and pulled on Tillie's arm, leading her away from Ernesto and the kitchen, while Ernesto watched her go, his eyes wide and his jaw clenched.

"So," Vincent reached out and cuffed Ernesto on the shoulder. "How are you doing, young man? I haven't spoken to you in quite some time."

Taking the cup of punch from Tillie's father, Ernesto gave a tight smile. "I'm fine, sir. Thank you."

"And what are you up to these days? Still working in the museum archives?" Vincent smiled and sipped his punch.

Ernesto's eyes flashed and he turned his eyes from Vincent's face to his own father's. "The Nazis destroyed my museum. I'm currently without employment."

There was an awkward silence. Tommy was unrecognizable sitting at the table in his Hitler Youth uniform. The red armband was bright against the brown button-down shirt. Ernesto's eyes darted from his brother to his father and back again.

"Actually," Ernesto continued, "I believe it was the Hitler Youth that destroyed my building. And they murdered a very dear friend of mine inside." Tommy swallowed and shifted in his chair. "You wouldn't know anything about that, would you Tommy?"

The room was tense and quiet when Tillie returned with pink cheeks and red lips. She met Ernesto's gaze and raised her eyebrows, but the doorbell rang, and the tension was broken. Tillie's father cleared his throat. "Yes, well, maybe let's keep the 'destruction' talk to a minimum, shall we?" Tillie could see the crease deepen on his forehead as he gave a backward glance to her and Ernesto standing at the counter, worry etched in the crinkles around his eyes. Ernesto's family and her parents left them standing alone in the kitchen, and she heard the front door open and loud greetings being exchanged.

She gave him a small nod and took a deep breath. "You need to keep it together tonight," she whispered. "I know you don't want to, and they don't deserve it, but we need to get through tonight unscathed." He grunted and didn't look at her. "For James," she breathed and this time he did look in her direction. His eyes quickly filled with tears, and he nodded, blinking them away. "Come on," Tillie said. "We need to go play nice." He didn't respond but followed her into the living room where the rest of the men were standing together, their red armbands joining them together like makeshift chains.

"Hello, gentlemen," Tillie said cheerfully, and all the men turned.

"Matilda!" Göring's loud, boisterous voice boomed in the small room. "You're looking lovely as always, darling." His smiling eyes went from Tillie to Ernesto. "Is this your fella?" He took two large strides to shake Ernesto's hand. "How are we doing, young man?"

Ernesto didn't smile but took Göring's hand. "Actually, we've met sir."

"Have we? Well, I meet a lot of people touring with the Führer, so forgive me for not recalling your face."

"No, I'm Ernesto Grandelis. I'm Anthony's oldest son." There was a pause and Göring's smile faltered. He recovered quickly, but Tillie and Ernesto caught it.

"Oh of course. My apologies." His eyes darted from Ernesto to Tillie, his face strained. "You look so much older than the last time I saw you." Ernesto nodded again, his lips in a grim line.

"I didn't realize your son would be joining us." Goebbels' soft voice came from behind Göring, and Tillie's stomach clenched. Göring's face had turned hard, and his eyes were narrow on Ernesto's face.

Tillie's mother broke in. "Is there a problem?"

Goebbels gave a small shrug. "I was under the impression Ernesto isn't a fan of our Führer. And that Ernesto seems to know what's better for Germany than our Chancellor does."

A thick silence settled over the room.

"You know," Ernesto grabbed Tillie's hand and pulled her arm so hard, her wrist cracked. "I can see we aren't welcome here. We should probably just go."

At that moment, the bell rang again, and they all froze, Ernesto's hand squeezing Tillie's finger bones hard.

"Ahhh," Goebbels smiled. "That'll be Heinrich. How wonderful."

Tillie's heart was beating so hard her chest hurt and the fear was making her legs tingly and wobbly. Ernesto's palm was starting to feel damp in hers and she could feel the distress coming off him in waves.

"Sorry I'm late everyone," Himmler bustled into the living room, a frumpy woman trailing behind him.

"You all know my wife, Margarete." A small blonde girl who looked about five, with her hair in braids, walked in between them.

"This is my daughter, Gudrun." He looked down at the small child with a smile on his face, his eyes warm. "I hope you don't mind her attendance at dinner this evening."

He looked up and his face changed, taking in the tense mood. "Is everything alright?"

"Heinrich, do tell us," Goebbels' voice was quiet and even, "what exactly gets you thrown into a labor camp these days?"

Tillie felt Ernesto stiffen next to her. Her father cleared his throat. "Why don't we head into the dining room and enjoy some appetizers before our meal?" Her father started walking but no one else moved. She met her father's eyes and for the first time, she saw very real fear behind them.

Heinrich laughed. "Oh, I would say just about anything could get you thrown into Dachau. It just depends on the kind of mood I'm in." His wife laughed and he winked at her. "Why do you ask?"

Goebbels settled his eyes on Tillie's. "Just making conversation." His lips curled and she fought a shudder. "You know, Vincent, you're right. I am a bit hungry." He set his punch glass down and nodded. "Why don't you lead the way?"

Her father nodded and led the dinner guests to the dining room where there were platters of crackers and cheese waiting. Tillie and Ernesto stood back to let Himmler and his family pass by. "We should probably go," Ernesto whispered in Tillie's ear. Tillie nodded.

"We'll wait for everyone to go into the dining room," she whispered back. "Then we'll just leave. I'll tell my father tomorrow I wasn't feeling well." They waited, their backs up against the wall drinking their punch and pretending to be in deep conversation until all the guests had filtered out.

Ernesto set his cup down and walked to the door, Tillie's hand tight in his. "Our coats!" Tillie pointed up the steps. He nodded and went up two steps at a time as quietly as he could.

"Going so soon?" a silky voice came from behind her. She turned and Goebbels stood in the doorway separating the hallway from the kitchen.

"Oh, yes. Unfortunately, I'm not feeling well." She smiled but it felt tight on her lips.

"I'm sure." He didn't move but raised his eyebrows while he stared at her. "Matilda, why do you insist on damning yourself?"

"I'm sorry?" She took a step back and looked up the stairs. Ernesto was at the top with their coats in his hand, but he stopped when he saw her face.

"You're spending all your time with these undesirables. You insist on aligning yourself with political dissidents. While I hold you in high favor, that cannot protect you forever. I just don't understand why you are engaging in such unladylike behavior."

Tillie felt a wave of anger. "With all due respect, why would you keep me on staff if you thought I was a Communist? Why would you keep me on staff if you had evidence that I was engaging with what you consider the enemy?"

Goebbels didn't respond right away so Tillie went on. "It doesn't even seem like you need evidence these days. You'll just throw anyone behind bars. Isn't that what Herr Himmler said? That it just depended on what mood he was in?" She started to feel bolder and took a step forward towards him. "Frankly, it seems like you're just angry that I have a male companion who isn't you."

She could feel her hands shaking but didn't want Goebbels to see she was terrified, so she clasped them behind her back. "Give my father my regrets. Ernesto and I will be going now."

At that, Ernesto came loudly down the stairs, their coats in hand. "You ready to go, darling?" He looked at Goebbels, his face hard. "She gets these headaches, I'm sure you'll give our apologies to the others." Goebbels stared at Ernesto, his thin lips in a slight frown.

Ernesto pulled Tillie through her parents' front door and when Tillie looked over her shoulder, Goebbels was standing in the doorway, his black eyes glittering, watching them walk away.

CHAPTER 30

August 1934

"Well, that's it then," Tillie overheard her father say as he and Herr Grandelis stood in his office doorway. She busied herself at her desk and tried to look as if she wasn't listening to their conversation.

Herr Grandelis nodded. "Hermann assured me that they have no doubt the Führer is going to take the presidency." He clapped his hands together. "It's all very exciting."

Tillie watched as her father's eyes lit up. He opened his mouth to speak, but Tillie interrupted him. "But it's a vote. How can they be so confident that Hitler, er, the Führer, is going to win?"

Both men turned to look at her. Her father's face looked disappointed and slightly embarrassed while Herr Grandelis looked livid. He turned back to her father.

"You see, Vincent? This is what I'm talking about. She is nothing but a menace to our business. She's not just apathetic to the party, she's a resistor. I don't understand why Joseph continues to believe it's just my son's influence that's causing her to be a problem. She is the problem, Vincent. She needs to be removed."

Tillie tried not to roll her eyes. "I was merely pointing out that it's still a vote, that still means there's a chance he might not become the president. I don't understand why you're throwing such a tantrum about it." She felt another wave of rage, like how she felt when Goebbels verbally attacked her at dinner.

"I'm not saying I hope one thing happens over the other." At that Herr Grandelis scoffed. "What I am saying is that if it's a fair vote, it's still up to the people."

Her father shook his head. "Matilda, what do I have to say to you to make you understand how much things will improve once the Führer is running the entire country? I just do not understand why you continue to keep company with those who only wish to serve themselves." He pinched the bridge of his nose. "I can't protect you forever." He turned to Herr Grandelis. "Anthony, she's clearly ill-informed. And she's only a secretary. What possible damage could she do?"

Herr Grandelis' eyes narrowed. "What damage could she do?" He gestured wildly. "She's only in every meeting, reading all our notes, listening in on all our phone calls. If she wanted to betray us," but with that, Tillie snapped.

"Oh, for heaven's sake." She slammed her hand down on the table. She could hear her heart thrumming in her ears. Both men turned back to her with wide, shocked eyes. "Who cares what I think if I'm just a lowly secretary? You really think I care at all what you people are doing here? You don't think I have anything better to be concerned about? It's all just so ridiculous." She was breathing hard, and her father tilted his head at her, a mixture of pity and amusement.

Her father blinked and then gave her a patronizing smile. "Of course, dear. You're young and shouldn't be concerned with the affairs of old men." Herr Grandelis had his arms crossed over his chest and was staring at her with contempt. "Anthony clearly, we're overreacting. Joseph would tell us if he thought Tillie was a problem and he hasn't mentioned anything to us about her performance." He paused. "I know he's not thrilled about her relationship with Ernesto, but even Heinrich said there's no evidence to support that Ernesto is engaging in any kind of Communist activity."

Her father turned his back to her as his phone started to ring. "Tillie, dear, just try to keep your tongue in check? You really can't be yelling at your employers."

He went into his office to answer his phone. Herr Grandelis turned, his eyes settling on Tillie. She avoided his gaze and focused on the papers on her desk, but he loomed over her, so close she could smell the soapy aftershave wafting from his neck.

"You know you and your little friends are living on borrowed time."

Tillie raised her eyebrows while she continued to set up her desk for the day. "Is that right? Most of my friends are either dead or have been run out of the country, so forgive me if I continue to be *apathetic*." Her breathing was coming in quick rasps through her clenched teeth.

He stepped dangerously close and took a lock of her hair between his fingers. "It doesn't matter that you're a perfect German specimen. You will still get exactly what you deserve."

Tillie froze and kept her eyes on her desk, while he ran her hair under his nose, inhaling deeply. He leaned in farther so she could feel his breath on her neck. "It's a shame too. What a waste for a pretty ass like yours to shrivel in a jail cell." He was pushing up against her and she could feel his arousal against her hip bone. "I bet," he continued, his voice a hoarse whisper, "what you need is a man to show you exactly what you're missing."

Tillie stayed as still as possible keeping her eyes glued to the ink pen on her desk. Her father was still on a call in his office. If she could see the light blinking on her phone, so could Herr Grandelis.

He wrapped his large hand around her wrist. "I think you should come with me to my office so we can discuss these client files further." His fingers were like a vice and Tillie knew there would be a bruise on her arm within hours.

"Please," she whispered. "Please just let me get my work done." As soon as she looked up, she saw that pleading with him had been a mistake. His face was dark and hungry, and she winced as his grip tightened further on her arm.

"You can work when we're done." He leaned in and, with his free hand, grabbed at the back of her hair. He yanked her head back and kissed her. His mouth was rough as he forced his tongue between her lips. His breath smelled like cigarettes and stale coffee. Tillie stifled a small cry of terror and pain, and he pulled back, looking into her eyes.

He pulled her hair even harder and growled, "Kiss me back you degenerate whore." He let go of her wrist and pulled her body into his, his hand still in her hair, her scalp on fire.

Then, he was off her and walking away. Tillie glanced down and the light on her phone was off, signaling the end of her father's call. She stood at her desk, unable to move. Her father opened his office door and said, "That was Herr Goebbels. He's going to be coming by to discuss a few final arrangements for election day. Tillie, can you run across the street to get pastries from the café? Just so he has something to snack on when he arrives."

Tillie's legs felt like lead as she walked through the front of the office. Her hands were shaking, and she kept trying to swallow, but her throat felt tight and hot. The red marks on her wrist glowed on her pale skin and her scalp throbbed.

Stepping out into the hot August sun, she sagged against the side of the brick building, feeling the cool of the bricks through her blouse. Closing her eyes, she felt Herr Grandelis' scratchy beard on her cheek and his tongue in her mouth and she leaned over to vomit in the bushes.

✝

"So, we're voting on whether or not Hitler becomes the president?" James looked up from the paper at the group congregated in their kitchen. Tillie was quiet. It had been a week since the incident at her office with Ernesto's father and she had told no one, but every time she closed her eyes to sleep, she could feel his grip on her wrist; his hand ripping her hair from her scalp. Like his touch was burned into her skin.

Adelaide cleared her throat and read the referendum in the paper out loud. "The office of the President of the Reich is unified with the office of the Chancellor. Consequently, all former powers of the President of the Reich are demised to the Führer and Chancellor of the Reich Adolf Hitler. He himself nominates his substitute. Do you, German man and German woman, approve of this regulation provided by this Law?" She set the paper down and sucked her teeth before continuing.

"It seems as though, on the surface, we will be voting for this," she said, slowly. "But I have my doubts as to how fair this vote will be."

She shook her head, looking up at Ruth and Tillie, her large brown eyes sad and tired. "Everyone has left," she murmured. "After the institute and Dora," her voice quivered, and she had to stop to collect herself. "Karl left to be with Dr. H. in France. Nissa left with her sister. I think they went to England. Helene has pledged her loyalty to The Reich and started going by the name Henry again." She wiped her eyes. When Ruth made a clicking sound with her tongue, Adelaide shrugged. "We do what we need to do to stay safe. She even moved back in with her parents and they're finding her a 'nice German girl' to marry."

She exhaled and rubbed her eyes with both hands. "Sorry, finding *him* a nice German girl to marry." She sounded bitter, and her eyes narrowed to slits. "The Nazis have destroyed our entire way of life. We're being erased, one by one. They killed Dora, they ran Dr. H., Karl, and Nissa out of the country, and Helene has become someone she's not just to stay alive.

"Erwin and Heinz are planning to leave and want me to go with them. I'm to pretend to be an aunt or cousin or some such thing. Erwin has family in Switzerland." She took a sip of her tea. "So, I guess they're running me out of the country, too."

James looked up. "When? When are you going to go?"

Adelaide shrugged. "Probably in the next six months. Erwin and Heinz are planning now and discussing it with Erwin's family. I'm even welcome at his parents' home. His parents must be quite lovely. I think they're hoping to leave by January."

After they discussed the forthcoming election as much as they could, Adelaide got up to leave. She paused at the door and looked back at them with a small smile. "You should consider talking with Erwin and Heinz about getting out. It's not safe here."

Closing the door behind Adelaide, Ernesto turned to the three sitting at the kitchen table. "Everyone is leaving." Tillie said nothing and sipped her tea.

James cleared his throat. "Adelaide is right. I think we should leave, too." Ernesto sat back in his chair and took James' hand, nodding. Tillie's eyes remained fixed on a spot in the woodgrain on the table. She knew exactly how Ruth would react to any suggestion of leaving.

"We're not leaving," Ruth said, as if on cue. "Did you hear what Adelaide said? They're *erasing* us. They want us to leave. What are they going to do? Jail all of us?" She scoffed. "Hitler will not be able to gain the presidency and we are not leaving." She laughed without humor into her tea mug. "Running away in fear. Doing nothing. It's so cowardly."

Tillie felt something inside her snap. Her wrist burned and her scalp throbbed and before she knew what she was doing, she had hurled her tea mug, full of tea across the kitchen where it struck the wall, shattering and spilling all over the floor. Three pairs of eyes, wide with surprise, turned to stare at her.

"Cowardly? Doing nothing, keeping yourself safe, trying to survive is cowardly? Helene is probably crying herself to sleep every night being forced to live as Henry again. Karl and Dr. H. have lost everything. Dora is dead because *they murdered her.* No one is running away in fear, they're running away to survive this. You think Hitler can't take the presidency? What is stopping him?"

She picked up the newspaper still sitting on the table with the referendum. "You think this vote will stop him? It won't. He will take the presidency and then the Germany that you're so hell bent on staying to defend is officially dead."

She threw the paper down. "You think they can't jail us all? What about the jail in Dachau? You don't think there will be another ten or twenty or hundred more just like it for all of us? They burned our books, they destroyed your jobs and closed your clubs, and they killed one of our best friends. What makes you think they're going to stop now?"

Tillie was standing, her throat hurt from screaming and her head was pounding. "You keep saying 'we're not leaving, we're not leaving.' Well, guess what, Ruth? The rest of us," she gestured wildly to James and Ernesto, "want to leave. We don't want to stay to see how this turns out. You think the people of Germany will suddenly show up for us and stop this from happening?"

Tillie gave a loud snort of bitter laughter. "The people of Germany don't care about us. We're outsiders. On the fringe of society." She shuddered as she felt Herr Grandelis' tongue in her mouth and tasted his stale breath. "We're degenerate whores. At least, according to your father," she turned to Ernesto, his eyes wide with shock.

Tillie took a shaky breath. "No one cared that Dora was dead outside on the pavement for God knows how long. I don't even know what happened to her body. I don't know where she's buried or if the Nazis just threw her into a pit someplace." A small cry escaped from Ernesto. "No one cared that they killed her, and no one will care if they kill us."

Tillie walked out of the kitchen, slamming her bedroom door behind her. She was so angry, her hands were shaking, and she couldn't catch her breath. A small click behind her made her clench her jaw. "Leave me alone right now, Ruth."

"Are you okay?" It was Ernesto. "What was that about my father?" She turned and he was staring at her, his large brown eyes full of tears. He reached out for her, but she recoiled, still thinking about his father and his hands. "Tillie," Ernesto's face was unreadable. "Did something happen with my father?"

At this, Tillie burst into tears. A week of replaying it repeatedly in her mind caused a fracture within her, and she could no longer keep the anguish contained. In between sobs, she told Ernesto what happened at her desk with his father.

When she finished, she dared to look at him. Ernesto's face was a deep shade of red, his jaw was tight, and his eyes were bright with fury. He stood and left the room without a word.

"Ernesto?" Tillie called after him. She could feel her stomach flip onto itself. Was he upset with her? Of course, she thought, of course he would be upset. She allowed his father to kiss her. In public, no less. She scrambled off the bed and went running after him calling his name.

In the kitchen, James was staring at the door. He turned to look at Tillie when she hurried into the room and said, "What the hell was that?"

"Did he leave?" Tillie ran to get her purse.

"Did you fight?" James was looking at her with raised eyebrows. "He looked furious." Ruth didn't say a word, her back to Tillie while she stood at the sink.

Tillie shook her head. "Did he say where he was going?"

James stared at her; his mouth slightly agape. "No. He walked through here, ignoring us, then was out the door." He looked back at the door. "What did you say to him?"

Tillie set her purse back down and collapsed into a kitchen

chair with exhaustion. "I told him his father kissed me." She didn't have any energy left so she laid her head down on the cool table. It felt soothing on her swollen face.

"What?" Ruth whirled around from the kitchen sink. "Ernesto's father *kissed* you? When?"

Taking a deep breath, without lifting her head from the tabletop, Tillie relayed the entire story a second time. It felt a little easier telling it again. The words didn't feel so big in her mouth when she spoke. She could still feel Herr Grandelis' hands pulling her hair and grabbing her wrist, but his stale breath was a little less potent and the burn on her forearm a little less intense.

Tillie could hear Ruth walking over and felt her cool hand on the back of her neck. Ruth stroked her hair and murmured something. James reached over and took Tillie's hand in his own.

"Tillie, sweetie, Ernesto's father didn't kiss you. He attacked you."

She lifted her head and looked at him. She watched as he and Ruth exchanged glances. "Did you tell Ernesto that story or just that he kissed you?"

"I told him exactly what I just told you."

Ruth nodded and looked back at James. "Then I expect Ernesto is on his way to beat the ever-loving shit out of his father." For a moment no one said anything.

"You don't think he's mad at me?" Tillie looked at James then at Ruth.

"Mad at you? Why?" Ruth's voice was sharp and incredulous.

"Because I just stood there. I didn't push him away or tell him to stop or anything. I was just frozen." Tillie rubbed her hands up and down her arms, aware that she was shivering. Ruth left and came back with the quilt from their bed.

"What could you have done?" Ruth asked, wrapping the quilt around Tillie's shoulders. "He's your boss and not just that, he's a high-ranking Nazi official. What were you going to do?

Hit him? You did what you could to get through it." Ruth kissed Tillie on her neck and whispered, "I'm sorry about what I said. About being cowardly. You are not a coward, doll."

Tillie let out a long breath. "So, I guess we just wait for Ernesto to come back." James squeezed her hand and then got up and went into his bedroom. Ruth sat down and looked over at the broken mug on the floor. "Do you want me to make you more tea?"

They both started giggling and couldn't stop.

Tillie wasn't awake when Ernesto returned but the next morning, he was sitting drinking coffee at the kitchen table. He had large scrapes on his knuckles.

"Are you alright?" She grabbed his free hand and he winced.

"Well, the good news is I'm not sixteen anymore. My father seemed to have forgotten that I grew several inches and put on some weight since the last time he hit me. If he bothers you again, let me know." He took another sip of his coffee as James strolled into the kitchen and kissed his forehead.

"So, are we voting against this ridiculous referendum today?" He sat down at the table with his coffee and absently played with Ernesto's hair as he sipped.

Tillie rubbed her face with her hands. "I suppose so. I'll go wake Ruth so we can get on with it."

They left the apartment and were immediately surrounded by Nazi flags, Hitler Youth, and the SS were everywhere, crowding around them on the streets. "Oh my God," Ruth mumbled. "What is going on?"

There were groups of people being escorted by SS agents, Hitler youth standing outside open polling stations, and large signs with big red letters shouting things like "Thank the Führer, vote yes," and outside private polling stations there were signs in black saying "Only traitors vote here."

"What do we do?" James breathed.

They huddled together against the wall of their apartment building, so as not to garner attention from any of the SS agents or Hitler Youth.

Tillie cleared her throat and tried not to seem anxious. "We go vote." They started walking together down the road surrounded by screaming Hitler Youth and other people being led to polling stations by men in all black with guns.

As they entered their polling location, it was like all the oxygen was sucked out of the room. It went from screaming and shouting to complete and utter silence passing through the doors. SS guards were stationed at every poll booth, the curtains removed, and were watching each person vote.

A small gasp escaped Ernesto's mouth and Tillie met Ruth's eyes. "I told you," Tillie whispered, and Ruth shook her head, her eyes wide and fearful.

They were each handed a ballot with the referendum listed at the top. The 'yes' circle was three times the size of the 'no' circle and the 'yes' was at the very center of the ballot, while the 'no' circle was set in the right-hand corner, almost off the paper. They all looked at one another then walked slowly to the voting stations.

Tillie picked up the pen and could feel the SS agent watching her, his eyes traveling up her body then back down to the ballot in her hand.

She lifted her chin and met his eyes. "May I help you?"

He didn't smile. "Just making sure you're doing what you need to do to thank the Führer for saving Germany."

She looked back down at the ballot in her hand, at the tiny 'no' circle off to the side. Before she could register her fear, she checked 'no' and turned, walking quickly away from the SS agent without looking at him again. "Filthy traitor," he shouted after her. She felt her face grow warm and she shoved her ballot into the ballot box in the center of the room, Ruth behind her.

"Let's go, before they decide to arrest us for treason." She grabbed Tillie's elbow and steered her out the door, the shouts of "traitor" and "Jew" following them from the SS agents inside. They hurried home, not waiting for the boys, and didn't speak until they made it back to their apartment. Fifteen minutes later, the boys arrived, looking as harried and flushed as they felt.

"Well." Ernesto sank into a chair. "That was quite an experience." Ruth grabbed vodka from the freezer and poured each of them a large drink.

James sat down and took a long sip from his glass. "Now what?"

Ruth downed her drink and looked at Tillie. "I guess now we get used to having Adolf Hitler as our president."

CHAPTER 31

January 1935

There was a quiet knock on the bedroom door. Tillie was sitting up reading the notes from her father's office she'd taken that day and Ruth was beside her reading a magazine.

"Come in," Tillie called, setting her notes down. James and Ernesto both walked in, wearing their robes. Ernesto sat on the edge of their bed next to Tillie's feet and James sat in the small chair next to the window.

Ernesto picked up one of the sheets of paper from Tillie's lap. "You're still doing this?"

Tillie shrugged. "It's kind of pointless now, isn't it. All the notes, all the meetings, every phone conversation, it's all the same. 'Heil Hitler, get on board, what laws can we pass to make life difficult for people not like us.'" Tillie picked up notes from a phone call from Ernesto's father and Goebbels. "This is from when he went to the Degenerate Art Exhibition." She sighed. "It's all very depressing. And all the same things over and over."

"Degenerate Art Exhibition." James scoffed at the window. "Well, their depravity know no bounds."

Ernesto dropped the paper and made a face. "Anyway. We're here to talk about," he glanced at James, "about what we're going to do."

James stood and walked over to the bed, sitting at Ruth's feet. "We've spoken to Heinz and Erwin. They're leaving soon. In a few weeks. We thought, after talking with them, if we were to all go, like friends going on holiday, it would be easier to get out."

Ernesto nodded. "Basically, avoiding attention by being as obvious as possible." James chuckled.

"We also thought that it might work better if we were newlyweds." Ernesto's face flushed. Ruth raised her eyebrows.

"What do you mean, newlyweds?" She looked from Ernesto to James.

"Well," Ernesto began, then looked to James for help.

"Ruthie, you and I would get married. And then Ernesto and Tillie would get married. Then we'd be, you know, two couples on a holiday with their friends for their honeymoon. It just seems more believable that way."

Ernesto placed his hand on top of James' on the bed. "It was actually Erwin's idea. They originally wanted to try that with Adelaide, but she was worried, you know." Ernesto looked down. "That they would be able to tell. That she wasn't born a woman," he added quietly, "so she's too afraid to try it."

"They did forge paperwork for her, though. She has a birth certificate listing her as Adelaide Rittenbach. Erwin's sister."

"Okay, stop." Ruth held up a hand. Both boys looked relieved to be interrupted. "You want us to marry each other. Then leave the country 'on a holiday' with Erwin, Heinz, and Adelaide. To go to Switzerland." She closed her eyes and rubbed her forehead, irritated. "You know that whatever they forged for Adelaide isn't going to work, right? She's going to get caught."

"Ruth," Tillie pulled the covers off and got out of bed. "You don't know that."

"Of course I do. Look, I know Adelaide has been Adelaide to all of us for the entire time we've known her." Ruth wiped a tear from her face. "But to them she's still a man in a dress."

Ernesto sighed. "I hope it will be fine." He sounded defeated. "I hope they'll get out. Who knows, maybe they won't even ask to see her papers. They're taking multiple trains so that Heinz's family doesn't try to find him."

Tillie looked up, frowning. "Heinz's family?"

James nodded. "Both his father and brother are high ranking. Like your dad and Herr Grandelis. It's only a matter of time before they turn him in for being gay and violating Paragraph 175."

Ernesto made a noise in his throat. "I'm surprised my father hasn't come after us yet, honestly."

Tillie took a deep breath. "It would certainly be more difficult for your father to come after you if you had a wife. Especially since my parents have always been under the assumption that we're a couple."

"You're not seriously considering this." Ruth folded her arms over her chest. "You want us to abandon who we are, just like that."

Tillie rolled her eyes. "For heaven's sake Ruth. No one is abandoning anything. It's a cover. It's to get out of the country. It's to keep Ernesto and James safe. I don't understand why this is so offensive to you. It's literally a piece of paper that keeps all of us from being thrown into a jail cell."

Ruth got out of bed and put on her robe. "It's not just a piece of paper. It's us letting them dictate our lives. It's them pushing us into the shadows because that's where they think we belong. I refuse to be stamped out."

"Ruth, they don't think we belong in the shadows, they think we belong in a grave." Tillie's voice was barely above a whisper. "They don't want to dictate our lives; they want to jail us. Kill us. They want us to cease to exist."

"Okay," James said. Both Ruth and Tillie jumped and looked over at him, having forgotten that he and Ernesto were still in their room. "We're going to leave you to discuss this."

He and Ernesto stood, joining hands. Tillie walked with them to the bedroom door and followed them out into the hallway. He lowered his voice to a quiet whisper. "Convince her. The sooner we get out of Germany, the better for all of us."

Tillie nodded then went back into the bedroom where Ruth stood, her hands on her hips, shaking her head. "I won't do it, Tillie. If I ever get married, it will be to you." Her eyes were bright with tears. "I know it's just a piece of paper. But it's so much more than that." At this, a strangled sob emerged from Ruth's throat. It was the first time Tillie saw Ruth really cry since Dora died. "I just want us to be able to live our lives. Like we used to." She got back into bed and curled into herself. "Why won't they just let us live our lives?"

Tillie got into bed next to her and wrapped her arms around Ruth's body, trying to calm her in between her sobs of anger and grief. "I know," she whispered, stroking Ruth's hair. They fell asleep in each other's arms, their fingers intertwined with one another.

The next morning, Tillie was sitting in the chair next to the window in their bedroom staring at the stack of notes on the little side table. The thoughts rolled around her brain like loose marbles. She could smell coffee wafting underneath their bedroom door but didn't feel up to seeing the boys yet. A rustle of bedclothes made her turn her eyes to Ruth, still buried under a pile of quilts.

"Fine." A hoarse voice emerged from under the mound of blankets and Tillie raised her eyebrows.

"What?"

Ruth fought against the covers to sit up and Tillie could see her eyes were red and swollen. "Fine." She sniffed. "Let's get married. If it will protect the boys, then I'm willing to do it." She rubbed her face. "I still don't know if I am willing to leave the city, though. I don't know if I can run." She lifted her gaze to meet Tillie's and her eyes looked dull and flat.

"Leaving this city is like leaving a best friend." Her voice caught in her throat. "I feel like I would be abandoning a friend to the wolves. To be shot and burned while the Nazis dance on her ashes." A tear trickled down her face. "How do I leave her behind? How do I just let them destroy my beloved Berlin?" Swallowing hard and not waiting for an answer, Ruth slunk back under the blankets and covered her head. She didn't say another word.

Tillie rose and padded out into the kitchen where the boys were having a hushed breakfast. She put her hand on Ernesto's shoulder. "She's in. At least for getting married. I'll keep working on convincing her to leave."

He nodded without looking at her. "That's a start."

✝

Going into the office was becoming more and more difficult. After Ernesto attacked his father on Tillie's behalf, Herr Grandelis mostly avoided her, but she still couldn't help the panicked feeling she would get anytime he would get anywhere near her. She preferred to be in the filing room where no one could see her from the offices or the lobby, and she'd taken to eating her lunch in the back corner.

"Tillie?" Her eyes snapped up from her sandwich. "Are you in here?" Her father's voice echoed from the doorway off the rows of metal filing cabinets.

"Yes Papa." She stood and hurried to the door, choosing to leave her sandwich in her corner to avoid awkward questions.

Her father was staring at her with a look of concern. "Are you alright, darling?"

She nodded without meeting his eye. "Is there something you need?"

Her father took a beat and then decided it wasn't worth investigating further.

"Yes, Herr Grandelis and I are having a meeting with a few of the other attorneys from the area. Can you run and place an order at the café across the street?" He handed her a piece of paper. "You don't need to attend the meeting; it's an informal gathering of like minds."

Tillie clenched her jaw. In other words, a meeting for Nazis. "Of course, Papa." She went to her desk to get her coat and bag when she heard footsteps behind her. "Is there something else?" She turned and felt her heart plummet. Herr Grandelis was standing a foot away talking to her father.

"You know, Vincent, I have a few things I need to catch up on. Can I borrow Tillie for a bit? Just to dictate some things to her." His eyes traveled from her father's face to her own and they were unreadable.

She swallowed hard. Her tongue felt thick and dry. She wiped her palms on her skirt.

"Of course, of course. If you could make it quick, though Anthony. We're expecting the other attorneys in about ninety minutes, so I was going to have her run out for our refreshments."

"Oh, we'll be quick." His eyes narrowed on Tillie's face and the corners of his lips turned up into a sneer. "Tillie, my office?"

She followed him carrying her coat and bag while her legs shook beneath her. She could feel the cold sweat beading along the base of her neck and her stomach flipped back and forth. As she entered his office behind him, she resisted the urge to scream, and bit her lip hard when she heard the door click shut behind her.

She stood, frozen to the spot, as Herr Grandelis moved to sit behind his desk. "Well?" He gestured for her to take a seat in one of the office chairs.

She stepped forward and sat down. He stared at her for a moment, then leaned forward onto his elbows on his desk. He moved so quickly that Tillie jumped. "Skittish, are we?" He continued to sneer at her, his eyes black and menacing.

"You know," he began, still watching her. "I had to wait for my nose and jaw to heal before I could return to work last year."

Tillie's eyes widened just the smallest amount and he nodded. "My son did quite a number on me. Broke my nose and my cheekbone and dislocated my jaw." He sucked on his teeth. "I couldn't very well return to work looking like that. What would my colleagues say? What would I tell them?"

At this he looked at her and tilted his head to the side. After the silence stretched out, he snapped, "Well, Matilda, what would I tell them?"

She jumped again, not realizing he expected her to answer. "I don't know, sir."

He nodded. "Exactly. I suppose I could have outed my son as the degenerate he is. Had him arrested and thrown into a labor camp." He leaned back in his chair and laced his fingers behind his head, like he was relaxing after a long day. "But then everyone would know my son is one of them and the stain would be on us all."

Tillie remained still, her heart beating so loud she thought the sound was echoing off the walls. Her coat rustled in her lap as her hands shook. She felt the beads of sweat run down between her shoulder blades.

"I thought you had notes to dictate to me, sir?" She felt trapped inside his office. The air felt heavy around her; with every breath she took, like there was less oxygen in the air. She was starting to feel lightheaded.

"There's a list, you know." His eyes went to her shaking pen, then back to her face.

"A list?" At this, she sat up a little straighter. "What kind of list?"

"We're arresting them left and right. The club owners, the men dressing as women, the traitors." Tillie must have looked confused because then he hissed, "*The homosexuals.*" He smoothed his tie, regaining his composure. "When one is arrested, he outs five more just to lessen his sentence in the camp."

He smiled to himself. "They're castrated, you know." He pointed a long, angry finger at her face. "It's only a matter of time before they arrest someone who outs Ernesto. And by process of elimination, who outs you. And that Jew girl you spend your time with. It's only a matter of time before you're all behind barbed wire fences where you belong."

Tillie stood, her inability to catch her breath overcoming her fear of Herr Grandelis. He watched her and she could see the smirk pulling up the corners of his lips. "Going so soon? We haven't even gotten to our dictation yet." She turned to hurry from his office, leaving him chucking behind her. "You know I'm helping Herr Himmler create an office." Tillie stopped with her hand on the doorknob and turned.

"What kind of office?"

"The kind where we hunt people like you."

Escaping to the restroom, Tillie was left gasping for air. She felt like she was having a heart attack in the bathroom stall. Hyperventilating and sweating, the tears came as she rested her face against the cool metal of the bathroom door, her coat and purse still clutched in her shaking fingers.

CHAPTER 32

September 1935

They all surrounded the table, the letter from Karl in France in between them. Ruth's head was in her hands and the tears dripped off her nose onto the table.

"He died of a broken heart," Ernesto was saying, in between sobs. "The Nazis destroyed his life's work, and it killed him. Just another murder to add to their list."

Tillie didn't say anything, she just stood, her back against the counter. Dr. Hirschfeld was dead, the institute was destroyed, all their friends had left. What was keeping them here?

James took Ernesto's hand in his own. He started murmuring under his breath and it sounded like he was saying a small prayer. The only other sounds in the room were the sniffling and stifled sobs coming from Ruth and Ernesto. When he finished, he raised his glass and the rest of them followed suit, giving a silent toast to Dr. Hirschfeld and all his work that no one else would ever see.

Setting down her glass, Tillie took a deep breath. "It's time." They all looked up at her. "It's time to go. We can't keep pretending things are going to get better. I'm the only one still with a job. Our friends are gone, our clubs are gone. It's time."

Ernesto swallowed and sighed, and James nodded. Ruth's head was still in her hands, her eyes on the letter from Karl in the center of the table. She slowly lifted her head to meet Tillie's eyes. They looked more green than hazel, wet with tears, and she leaned back in her chair. She opened her mouth to say something when she was interrupted by a soft knock on the front door.

Tillie opened the door slowly and a clean-cut stranger in a blue coat and white buttoned-down shirt stood before her. "May I help you?"

Smiling sadly, the stranger said, "Hiya, Tills."

Opening her eyes wide, she gasped. "*Helene?*" Her stomach sank. "Oh sweetie. Come in." She moved aside and Helene walked in, moving stiffly in her pants and shiny black shoes.

"You have no idea how nice it is to hear my name." Helene's eyes were filled with tears. "I came because I got a letter from Karl. I wanted to see if he sent you one as well." They all nodded, and Helene sunk into a chair at the table. Tillie rushed to pour her a drink. "I can't believe he's dead." She shook her head and took the vodka from Tillie.

Ruth reached out and laid a hand on Helene's arm. "Oh, Helene. How are you doing?"

She sighed. "Well, I have to go by Henry now. It was the only way my parents would let me stay with them. I'm marrying my third cousin next week." She shrugged. "Her name is Elizabeth. She seems nice enough."

A tear trickled down Helene's face. "I just didn't have the money to leave, and my parents wouldn't help me get out. I could stay with them as their son, or I could go it alone, figure it out." Shaking her head, she took another drink. "I was too afraid to try to be on my own. Without the institute, without Dora, I didn't have anything left."

Ernesto reached out and took Helene's hand. "Why didn't you try to leave with Heinz and Erwin? With Adelaide? I'm sure they could have gotten you out."

Helene's face crumpled and she shook her head. "Didn't you hear?"

They all exchanged glances and Tillie shook her head. More tears spilled from Helene's eyes. "They tried to pass off Adelaide as Erwin's cousin and were caught. They were all arrested."

Ernesto's hand flew to his mouth and Ruth moaned. Helene continued. "I got a letter from Heinz. His favorite uncle works in transportation, so he was able to get out. But he had to leave Erwin behind. He said he's been trying to get any information to find Erwin, but his uncle refuses to help him further. Adelaide is dead. Or at least Heinz assumes as much."

The silence closed in around them. "Where is Heinz now?" James' face was creased with grief and worry.

"Switzerland. Erwin's family took him in. They figured it was the best chance to find Erwin. But I'm not optimistic." Helene wiped her face. "Anyway," she finished her drink and stood, "I just wanted to make sure you heard about Dr. Hirschfeld. I should go, my parents are keeping a close eye on who I visit." She sighed and turned to the door.

"This time next week, I'll have a wife. Strange how quickly life can change." She laughed to herself, but Tillie could see the tears in her eyes. Helene gave each of them a quick hug and walked out, her black shoes clicking on the linoleum floor as she went.

They all stared at the door in silence after she left. It was James who broke the quiet. "Well. That's another two people to add to the list, I suppose, Adelaide and Erwin." James shrugged. "No one is going to see them again. Heinz can keep trying to find Erwin, but he's not going to. He's as good as dead. Just like Adelaide, Dora, and Dr. H. Did you see Helene's face? She's miserable. Having to live as Henry? Getting married?" James shook his head in disgust. "At least our marriages will be fake."

Ruth stood up abruptly, her eyes flashing. "And we're just supposed to leave?" They all turned toward her. "That's what you're all going to say, right? That we should leave. With Erwin in a labor camp someplace and Adelaide probably dead, and Helene living as Henry now, that we should just go."

Ernesto met James' eyes and they shifted in their chairs. Tillie leaned back against the front door but didn't respond right away. Ruth picked up Helene's glass and began to wash it angrily. "We just leave Helene and Erwin and all the other people just like us to fend for themselves. We just *run*." She shook her head as she scrubbed the glass clean.

"Ruth," Tillie kept her voice quiet. When Ruth didn't turn, she crossed the tiny kitchen and took the clean glass from her shaking hands. Ruth's face had tears dripping from her chin into her collar. "Ruth." Tillie set the glass down and wrapped her arms around Ruth's bony shoulders. "Shhh, it's okay." Ruth sobbed into Tillie's neck.

"What are we going to do? How do we leave everyone to fend for themselves?" Tillie stroked her hair as she cried. She met Ernesto's eyes, and they were creased with worry. She frowned and gave her head the smallest shake. He nodded and took James' hand, leading him to their bedroom.

"We don't have to talk about leaving right now. I know you don't want to leave." Ruth continued to cry into Tillie's hair. "But we're going to have to talk about it eventually. You agreed to the marriages, leaving is the next part of the plan." She could feel Ruth nodding into her neck.

She let go and led Ruth to the kitchen table. They sat and Ruth wiped her face. "Ruth, we have to talk about this." Tillie took Ruth's hand in her own. "With everything we know, with everything we've seen from my father's notes, even if we pretend to be married, it's not going to be safe here for you and for James."

"This city is our home, Tills. This is where we fell in love, this is where we grew up. How do we just leave our city for them to destroy? How do we leave our friends to fight on their own?"

"Ruth, all our friends are gone." Tillie reached over and wiped a tear from Ruth's cheek.

"And if we get caught?" Ruth's voice turned sharp. "Then what? We all end up in a jail separated? Or killed outright like Adelaide?"

"We won't be caught, Ruth. You said yourself that Adelaide was different. You could tell, you know. They would have had a better chance if Adelaide pretended to be Erwin's brother while they tried to get out. We're not in the same situation they were. We're just two married couples going on holiday. It's completely different." Tillie's voice had turned whiny, but she didn't care. She had to get Ruth to understand how important it was to make a plan.

Ruth wiped her face. "I can't do it, Tills. I can't leave." She blew out a long breath. "What if we leave and our city is destroyed?"

Tillie could feel the sting of tears behind her eyes. "Ruth, what if our city is destroyed and we stay?" They sat at the table holding hands in the quiet, still kitchen late into the night before Tillie gave up and went to bed without saying anything else.

†

She was just sitting down at her desk, ready to start another day of work when a courier brought in a stack of *Der Angriff* that was twice the amount they usually receive.

"What on earth?" Tillie stood and hurried to take some of the burden out of the young man's hands. "There must be some mistake, we normally only get half this amount of the paper."

The courier shook his head. "No ma'am. These are a special printing. Herr Goebbels told me to give instructions for you to begin handing them out to anyone walking by as well."

She fought the annoyance blooming in her chest. As if she had nothing better to do than to hand out newspapers to random strangers on the street. "Did he, now?" she muttered.

He raised his eyebrows at her, and she forced a smile. "Thank you so much for delivering them," she said tightly.

He nodded, still watching her with slight apprehension. As he turned to go, he saluted her. "Heil Hitler," he said, his voice full of conviction.

She stood in front of him, her heart beating in her ears. The irritation with Goebbels interrupting her workday and the exhaustion from dealing with Ruth from the night before took over and before she knew what she was doing, she set the papers down on her desk and crossed her arms. "Thank you for the delivery." *Screw Hitler,* she thought.

The delivery boy's eyes grew round, and his face flushed. "You could be reported you know."

She fought not to roll her eyes. "Then report me." She turned away before he could respond and walked to the kitchen, feeling slightly giddy at her tiny act of defiance. She waited at least five minutes in the back to be sure he had left before returning to her desk.

Dropping into her chair, she picked up one of the papers. "What could be so bloody important that I have to hand these out outside?" she murmured to herself.

The headline made it clear immediately. A large picture of Hitler at the Nuremberg Rally from over the weekend was placed directly under the words *"Laws for the Protection of German Blood."* Her stomach tightened as she continued to read the new laws that Hitler's Germany had just put into place.

†

Her feet dragged with exhaustion as she walked into her apartment. She was startled to see all the notes from her father's office strewn over the kitchen table, with Ruth sitting in between Helene, wearing a purple dress and scarf, and another woman whom Tillie did not know.

"What's going on?" Tillie shut the door behind her, while Ruth stood, her face flushed with excitement.

"Tillie, this is Helene's wife, Elizabeth."

Elizabeth stood and smiled, holding out her hand. Tillie took it and mumbled, "Nice to meet you." Clearing her throat, she said louder, "What are you doing with all my notes?"

Ruth beamed and even Helene was smiling. "It turns out, Elizabeth is part of the underground SPD. The Social Democrat Party."

Elizabeth nodded and said, "Our party was made illegal back in '33. But we just went underground. When I walked in on Henry," Ruth cleared her throat, loudly. Elizabeth shook her head a little. "I mean, Helene, trying on my clothes, I made her tell me everything. After we talked about her life up to now and you and Ruth, I knew I needed to meet you."

Tillie looked from Ruth to Elizabeth to Helene. "I'm sorry, so why did you need to meet us?"

Elizabeth smiled even broader. "Because you're resistors. You're part of our team. The opposition to the Nazis. And not only that, but you also have all this insider information." She waved at the notes on the table. "You are going to be invaluable to our efforts."

Tillie's eyes fell onto Ruth's face, her excitement showing in her glowing, pink cheeks. "Do James and Ernesto know about this?"

Ruth shook her head. "No, Elizabeth and Helene just came by today. Come sit down. You know these notes better than I do."

Tillie could feel the anger and frustration building from the pit of her stomach, the copy of *Der Angriff* she brought home feeling heavier by the minute in her work bag. "I'm so tired, can you give me a few minutes to change and splash some water on my face?" Ruth smiled up at her and nodded.

"Of course, doll."

Elizabeth checked her watch. "Actually, we need to get going." She turned to Helene. "You should probably get changed." Helene nodded and headed to the bathroom. Turning back to Ruth, Elizabeth said, "We're having a meeting at our house next week. Please come. Helene can give you the address, and our cover is a game night." She winked. "Just nice German couples playing cards."

Ruth laughed. "That sounds wonderful, we'll be there." Helene emerged from the bathroom dressed as Henry, and Tillie moved to the side while Ruth walked them out. She was sitting at the kitchen table when Ruth returned.

"Isn't this exciting, Tills? It's like a sign. This is why we need to stay. There are others, like us, others resisting, trying to save Berlin and the rest of Germany. We can help them."

Tillie sat at the table, staring at the notes still littering the table and parts of the floor. "Ruth. Have you lost your mind?"

Ruth laughed, but then looked at Tillie's face. "Wait. Are you angry with me?"

Tillie stood up, banging her fist on the table. "We had a plan!" She was yelling, but she didn't care. "Being part of some underground resistance with Ernesto's old roommate and her new wife was not part of the plan, Ruth. *This* is what is going to get us thrown into jail or killed. Not trying to leave."

Tillie pulled the copy of *Der Angriff* out of her bag. "Have you seen this, Ruth?" She slammed the paper down onto the table under her palm. "Do you know what they've done?"

Ruth stood, her face red with rage. "No, unlike you, I don't read their propaganda."

Tillie clenched her jaw. "Oh, well. Let's read it together, shall we?" She wrenched open the paper while Ruth stood before her practically vibrating with anger. "*Law for the Protection of German Blood and German Honor.*"

She looked up at Ruth before continuing to read. "Marriages between Jews and citizens of German or related blood are forbidden and any marriages conducted are invalid, including those conducted abroad. Extramarital relations between Jews and citizens of German or related blood are forbidden. Jews may not employ female citizens of German or related blood who are under forty-five years old. Jews are forbidden from flying the flag or the colors of the Reich."

She paused as Ruth crossed her arms in front of her. "Okay, so they made laws keeping Jews from marrying Germans. Cecilia and her husband have already left, so they're safe. It's terrible, but not something that directly causes me all that much concern. In case you forgot, James is also Jewish, so my *marriage*," her voice took on a mocking tone, "will be perfectly legal."

Tillie didn't respond. She looked back down at the paper and kept reading, her voice still even and unwavering. *"Reich Citizenship Law."* She cleared her throat. "The Reichstag has unanimously enacted the following law, which is promulgated herewith: A Reich citizen is a subject of the state who is of German or related blood and proves by his conduct that he is willing and fit to faithfully serve the German people and the Reich."

She looked back up and saw Ruth's face falter. "What?" Her eyes were narrow, and her brow furrowed.

"It means, Ruth, that you are no longer a citizen of Germany. Starting now." She flipped to the third page of the paper. "There's a chart." She jabbed at the last column with the heading *Jude*. "That's you. You don't qualify for a citizenship certificate. You're officially no longer a citizen of Germany, Ruth."

Ruth's cheeks lost their color, and she snatched the paper off the table. Her mouth opened and closed several times as she re-read the words printed in front of her. "They stripped our citizenship?" Her voice was soft and full of disbelief.

Tillie felt her heart soften and reached out to take Ruth's hand. "You see, Ruth? We can't stay. It's just going to get worse. We have to stick to the plan."

Ruth slowly lowered the paper and swallowed, her eyes far away. She blinked several times before her face hardened. "Then I'll be part of the resistance. I'll be part of the resistance and you and Ernesto and James can run."

She started scooping up the notes to put back into the closet. "But you know as well as I do that you won't leave without me. And I'm not leaving. So, I guess you're stuck here. You're stuck here and you're not helping us. You have all this knowledge, and you're not helping us. What does that make you, Matilda?" She shoved the notes into the pantry and stalked off to the bedroom, slamming the door behind her, leaving Tillie in the kitchen, her stomach in knots.

CHAPTER 33

February 1936

Tillie sat turning the plain gold band around her left finger while she waited for her father to arrive. The anticipation of having to tell her father that she and Ernesto were married over the weekend made her feel like she'd swallowed a beehive.

The door opened and she stood slowly, listening to the heavy footsteps. Her father appeared in the lobby and took off his hat, crossing to his side of the office. Seeing her standing, his face went from surprised to concerned.

"Tillie, you're in early. Is everything alright?"

"Yes, Papa. I just," She took a deep breath, "I needed to talk to you before the others arrived for the day."

Her father's eyes flickered toward Herr Grandelis' side of the office. "Of course. Let's go into my office."

Once inside, she waited while her father hung up his coat and settled behind his desk. "So," he smiled up at her, his face looking much older than his forty-some odd years. "What can I do for you, my dear?"

She pinched her lips together. Better to just rip off the bandage, she thought. "Ernesto and I were married on Saturday." She swallowed and carefully watched his facial reaction. For a moment he sat there, the smile frozen on his face. Then, like melting ice cream, the smile vanished from his face, and he stood, walking to his door and closing it, clicking the lock.

"Matilda Rose Weber. What could you have been thinking?" His voice was a harsh whisper and his eyes dropped to her left hand where she was still fingering the gold band.

She shook her head. "I'm sorry that I didn't tell you beforehand, it was just a last-minute decision." She had practiced this speech with Ruth and the boys before she left the apartment that morning.

"Make it seem like you were overcome with passion and love," James had said, laughing. He and Ernesto had smiled at one another and kissed while Ruth avoided Tillie's gaze and refused to give her any advice.

When they went out to dinner that night after they had all gotten married, she and Ruth had pretended they had married each other, posing for a photo in their matching white outfits. But then Ruth was quiet the rest of the weekend and didn't kiss Tillie goodbye when she left for work this morning.

"We are just so in love, Papa," she started to say, but he held up his hand.

"You cannot afford to be married to him, Tillie."

Tillie shook her head. "Well, the Nazis destroyed the museum where he worked. I'm sure he'll be able to find work again soon, it's just …" her father cut her off.

"That is *not* what I mean." He sat back down at his desk and put his head in his hands. "Do you know what Anthony says about his son? The things he says his son has done?"

Tillie's heart started to beat faster, and she lowered herself into a chair. "Like what?" She couldn't keep the quiver of fear out of her voice.

"That he's a socialist. That he's actively working against the Führer. That it's only a matter of time before he gets thrown into Dachau." He lowered his voice further. "And the things Herr

Goebbels and Herr Göring have said are even worse." He rubbed his face and Tillie was startled to see there were tears in his eyes.

"They're saying that he's violating Paragraph 175. That he's," he paused, clenching his jaw, "that he's a *homosexual.*" The word came out as a whisper. He seemed to be drained of all color.

"If they find evidence of that, or even if they don't and they decide Anthony's position no longer offers protection for Ernesto, they will arrest him. They will send him away." He stared at her, his eyes pleading. "Tillie, they will arrest you too. For aiding in his crimes. You cannot tell anyone what you've done. You must take off that ring and hide it. Herr Goebbels *cannot* know about this. I can't keep you safe."

White hot anger burned inside her and threatened to boil over. She stood and put her hands on her father's desk, leaning toward him.

"You can't keep me safe?" she hissed at him. "You should have thought of that when you were busy becoming one of them." Her father stared up at her in surprise, and for the first time Tillie thought about how small and frail her father seemed.

"You coward." She spat out the words, furious. The numbness over all the things they'd lost had evaporated and left behind only rage. "You let those men take over our country and you did *nothing.*" Her voice was getting louder, despite her attempts to keep it low.

"All you saw was power. You didn't see that Ernesto and I would be in danger. You didn't care that this group of men destroyed our lives." She was crying now, hot angry tears streaming down her face.

"Tillie." Her father's voice sounded sad and desperate. "The Führer brought jobs back to our country. He's revitalized the military. He's made Germany great again. And he's doing that by eliminating the people who dragged the country down in the first place."

"Oh. Eliminating them? You mean by stripping away their German citizenship? You mean by throwing them in jail? Or by having them murdered?"

His face looked stricken. "Who? Who was murdered?"

"My friend Dora for one. She was murdered by the Hitler Youth." Tillie slammed her palms onto her father's desk. "They set Dora on fire," she shouted. "Our friend Adelaide. She was murdered. Or at least that's the rumor. She was caught trying to sneak out of the country with two of our other friends. Only one of them got out safely. No one knows about Adelaide or Erwin."

Her father shook his head. "If they were sneaking out of the country without the proper paperwork, then of course they're going to get into trouble. Are you suggesting criminals deserve no consequences?"

Tillie's mouth dropped open. "Criminals? They were just trying to leave. And Adelaide and Erwin were arrested for your ridiculous Paragraph 175. And Dora? She wasn't doing anything." She fought back a sob.

"Dora was a kind, lovely woman. She did nothing but care about everyone around her. Ernesto and I included. She was like a mother to Ernesto. And the Nazis *killed* her."

Her father raised his eyebrows and said, "Being arrested for Paragraph 175 isn't ridiculous, it's to protect the rest of the country from their perverted ways. And your other friend," he paused, "well, what was she doing when she was killed?"

Tillie just stared at him, her mouth still agape. "Is that what you'll ask when they kill me? What did I do to deserve it?"

He waved his hand and stood, walking around his desk. Putting his hands on her shoulders, he gave her a little shake. "No one is going to kill you, Matilda. You're going to do the right thing. Go home and end whatever is going on with Ernesto."

He tried to catch her eye, but she refused to look at him. "I'm not sure if you were ever really a couple, if what Herr Goering says is true about him or if he's just a dissenter. But either way, you cannot be with him. It's not safe for you."

He dropped his arms. "You are a good German girl and I know that we can get you out of this marriage. All I have to do is make a call and it will be erased from any record. It's quite easy to get a marriage invalidated, especially if one party is engaging in illegal activities. We can say you were led by his influence but have come to your senses." He picked up the phone and started to dial.

The rage inside her fizzled and she suddenly felt exhausted. She leaned over and put her hand over his to stop him from dialing. She took the ring off and put it in her pocket.

"Fine, Papa. I won't tell anyone else." She dropped into the chair. "But I'm not going to end the marriage either." She raised her eyes to meet her father's. "I won't abandon the people that I love."

†

When Tillie arrived home, the boys were in their bedroom, but Ruth was gone. Tillie went straight to her bed and collapsed, burying herself under a mountain of blankets, not even bothering to take off her shoes.

She pulled the pillow over her head and pressed her eyes shut as tight as she could. She counted the small explosions bursting on the backs of her eyelids while she screwed up her face, squeezing her eyes together so hard that her head started to hurt. Slowly, she drifted off into a restless sleep.

"Tills?" Ruth's worried voice sounded very far away. "Are you alright, doll? Are you sick?" The bed sunk down near Tillie's midsection and she slowly lifted the pillow off her head. Ruth quickly stifled a laugh and Tillie reached up to feel her curls, sticking out in all directions. She stuck her tongue out.

Ruth's face relaxed and she reached over to feel Tillie's forehead. "You okay?"

Tillie nodded. "Just a long day." Pulling herself up into a sitting position, she tilted her head. "Where were you?"

Ruth stood and took off her coat. "I was at Helene and Elizabeth's. For the SPD meeting."

"Oh."

Ruth sighed. "I know you don't approve, but they're doing very real things. We're making pamphlets to leave in public toilets, with information about what's really going on behind the scenes. Things about Dachau, about the arrest of dissidents and people like us." Ruth rubbed her hands over her face.

Ruth dropped her hand and gazed down at her own gold band. She bit her lip. "I'm sorry that I've been ..." she stopped, searching for the word.

"Cranky?" Tillie interrupted.

Ruth made a face. "I was going to say 'melancholy' but sure, I guess cranky works too." She sighed and moved to nestle in next to Tillie under the covers. "Watching you marry another person was upsetting. I didn't like it."

Tillie rested her head on Ruth's chest. "I know. It was weird for me too. Watching you marry James. But it's not real, Ruthie." She lifted her chin to look up at Ruth's face. "You and me? That's real. This. Us." Ruth nodded but didn't say anything.

"I think I understand your refusal to leave Berlin now, though."

Ruth sat up and looked down into Tillie's tired face. "Really?"

"Yes. Today my father told me Ernesto is as good as arrested at this point. We're on borrowed time. And he told me to leave him, to abandon him and pretend Ernesto never existed. That he could get the marriage erased and doing that was the only way for me to be safe."

"Oh my," Ruth breathed and took Tillie's hand.

"I told him I wasn't going to abandon the people I love. The idea that I just leave Ernesto to save myself."

Tillie brought Ruth's hand to her lips and kissed her fingertips. "I couldn't imagine it," she murmured.

Tillie let her lips work their way up Ruth's pale arm and to her neck. Ruth made a little noise in her throat while Tillie ran her tongue down Ruth's prominent collar bone.

"Wait, wait." Ruth squirmed away while Tillie dragged her fingers up the inside of Ruth's thigh. "Does this mean they know about Ernesto? Why is he on borrowed time? I thought this plan was supposed to work? At least for now?"

Tillie made a small growl and went back to kissing Ruth's neck. "Can we talk about this later?" she whispered into Ruth's ear as she ran her fingers through Ruth's hair.

"Fine," Ruth whispered back. She grabbed Tillie's chin between her thumb and her forefinger and forced Tillie to meet her hazel gaze. "But don't you think I'll forget."

Tillie smiled and pulled Ruth's shirt over her head. "I'll make you forget." Ruth laughed and they fell into the pile of blankets, their bodies intertwined while the setting sun threw shadows onto their bedroom wall.

†

They all sat wrapped in quilts drinking tea at the kitchen table. Ernesto was quiet and James rested his hand on Ernesto's thigh. "We knew this would happen eventually," James said. Ernesto nodded.

Ruth and Tillie exchanged glances. Tillie chewed the inside of her lip. Ruth gave a shrug. "Well, we might still have a little time. They have no proof against you." Ernesto gave a little laugh. "Plus, I think your father's position is still protecting you."

Ernesto let out his breath and leaned back in his chair, his hand dropping to rest on the back of James' neck. "I just thought that getting married would buy us more time." He looked over at Tillie. "Your dad makes it sound like we should leave now." When Tillie didn't respond, he leaned forward again. "Right? Isn't that what it sounds like?"

"Well," Tillie began, keeping her eyes on her teacup. "I don't know if we need to leave right now. We could stay, just for a little longer. Besides, outside of your father and mine, it's all speculation at this point." James snorted and Ernesto rubbed his eyes.

Tillie felt Ruth squeeze her knee under the table, then Ruth addressed Ernesto. "We could stay a little longer and help Elizabeth with the resistance. Continue to funnel them information from the law office."

Tillie couldn't ignore the concerned glance between Ernesto and James when Ruth suggested again that they all stay.

"Ruth, the Nazis don't care about proof. The minute my father's position is no longer an issue, they're going to come after us." His eyes made their way around the table. "After all of us."

CHAPTER 34

July 1936

Goebbels' voice was quiet, and Tillie had to lean forward to ensure the notes she took were correct. "The goal is for those coming to our beloved Germany to see the splendor and prowess of the German athlete." The other men around the table nodded. "The Führer initially was less than excited about having the Olympic games here in our city." He paused and raised his black eyes to the men around the table. "However, I explained to him how beneficial it would be to have so many other countries here to see the Germany we've become under his guidance and rule." Tillie watched as the men continued to nod and whisper to one another in agreement.

"I've been tasked with making a film highlighting our athletes and their heightened physical abilities. The Führer has given me an extensive budget to do so and I'm in the process of finding the perfect director." He glanced at Tillie's father. "I would like you to draft a contract for the director as well as any athletes we feature."

Her father nodded and scribbled something in his notes. Goebbels steepled his fingers. "We want to present a new, strong, technologically advanced Germany. And I believe it's possible to do so."

A man from the end of the table cleared his throat. "I've come up with an idea." All eyes turned to him.

Goebbels gave a small, foxlike smile. "Please continue, Herr Mueller."

Herr Mueller nodded. "It has come to my attention, through several of our own party's researchers, that fire and flames were of great importance to the ancient Olympians." Tillie watched as Goebbels gestured for him to continue. "I propose a relay. A monumental relay. One that begins in Olympia and travels to our new stadium."

"A relay," Goebbels repeated.

"A relay, featuring all our best, Aryan athletes. Carrying a torch." Goebbels jerked his head up and tilted it to the side.

"A torch? You mean a flame?"

Herr Mueller smiled. "Yes. When the last athlete arrives at our beautiful stadium, he will climb a grand white staircase and use the torch that has just travelled two thousand miles to light the massive pyre in the center of our stadium. In front of thousands of onlookers and our Führer."

Goebbels smiled. "We could line the streets with all the people of our great nation and have them salute the Führer as the torch passes."

Mueller nodded. "It would be a brilliant display of our power as a nation as well as the talent of our athletes."

Goebbels looked at Herr Grandelis. "Take this to the Olympic committee. Ensure they are aware that the idea and the organization and execution of this idea are strictly German."

Herr Grandelis nodded. "Of course, sir."

The men talked among themselves while Tillie transcribed what was being said at the meeting. Herr Grandelis cleared his throat. "There is one other thing." He paused and pursed his lips. "It should be noted that a few athletes from the United States, among other nations, are planning to attend a separate event in Barcelona, in protest of the Führer."

Goebbels shrugged. "That may be, but we will display such hospitality and such generosity toward the other countries visiting us that no one will remember such a protest even happened." He paused, rubbing his chin. "I do think it prudent to remove some of our more aggressive language. If only while our visitors are here."

Another man Tillie only met once before raised his hand. "We can get both the Hitler Youth and The League of German Girls to paper more welcoming flyers over the more distasteful images in Berlin. Send them to shops to have them remove signs not allowing Jews into their establishments."

Goebbels nodded. "That would be helpful, thank you Herr Schirach. As for any other, shall we say, unpleasant imagery, the Führer would like to ensure that our guests remain ignorant of its existence."

Tillie's father tapped his pencil on his notebook. "Did you know," he began, "that in the United States, Black people have to ride in the back of buses and trains? In some cases, they're forced to stand so all the white people can sit."

The group was briefly quiet. Tillie watched as a small smile spread over Goebbels' face. "Well, we'll just have to make sure our citizens know they're expected to be extra welcoming to those visiting who are," he paused, "of *African* descent." He spat out the word *African* like it tasted badly in his mouth. "No sitting in the back of buses in Germany." His eyes glittered and the men around the table chuckled.

Goebbels dismissed the meeting before raising his hand and saying loudly over the din of papers being gathered and chairs being scraped along the floor, "And I think it goes without saying, no Jew athletes will be permitted to participate."

Tillie kept her eyes on her notes as all the men in the room laughed.

†

Elizabeth's eyes narrowed and Ruth picked up a piece of paper Tillie had set in the middle of the kitchen table. "I don't understand. They think they'll be able to just scrub away all evidence of the things they've done, and no other country will notice?"

Tillie shrugged. "I'm not sure other countries really care." She gestured to the notes. "Aside from those few athletes going to Spain instead of coming here, I'm not sure anyone is that concerned about what the Nazis are doing."

Helene crossed her legs. "Heinz made it to New York last month. I got a letter from him stating as much. There are headlines in every paper in the United States about Germany and what's happening." She rubbed her forehead. "They know what's going on here," Helene said, shaking her head. "They just don't care."

Tillie sipped her tea, contemplating. "They want Germany to appear sparkling, brand new. Like The Great War never happened. That's the goal." She leaned back into the comfortable armchair and sighed. "They want to show that by following along with Hitler and his regime, Germany has become a powerhouse. Hitler wants to show that he has created the perfect nation."

Ruth made a noise in her throat but didn't respond. James leaned forward. "But if that's true," he paused, "I just don't see how that will be accomplished."

"Goebbels is producing some movie, which we know is what he does best. He's looking for a director now. The Hitler kids are going to be cleaning up Berlin before the arrival of the other countries. It's not like they're going to see the labor prisons."

Elizabeth nodded. "And, keep in mind, most of Germany is on board. We're the minority right now. If I was reading horrible things happening in another country, but then went there and everyone I saw was happy, healthy, and well fed and seemingly supportive of the government, I'm not sure I would believe what was being printed in the papers about that country."

Tillie nodded. "The other countries are going to come here, see how beloved and revered Hitler is, and think the papers are exaggerating. And that's exactly what Goebbels and the rest of them want. This torch nonsense is just going to be icing on the cake, unfortunately."

James looked at his watch. "We should get going."

Ruth nodded and stood. She gave Helene a smile as she carried her cup and saucer to the kitchen. "Thanks ladies. Perhaps we can figure out some small act of defiance in the days leading up to the Olympics."

Helene nodded, though her eyes seemed troubled. Elizabeth rubbed her arms and looked down at all the notes scattered on the kitchen table. "I don't even know what we could do, honestly. How do we make people see what it's really like here? That's the question."

Tillie cleared her throat. "I'm not sure we can do anything. Announcements are being made to remove all the signs banning Jews from stores and Goebbels has already ordered several articles to be placed in *Der Angriff* reminding people to be good hosts."

Ruth snorted. "Good hosts to Jews from other countries while we're no longer citizens. Of course."

Elizabeth sighed. "Well, keep us posted of any updates and we'll keep brainstorming. But I think you might be right, if they're determined to show a country that doesn't really exist, I'm not sure we'll be able to do anything to change that."

†

Tillie peeled off her blouse, feeling sticky and gritty from the heavy hot air outside their apartment. Ruth was holding a cold towel to the back of her neck.

"I think we got out enough pamphlets," Ruth said, as Tillie pulled her hair up to get it off her sweaty neck. "At least enough to last until the Olympians arrive."

Tillie nodded but she could feel the tension on her face.

"What's wrong, doll? We did a good thing today, helping Helene and Elizabeth."

Tillie shrugged. "It just feels like it doesn't really matter." She met Ruth's eyes. "I hate it here."

Ruth didn't say anything. Her eyes stayed on Tillie's and Tillie could see her jaw clenching and unclenching.

Tillie blinked and she realized she felt the hate in her bones. "I mean it Ruth. I absolutely hate it here. We are miserable, we're constantly afraid, I'm the only one with a job. I mean, I love this city, I do. But I hate what it is now."

She gestured to the boys' room down the hall. "And that's not even talking about the stress Ernesto and James must feel. The idea that they could be arrested at any moment. Having to live with that day in and day out. No wonder Ernesto constantly looks like he's on the verge of tears. He probably is."

Ruth stood very still and Tillie could see she was trying to keep her breathing even. "Ruth."

Tillie's voice dropped to almost a whisper. "I know you keep saying that you don't want to leave, but Ernesto and James are in very real danger. You are in very real danger. I just don't think it's worth it anymore."

She pulled a clean shirt out of her drawer and pulled it over her head. She could feel Ruth's eyes on her back, drilling a hole into her skin. She turned and Ruth's jaw was set, her eyes glittering. "I'm not afraid."

Tillie stared at her and for the first time, she felt real rage over Ruth's stubbornness. "Well," she said, walking past her to their bedroom door. "Congratulations, because you might be the only one that isn't."

Tillie stalked into the kitchen and started to busy herself with cleaning up dishes, shutting the cupboards louder than necessary when the phone rang.

Muttering to herself, she picked it up and tried to disguise the bitterness in her voice. "Hello?" She leaned her head against the wall and closed her eyes, willing herself to calm down.

"Tillie?" A scared whisper came through the other line.

"Elizabeth?" Tillie's eyes popped open, and she stood up straight. "Are you alright?"

"Helene." She heard Elizabeth gasping for air. "She was arrested. They took her, Tillie."

Tillie's heart began to pound. "Are you at home? Where are you?"

Elizabeth gave Tillie the address of a diner in another neighborhood. Tillie nodded.

"Ruth and I will be right there." She hung up the phone and Ruth materialized in the doorway, her face still a mask of cold indifference.

"Who was that?"

"That," Tillie said, unable to keep the irritation out of her voice, "was Elizabeth. Helene has been arrested." She sat down to pull on her shoes while Ruth stood in the doorway, the blood draining from her face.

"We're to meet her at a diner up the road." Tillie looked up at Ruth and raised her eyebrows. "You afraid yet?"

She turned and walked out, not bothering to see if Ruth was following her.

She felt Ruth hurry next to her and her voice was soft. "Tills." Tillie didn't respond and kept her eyes forward, focusing on getting to Elizabeth. "Tillie." Ruth reached out and grabbed her arm, pulling her to a stop so that their eyes met.

"What?" Tillie crossed her arms in front of her.

"I'm sorry." Ruth's eyes were bright with tears.

"You're always sorry, Ruth. But you just keep pushing me with this. Why? Why is it so important to you that we stay here?"

Ruth shook her head, the tears dribbling down her cheeks. Tillie had to fight not to make a scene. She leaned forward so Ruth could hear her.

She barely moved her lips, but her words tasted of venom and anger. "We are not making one ounce of difference. You think this government will fall because we're printing anti-Nazi magazines disguised as recipe books and how-to manuals? You are fooling yourself thinking you're doing anything worthwhile to bring about any kind of change."

Tillie breathed in through her nose and then hissed, "Is the risk worth it? Is it worth being arrested and beaten and raped and God knows what else just to get under the skin of a couple of Nazis?"

Ruth wiped her face and lowered her eyes. "Everyone thinks like you do, that it won't make a difference. That's why our numbers are so small right now." She wasn't crying, but Tillie heard the lack of conviction in her voice.

"You don't believe that." Tillie waved her hand and kept walking. "That's just what all those SPD people keep telling you to keep you showing up with information. The information that you're getting from *me.*"

A thought struck her. "And tell me, Ruth, what have they done with all the stacks and stacks of information, of locations of high-ranking officials, of meetings, of the Nuremberg schedule that I've been feeding to them over the last few months? Have they done *anything?* Anything at all?" The rage that she felt back at the apartment returned. "No. They haven't."

They continued walking in silence toward the diner and they didn't speak again until they sat down across from a tear-soaked Elizabeth. She was drinking a cup of coffee, but every time she picked up her cup, it rattled in the saucer.

"Elizabeth," Tillie reached out toward her friend, "What happened?"

She shook her head and dropped her eyes. "She was putting pamphlets in one of the drop points. One of the bathrooms when an SS officer walked in. Someone Helene knew from before. I'm not exactly sure."

Ruth furrowed her brow. "Someone she knew from before? Who was it?"

Elizabeth shrugged and brushed new tears away. "Erik was across the street leaving booklets at a cafe. He heard her calling the officer 'Friedrich.'" She looked up. "Does that name mean anything to you?"

Tillie dropped her head into her hands. "Yes."

Ruth made a noise in her throat. "That snake."

"So, it was someone from before?" Elizabeth looked from Ruth to Tillie.

Tillie nodded. "Friedrich used to work at the institute with all of us. He knew Helene. He knew all of us; he was a groundskeeper and a gardener. He gave his allegiance to the Reich after they attacked the institute when Dora died." She rubbed a spot on the back of her neck. "I'm sure he recognized Helene, even dressed as Henry. Just bad luck."

Elizabeth sniffed. "She's not going to get back out," she whispered. "No one does. That's it. We're never going to see her again."

"No," Tillie agreed. "That's it."

Ruth leaned forward. "Does this mean the end of your work with the SPD?"

Elizabeth's eyes widened. "Of course not. We'll just have to be more careful. The good news is, when the officer informed me of her crimes, he said Helene was arrested for Paragraph 175. Which means she couldn't have had any of our literature still on her when she was taken in. Otherwise, she would have been charged as a dissident. So, the SPD is still protected."

Ruth nodded. "That is good news."

Tillie tightened her grip on her coffee cup and didn't speak to Ruth again for the rest of the evening.

CHAPTER 35

October 1936

Ernesto was in the kitchen when Tillie went to get her morning tea. He was sitting at the table, just staring at the wall. "Oh, good morning." She gave him a small smile. "I didn't expect anyone to be up yet."

He met her gaze and she saw deep purple circles under his eyes. "I haven't been to bed yet," he said.

She watched as tears started to fill his eyes. "Ernesto, what's wrong?" She sat next to him and took his hand.

He cleared his throat and rubbed his hand over his face. "James wants to leave now. He's tired of waiting and with most of our contacts with the SPD arrested, we don't have a reason to stay." He looked at her. "He wants to leave at the end of the year, at the latest."

She nodded. "I knew this would happen eventually. At some point, it would become so dangerous for you that we'd have to make a decision."

He took her hand. "I don't want to leave without you. I'm not sure it would even work; just me and James trying to leave without you and Ruth." Tears dripped onto the dark wood of the kitchen table. "James is terrified all the time. I owe him this, to get him out."

She nodded. "You would need to get papers changing James' last name. Would you try to be brothers? Or cousins, maybe?"

He shook his head. "I don't know. I'm not sure we could pass as brothers. I'm just so worried that without wives, we'll be questioned. That they'll know." He fought to keep in the sobs, and she felt her eyes prickle.

She squeezed his hand. "We'll figure something out. It'll be okay, Ernesto. We'll get you and James out." She wiped her eyes and stood. "You need to go get some rest and I have to get to work."

His mouth quirked into half a smile. "Okay, Tills. I'll see you when you get home." She kissed the top of his head and walked out the door, trying to focus on anything besides the fear she saw behind his eyes.

✝

Tillie sat at her desk, staring at her typewriter. She hadn't moved in over ten minutes, and she was still wearing her coat. She kept thinking about how it would look if the boys left without them. If she and Ruth stayed behind. The only contact they had left in the SPD was Elizabeth and the resistance group was down to five or six members. After Helene's arrest, some of the resistors went further underground in their fight against the Nazi government, but the ones she knew, they had nearly all their work.

She and Ruth would just be here, while she continued to work for her father. Eventually they would be found out, they would be arrested, and they would be separated. She could feel the goosebumps on her arms.

"Tillie?" She jumped at her father's quiet voice behind her. She turned and her father was standing in the doorway. He looked tired, his face lined and pale. She noticed for the first time that he looked like he had lost weight. "Tillie, darling, I have a meeting with Herr Grandelis and Herr Himmler. Can you come take notes please?"

She nodded; her stomach clenched. Shrugging off her coat, she followed her father into the conference room, her notepad and pen in hand. "Good morning gentlemen," she said as she took her seat. Himmler, who she had only ever seen at dinner parties, smiled at her. He was smaller than her father and Ernesto's father, with a blond mustache and a pointed face. His tiny round glasses made his face look even smaller.

"Tillie, it's so lovely to see you." He bowed his head in her direction. "I think what we're talking about today will interest you immensely." He winked at her.

Tillie shifted in her seat but didn't respond. As her father took his spot at the table, he opened a folder and said, "Well, let's get started, shall we?"

Himmler folded his hands in front of him on the table. "We are concerned about the declining birth rate in Germany." Tillie started transcribing. "Birth rates have been dropping since 1934. I have had an idea to support families and children who are," he paused, choosing his words, "biologically valuable."

Tillie looked at him, then to her father, who was jotting down notes. He sucked his bottom teeth and then looked to Herr Grandelis. "Well, I think it's doable to set up some sort of foundation. We can draft goals, a contract, make it a requirement for SS members to join said foundation."

Himmler nodded. "I'm going to call it *Lebensborn*. The goal will be to give support to racially valuable families who have many children or to give support to those who might not have children yet, where it would be beneficial to Germany for those women to pass on their genetics."

There was another pause and Tillie realized the scratching of her father's pen had stopped. She broke her eyes away from the two words she had written and looked up at the rest of the table, Himmler was looking directly at her, a smile on his lips. "Financial support, food, lodging; we would get whatever these women would need. Women who would birth racially, biologically valuable offspring for our great country." Tillie felt frozen under his gaze.

Her father cleared his throat, breaking Himmler's stare. "I think we can help you draft something."

Himmler clapped his hands. "Wonderful. I would also like to involve the League of German Girls to help recruit young women. We could pair up recruited women with members of the SS and end up with an army of good breeding partners. I would like to address the SS officers at the Rally of Freedom this month. So, let's have something by then."

Both her father and Herr Grandelis stood, shook his hand, and walked him out, leaving Tillie sitting at the table staring down at her paper, the only words she'd managed to write glaring back at her. *Biologically valuable.*

✝

"Well." James shook his head. "That's disgusting."

Tillie had to laugh in spite of herself. "I know, it really is." She poured another vodka and began sipping it slowly. She, James, and Ernesto were sitting around the table while she told them about the meeting with Himmler.

"It's like they're talking about breeding dogs." Ernesto shuddered. "It's so bizarre." He took a deep drink from his own glass. "What are you going to do if they want to send you away, Tills?"

She waved a hand. "My father would never let that happen. I'm not worried about it." She thought about the cold stare from Himmler during the meeting. She shook her head, trying to shake loose the image. "No. He wouldn't let that happen."

They were all sitting drinking when Ruth walked in, her face pink with cold.

Tillie tried to keep her voice even. "Where have you been?"

Ruth dumped her bag onto the table. "Leaving out pamphlets, walking the streets." Her words were short and cold.

Tillie watched James and Ernesto's eyes meet and Ernesto made the smallest face. Ruth missed it, but James had to duck his head to hide a giggle.

"So, you and Elizabeth are single handedly keeping the SPD alive, huh?" James couldn't keep the humor out of his voice. He raised his eyebrows when she looked in his direction. "Ruthie." He set his glass down. "Ruth. It's over. It's time."

Tillie kept her eyes on her glass and kept drinking.

"There's more than just me and Elizabeth." Ruth sounded irritated. "There are several other members that are still working on literature and other ways to fight back."

Ernesto gave Ruth a sad smile. "We're leaving at the end of the year. Heinz is getting us fake papers. You can join us if you'd like, we just have to get you papers."

He stood and took his glass to the sink before standing behind James, his hands on James' shoulders. "We can't keep waiting for you. We want you to come with us, but if you decide not to, we understand."

James stood and they both left the kitchen, leaving Ruth standing, still in her coat, and Tillie drinking the rest of her vodka.

"Are you going too?"

Tillie took a deep breath through her nose. "No, Ruth. Despite how angry I am with you right now. I'm not going to leave you behind." She looked up at her girlfriend. "So, I guess the upside of being arrested and sent away is that we'll be together."

Ruth let out a sigh. "Tills." Her voice was quiet and soft. "Doll."

Tillie held up her hand. "Don't. You're asking me to choose between you and my best friend. They are in more danger than we are, so they need to go. And I will obviously choose you because I love you and you are my life." She looked up at Ruth.

"But it's going to take me a while to forgive you."

Ruth gave a nod and Tillie stood. She stopped just outside their bedroom without turning back around. "I hope you know what you're doing, Ruth."

CHAPTER 36

December 1936

Tillie sat at her desk, staring at the blinking light on her desktop phone. After the massive turnout at the Nuremberg rally in September, her father and Herr Grandelis had an influx of clients, mostly SS officers, and it was rare for Tillie to have a quiet moment in the office.

She'd been required to attend meetings with other lawyers, as there was discussion of pulling in more attorneys and new assistants that Tillie would be in charge of training. She'd never seen her father so pleased about how work was going. "What did I tell you, Tillie?" he kept saying. "The Führer is rescuing the German people, just like he said he would."

Tillie didn't bother to mention that most of the German people she knew had either fled the country, were locked away someplace, gone without a trace, or dead.

"Matilda," a low, gravelly voice broke her stare. Looking up, she saw Goebbels limping toward her across the office. Sighing to herself, she forced a smile.

"Hello Herr Goebbels. How are you today, sir?"

"Fine." His voice was sharp and his eyes narrow and menacing. He stopped next to her chair and tilted his head to the side, splaying his fingers over the edge of her desk. "I'm here to have a meeting with you and your father."

Tillie tried to mask her confusion. "A meeting with both of us?"

He nodded. "Yes. Let him know I'm here." At that moment, Tillie's father opened his door. "Joseph. Wonderful to see you. Tillie, would you join us, please?" Tillie stood, a pen and notepad in her hand. Her father wouldn't meet her eyes.

Once they were all seated, her father cleared his throat. Tillie could see him fidgeting in his seat and there were small beads of sweat above his lip.

"Well. Best get to it." He looked up at her. "Tillie, you will be moving to the Ministry of Propaganda and Public Enlightenment after the Christmas holiday. Herr Goebbels has requested to have you as one of his personal secretaries."

Tillie sat very still, keeping her eyes on the pen in her hand. Goebbels spoke, but his voice sounded extremely far away, like she was underwater. "We have a large office, in charge of the press, film, radio, plus the printing of *Der Angriff*. I really do need multiple secretaries to help me. After speaking with your father, Herr Himmler, and Anthony, removing you from Berlin to come to work in my office is the best option for you. I will also be introducing you to several SS officers that I have chosen to be appropriate suitors." He rose from his seat and her father copied him.

"A replacement has been hired and will be trained by you here before you relocate to my office." He adjusted his tie and turned to the door. "You will start in two weeks, just after the first of the year. That gives you several days to train your replacement before the holiday and next week your lodgings can be secured."

He looked at her with his dark, narrow eyes, his face foxlike. "Many of the girls who work for our office reside in a girl's boarding house about a block from the building. I shall have my other assistant pass along the information to your father."

He limped to the door, pausing just outside the door frame, his back still to her. "That also gives you two weeks to remove Anthony's son from your life. Your marriage will be annulled when you begin working at my office. You are not to see that criminal again." He continued walking, while Tillie and her father stood in silence in his office.

Trembling, Tillie turned to her father, his face a white sheet. "Papa, what is happening? What have you done?" She couldn't keep the panic from creeping in and her voice shook.

Her father looked down at his desk. "Herr Goebbels is trying to protect you from making mistakes." His voice was quiet and resigned. "Ernesto is going to be," he paused without looking up. Clearing his throat and looking strained, he seemed to have to force himself to continue. "Ernesto is going to be detained. I imagine it will happen when you are moved to your new position. I doubt it will happen this week, as Christmas is on Friday." He looked up at Tillie's stricken face. "The longer you stay with him, the more danger you are in."

It took her a moment to find her voice. "Papa. This is Ernesto we're talking about. The skinny little boy who used to walk me to school every day. How can you talk about him like he is some criminal?"

Her father suddenly banged his fist on his desk, causing Tillie to jump, her heart pounding loudly. "He *is* a criminal!" Her father was shouting at her now. "He is what keeps good Germans from reaching their potential. Good Germans like you, Matilda."

He pointed a shaking finger at her face. She took a step backward when her father's face twisted into a mask she didn't recognize. His voice dropped to a hiss. "Anthony told me why he was kicked out all those years ago. He told me Ernesto isn't a Communist." Her father's face was purple with rage. "I trusted you. And you lied to me. You made me believe he was a good man, that he wanted to take care of you."

Tillie's breath was coming in short gasps, and she couldn't form words. Her face felt hot, but the rest of her body felt cold and she couldn't stop shivering.

"This entire time, he was a disgusting pervert and he used you to protect himself. And you let him. How could you? What was in it for you? Why would you involve yourself in such a ridiculous situation? Your mother and I raised you better than this." A small tear slid down Tillie's face and dripped onto the notepad still in her hands. Her father composed himself and straightened his tie.

"Well, it doesn't matter anymore. He will be arrested, you will be moved to Joseph's office where he can keep an eye on you, your ridiculous marriage will be erased, and you'll meet a nice German SS boy. This entire thing will be just a minor hiccup in your life." Her father sat back down at his desk, clearly dismissing her. "Your first day at Joseph's office will be Monday, January fourth. Your replacement will be here tomorrow for you to train."

Tillie stood for a moment, unsure what to do next. The words were stuck in her throat, while hot tears streamed down her face. Her father glanced up. "Is there something you'd like to say?"

She was about to squeak out the word "no" when her father leaned back in his chair. "An apology perhaps?" There was a look of smugness on his face she didn't recognize. Her belly filled with red-hot anger.

She wiped her tears and clenched her jaw. "Ernesto was never my boyfriend."

Her father snorted. "You don't say," his voice was bitter and cold.

"He was never my boyfriend because I've been with the same woman for the last ten years. Her name is Ruth. She and I have lived together for close to nine years. You met her once, actually, when you saw me on the street, and you thought we were at Ernesto's building. She came outside. That's the apartment that *we* share."

Her voice grew stronger. "The institute where Ernesto worked? I worked there too, in the library on weekends. Those perverts Himmler and Hitler and the rest of them keep arresting and throwing in labor camps are my friends and my family." She leaned forward on his desk, getting close to his face, his eyes wide with shock. "I'm one of them, Papa. And we are better Germans than you and all your Nazi friends will ever be," she spat, her voice sharp and angry.

She threw the notepad and the pen onto her father's desk. "Train your own new secretary." She turned and strode out of the office, stopping only to grab her purse from her desk, before slamming the front door behind her.

†

"Wait, slow down." Ernesto was following Tillie's pacing with his eyes. "I'm going to be arrested?"

"Yes," Tillie was frantic, wringing her hands and taking laps around their small kitchen. "And they're forcing me to go work for Goebbels at his office telling lies to the German people."

She stopped, remembering all the things she told her father. She suddenly felt sick and exhausted. She moaned and slid into a chair.

For a split second, no one moved. Then James jumped up. "We have to get out of here." His eyes were wild. "Where can we go?"

Ruth was already walking to the phone. "I'll call Elizabeth. You can stay there for the time being. She has a wine cellar that we converted to the meeting space and the doorway is hidden. You can hide there." She picked up the phone and started dialing. "Go. Go now. I'll pack your stuff for you and bring it over."

Ernesto nodded and they grabbed their coats and hats before hurrying out the door. Tillie could hear Ruth explaining things to Elizabeth, but she wasn't really listening.

After Ruth hung up the phone, she came and sat with Tillie. "I'm sure they have time to get out before they come to arrest him. I doubt they'll do anything before the weekend."

Tillie didn't say anything right away. Then she said, "I told my father about you." She put her head into her hands, feeling the tears prick her eyes.

"You what?" She heard Ruth's chair scrape the linoleum floor and Ruth knelt down at Tillie's feet, putting her hands on Tillie's knees. "You told your father about me?" Her voice was soft.

Tillie looked up and met Ruth's gaze but couldn't read her expression. "Are you upset with me?" She couldn't keep the tears in, and a sob escaped her throat. "I'm so sorry, I know I shouldn't have. But I was just so angry. He looked so pleased with himself, demanding I apologize to him. Me. Apologize to him. After they ruined our lives." She wiped her nose with her sleeve.

Ruth cupped Tillie's face in her hand. "No. I'm not angry," she said quietly. "I'm actually really happy."

Tillie straightened. "Happy?"

"Yeah." Ruth shrugged. "You told him the truth. You said it out loud to your father that you love me. That's a big deal, Tills."

Tillie dropped to the floor and took Ruth's hands in her own. "But what if they come after us? After you? What if I just did something stupid?"

Ruth shook her head and leaned forward to take Tillie into her long arms. "Your father won't tell anyone. There's already a plan in place and as angry as he probably is about Ernesto, I don't think he would have you arrested. He's not like Ernesto's father. He'll protect you, especially now that you're going to work for Goebbels."

"I can't. I can't go work for him." She buried her face in Ruth's neck. "What are we going to do?" she whispered.

She felt Ruth's body tense. "It'll be okay, we'll figure something out." She leaned back on her heels. "In the meantime, I'm going to go pack a suitcase for the boys. Just in case they end up having to stay there until their papers come."

Tillie nodded, watching Ruth stand and walk into the boys' bedroom, bustling around grabbing changes of clothes and toothbrushes. She felt a nagging in the back of her brain, as Ruth busied herself with zipping up the bag and wrapping a scarf around her head in preparation for the quick train ride across town.

"We'll get to have the apartment to ourselves tonight, that'll be fun, huh?" She gave Tillie a quick grin with bright red lips before walking outside and closing the door quietly behind her.

Tillie felt glued to the floor. This was it; the reason they had been waiting for, without realizing they were waiting. She was being forced to relocate and to work directly for Goebbels. Ernesto and James were going to be arrested and taken to some horrible place, never to be seen again. Ruth would be left here in this apartment all alone. It was time to leave. They had gotten married, which was the beginning of the plan. Time to follow through with the rest.

She stood and dug through her letters until she found what she was looking for and picked up the phone, dialing carefully in the hopes a familiar voice answered.

When Ruth returned, Tillie was sitting at the kitchen table drinking a cup of tea. She walked in with a bag of treats from the bakery near Elizabeth's house and sighed as she sat down.

"Okay, the boys are all set at Elizabeth's. They can stay as long as they need to."

Tillie nodded without speaking.

Ruth leaned forward to take Tillie's hand. "It'll be okay. Just think about how much intel you'll be able to get working for Goebbels. I talked about it with Elizabeth and Erik, and you'll be like a spy. You'll get to see everything that the Nazis are doing. This could be good for us and for the resistance."

Tillie raised her eyes from her tea. "I spoke with Heinz. I called him after you left. He's sending us paperwork. New passports to get out. He's changing Ernesto's name on the paperwork to Aaron Wagner since they're looking for him now. He promised to rush the new papers and to get us everything by next week so that we can leave on New Year's Day."

She took a sip of her tea and Ruth let go of her hand. "That gives me next week to pretend to move into the new lodgings and check in with Goebbels, then we'll have the long weekend to get out of Germany. We'll be in Portugal before anyone realizes we've left."

"Doll." Ruth's voice was calm and even, but Tillie could see the shock in her eyes. "We can't leave now. I know it seems like the SPD is floundering, especially after Helene. But we're just starting. Think of all the good you can do working in the Ministry. You can funnel information to Elizabeth and to Erik. We can use you. Helene, Erwin, Adelaide, Dora. They can't have died in vain. We have to keep working."

Tillie pursed her lips. "I don't want to be used. I want to be safe. I want the people I love to be safe." She stood, carrying her cup and saucer to the sink, hoping Ruth couldn't hear the delicate China rattling under her shaking hands.

"Do you expect to go into hiding at Elizabeth's house? What happens when I'm forced to leave, and the boys leave and you're here all alone? Are you going to hide out at Elizabeth's for a year? Two? Five? We don't know how long this is going to go on." She set her cup gently into the sink.

"And, frankly Ruth, I realize that you enjoy all this cloak and dagger nonsense, but I do not. And I'm not going to work for Goebbels." She took a deep breath and turned to face the woman she had loved for the last ten years. "We are leaving a week from Friday." Their eyes met. Ruth's were filled with tears and Tillie's voice dropped to a desperate whisper. "Please, Ruth. Please. It's time."

When Tillie awoke the next morning, Ruth was gone. She wrapped a blanket around her shoulders and wandered into the freezing kitchen to make a cup of tea when she heard loud footsteps in the hallway outside the apartment. Pausing with the box of tea in her hand, she took two steps toward the door when it burst open, her kitchen flooded with shouting SS officers, their guns drawn and pointed in her direction.

She screamed and threw her hands up to shield her face, her blanket dropping to the ground exposing her thin nightdress.

"Where is he?" A calm voice rose over the chaos of the officers tearing through the small apartment shouting at one another.

Tillie lowered her hands when she saw Himmler standing in front of her, his hands clasped behind his back. He was dressed all in black with the SS symbol on his lapel and the blood red cuff around his upper arm.

"Who?"

"Ernesto Grandelis. We're here to arrest him for crimes in connection with Paragraph 175." Out of the corner of her eye, Tillie caught an SS officer opening the pantry door in her kitchen and her heart thudded loudly.

"He's not here," she said, louder than she intended, while she snatched up her blanket to cover herself, and walked over to close the pantry door. She knew her notes were well hidden, but that didn't mean the officers wouldn't find them.

She cleared her throat and looked back at Himmler, who hadn't taken his eyes off her. "I don't know where he is. He wasn't here when I came home from work."

"I thought he was your husband?" Himmler wore a smirk, and his eyes were cold and dark. "It seems inappropriate that your husband would leave you here alone." She heard the question in his voice. She felt her stomach lurch. Could her father have told him about Ruth?

"I telephoned him when I left my father's office to inform him of the plan my father and Herr Goebbels have concocted for me." Tillie wasn't sure how much Himmler knew, but she assumed it was enough. "He was gone when I arrived home."

She shrugged, trying to seem indifferent. "I have ten days to relax and enjoy my holiday before I'm forced to work for Goebbels, so that's what I'm planning to do."

Himmler nodded slowly and a small smile appeared on his lips. He turned to one of the other soldiers. "Anything?"

The man shook his head. "They don't share a bedroom, though, that's for sure." His eyes went to Tillie, a mixture of disgust and anger on his face. Tillie shuddered under the soldier's hateful stare.

"Oh, I have no doubt about that." Himmler turned back to Tillie. "Harboring a criminal is a punishable offense, my dear." His voice was pleasant, but Tillie could hear the warning swimming just under the surface of his words. "Joseph's little obsession with you will only keep you safe for so long."

Himmler called to the rest of the soldiers, now standing around in the hallway and spilling into Tillie's kitchen. "Gentlemen, it seems we have a fugitive on our hands." The rest of the soldiers began to file out Tillie's front door, Himmler waiting until everyone was out before turning back to Tillie.

"Good luck with your new position, Matilda. Let Ernesto know we're looking for him." He disappeared into the dimly lit stairwell behind the other soldiers and Tillie closed the door behind him, before her knees buckled and she slid to the floor, too shocked and terrified to even cry.

✝

She walked across the train platform, keeping her eyes down. Very few people were out, as the snow swirled around her, just SS and last-minute shoppers trying to get a few errands in before everything closed up for Christmas. Tillie hurried through the cold on her way to Elizabeth's, knowing that would be where she would find Ruth.

After the visit from Himmler, she phoned them from a pay phone to tell Ruth and the boys not to return home. She didn't know if or when they would be back, and she didn't want to chance it. The conversation hadn't gone smoothly. Tillie replayed every word in her mind for what seemed like the millionth time.

"Himmler told me Goebbels is obsessed with me. We have to leave, Ruth. I know you don't want to, but the danger we're in isn't abstract anymore. It's real." Ruth was quiet and didn't answer right away. "We could just stay here. They don't know our connection to Elizabeth. You could go work for Goebbels and report back when you're able."

"And when he forces me into a marriage with some Nazi he picks out especially for me? Then what, Ruth? Then what do I do? You're willing to sacrifice me to some SS officer all for a floundering resistance?" Tillie knew that would be the breaking point.

Ruth sighed. "Of course not." She paused. "You're right. You can't stay here."

"We can't stay," Tillie had corrected her.

"*We*. We can't stay."

She knocked on the dark wooden front door and smiled when Elizabeth opened the door. "Hello, Tillie!" Her round face was slightly flushed, and she held a glass of champagne in her hand. "Please, come in, come in. Merry Christmas." She widened the door and Tillie saw Ruth, James, Ernesto, and several other faces she didn't recognize around the small sitting room. Everyone had a drink in their hand, everyone looked happy and smiling. There seemed to be no concern over Himmler, the SS, or her impending move to Goebbels office.

"Hello everyone." Tillie gave a strained smile and Erik handed her a glass of champagne. Upon closer inspection, James and

Ernesto's smiles looked forced and tight. She raised her eyebrows and Ruth stood. James and Ernesto followed suit. Ruth cleared her throat. "Elizabeth, can we use your parlor for just a moment?"

Elizabeth nodded and pointed in the direction of a set of pocket doors to the left. Ruth led the way while James, Tillie, and Ernesto followed. Ernesto quietly pulled the doors closed behind them.

Tillie took a deep breath and downed her entire glass of champagne, feeling the warmth spread through her gut and down to her toes.

"Well?" James had his eyes on Tillie and his face was pale, his eyes concerned and full of questions.

"Our new paperwork should be here by the middle of next week. Wednesday at the latest. You will be my brother; Ernesto will be my husband. That makes Ruth my sister-in-law. His passport will have a fake name, yours and Ruth's will just be a different last name. To hide your Jewish heritage." James nodded and Ernesto looked relieved.

"I think it will be okay to come back to the apartment to pack up a few more things the night before we leave. Since I'm supposed to be getting ready for my new job and moving, I don't think the SS officers will be back. At least not for a while."

Ruth spoke. "Elizabeth will be applying at the Ministry the week after we leave, with the hopes of getting the position you were supposed to take. Maybe we'll get lucky." She quickly corrected herself. "I mean, the SPD. Maybe the SPD will get lucky."

"So, you're going to go meet with this other secretary to get your new apartment on Monday, our paperwork should be here Wednesday, and we'll leave on Friday morning." Ernesto talked it through, more to himself than anyone else. James took his hand and kissed his fingertips.

"It'll be okay, love." James smiled gently at Ernesto and Tillie caught Ruth watching them, her face sad.

She turned, as if feeling Tillie's gaze. "I'm going to come home with you tonight. That Himmler doesn't scare me," she joked, winking. She smiled at Tillie, but her eyes still looked sad. "We'll have a whole week with just us in the apartment. It'll be like a honeymoon."

Tillie forced a little laugh. "That sounds lovely." Tillie couldn't help but notice the glance between James and Ernesto, their eyes full of worry.

†

"You're responsible for getting yourself to and from the office, but we all typically leave at the same time." The girl's black heels clicked down the long hallway of the boarding house, her blond hair bouncing as she walked.

"Herr Goebbels is a lovely boss," she was saying. "He's so thoughtful and considerate. And his wife, Magda, is a close personal friend of the Führer's. Not that Herr Goebbels isn't," she added quickly. "But it's just so refreshing to see a German woman sitting at the table, as it were." She cleared her throat, evidently embarrassed that she was gushing.

"Anyway, your room is at the very end of the hall. Curfew is nine p.m., lights out at ten."

Tillie stopped walking. "We have a bedtime?"

The girl shrugged. "The couple that run the boarding house like it quiet. It's not that bad once you get used to it."

Another woman walked past them down the hallway, clearly quite pregnant. Tillie watched her, her eyes wide. The girl giving the tour said a polite hello to the pregnant woman, while continuing to walk.

The girl's voice dropped to a whisper. "There are pregnant girls who come through every so often. They leave once their babies are born, but the rumor is that the babies get adopted by high level officials."

The girl shrugged again, but Tillie knew the rumors were true. She was in the meeting when Himmler proposed the program. She fought a shudder and gave the girl a tight smile.

"I'm sure I'll be very comfortable here, thank you for showing me around." Tillie put down the empty suitcase in the closet of what was supposed to be her new bedroom. "I'll be coming and going over the next few days, moving my things." The girl nodded; her arms folded across her chest. Tillie tried to keep her voice even and kept eye contact. "I'm going to be visiting a friend for New Years, so I won't be back until the third. Just so you know."

The girl's eyes narrowed for a fraction of a second and then she cocked an eyebrow. "A friend? Or a *friend.*"

Tillie realized the girl just wanted to gossip and she faked a giggle. "Oh, you know how it is. Gotta get one more fun weekend in before moving to the convent."

The girl let out a laugh. "Don't I know it. Well, if I don't see you before then, have a good time. I'll see you on the third."

CHAPTER 37

January 1937

The air was dry and cold when they awoke in the dark. Tillie rolled out of bed and gasped as her bare feet hit the freezing floor. "Ruth," she whispered. "Time to get up."

Ruth rolled over and Tillie put her hand to Ruth's swollen face. She'd been crying and had deep purple circles under her eyes. "Didn't you sleep at all?"

Ruth shook her head. "I couldn't. I think I might have dozed off around three." She dropped her eyes from Tillie's gaze and got out of bed with her back to Tillie. "We should get ready to go and make sure the boys are here." Her voice was flat and emotionless.

Tillie watched Ruth's back as she pulled on a pair of black pants and a crisp, blue blouse. She walked out of their room without a second glance back at Tillie and closed the door behind her. Tillie stared at the closed door, her heart pounding, her stomach in knots.

The boys were back from Elizabeth's, but the lights were off and it felt even colder than the bedroom. Tillie could see steam rising from the mugs of coffee set on the table waiting for them.

"Let's go over it one more time." Ernesto's face was tight and pale. He kept glancing at the door, as if expecting SS officers to storm in any minute. James sighed and picked up his forged passport.

"I'm James Weber. Tillie's brother. Married to Ruth. Son of Alice and Vincent. You are Aaron Wagner, married to Tillie Wagner. But you've just gotten married which is why her passport still has her maiden name. We're just a group of German friends getting ready to go on holiday to celebrate our marriages."

Ernesto nodded and turned to Ruth. She rolled her eyes. "I think I can remember our cover story well enough. It's not like we changed anything important." Tillie rested a hand on the small of Ruth's back.

"We just want to be prepared for any questions." Tillie picked at the food in front of her, finding herself, once again, without an appetite. She felt slightly sick and pushed her plate away. "I can't eat. I'm too nervous."

Ernesto set the train tickets to Portugal down in the center of the table. "We're all nervous, Tills." His mouth was set in a grim line and James took his hand. Ernesto rubbed his thumb in mindless circles on the back of James' hand and then sighed. "We should have left back in '34. As soon as he became president, we should have left."

They all looked around the dark kitchen. Ruth took a deep breath and let it out slowly. "So, I guess this is it for our apartment." James put his hand over Ruth's and gave her a sad smile.

"Maybe we'll be able to come back. Once this is all over." He squeezed her hand, trying to be reassuring. She smiled back and took a long sip of coffee.

Ernesto cleared his throat. "We should probably get going." They all nodded and washed their mugs in the sink.

"What will happen? To all our things?" Tillie looked around at their small apartment. They could only pack one suitcase each. It couldn't look like they were leaving permanently, so almost everything they owned was in its place, save for a few sets of clothing and a hatbox full of photos Tillie carried.

Ruth shrugged. "Does it matter?" She put her mug back in the cupboard.

Tillie's eyes fell on the pantry. "Should we destroy the notes? From my father's office? Or take them with us?" Ruth spun from the sink.

"No!" Her voice was sharp and sounded like a thunderclap in the quiet of the early morning. James and Ernesto stared at her, and Tillie shrunk back.

"Oh, okay. I just thought ..." she trailed off, trying to read Ruth's stone face.

"No, I just mean when Elizabeth realizes we left, she could come and get them. They could be helpful to the SPD. We should just leave them here."

Tillie watched Ruth for a moment; the tension in the kitchen was thick. No one dared to breathe. Ruth was standing rigid, blocking the pantry door. "We shouldn't destroy them," she said again.

James licked his lips. "Well, then I guess we should leave them." He and Ernesto exchanged a glance. Ernesto checked his watch and raised his eyebrows. James nodded. "Ruthie," he held out his hand. "You ready?"

Ruth looked at James' outstretched hand. She was so pale and the purple circles under her eyes so dark, she looked ill. She nodded and took his hand. They all walked out and didn't bother locking the apartment door behind them.

They walked with purpose to the train station, James holding Ruth's hand, Ernesto's arm looped through Tillie's elbow. From now until they arrived in Portugal, they were two married couples.

Tillie's eyes fell on the shops and clubs in their neighborhood. Most of the windows were broken or boarded up, large red flags with big black swastikas glowed in the darkness throughout the street, hanging off doors and overhangs. In several places, JUDE in large yellow letters jumped out at them as they walked.

"Can we walk past the institute? We have a little time." Ernesto's voice was small and quiet, and Tillie's eyes stung.

"I think so." They turned and took the familiar walk through the avenues where the clubs used to be, all closed now. Notices of closures and glass littered the ground surrounding all the buildings they used to frequent. The club owners had long since been arrested or fled to another country.

Tillie's eyes fell on The Belle Club. The windows were covered in long, weathered plywood and the sign overhead was missing letters. Ruth stopped and stood in front of her club her eyes bright with tears.

The sun was beginning to rise, turning the sky a brilliant pink. With the sun came the daytime officers, patrolling the streets and swinging their batons. "Ruth," Tillie said gently, "we should probably keep moving."

Tillie could see Ruth swallowing, her jaw clenched to keep the tears from falling. She reached out and touched the handle of the door, like it was a sleeping child. Then she nodded and turned, taking James' hand once more as they continued their walk to the institute.

"Oh." Ernesto let out a small gasp as they rounded the corner.

The beautiful building that had once been home for Ernesto and Ruth, for all of them really, stood stark and barren in front of them. No windows or doors were left, and scorch marks were etched like scars on the sides of the brick where the building had burned. Dr. Hirschfeld's statue was gone, though Tillie knew it would be, having seen it thrown into fire four years earlier.

Ruth made a noise in her throat and Tillie looked over. Ruth's eyes were narrowed, and her face was set with rage. Tillie followed her gaze to the back building, the one that had once served as a residence for Dr. Hirschfeld and Karl. Its garden was well tended and there was a flutter of activity between it and the entrance to the main building where Ernesto's dormitory used to be.

Nazi flags hung from every window. The red flags looked like flames in the brightness of the rising sun. Tillie's nose and feet were numb with cold, but her cheeks burned with anger. "What did they do?" she heard Ernesto hiss.

Tillie stood for a moment, then took the little path that led to the back of the building. Ernesto called after her to come back, but she ignored him, continuing on to the back of the building. Careful not to look at the place where Dora died, she saw a man leaning against the wall smoking a cigarette.

"Excuse me," she smiled as she walked up to the man. He looked at her, his eyes tired and suspicious. "Could you tell me what's going on in this back building?"

He said nothing but put out his cigarette and stood up from the wall, folding his arms in front of his chest. Tillie hurried on. "I'm supposed to have a job interview for a secretary position and I'm just not sure I'm in the right place."

At this, his face relaxed. "Oh. That back building is the Institute of Studies. They do racial hygiene classes and study things related to the Jewish Question." Tillie nodded, trying to keep her face even. "And this building," he gestured to the back half of the dormitory building, "has Arthur Gutt's office. His labs are in there as well."

Tillie must have looked confused because the man continued. "He does the prevention of children with hereditary diseases." He shrugged. "Keeping anyone who would birth a less than suitable German from having children."

Tillie gave the man a tight smile. "Thank you." She turned to walk away when the man grabbed her elbow.

"I can walk you to your interview if you like. I'm on break for another ten minutes."

Tillie smiled again and shook her head. "Turns out I'm not in the right place. Have a nice day." The man's eyes narrowed at her again.

"Heil Hitler." His voice was hard. He had his back to the rising sun, his face shrouded in shadow.

"Heil Hitler," Tillie answered quietly.

Walking to the front of the building back to her friends, she hissed at them as she approached. "Turn and keep walking."

They didn't speak again until they turned the corner and Dr. Hirschfeld's institute disappeared behind them.

Ruth grabbed Tillie's arm. "What was that about?"

Tillie's voice shook. "The Nazis took over Dr. H.'s house. To study something called 'racial hygiene.'" Tillie closed her eyes to fight the wave of sickness pulling her under. "And in his labs, in the dormitories, is where the doctor who does the surgeries." She shuddered. "The surgeries to keep people from having children."

Ruth shook her head and pulled Tillie into a hug. She felt Ernesto's hand squeezing her shoulder. "Using Dr. H.'s buildings for that. It's unconscionable."

James wiped his eyes. "We should keep moving. Get to the train station. It was a mistake to come here."

Ernesto nodded. "I just wanted to say goodbye to Dora. Our life here." His voice was thick and choked.

They kept walking with their eyes down, past multiple SS agents. Tillie could smell the sweat from Ernesto, despite the freezing temperatures. He smelled like fear.

Arriving at the train station, Tillie's heartbeat quickened. There were SS agents swarming the station's platforms like ants, stopping travelers every few feet demanding to see their paperwork. She felt Ernesto's hand tighten on her forearm and she gave a squeeze back, trying to be reassuring.

She glanced at Ruth walking on the other side of her. Ruth's face looked clammy; her mouth set in a grim line. She did not return Tillie's glance. Frowning, Tillie wanted to reach out, take Ruth's hand, but she didn't dare. Not with all the agents surrounding them.

"We're almost there," she whispered to Ruth. Then, even quieter, "I love you. We're okay."

Ruth nodded her head once but continued to keep her eyes forward and didn't respond.

They spotted their train and began to walk toward it when a large man with blank, dark eyes stopped them. "Papers." He sounded bored. Ernesto pulled the stack of papers out of his coat pocket that included their birth certificates and passports.

James followed Ernesto's lead and handed over his forged birth certificate listing him as Tillie's brother and Ruth's paperwork listing her as his wife. Their real birth certificates and passports were hidden inside the front of Tillie's suitcase, sewn into the lining.

The SS agent looked at each of their pictures carefully and then at each of their faces. Tillie wanted to fill the silence with chatter but remembered Heinz's advice about staying quiet when faced with any of the Stormtroopers.

"Where are you heading?" The SS agent raised his gaze to Ernesto, then looked at James. James smiled.

"We've all just been married. We decided to take a holiday to celebrate. Just for a long weekend." The SS agent nodded.

"What day will you be returning?"

This time Ernesto answered. "Sunday afternoon."

"Make sure you check in with the proper authorities upon your return." The SS agent handed back their paperwork and gestured to the train behind him, signaling they were free to go. Tillie tried not to release the breath she had been holding all at once. She didn't want to draw any attention to themselves.

They walked to the back of the train and Tillie sank into one of the chairs. Closing her eyes, she felt the relief wash over her. Another few days, they'll be at Ernesto's cousin's house in Portugal and then hopefully on their way to America, if they were lucky. But at least Portugal would be safe for the time being. She felt Ruth stir next to her and Tillie opened her eyes. "Are you alright?"

Ruth looked behind her back up the train, biting the edge of her fingernail. She nodded, not making eye contact with Tillie. "Yes, I'm fine."

A whistle sounded. Tillie patted the top of Ruth's hand. She whispered, "It's going to be fine, in a few more hours we'll be out of Germany and home free." Ruth nodded, still not making eye contact. Her eyes were darting around the train. She turned to Tillie.

"I'm going to use the restroom before the train gets going," She turned to Tillie and looked deep into her eyes. "I love you." She said it with so much force that Tillie stared at her, taking in her pinched, serious face.

"Ruth, what's wrong?"

Ruth nodded, still looking into Tillie's eyes. Then she smiled, but Tillie thought it seemed forced. "Nothing. I'm fine. I'm just a little nervous."

Tillie rubbed Ruth's forearm. "I know. But we'll be moving in a few minutes and out of Germany in a few hours. We're going to be okay now." Ruth broke her gaze and looked down at her lap.

"Alright, I'm going to the restroom." Tillie nodded and closed her eyes again, waiting for the train to start moving.

She heard a throat clear from across the aisle and she opened her eyes again. "Is Ruth okay?" Ernesto asked. He and James were sitting together, but James looked as unsettled as Ruth.

"I think so. She's just feeling a bit nervous." A second whistle sounded, and the train gave a lurch. Tillie leaned forward to rub a tense spot in her neck and happened to glance out the window.

There, standing on the platform, was Ruth, looking back at her, her suitcase by her feet. Tillie's stomach dropped and she shot to her feet. The train lurched again, and she started looking around for the exit, but before she could get to it the train started to move.

"NO!" Tillie screamed and she turned and started banging on the window. "Stop, someone tell them to stop the train." She was banging on the window so hard that she heard a crack in the glass. She felt hands on her shoulders, and she was being pulled back. She was still screaming, and her insides felt like ice.

"Tillie, stop it," Ernesto hissed into her ear. "People are staring." He tried to get her to sit down, but the adrenaline was too much for him and she wrenched out of his grip screaming Ruth's name and continuing to bang on the window. "James, help me!" Then Tillie felt a second set of hands on her arms pulling her back.

She heard a deep voice asking if there was a problem, and she looked wild-eyed into the aisle to see an SS officer standing staring at them. The red armband he wore hurt Tillie's eyes. She turned back to the window and saw Ruth standing there, tears streaming down her face.

James apologized to the guard while continuing to try and get Tillie to sit down and Ernesto stepped into the aisle. Very quietly he leaned into the guard and said, "My wife and I recently lost our daughter, Ruth. She's very distraught at taking this holiday to the country, feels she's leaving our daughter behind. I'm sure you understand." The officer stared at Ernesto then looked to James, his hands still on Tillie's shoulders while she sobbed against the window.

"Who's he?"

"That's my brother-in-law, her brother. I have all our paperwork in my bag if you'd like to see it."

The officer stood a few beats longer and then said, "Get her under control then. If you cannot, you'll be escorted off the train." He walked away.

Tillie heard James whisper into her ear, "Tillie, you have to be quiet or they're going to kick us off the train." She turned to look at him and saw he was crying too.

As the train picked up steam, she watched as Ruth's bright red lips mouthed the words, "I'm sorry. I love you," then she blew her a kiss.

Tillie heard a sound like an animal dying and realized it was coming from somewhere deep inside of her. She sank back into the chair, her hands still on the window, her body wracked with sobs. The train pulled out of the station and Ruth was gone.

CHAPTER 38

June 1991

Ruth took a deep breath, her eyes closed, her wrinkled hands on the table. Opening her eyes, she gave Thea a smile. "You look a little like her, when we were young." Thea smiled back.

"So." She let out a long breath. "What do you know, exactly?"

"Not much." Thea bit her lip. "I did find these." She reached into her bag and pulled out all the paperwork she'd found. The birth certificates and passports, hidden away in the bottom of her grandmother's bookshelf. "There are duplicates of both yours and my uncle's."

Ruth reached out a shaking hand and took one of the passports from Thea. "Oh man, I was a looker." She sighed, then held up the passport. "Look at me here, Robert. Look at that bone structure."

Robert chuckled. "Yes, Aunt May. You were quite pretty." Thea looked over at him and he was shaking his head and rolling his eyes.

Ruth touched her own young face in the photo. "I know." She lifted her eyes, glittering and crinkled with humor, to the other papers in front of Thea. "This is the fake passport. The one that says I was married to James. I assume the real one is in that pile as well?"

Thea nodded and handed over the passport with the large J scrolled across one side. Ruth took it and shook her head. "You know, we almost left in '35. Our passports were still valid then. But ..." she trailed off. "Well. Things happened, so we waited. And then it was too late. We had to turn in our passports to be stamped. We didn't think they would let us leave with these passports, so Tillie sewed them into her suitcase, and we had some friends send us fake papers. Birth certificates and passports that claimed Tillie and James were brother and sister. And that I was Tillie's sister-in-law." She closed the passport and slid it back across the table.

"My grandfather has one that has a completely different name. Do you know why?"

Ruth pursed her lips. "By the time we left, your grandfather was a wanted man. He needed a passport with a fake name because the authorities were actively looking for him."

Thea shook her head but couldn't find any words.

Ruth took a deep breath. "I assume you know that your grandmother and I were a couple. And James and your grandfather were also together." Thea nodded. "Did you know Berlin was the considered the gay capital of the world in the 1920s?"

Thea must have looked surprised because Ruth laughed, a deep and throaty sound. "I know. Crazy, right? I was a dancer at a club specifically for gay clientele. So was your uncle James. He dressed in drag every night and performed. So did I, for that matter, although I don't know if my outfits would be considered drag now." She shrugged. "Pants and a top hat were considered quite risqué for the time period."

Thea laughed. "I can't believe my uncle dressed in drag. He was so strait laced." Ruth smiled.

"James was such a kind soul. He loved your grandfather so fiercely." She reached for the rest of the pile of papers and started looking through them. "Your grandfather worked at The Institute for Sexual Science. For a very brilliant man, Dr. Hirschfeld. We used to call him Dr. H."

Her face softened. "James worked there for a bit. And your grandmother volunteered there in the library." She smiled; her eyes lost in memories. "It was such a fun time to be living in our beautiful city. And the institute was a lifeline for us." She blinked and looked down at her bright red fingernails. "For people like us, I mean."

She bit her lip. "Anyway, we had to get out. People were being carted away in the dead of night, arrested right and left. It was only a matter of time until they came for your grandfather and for James." She paused. "Did you know your great-grandparents were Nazis?" Miriam gasped and Thea gave a start.

Thea couldn't mask her confusion. "But Dora? Everyone always talked about how wonderful she was. She couldn't have been a Nazi."

Ruth reached out and took Thea's hands. "You weren't named after Ernesto's birth mother. Her name was Ursula. She was dreadful as a person and a Nazi on top of that. As was Ernesto's father, Anthony. Ernesto's brother, Tommy, who would have been your great-uncle, was in the Hitler Youth. Tillie's father Vincent was high up in the party, too. Both Tillie's father and Ernesto's father worked quite closely with Joseph Goebbels in the beginning. They were lawyers on retainer for Goebbels and Göring. Maybe Himmler, too. At least in the early days."

Thea's head swam. She blinked, trying to clear her vision. She felt a hand on her shoulder. "Can I get you a glass of water?" Robert's face was in front of hers and she nodded.

"I lost track of them when I was sent to Dachau, but I know they were very committed to the Nazi cause." She paused, lost in thought. "I wonder if Tommy is still alive." Shaking her head, she went on. "Anyway, that's not who you're named for."

At that, she stood and walked out of the kitchen while Thea, Robert, and Miriam exchanged confused glances. A few moments later, Thea heard the thumping of a cane, and Ruth returned with a frame in her hand.

Thea recognized the photo. It was the one from her grandmother's hatbox, the one with Dora written on the back. She leaned down and took her grandmother's copy out of her purse. Seeing the photo, Ruth smiled. "I should have known Tillie would've kept that picture. I think it's the only one with Dora that still exists."

She pointed to a taller woman in the back of the group behind her grandfather. "See? That's Dora. That's who you're named after."

"Who was she?" Thea squinted at the photo to try to see her namesake better.

"Ernesto considered her his mother. He was kicked out of his house at sixteen, I think, and Dora lived at the institute. That's the big building in the backdrop of the photo. We all lived there briefly except for your grandmother. Your grandfather lived there with James, until they had to move out after it was destroyed. Dora was like a mother hen."

Ruth's eyes grew wet. "She loved everyone who set foot in that building. Took care of anyone who needed it. She was the best of us. Even Dr. Hirschfeld thought so."

"What happened to her?"

Ruth set the photo down and wiped her eyes. "They killed her."

Thea nodded. "In a concentration camp?" Her knowledge of the Holocaust wasn't extensive, but she knew some things.

Ruth shook her head. "Actually no. The Hitler Youth attacked the institute. Right before they burned all our books. Dora was inside, trying to make sure everyone else was safe. And they murdered her."

Ruth looked up at Thea and met her eyes. "They set her on fire. Because she was different." Then she murmured, "I'm sure they did more than set her on fire, too."

Thea felt sick and broke Ruth's sharp gaze to take a drink of water. After a minute of quiet, she looked back at Ruth. "Why didn't you leave then?"

Ruth looked down at her hands. "You know that old wives' tale about the frog, not knowing they're being boiled until it's too late? It was like that. No one was really paying attention to them." She rubbed her face. "The Nazis, I mean. Hitler and the rest of them. They lost their first big election and so no one really took them seriously in the beginning. And then, suddenly, we were boiling."

The table grew quiet again.

"Anyway." Ruth took a sip of tea from the mug in front of her. "They wanted to leave but I wanted to stay and fight back. I loved Berlin. Tillie did too, but she looked at leaving as a way to preserve our lives. Our lifestyle. I thought leaving our city to the wolves was giving up."

"I can't believe she left without you." Thea touched the photo in front of her, their smiling faces looking back.

Ruth shifted and wiped her eyes. "She didn't." Miriam reached across and handed Ruth another tissue. Ruth wiped her eyes. "It was me. We were sitting on the train, getting ready to leave, and I couldn't do it. I couldn't leave my city."

She was crying freely now, the tears running down her face and Miriam was sniffling and dabbing her eyes. "I got up and told her I was going to the bathroom and just got off the train. That was the last time I saw her. January of 1937."

"But she wrote to you?" Thea took Ruth's papery hand in her own.

"She did. She forgave me. She was always so much more reasonable than I was." She laughed through a sob. "I would have been furious. But not Tillie. She understood. We wrote to one another as often as we could. Until I got sent to Dachau."

Miriam sniffed again and interrupted. "My family ended up there. Me and my parents. I was little, five or six. A neighbor sent her children on the Kindertransport and tried to convince my parents to do the same. But my father didn't want us to be separated." Her voice dropped. "They died. But May had become friends with my mother and when she died, May took care of me. We lived through it. And then we left. We left it all behind. Even our names. It was easier." She clenched her jaw and Thea could see her eyes were bright with tears. "When you become a new person, you don't have to remember everything you've lost." Miriam took a sip of tea and it seemed to steady her.

Ruth reached out her other hand to take Miriam's. "I lied and said Miriam was my niece so we could stay together. I wanted to try and find Tillie. I truly did. But Miri and I went from Dachau to a refugee camp in France, and then we ended up in Canada after being sponsored by my mother's second cousin. Once we were in Ontario, I had to get a job and raise Miri. And then my job brought us here. When we ended up in the U.S., I assumed they had stayed in Portugal. I thought about looking for her for years, but I didn't even know where to start."

She mopped her eyes again. "So, I gave up." She gave a shaky sigh, and her voice was thick. "I owed her more than that, but I just didn't know where to start."

†

Robert walked Thea to the door, his hand on her back. Her eyes felt red and swollen and she clutched a tissue between her fingers.

They stood in the doorway, quiet for a moment, before Thea wiped her nose and said, "Did you know any of this?"

He took a deep breath. "Some of it?" He rubbed the stubble on his chin. "I had known that my grandparents were killed during the Holocaust and that my mother and aunt were in the camps with them. They never discussed it, so I never really asked." He shrugged. "Some people deal with trauma by talking about it to anyone who will listen, and some people pretend it never happened."

Thea rubbed her arms, trying to warm herself, despite the thick summer air. "But did you know about my grandmother? About your aunt's past before the camps and everything?"

He gave a little shrug. "I knew she was gay if that's what you mean. She never hid that part of her life. I don't remember her ever having a partner, though. At least, not a serious one. But I always knew. So did my mom. I knew what Berlin was like before the Nazis desecrated it. She talks about that city like it was a person she loved."

Thea reached into her purse and took out the group photo with her grandparents, Ruth, and Dora in front of The Institute for Sexual Science. Robert tilted his head and looked at it. He pointed at each smiling face. "That's Heinz and Erwin." He pointed to a smiling woman in front of Heinz. "That's Adelaide, and next to her is Helene, and the blonde in back is Nissa. And that man with the glasses and the mustache is Dr. Hirschfeld, and next to him is his partner, Karl. And then there's Aunt May and your grandmother, your grandfather and James, and behind your grandfather is Dora."

"Why didn't she tell me any of this?" Thea whispered, more to herself than to Robert.

"Maybe she thought it would be too hard. Maybe she was lonely. Or she didn't know how. I think for my aunt, it was a way to keep herself connected to your grandmother. But, if your grandmother thought my aunt was dead, maybe it was just too painful."

Thea nodded. Gazing at the photo, she wondered out loud, "What happened to the rest of them?"

"I know that part, too." He let out a long breath. "They died. Every single one of them."

✝

Thea sat in the cool, dark hotel room staring at the photo on the desk. Robert's words echoed in her brain like a shout in a cave. *"They died. Every single one of them."* She took a deep breath and picked up the phone to call Michael back home.

He answered after one ring. "Hello?"

"Hi Michael. How's it going?"

"Oh Thea," he breathed. "I was going crazy wondering how it went." When she didn't answer right away, he said, "Thea, are you there?"

"I'm here. It's just …" she trailed off, "it's all so sad."

"Was it her? Did you find her?" Michael's voice was tense with excitement.

"It's her. She had the same photo of all of them in front of that building in Berlin." Michael let out an excited gasp. "She ended up in Dachau. That's why Gram's letter was returned."

"Oh my God."

"They were all part of this culture in Berlin. This huge gay culture." Thea paused. "Clubs and restaurants. Uncle Jimmy was a performer." She gave a little laugh. "He dressed in drag and performed. On a stage."

Michael gave a loud laugh. "No!"

"I know. It sounds crazy. They had jobs and lives and friends and this community in Berlin. And then."

"And then?"

Thea picked up the photo. "The Nazis came and destroyed all of it. Erased them. Erased it all."

Michael was quiet on the other end of the line. She could hear his breathing become labored, and she wiped her eyes. "They destroyed everything. They had to run with fake papers and fake marriages. They escaped to Portugal in 1937, then I guess sometime around 1941, they left Portugal to come here. Ruth didn't know they had come to the States. That they'd been here all this time."

"Does Ruth know about your grandmother? Her memory?"

"She does. I told her. She still wants to visit though. She said she doesn't care if Gram remembers her or not. But I don't know." Tillie bit her lip and felt the tense worry creep into her neck and the base of her skull. "What if she comes to visit and Gram freaks out? Or doesn't remember her at all?"

She rubbed her temples trying to fight the oncoming headache. "It's not just that. That picture I showed you? Of the group? I asked what happened to the rest of the people in that photo. They all died. All of them. Ruth and Gram are the only ones left. It's just ..." A sob caught in her throat. "It's not a happy story. It didn't end well for any of the people in that photo."

Michael's voice was quiet. "Well, it was a long time ago."

"Dora, the woman I'm named after? The Hitler Youth set her on fire." Her voice was sharper than she intended, and she felt the flames of rage flickering up her throat. "She was just living her life and they murdered her because of it."

"Jesus."

"I just don't know if I even want Gram to have to remember." She flipped the photo over and looked at her grandmother's neat cursive on the back. Berlin, 1929. "It's like she had an entire life that we know nothing about. She didn't talk about it; do we really want to force her to remember it?"

CHAPTER 39

March 1941

Tillie stood in the kitchen of their tiny Portugal apartment washing dishes. The radio played in the background, but she wasn't listening. She only kept it on to hear updates about the war, about Germany, about when this all might be over. Portugal was still neutral, but James and Ernesto had been talking about leaving for the United States if the war continued. They didn't believe anywhere in Europe would be safe.

Tillie gazed out the window and wondered for the millionth time what Ruth was doing. If she was safe. If she was cold or hungry. Because she was still in Germany and they were sure mail was being searched and read, it wasn't safe for Ruth to give her any information, other than the vague impression that she was doing something helpful.

The letters were usually just love letters anyway, they didn't have time for details when all they wanted was to constantly remind one another of their love. She'd tried to convince Ruth to come to Portugal, but now it was far too dangerous for her to try to leave. It had been terrifying to leave in 1937, but now that the Germans were at war it was impossible.

A chair scraping behind her jolted Tillie out of her thoughts.

She blinked and turned around. "James, what are you doing here?" James sat down at the kitchen table.

He smiled. "I came home for lunch." He lifted his lunch pail and set it on the kitchen table. She smiled back.

"Where's Ernesto?"

James bit into his sandwich. "He should be right behind me. We both were in the same section of the vineyard today."

Tillie nodded and pulled cold chicken out of the icebox to make her own lunch. She heard voices at the door and set the plate down. "I'm sure that's him." James nodded; his mouth too full to respond.

She walked down the hall and called out, "Ernesto, do you want some cold chicken for lunch?" He was standing in the doorway, talking to their landlord. "Oh, hello Herr Saleiro. Can I interest you in some lunch?" As she got closer, she saw that their lips were set in grim lines and Herr Saleiro had something in his hand. "Is everything alright?"

Herr Saleiro gave her a small smile and bowed his head. "No lunch for me today, Miss Matilda." He nodded again to Ernesto, then turned and left.

"What was that about?" She raised her eyes at Ernesto, but he wouldn't meet her gaze.

He cleared his throat. "Herr Saleiro was just dropping off our mail." He raised his eyes to meet hers.

"Oh. Well, that was nice of him." She stared at him. His face was white, and his eyes were wide, watching her. "Ernesto, what on earth is the matter?" She reached her hand out to take the letter from him.

He handed the envelope to her. Looking down, she recognized her own slanted writing, the Portugal flag stamp she purchased several weeks ago, and smear of ink on the bottom corner where she accidentally set the pen down and it leaked. "What," the word escaped her lips as she took in the large, red letters.

RETURN TO SENDER. RETURNED BY CENSOR. UNDELIVERABLE.

Tillie looked up at Ernesto. His large eyes were wet with tears. "What does this mean?" Her voice bordered on shrill. "What does this mean, 'undeliverable'? Where is she?" She realized her hands were shaking and her knees suddenly gave way.

James and Ernesto helped her to the small wooden kitchen table, and she stared at the swirls in the grain, trying to hold her body together. They were talking in low voices, while Ernesto rubbed her arm. One of them had put a blanket around her shoulders, but she was still shaking, despite the warm temperatures outside.

She kept swallowing, the hard lump of panic in her throat refusing to go down. "Ernesto." It came out like a croak. She couldn't look at them, she was barely keeping her body from dissolving into hysterics. "Where is she?"

James sighed and Ernesto squeezed her forearm. "I don't know Tills." James sniffed and she finally looked up. Seeing his puffy eyes and wet face made the panic and fear overtake her. She folded in on herself, the grief pouring out of her like an ocean. She felt like it would never stop.

✝

Ernesto and James sat on the couch in the sitting room and were staring at her when she walked out of her bedroom. "What?" she snapped.

"Tillie." James' voice was gentle but firm. "Can you come sit down please?" She paused but wrapped her bathrobe tighter around her body and walked over to the overstuffed armchair by the window. She pulled her legs up to her chest when she sat, the only way to keep the hole in her chest from overtaking her.

"It's been six months with no word." Ernesto's voice was soft. "We've written to everyone we can think of, and no one knows where she is. And Elizabeth hasn't responded to any of the letters we've sent."

Tillie felt like she was being filled with ice water.

James leaned over and put his hand on her knee. "We're not sure how much longer it will be safe in Europe. We've made enough money here that we can leave soon for the United States. We'll be safe there."

Tillie stared at James' hand on top of her pink bathrobe. The ice water traveled through her stomach and down into her legs, filling her up from head to toe. And then it turned to fire.

"So, I just leave? I leave her behind. Again. And I go to the United States with you two. And then what? How will she find us once the war is over? How will we find her?"

Her eyes stung and she could feel bile rising in her throat. She swallowed hard.

James and Ernesto exchanged a glance. It was quick, but Tillie caught it. Staring at them both, she jumped out of the chair, feeling the panic and anger and grief so sharply, she thought lightning was going to shoot out of her fingertips. "You think she's dead." Pressing a hand to her mouth, she didn't wait for them to respond. She ran to the kitchen and vomited in the sink.

Two weeks later, Tillie packed up her suitcase and pulled down all the photos from their lives in Berlin, placing them back in the pink hatbox. Lifting her pillow, she picked up the letter she sent to Ruth that was returned. Touching it with her fingertips, she placed it on top of the photos in her hatbox. She didn't say a word to James or Ernesto as they left the apartment and walked to the train station, silent tears streaming down her face.

CHAPTER 40

July 1991

"Hello?"

"Hi Miriam, it's Thea."

"Oh, Thea, hi sweetie. How are you?"

Thea breathed a sigh of relief. She was worried Miriam would be cold on the phone with her. It had been a month since she'd surprised them with her grandmother's letter and they spent the weekend going through all the photos Ruth had left, plus talking all about her life at Dachau, then afterwards. They had all been emotionally spent by Sunday night.

"I just wanted to check in and see how you were, how Ruth, I mean, May, is doing."

Miriam let out a long, low whistle. "Well, she's a stubborn old woman, so she's insisting we visit. I believe her exact words were 'put me in the car and let's go already.'"

Thea laughed. "I know. Michael wants her to visit too." She chewed the inside of her cheek. "I'm just so worried."

"Well, she's in pretty good shape, I know she carries a cane, but she moves well. I think she could make the flight. Especially if we get her a wheelchair for the airport." She paused. "Although she'd hate that."

"No, I know she'd be fine. I'm more worried that she'll get here, and my grandmother won't have any idea who she is." She felt the tears pooling in her eyes. "Her bad days certainly outnumber her good ones." Her voice grew thick. "It would be so hard to see her not remember your aunt."

Thinking about how many years they lost, how lonely they both must have been all this time, she couldn't help it. She started crying.

"Oh sweetie. I know. But what a tragedy it would be to not even try?"

Thea nodded through her tears. "I know."

"So," Robert's voice came through in the background. "Am I booking a flight?"

"Yes." She was surprised at how strong her voice was. "Book the flight. Let's do this."

The next morning, Thea went to visit her grandmother. Knocking softly on the door, she walked in and saw her tiny grandmother sitting in her giant chair, staring out the window. "Hey, Gram." She kept her voice low and gentle. "How are you doing?"

Her grandmother tilted her head to the side. "I'm fine, dear. I'm sorry," she put a finger to her thin lips. "I can't quite place you. Are you my nurse?"

Thea walked over and sat on the floor, taking her grandmother's dry hands in her own. "I'm your granddaughter, Theadora. Remember?"

"Dora," her grandmother said slowly.

"Yes, that's right. I was named after your friend Dora. From the institute." She squeezed her grandmother's hands.

"Oh. She died." Beads of tears formed on her grandmother's lashes.

"I know. I know she did. A lot of your friends died, didn't they? That must have been hard for you." Now her own tears started to spill down her cheeks.

"It was." Her grandmother's blue eyes filled and when she blinked, the tears fell, and her nose started to run. Thea grabbed a tissue from the side table and handed it to her.

"Not everyone died, though, Gram. Ruth didn't die." Thea wiped her own eyes.

"Ruth." Her grandmother closed her eyes and leaned back into her chair. "We left her behind. She was so brave, she wouldn't leave. I left. I was a coward." Her eyes were still closed, and the tears streamed down her face, forming small pools around her mouth.

"You did what you needed to do, Gram, to keep yourself safe. To keep Grandpa and Jimmy safe."

She opened her eyes and smiled, causing the pools to spill over. Wiping her face with her hands, she sighed. "Some people live their whole lives without being in love. I got to have all those years with Ruth before things were ruined. Before my father and Ernesto's father and all their evil friends ruined us. We got to have a life together, even if it was a short one."

She took a deep breath. "I wish she could have met Jenny, though. And Theadora, my granddaughter. She would have loved them both."

Closing her eyes again, she rested her head back on her chair. Thea sat for a moment on the floor, before getting up, giving her grandmother's hands one more quick squeeze, and walking out the door.

✝

A week later, Michael pulled into the parking lot, the assisted living facility looming in front of them. Thea pivoted in her seat to look back at Ruth and saw her sitting with a serene smile on her face, her eyes closed, Robert's hand grasped in her own.

"Um, Aunt May?" Robert's voice was tentative. "We're here."

She opened her eyes, and her smile grew. "So, we are." Thea met Robert's gaze and he gave her a tiny smile and winked.

They all started getting out of the car when Ruth reached into her purse and pulled out a small mirror and a tube of lipstick. "Just a moment." She proceeded to paint her lips a frightening color of red and Thea had to laugh.

"Gram used to wear almost the exact same shade." She watched as Ruth's face looked shocked, then amused.

"My Tillie, wearing red lips? I would have paid good money to see that." She smiled into her reflection, checking her teeth. "She would hardly even rouge her cheeks back in Berlin." Ruth took Robert's hand again and he helped her out of the backseat.

They made their way through the sterile hallways, Ruth smiling at the patients who walked by them. Thea could see the old woman was nervous. Despite the cold air being pushed through the building, there were small beads of sweat on her pale forehead.

They met Vanessa at the doors into Memory Care. She gave Ruth a brilliant smile. "When Michael told me your story, I cried like a baby." Vanessa gave Ruth's hands a squeeze. "I'm so glad to meet you, Ms. Birnbaum." Ruth smiled back and placed a hand on Vanessa's smooth face.

"Call me May. I'm glad to meet you too, dear. Anyone taking good care of my Tillie is on my nice list." Vanessa laughed and unlocked the doors, letting them into the wider hallways of the Memory Care section.

"I hope you have a nice visit, May." Vanessa waved as she turned to go back to her office.

Briefly Ruth's brow furrowed.

"What's wrong?" Robert steadied her by placing his hand on her elbow.

"Well, it's just, I should probably tell the staff here to call me Ruth, not May." She turned to Robert. "Tillie will get confused."

Robert met Thea's eyes again, this time his brown eyes were full of sadness. She gave him a small nod and he leaned into his aunt.

"Aunt May, you really shouldn't get your hopes up." His voice was gentle and soft, but she waved him away.

"May," Thea began, but saw the hazel eyes narrow, the green flecks almost glowing. She started again. "Ruth. My grandmother has good days, but they are few and far between now. Most days she doesn't know me, she doesn't know where she is, or that my grandfather and Jimmy are dead." Ruth took her hand off her cane and crossed her arms, her face full of indignation.

"I realize what dementia is, thank you." Her voice was stern, but not angry.

"We're just trying to protect you from being disappointed, Aunt May." Robert stood next to his aunt, not sure what to do with his hands. He kept reaching up to help her and she kept waving him off.

Her tone grew softer. "Finding her again is a miracle. The idea that she wouldn't remember me now." She dropped her eyes to her feet and bit her lip. "Well," she said in a whisper, "it's just impossible."

Thea chewed the inside of her cheek and, not for the first time, wondered if bringing Ruth here was a mistake. She was going to be devastated when her grandmother had no idea who she was. They all stood outside her grandmother's room, the air tense.

Ruth put her hand on the doorknob. "Here we go."

Pushing the door open, Ruth went first, followed by Thea, then Michael, then Robert bringing up the rear of the group. Her grandmother's room was dark, the only light coming from the window. Thea could see her grandmother sitting in her armchair looking out onto the courtyard, her tiny hands curled on her lap.

Thea opened her mouth to speak but Ruth broke the silence first. "Tillie?" Her grandmother slowly turned; her face confused. Ruth smiled and took a step forward. "Hi, doll. I missed you."

Thea watched as her grandmother rose from her chair. She heard Robert inhale behind her and she dropped her arm down to her side, searching for Robert's comforting larger hand. Her heart was beating so fast, she was sure everyone in the room could hear it.

Tillie took two steps, her face a mixture of confusion and concentration. "I know you," she said slowly, in a low voice.

Ruth gave her a strained smile, her eyes brimming with tears. "Yes, you do." She turned and reached for her handbag, pulling out a grainy photo. The paper trembled in her fingers as she held it out to give it to Tillie. "Do you remember that day?"

Two beautiful young women stood hand in hand in white dresses, smiling at the camera. One tall with jet black hair set in finger waves, the other short with soft brown hair, curls pulled back off her face.

There was a long silence as Tillie stared at the picture. Ruth touched Tillie's hand. "That's us, doll." Her voice was quiet and patient. "When we married the boys. We lived together in Berlin, and we married the boys. Remember? I married James and you married Ernesto."

When Tillie still didn't respond, Ruth kept going. "But we pretended we married each other." She gave a small laugh. "Do you remember?"

Tillie sat back down on her bed and opened the side table drawer, pulling out the pink hat box. She pried the lid off and pulled something out from inside. Thea could see it was the exact same picture. Looking at it, then at the photo Ruth handed her, her brow furrowed. She stood, both photos in her shriveled fingers.

Tillie's eyes lifted from the photo to settle on Ruth's face. Tears were streaming down her face. Her voice was so soft, Ruth had to lean forward to hear her. "Ruthie." The photos fluttered to the floor as Tillie dropped them, her eyes wide and full of tears.

Ruth gave a small sob of relief, and she took Tillie's hand in her own. "That's right, doll." She was crying as they gripped one another's hands.

Tillie shook her head. "But they killed you. I thought they killed you."

Ruth gave a small shrug. "They tried to. But I got out, my niece and I. We went to France first, then Canada, then Vermont."

"Vermont." Tillie gave a little laugh.

"I thought you and the boys stayed in Portugal. I wanted to look for you, but my niece was so young." Ruth's voice was thick and full of despair. "She was so young, and we were starting all over."

Tillie reached up and touched Ruth's face. "It's okay," she whispered.

Thea wiped her face with the back of her hand and heard a sniff behind her. She turned and saw Robert's face was wet with tears. Michael had his hands over his mouth like he was trying to hold in all the emotion she saw in his eyes. She motioned for them to follow her out of her grandmother's room.

Her grandmother noticed the movement and called out. "Jenny, is that you?"

But before Thea could respond, Ruth looped her arm through her grandmother's elbow and said, "No, doll. That's Thea. Your granddaughter. She was named for Dora, isn't that right?"

Thea watched as the wheels turned behind her grandmother's eyes and she nodded slowly.

"Yes. Yes, I think that's right." Thea felt Robert's hand squeeze her own.

"It is right. Dora would be so pleased, don't you think?" Again, Tillie nodded, but Thea wasn't sure she really remembered Dora or that she was named after her.

Her grandmother turned to Ruth, a crease above her blue eyes. "Ruthie?"

"Yes love?" Ruth lowered herself onto the bed and Tillie followed.

She looked around. "Where are the boys?"

Thea's heart sank and she heard Robert sigh behind her, then felt his reassuring hand squeeze her shoulder. She rubbed her arms, suddenly very cold.

But Ruth just smiled. "Oh, well, James is at the club. He had a performance tonight. And Ernesto is there watching." She patted the top of Tillie's hand and for a moment Tillie looked placated.

Ruth put a wrinkled arm, pale and lined with bright blue veins around Tillie's thin shoulders. Tillie gazed up at Ruth, her eyes bright and her face calm and relaxed, and Thea knew her grandmother no longer remembered that they were all standing in the doorway, watching.

"Ruthie?" she breathed, leaning into Ruth's body.

"Yes Tills?" Ruth rested her head on top of Tillie's soft pile of white hair.

"Where are we?"

Ruth pulled away just enough to look into Tillie's eyes. She gave Tillie a small kiss on the end of her nose. Her voice was soft, and she gazed into Tillie's eyes. "Oh, doll. We're in Berlin."

✝ THE END ✝

AFTERWORD

Dr. Magnus Hirschfeld opened The Institute of Sexual Science in 1919 not far from the Reichstag building in Berlin. The institute was a haven for the local LGBTQ community and housed a large archival area, psychiatric and medical offices, a museum, and dormitories for the transgender women that lived and worked at the institute for Hirschfeld. Dr. Hirschfeld also worked with the local police forces during this time period to issue certificates for the trans people in the community. These certificates would keep the trans people under Dr. Hirschfeld's care from being arrested for cross-dressing, a violation of Paragraph 175.

Dr. Hirschfeld recognized that as a Jewish gay man, he would no longer have a future in Germany and in 1930, he left to go on a speaking tour. This tour was actually a way for him to explore several other countries to see where the safest place for him would be to settle and rebuild his practice. He visited the United States, Asia, Africa, and finally settled in France. He died of a heart attack in 1935 and was never able to rebuild his vast amount of research after most of it was destroyed by the Nazis.

Dora Richter was one of the first transgender women to receive gender-affirming surgery at Dr. Hirschfeld's Institute for

Sexual Science. She was born in 1891 and, at the age of nine, her parents allowed her to live as a girl. After being arrested multiple times for cross-dressing, the police released her to the custody of Dr. Hirschfeld and the institute, where she lived and worked, along with other transgender women (the characters of Helene, Adelaide, and Nissa were based on these other women, although there is no record of their names). Dora's surgery and case study done by Dr. Levy-Lenz was what led Lili Elbe (*The Danish Girl*) to the institute for her own gender-affirming surgery in 1932.

When the Hitler Youth and the Stormtroopers attacked the institute on that night in May of 1933, Dr. Hirschfeld was already out of the country. Because the transgender women lived there, it is assumed they were present when the Nazis and Hitler Youth arrived to destroy the building and seize all the books housed in the library. While no one knows exactly what happened to Dora, she disappeared that night. It was likely that she was either arrested and sent to a camp or murdered upon the Nazis entry into the institute. Because there is no record of the names of the other trans women who lived and worked within the walls of the institute, there is also no record of what happened to them.

Dora was forty-two when she disappeared. I attempted to find a memorial or grave—I even searched her birth name in the records of those who died in the camps—anything that would give me an idea of what happened to her that night in May, but I came up empty-handed.

ACKNOWLEDGMENTS

When the world stopped back in March of 2020, something took hold of me that I can't quite explain. This story, these characters, this moment in time had lodged themselves deep inside my brain and, mostly because there was really nothing else to do, I started writing.

It started as a fun little hobby while my children entertained themselves in our backyard. While they jumped on trampolines and climbed trees and watched movies on rainy days, I would sit in front of my computer and read article after article about Dr. Magnus Hirschfeld, google photos of Dora Richter and her friends, and look up translated PDFs of Joseph Goebbels' newspaper. But by the end of that summer, something new had blossomed and a new dream took shape.

I wanted this story to be told and I wanted people to know these characters. I wanted other people to know Dora and Dr. Hirschfeld and the lives they'd lived. I wanted Tillie and Ruth and James and Ernesto to become real to other people and for an audience to learn about Berlin during the 20s and 30s. I wanted other people to fall in love with this community the way that I had and there are many people who have made that dream a reality.

To my beta reader, Emily, who read the first version of the first chapter, thank you for never making me feel silly or stupid for embarking on this journey. For always being a cheerleader and encouraging my dreams of finally finishing this story.

To my agent, Mira Perrizo, for loving this book as much as I do and for believing that it deserved to see the light of day. I'm so thankful that you kept trying to find this novel a home and I appreciate your help every step of the way.

To Lisa, Kristy, and the rest of the amazing humans at Amphorae Publishing. You guys have been an absolute blast to work with. I've found a kindred spirit in Lisa and I hope we're able to work together again.

To my amazing daughters, Blaine, Charlotte, Eliza, and Rosie. You never complained that I was working too hard or that I wasn't paying enough attention. You all could see how important this was to me and I hope that I've shown you that you are never too old to go after your dreams. I should also mention my parents, Tim and Tracey, here, because they served as babysitters more times than I can count just so I could write uninterrupted.

Even though I dedicated this book to my spouse, it's important for me to thank him again. Dave, this book literally wouldn't exist if it weren't for you. Thanks for being my person.

And finally, I would like to express my immense gratitude to all the queer humans who came before me, who laid the path for, not just my liberation, but the liberation of us all. Those whose stories have been told and those whose stories have been lost to history.

To the reader. If you've made it this far, please take five minutes today and learn about one queer person from history that you might not already know about. Tell their story to someone else. Our queer ancestors deserve to have their stories told.

ABOUT THE AUTHOR

As the mother of a transgender child, author Katherine Bryant became increasingly interested in LGBTQ history, in particular, Dr. Magnus Hirshfeld and The Institute of Sexual Science in Berlin. Tillie, Ruth, James, and Ernesto came to life as she studied the Nazi destruction of The Institute of Sexual Science and their burning of all of Dr. Hirshfeld's research on the LGBTQ community members of Berlin and the surrounding areas. This is her debut novel.